Mrs Craddock

William Somerset Maugham was born in 1874 and lived in Paris until he was ten. He was educated at King's School, Canterbury, and at Heidelberg University. He afterwards walked the wards of St Thomas's Hospital with a view to practice in medicine, but the success of his first novel, *Liza of Lambeth* (1897), won him over to letters. Something of his hospital experience is reflected, however, in the first of his masterpieces, *Of Human Bondage* (1915), and with *The Moon and Sixpence* (1919) his reputation as a novelist was assured.

His position as one of the most successful playwrights on the London stage was being consolidated simultaneously. His first play, *A Man of Honour* (1903), was followed by a procession of successes just before and after the First World War. (At one point only Bernard Shaw had more plays running at the same time in London.) His theatre career ended with *Sheppey* (1933).

His fame as a short-story writer began with *The Trembling of a Leaf*, sub-titled *Little Stories of the South Sea Islands*, in 1921, since when he published more than ten collections.

Somerset Maugham's general books are fewer in number. They include travel books, such as *On a Chinese Screen* (1922) and *Don Fernando* (1935), essays, criticism, and the self-revealing *The Summing Up* (1938) and *A Writer's Notebook* (1949).

He settled in the South of France in 1929 and lived there until his death in 1965.

Also by W. Somerset Maugham
in Pan Books

W. Somerset Maugham

Mrs Craddock

Pan Books in association with Heinemann

First published 1902 by William Heinemann Ltd
This edition published 1978 by Pan Books Ltd,
Cavaye Place, London SW10 9PG
in association with William Heinemann Ltd
9 8 7 6 5 4 3
ISBN 0 330 25495 2
Set, printed and bound in Great Britain by
Cox & Wyman Ltd, Reading

PREFACE

THIS novel was written in 1900. It was thought extremely daring, and was refused by publisher after publisher, among others by William Heinemann; but it was at last read by Robertson Nicoll, a partner in the firm of Hodder and Stoughton, and he, though of opinion that it was not the sort of book his own firm should publish, thought well enough of it to urge William Heinemann to reconsider his decision. Heinemann read it himself and, on the condition that I took out passages that he found shocking, agreed to publish it. This was in 1902. It must have had something of a success, since it was reissued the following year, and again in 1908. Thirty years later it was republished. The new edition was printed from the original manuscript with the offensive parts left in, for I could not for the life of me imagine what they were, and I had not the patience to compare the manuscript with the printed copy. On the contrary, the propriety of the book seemed to me almost painful. I made, however, certain corrections.

The author had been dead for many years, and I used the manuscript as I would that of a departed friend whose book, unrevised by him, had been entrusted to me for publication. I left it as it was, with all its faults, and contented myself with minor emendations. The author's punctuation was haphazard, and I did my best to put some method into it. I replaced the dashes which he used, I fear from ignorance of a complicated art, with colons, semi-colons and commas; I omitted the rows of dots with which he sought to draw the reader's attention to the elegance of a sentiment or the subtlety of an observation, and I replaced with a full stop the marks of exclamation that stood all over the page, like telegraph poles, apparently to emphasize the author's astonishment at his own acumen. I cannot imagine why he had the affectation of treating the letter H as a vowel, and wrote of *an* horse, *an* house and *an* home; I struck out all I could find of these otiose Ns; but if any still remain, the reader is besought to pardon an aberration of youth and the carelessness of the editor. It is not an easy matter to decide how you should treat this particular letter and, searching for guidance, I have consulted a number of grammars. So far as I can make out, whether you treat H as a vowel or a consonant depends on the stress you naturally lay on the syllable it accompanies. So, it would be absurd to tell a friend, who wanted to write still another war novel, to have *an* heart; but not unreasonable to suggest that, if he must write, he would be better advised to write *an* historical romance.

A pleasant story is told about Alfred de Musset. He was sitting down one day at George Sand's to wait for her, and he took up one of her novels that lay on a table. He thought it uncommonly verbose. When she came in, she found him, pencil in hand, crossing out all the unnecessary adjectives; and they say that she did not take it very well. I sympathize with his impatience and with her irritation. But in this matter I used moderation. Some of the author's favourite words have now a strangely old-fashioned air, but I saw no reason to change them, since there is nothing to show that the modern ones which I might have put in their stead will not in a few years be just as dated. An epithet has its vogue and is forgotten, and the *amusing* of the moment will doubtless in a little ring as false as the *horrid* of the eighteen nineties. But I crossed out a great many *somes*, *certains* and *rathers*, for the author of this book had an unhappy disinclination to make an unqualified statement. I was ruthless with the adverbs. When he used five words to say what could have been said in one, I replaced them with the one; and when it seemed to me that he had not said what he wanted to, I ventured to change what he said for what I could not but think he meant. English is a very difficult language, and the author, with whose work I was taking the liberties I have described, had never been taught it. The little he knew he had picked up here and there. No one had ever explained to him the difficulties of composition or the mysteries of style. He began to write as a child begins to walk. He took pains to study good models, but, with none to guide him, he did not always choose his models wisely, and he devoted much care to writers who now seem to most of us affected and jejune.

Some months ago, a gallery in Cork Street had an exhibition of small French pictures painted early in the present century. Since I was often in Paris at that time and used to wander in and out of the shops in the Rue de la Boëtie or on the other side of the Seine where pictures were on view, I must have seen them, or others like them; but if I did, I would have dismissed them with a shrug of the shoulders as Salon pictures, and commonplace, for I had recently discovered Manet, Monet and Pissarro; and these little pictures of Paris, the quais, the boulevards, the shabby streets, the Champs-Élysées, said nothing to me; but when, after this long lapse of time I saw them again, I found them enchanting. The *fiacres*, the horse-drawn buses, the victorias with their pair of 'spanking' horses in which drove women, *femmes du monde* or celebrated *cocottes*, dressed in the height of fashion, on their way to the Bois, the queer uniforms of the little soldiers, the *nounous* with long satin streamers to their caps, pushing prams in the gardens of the Luxembourg – one had taken it all for granted; one had no idea that life was so gay and colourful. Whether these pictures were well painted or not, and most of them showed the competence of a sound training at the Beaux Arts, was no matter; the years had given them a nostalgic charm that one had no wish to resist. They were *genre*. And now that for this new edition of *Mrs Craddock* I have re-read it, it is as a genre picture that I regard it. I smile and blush at its absurdities, but leave them because they belong to the period; and if the novel has any merit (and that the reader must decide for himself), it is because it is a picture, faithful, I believe, of life in a corner of England during the last years of the nineteenth century.

The action takes place between 1890 and 1900. The world was very different from what it is today. The telephone and the gramophone had been invented, but they were not till many years later necessities of life to be found in every house. The radio, of course, was unknown. The motor-car was still in the future, and it was not till 1903 that the Wrights produced the first flying machine. The safety bicycle was all the rage and parties were made to ride it in Battersea Park or in country lanes. Women wore their hair long, piled up on their heads, and if they hadn't enough, added a long switch made out of their combings. Perched up atop of these imposing erections, they wore large hats covered with flowers, fruit and feathers. They wore high collars and full skirts that reached the ground; corsets stiffened with whalebone and pulled as tight as they could bear it. Girls boasted of their eighteen-inch waists. For some years leg of mutton sleeves were vastly fashionable. Towards the end of the decade, in England at least, the hair was no longer brushed up on the top of the head, but done in a 'bun' on the nape of the neck, and every woman wore an elaborate (and often false) fringe. Maids wore caps and neat aprons, and a mistress would have looked upon it as an impertinence if one of hers appeared before her bare-headed.

Men wore top hats and frock coats to pay calls and to go to their clubs and offices. A few bold fellows wore morning coats with, of course, a silk hat. Bowlers were worn by bus conductors, drivers of hansom cabs, clerks and bounders. At night men wore full evening dress with black waistcoats and white ties. It was only the heavy swells who sported white waistcoats. The dinner jacket was unknown. Even in the country, when they were in tweeds and knickerbockers, not yet known as plus fours, men wore high, stiff collars and starched shirts.

It was the end of an era, but the landed gentry, who were soon to lose the power they had so long enjoyed, were the last to have a suspicion of it. Owing to the agricultural depression, land was no longer a source of profit, but, except for that, they were quite satisfied that things should go on as they had in the past. They had only disdain for the moneyed class that was already beginning to take their place. They were gentlefolk. It is true that for the most part they were narrow, stupid and intolerant; prudish, formal and punctilious. But they had

7

their points, and I do not think the author was quite fair to them. They did their duty according to their lights. That some should be born to possess a fine estate, and others to work upon it at a miserable wage, was in the nature of things; and it was not for them to cavil at the decrees of inscrutable Providence. The landed gentry were on the whole decent, honourable and upright. They were devoid of envy. They had good manners and were kindly and hospitable. But they had outworn their use, and perhaps it was inevitable that the course of events should sweep them away. Their houses now lie derelict or are schools or homes for the aged, and on the broad acres which they have sold, enterprising builders have built houses, pubs and cinemas.

As is the common practice with novelists, the author of *Mrs Craddock*, with one exception, took as his models for the persons who play their parts in it persons he knew. The exception is Miss Ley. She was founded on the portrait-statue of Agrippina in the museum at Naples. This sounds improbable, yet happens to be a fact. But on re-reading this book it is the character of the author, manifest throughout, that has chiefly attracted my attention. He was evidently not a very nice young man. He had absurd prejudices. I cannot imagine why he despised Georgian architecture. I should have thought that nowhere has domestic architecture reached such a pitch of excellence as in England under the Georges. Its houses were dignified, elegant and commodious. Yet he never mentions the house in which his heroine lived without a sneer. He called it a blot on the landscape. I have an uneasy feeling that he greatly admired the red brick villas with casement windows and dormered roofs which architects were erecting all over the country. But this is merely a question of taste and, as we know, a man may have an indifferent character and exquisite taste. I do not know why, unless he had learnt it from Matthew Arnold, he was of opinion that the English were philistines; and that for wit, brilliance and culture you must go to the French. He never missed a chance to have a fling at his own countrymen. With a certain naïveté he took the French at their own estimate of themselves, and never doubted that Paris was the centre of civilization. He was better acquainted with the contemporary literature of France than with that of his own country. It was through the influence it had on him that he adopted some of the mannerisms, such as the rows of dots to which I have already referred, which the French writers of the time made excessive use of. The only excuse I can make for his attitude, besides his youth, is that for him England signified constraint and convention, whereas France signified freedom and adventure. I highly disapprove of a way he had now and then of stepping out of his novel and in sarcastic terms directly addressing the reader. Where he learnt this bad practice I cannot tell.

Because for his age the author of *Mrs Craddock* had travelled exten-

sively in Europe and could speak quite adequately four foreign langu-
ages, because he had read much, not only in English and French, but
also in German, Spanish and Italian, he had a very good opinion of
himself. During his various sojourns on the Continent he came in contact with a number of men, some young, some not so young, who
shared his prejudices. With private means adequate to those inexpen-
sive days, they had come down from Oxford or Cambridge with a pass
degree and led desultory lives in Paris, Florence, Rome and Capri. He
was too ingenuous to see how ineffectual they were. They did not
hesitate to call themselves aesthetes and liked to think that they burnt
with a hard, gemlike flame. They looked upon Oscar Wilde as the
greatest master of English prose in the nineteenth century. Though not
insensible to the fact that they thought him immature, in fact a bit of a
philistine, he did his best to meet their high standards. He dutifully
admired the works of art they admired and despised those they despised. He was not only a foolish young man; he was supercilious, cock-
sure and often wrong-headed. If I met him now I should take an
immediate dislike to him.

1955   W.S.M.

1

THIS book might be called also *The Triumph of Love*.

Bertha was looking out of the window at the bleakness of the day. The sky was grey and the clouds were heavy and low; the neglected drive leading to the gates was swept by the bitter wind, and the elm trees that bordered it were bare of leaf; their naked branches seemed to shiver with horror of the cold. It was the end of November and the day was cheerless. The dying year seemed to have cast over all nature the terror of death; the imagination would not bring to the wearied mind thoughts of the merciful sunshine, thoughts of the spring coming as a maiden to scatter from her baskets the flowers and the green leaves.

Bertha turned round and looked at her aunt cutting the leaves of a new *Spectator*. Wondering what book to get down from Mudie's, Miss Ley read the autumn lists and the laudatory expressions that the adroitness of publishers extracts from unfavourable reviews.

'You're very restless this afternoon, Bertha,' she remarked, in answer to her niece's steady gaze.

'I think I shall walk down to the gate.'

'You've already done that twice in the last hour. Do you find in it something alarmingly novel?'

Bertha did not reply, but turned again to the window; the scene in the last two hours had fixed itself upon her mind with monotonous accuracy.

'What are you thinking about, Aunt Polly?' she asked, suddenly turning back to her aunt and catching the eyes fixed upon her.

'I was thinking that one must be very penetrative to discover a woman's emotions from the view of her back hair.'

Bertha laughed: 'I don't think I have any emotions to discover. I feel – ' she sought for some way of expressing the sensation. 'I feel as if I should like to take my hair down.'

Miss Ley made no rejoinder, but looked down at her paper. She hardly wondered what her niece meant, having long ceased to be astonished at Bertha's ways and doings; indeed, her only surprise was that they never sufficiently corroborated the common opinion that Bertha was an independent young woman from whom anything might be expected. In the three years they had spent together since the death of Bertha's father, the two women had learned to tolerate one another extremely well. Their mutual affection was mild and perfectly respectable, in every way suitable to ladylike persons bound together by ties of convenience and decorum. Miss Ley, called to the death-bed of her brother in Italy, made Bertha's acquaintance over the dead man's grave, and she was then too old and of too independent character to accept a stranger's authority; nor had Miss Ley the smallest desire to exert authority over anybody. She was a very indolent woman, who wished nothing more than to leave people alone and be left alone by them. But if it was obviously her duty to take charge of an orphan niece, it was also an advantage that Bertha was eighteen and but for conventions of decent society could very well take charge of herself. Miss Ley was not unthankful to a merciful providence on the discovery that her ward had every intention of going her own way and none whatever of hanging about the skirts of a maiden aunt who was passionately devoted to her liberty.

They travelled on the Continent, seeing many churches, pictures and cities, in the examination of which their chief desire appeared to be to conceal from one another the emotions they felt. Like the Red Indian, who will suffer the most horrid tortures without wincing, Miss Ley would have thought it highly disgraceful to display feeling at some touching scene. She used polite cynicism as a cloak for sentimentality, laughing that she might not cry – and her want of originality herein, the old repetition of Grimaldi's doubleness, made her snigger at herself; she felt that tears were unbecoming and foolish.

'Weeping makes a fright even of a good-looking woman,' she said, 'but if she is ugly they make her simply repulsive.'

Finally, letting her own flat in London, Miss Ley settled down with Bertha to cultivate rural delights at Court Leys near Blackstable, in the county of Kent. The two ladies lived together with much harmony, although the demonstrations of their affection did not exceed a single kiss morning and night, given and received with almost equal indifference. Each had considerable respect for the other's abilities, and particularly for the wit that occasionally exhibited itself in little friendly sarcasms. But they were too clever

12

to get on badly, and since they neither hated nor loved one another excessively, there was really no reason why they should not continue to live together on the best of terms. The general result of their relations was that Bertha's restlessness on this particular day aroused in Miss Ley no more question than was easily explained by the warmth of her young blood; and her eccentric curiosity in respect of the gate on a very cold and unpleasant winter afternoon did not even elicit from her a shrug of disapproval or an upraising of the eyebrows in wonder.

Bertha put on a hat and walked out. The avenue of elm trees reaching from the façade of Court Leys in a straight line to the gates had once been rather an imposing sight, but now announced clearly the ruin of an ancient house. Here and there a tree had died and fallen, leaving an unsightly gap, and one huge trunk still lay upon the ground after a terrific storm of the preceding year, left there to rot in the indifference of bailiffs and tenants. On either side of the elm trees was a broad strip of meadow that once had been a well-kept lawn, but now was foul with docks and rank weeds; a few sheep nibbled the grass where upon a time fine ladies in hoops and gentlemen with tie-wigs had sauntered, discussing the wars and the last volumes of Mr Richardson. Beyond was an ill-trimmed hedge and then the broad fields of the Ley estate. Bertha walked down, looking at the highway beyond the gate; it was a relief no longer to feel Miss Ley's cold eyes fixed upon her. She had emotions enough in her breast, they beat against one another like birds in a net struggling to get free; but not for worlds would she have bidden anyone look into her heart, full of expectation, of longing and of a hundred strange desires. She went out on the high-road that led from Blackstable to Tercanbury; she looked up and down with a tremor and a quick beating of the heart. But the road was empty, swept by the winter wind, and she almost sobbed with disappointment.

She could not return to the house; a roof just then would stifle her, and the walls seemed like a prison; there was a certain pleasure in the biting wind that blew through her clothes and chilled her to the bone. The waiting was terrible. She entered the grounds and looked up the carriage-drive to the big white house that was hers. The very roadway was in need of repair, and the dead leaves that none troubled about rustled hither and thither in the gusts of wind. The house stood out in its squareness without relation to its environment. Built in the reign of George II, it seemed to have acquired no hold upon the land that bore it; with its plain front and many windows, the Doric portico exactly in the middle, it looked as if it were merely placed upon the ground as a house of cards is built upon the floor, with no foundations. The passing years had given it no beauty, and it stood now, as for more than a century it had stood, a blot upon the landscape, vulgar and new. Surrounded by the fields, it had no garden but for a few beds planted about its feet, and in them the flowers, uncared for, had grown wild or withered away.

The day was declining and the lowering clouds seemed to shut out the light. Bertha gave up hope. But she looked once more down the hill, and her heart gave a great thud against her chest. She felt herself blushing furiously. Her blood seemed to be rushing through the vessels with sudden rapidity, and in dismay at her want of composure she had an impulse to turn quickly and go back to the house. She forgot the sickening expectation and the hours that she had spent in looking for the figure that tramped up the hill.

He came nearer, a tall fellow of twenty-seven, massively set together, big-boned, with long arms and legs and a magnificent breadth of chest. One could well believe him as strong as an ox. Bertha recognized the costume that always pleased her, the knickerbockers and gaiters, the Norfolk jacket of rough tweed, the white stock and the cap – all redolent of the country which for his sake she was beginning to love, and all intensely masculine. Even the huge boots that covered his feet gave her by their very size a thrill of pleasure; their dimensions suggested a firmness of character and a masterfulness that were intensely reassuring. The style of dress fitted perfectly the background of brown road and ploughed field. Bertha wondered if he knew that he was exceedingly picturesque as he climbed the hill.

'Afternoon, Miss Bertha,' the man said as he passed.

He showed no sign of stopping, and the girl's heart sank at the thought that he might go on with only a commonplace word of greeting.

'I thought it was you I saw coming up the hill,' she said, stretching out her hand.

He stopped and shook it. The touch of his big, firm fingers made her tremble. His hand was as massive and hard as if it were hewn of stone. She looked up at him and smiled.

'Isn't it cold?' she said.

It is terrible to be desirous of saying all sorts of passionate things while convention prevents you from any but the most commonplace.

'You haven't been walking at the rate of five miles an hour,' he said cheerily. 'I've been into Blackstable to see about buying a nag.'

He was the very picture of health. The winds of November were like summer breezes to him, and his face glowed with the pleasant cold. His cheeks were flushed and his eyes glistened; his vitality was intense, shining out upon others with almost a material warmth.

'Were you going out?' he asked.

'Oh, no,' Bertha replied without strict regard to truth. 'I just walked down to the gate and I happened to catch sight of you.'

'I'm very glad. I see you so seldom now, Miss Bertha.'

'I wish you wouldn't call me Miss Bertha,' she cried. 'It sounds horrid.'

It was worse than that, it sounded almost menial.

'When we were boy and girl we used to call each other by our Christian names.'

He blushed a little, and his modesty filled Bertha with pleasure.

'Yes, but when you came back six months ago you had changed so much – I didn't dare; and besides, you called me Mr Craddock.'

'Well, I won't any more,' she said, smiling. 'I'd much sooner call you Edward.'

She did not add that the word seemed to her the most beautiful in the whole list of Christian names, nor that in the past few weeks she had already repeated it to herself a thousand times.

'It'll be like the old days,' he said. 'D'you remember what fun we used to have when you were a little girl, before you went abroad with Mr Ley?'

'I remember that you used to look upon me with great contempt because I *was* a little girl,' she replied, laughing.

'Well, I was awfully frightened the first time I saw you again, with your hair up and long dresses.'

'I'm not really very terrible,' she answered.

For five minutes they had been looking into one another's eyes, and suddenly, without obvious reason, Edward Craddock blushed.

Bertha noticed it, and a strange little thrill went through her. She blushed too, and her dark eyes flashed even more brightly than before.

'I wish I didn't see you so seldom, Miss Bertha,' he said.

'You have only yourself to blame, fair sir,' she replied. 'You perceive the road that leads to my palace, and at the end of it you will certainly find a door.'

'I'm rather afraid of your aunt,' he said.

It was on the tip of Bertha's tongue to say that faint heart never won fair lady, but, for modesty's sake, she refrained. Her spirits had suddenly gone up and she felt extraordinarily happy.

'Do you want to see me very badly?' she asked, her heart beating at quite an absurd rate.

Craddock blushed again and seemed to have some difficulty in finding a reply; his confusion and his ingenuous air were new delights to Bertha.

'If he only knew how I adore him!' she thought; but naturally could not tell him in so many words.

'You've changed so much in these years,' he said. 'I don't understand you.'

'You haven't answered my question.'

'Of course I want to see you, Bertha,' he said quickly, seeming to take his courage in both hands. 'I want to see you always.'

'Well,' she said, with a charming smile, 'I sometimes take a walk after dinner to the gate and observe the shadows of night.'

'By Jove, I wish I'd known that before.'

'Foolish creature!' said Bertha to herself with amusement. 'He doesn't gather that this is the first night upon which I shall have done anything of the kind.'

Then aloud, she bade him a laughing good-bye and they separated.

2

WITH swinging step Bertha returned to the house, and, like a swarm of birds, a hundred amorets flew about her head; Cupid leapt from tree to tree and shot his arrows into her willing heart; her imagination clothed the naked branches with tender green and in her happiness the grey sky turned to azure. It was the first time that Edward Craddock had shown his love in a manner that was unmistakable; if, before, much had suggested that he was not indifferent, nothing had been absolutely convincing, and the doubt had caused her every imaginable woe. As for her, she made no effort to conceal it from herself; she was not ashamed, she loved him passionately, she worshipped the ground he trod on; she confessed boldly that he of all men was the one to make her happy, her life she would give into his strong and manly hands; she had made up her mind firmly that Craddock should lead her to the altar.

'I want to be his wife,' she gasped, in the extremity of her passion.

Times without number already had she thought of herself resting in his arms – in his strong arms, the very thought of which was a protection against all the ills of the world. Oh, yes, she wanted him to take her in his arms and kiss her; in imagination she felt his lips upon hers, and the warmth of his breath made her faint with the anguish of love.

She asked herself how she could wait till the evening, how on earth she was to endure the slow passing of the hours. And she must sit opposite her aunt and pretend to read, or talk on this subject or that. It was insufferable. Then inconsequently she asked herself if Edward knew that she loved him; he could not dream how intense was her desire.

'I'm sorry I'm late for tea,' she said, on entering the drawing-room.

'My dear,' said Miss Ley, 'the buttered toast is probably horrid, but I don't see why you should not eat cake.'

'I don't want anything to eat,' cried Bertha, flinging herself on a chair.

'But you're dying with thirst,' added Miss Ley, looking at her niece with sharp eye. 'Wouldn't you like your tea out of a break-fast cup?'

Miss Ley had come to the conclusion that the restlessness and the long absence could only be due to some masculine cause. Mentally she shrugged her shoulders, hardly wondering who the creature was.

'Of course,' she thought, 'it's certain to be someone quite ineligible. I hope they won't have a long engagement.'

Miss Ley could not have supported for several months the presence of a bashful and love-sick swain. She found lovers invariably ridiculous and felt that they should be hidden – just as the sons of Noah covered their father's nakedness. She watched Bertha gulp down six cups of tea. Of course those shining eyes, the flushed cheeks and the breathlessness indicated some amorous excitement; it amused her, but she thought it charitable and wise to pretend that she noticed nothing.

'After all, it's no business of mine,' she thought, 'and if Bertha is going to get married at all, it would be much more convenient for her to do it before next quarter day, when the Brownes give up my flat.'

Miss Ley sat on the sofa by the fireside. She was a woman neither short nor tall, very slight, with a thin and much-wrinkled face. Of her features the mouth was the most noticeable, not large, with lips that were a trifle too thin; it was always so tightly compressed as to give her an air of great determination, but there was about the corners an expressive mobility, contradicting in rather an unusual manner the inferences that might be drawn from the rest of her person. She had a habit of fixing her cold eyes on people with a steadiness that was not a little embarrassing. They said Miss Ley looked as if she thought them great fools, and as a matter of fact that usually was precisely what she did think. Her thin grey hair was very plainly done, and the extreme simplicity of her costume gave her a certain primness, so that her favourite method of saying rather absurd things in the gravest and most decorous manner often disconcerted the casual stranger. She was a woman who, one felt, had never been handsome, but now, in middle age, was of distinctly prepossessing appearance. Young men thought her somewhat terrifying till they discovered that they were to her a constant source of amusement, while elderly ladies asserted that, though of course a perfect gentlewoman, she was a little queer.

'You know, Aunt Polly,' said Bertha, finishing her tea and getting up, 'I think you ought to have been called Martha or Matilda. I don't think Polly suits you.'

'My dear, you need not remind me so pointedly that I'm forty-five – and you need not smile in that fashion because you know that I'm really forty-seven. I say forty-five merely as a round number; in another year I shall call myself fifty. A woman never

18

acknowledges such a nondescript age as forty-eight unless she is going to marry a widower with seventeen children.'

'I wonder why you never married, Aunt Polly?' said Bertha looking away.

Miss Ley smiled almost imperceptibly; she found Bertha's remark highly significant.

'My dear,' she said, 'why should I? I had five hundred a year of my own. Ah, yes, I know it's not what might have been expected; I'm sorry for your sake that I had no hopeless amour. The only excuse for an old maid is that she has pined thirty years for a lover who is buried under the snowdrops or has married another.'

Bertha made no answer; she was feeling that the world had turned good, and wanted to hear nothing that could suggest imperfections in human nature. Going upstairs she sat at the window, gazing towards the farm where lived her heart's desire. She wondered what Edward was doing. Was he awaiting the night as anxiously as she? It gave her quite a pang that a sizable hill should intervene between herself and him. During dinner she hardly spoke, and Miss Ley was mercifully silent. Bertha could not eat. She crumpled her bread and toyed with the various meats put before her. She looked at the clock a dozen times and started absurdly when it struck the hour.

She did not trouble to make any excuse to Miss Ley, whom she left to think as she chose. The night was dark and cold. Bertha slipped out of the side-door with a delightful feeling of doing something venturesome. But her legs would scarcely carry her, she had a sensation that was entirely novel: never before had she experienced that utter weakness of the knees so that she feared to fall; her breathing was strangely oppressive, her heart beat painfully. She walked down the carriage-drive hardly knowing what she did. And supposing he was not there, supposing he never came? She had forced herself to wait in-doors till the desire to go out became uncontrollable, she dared not imagine her dismay if there was no one to meet her when she reached the gate. It would mean he did not love her. She stopped with a sob. Ought she not to wait longer? It was still early. But her impatience forced her on.

She gave a little cry. Craddock had suddenly stepped out of the darkness.

'Oh, I'm sorry,' he said, 'I frightened you. I thought you wouldn't mind my coming this evening. You're not angry?'

19

She could not answer, it was an immense load off her heart. She was extremely happy. Then he did love her; and he feared she was angry with him.

'I expected you,' she whispered.

What was the good of pretending to be modest and bashful? She loved him and he loved her. Why should she not tell him all she felt?

'It's so dark,' he said. 'I can't see you.'

She was too deliriously happy to speak, and the only words she could have said were, '*I love you, I love you!*' She moved a step nearer so as to touch him. Why did he not open his arms and take her in them and kiss her as she had dreamt that he would kiss her?

But he took her hand, and the contact thrilled her; her senses were giving way, and she almost tottered.

'What's the matter?' he said. 'Are you trembling?'

'I'm only a little cold.'

She was trying with all her might to speak naturally. Nothing came into her head to say.

'You've got nothing on,' he said. 'You must wear my coat.'

He began to take it off.

'No,' she said, 'then you'll be cold.'

'Oh, no, I shan't.'

What he was doing seemed to her a marvel of unselfish kindness. She was beside herself with gratitude.

'It's awfully good of you, Edward,' she whispered, almost tearfully.

When he put it round her shoulders the touch of his hands made her lose the little self-control she had left. A curious spasm passed through her and she pressed herself closer to him; at the same time his hands sank down, dropping the cloak and encircled her waist. Then she surrendered herself entirely to his embrace and lifted up her face to his. He bent down and kissed her. The kiss was such utter rapture that she almost groaned. She could not tell if it was pain or pleasure. She flung her arms round his neck and drew him to her.

'What a fool I am,' she said at last, with something between a sob and a laugh.

She drew herself a little away, though not so violently as to make him withdraw the arm that so comfortably encircled her. But why did he say nothing? Why did he not swear he loved her?

20

Why did he not ask what she was so willing to grant? She rested her head on his shoulder.

'Do you like me at all, Bertha?' he asked. 'I've been wanting to ask you ever since you came home.'

'Can't you see?' She was reassured; she understood that it was only timidity that clogged his tongue. 'You're so absurdly bashful.'

'You know who I am, Bertha; and – ' he hesitated.

'And what?'

'And you're Miss Ley of Court Leys, while I'm just one of your tenants with nothing whatever to my back.'

'I've got very little,' she said. 'And if I had ten thousand a year my only wish would be to lay it at your feet.'

'Bertha, what d'you mean? Don't be cruel to me. You know what I want – but – '

'Well, as far as I can make out,' she said, smiling, 'you want me to propose to you.'

'Oh, Bertha, don't laugh at me. I love you. I want to ask you to marry me. But I haven't got anything to offer you, and I know I oughtn't. Don't be angry with me, Bertha.'

'But I love you with all my heart,' she cried. 'I want no better husband. You can give me happiness, and I want nothing else in the world.'

Then he caught her again in his arms quite passionately and kissed her.

'Didn't you see that I loved you?' she whispered.

'I thought perhaps you did; but I wasn't sure, and I was afraid that you wouldn't think me good enough.'

'I love you with all my heart. I never imagined it possible to love anyone as I love you. Oh, Eddie, you don't know how happy you've made me.'

He kissed her again, and again she flung her arms around his neck.

'Oughtn't you to be going in?' he said at last. 'What will Miss Ley think?'

'Oh, no – not yet,' she cried.

'How will you tell her? D'you think she'll like me? She'll try and make you give me up.'

'Oh, I'm sure she'll love you. Besides, what does it matter if she doesn't? She isn't going to marry you.'

21

'She can take you abroad again, and then you may see someone you like better."

'But I'm twenty-one tomorrow, Edward – didn't you know? And I shall be my own mistress. I shan't leave Blackstable till I'm your wife.'

They were walking slowly towards the house, whither he, in his anxiety lest she should stay out too long, had guided her steps. They went arm in arm, and Bertha enjoyed her happiness.

'Dr Ramsay is coming to luncheon tomorrow,' she said. 'I shall tell them both that I'm going to be married to you.'

'He won't like it,' said Craddock rather nervously.

'I'm sure I don't care. If you like it and I like it the rest can think what they like.'

'I leave everything in your hands,' he said.

They had arrived at the portico, and Bertha looked at it doubtfully.

'I suppose I ought to go in,' she said, wishing Edward to persuade her to take one more turn in the garden.

'Yes, do,' he said. 'I'm so afraid you'll catch cold.'

It was charming of him to be so solicitous about her health, and of course he was right. Everything he did and said was right; for the moment Bertha forgot her wayward nature and wished suddenly to subject herself to his strong guidance. His very strength made her feel strangely weak.

'Good night, my beloved,' she whispered passionately.

She could not tear herself away from him; it was utter madness. Their kisses never ended.

'Good night!'

She watched him at last disappear into the darkness and finally shut the door behind her.

3

WITH old and young great sorrow is followed by a sleepless night, and with the old great joy is as disturbing; but youth, I suppose, finds happiness more natural and its rest is not disturbed by it. Bertha slept without dreams, and awaking, for the moment did not remember the occurrence of the previous day; but suddenly it came back to her, and she stretched herself with a sigh of great content. She lay in bed to contemplate her well-being. She could hardly realize that she had attained her dearest wish. God was very good and gave His creatures what they asked; without words, from the fullness of her heart she offered up thanks. It was quite extraordinary, after the maddening expectation, after the hopes and fears, the lover's pains that are nearly pleasures, at last to be satisfied. She had now nothing more to desire, her happiness was complete. Ah, yes, indeed, God was very good!

Bertha thought of the two months she had spent at Blackstable. After the first excitement of getting into the house of her fathers she had settled down to the humdrum of country life. She spent the day wandering about the lanes or on the sea-shore watching the desolate sea. She read a great deal and looked forward to the ample time at her disposal to satisfy an immoderate desire for knowledge. She spent many hours looking at the books in the library, gathered mostly by her father, for it was only with falling fortunes that the family of Ley had taken to reading books; it had only applied itself to literature when it was too poor for any other pursuit. Bertha looked at the titles, receiving a certain thrill as she read over the great names of the past, and imagined the future delights that they would give her. Beside the vicar and his sister, Dr Ramsay, who was Bertha's guardian, and his wife, she saw no one.

One day she was calling at the vicarage, and Edward Craddock, just returned from a short holiday, happened to be there. She had known him in days gone by; his father had been her father's tenant, and he still farmed the same land, but for eight years they had not seen one another, and now Bertha hardly recognized him. She thought him, however, a good-looking fellow in his knickerbockers and thick stockings, and was not displeased when he came up to speak to her, asking if she remembered him. He sat down, and a certain pleasant odour of the farmyard was wafted over to Bertha, a mingled perfume of strong tobacco, of cattle and horses. She did not understand why it made her heart beat; but she inhaled it voluptuously, and her eyes glittered. He began to talk, and his voice sounded like music in her ears; he looked at her, and his eyes were rather large and grey; she found them highly sympathetic. He was clean-shaven, and his mouth was very attractive. She blushed and felt herself a fool. She took pains to be as charming as possible. She knew her own dark eyes were beautiful, and kept them fixed upon his. When at last he bade her good-bye and shook hands with her, she blushed again; she was extraordinarily troubled, and as, with his rising, the strong, masculine odour of the countryside again reached her nostrils, her head whirled. She was very glad Miss Ley was not there to see her.

She walked home in the darkness, trying to compose herself. She could think of nothing but Edward Craddock. She recalled the past, trying to bring back to her memory incidents of their old acquaintance. At night she dreamt of him, and she dreamt he kissed her.

She awoke thinking of Craddock, and felt it impossible to go through the day without seeing him. She thought of sending him an invitation to luncheon or tea, but hardly dared to; and she did not want Miss Ley to see him yet. Suddenly she thought of the farm; she would walk there, was it not hers? The god of Love was propitious, and in a field she saw him, directing some operation. She trembled at the sight, her heart beat very quickly; and when, seeing her, he came forward with a greeting, she turned red and then white in the most compromising fashion. But he was very handsome as with easy gait he sauntered up to the hedge; above all he was manly; the thought passed through Bertha that his strength must be quite herculean. She scarcely concealed her admiration.

'Oh, I didn't know this was your farm,' she said, shaking hands. 'I was just walking at random.'

'I should like to show you round, Miss Bertha.'

He opened the gate and took her to the sheds where he kept his carts, pointing out a couple of sturdy horses ploughing an adjacent field; he showed her his cattle and poked the pigs to let her admire their excellent condition; he gave her sugar for his hunter, and took her to the sheep, explaining everything while she listened spell-bound. When with great pride Craddock showed her his machines and explained the use of the horse-tosser and the expense of the reaper, she thought that never in her life had she heard anything so enthralling. But above all Bertha wanted to see the house in which he lived.

'D'you mind giving me a glass of water?' she said. 'I'm so thirsty.'

'Do come in,' he answered, opening the door.

He led her into a little parlour with an oilcloth on the floor. On the table, which took up the middle of the room, was a stamped red cloth; the chairs and the sofa, covered with worn old leather, were arranged with the greatest possible stiffness. On the chimney-piece, along with pipes and tobacco-jars, were bright china vases with rushes in them, and in the middle a marble clock.

'Oh, how pretty!' cried Bertha with enthusiasm. 'You must feel very lonely here by yourself.'

'Oh, no. I'm always out. Shall I get you some milk? It'll be better for you than water.'

But Bertha saw a napkin laid out on the table, a jug of beer and some bread and cheese.

'Have I been keeping you from your lunch?' she asked. 'I'm so sorry.'

'It doesn't matter at all; I just have a little snack at eleven.'

'Oh, may I have some too?' she cried. 'I love bread and cheese, and I'm perfectly ravenous.'

They sat down opposite one another, seeing a great joke in the impromptu meal. The bread, which he cut in a great chunk, was delicious, and the beer, of course, was nectar. But afterwards, Bertha feared that Craddock must be thinking her rather queer.

'D'you think it's very eccentric of me to come and lunch with you in this way?'

'I think it's awfully good of you. Mr Ley often used to come and have a snack with my father.'

'Oh, did he?' said Bertha. Of course that made her proceeding quite natural. 'But I really must go now,' she said. 'I shall get in awful trouble with Aunt Polly.'

He begged her to take some flowers, and hastily cut a bunch of dahlias. She accepted them with embarrassing gratitude; and when they shook hands at parting her heart went pit-a-pat again in the most ridiculous fashion.

Miss Ley inquired from whom she had got her flowers.

'Oh,' said Bertha coolly. 'I happened to meet one of the tenants and he gave them to me.'

'H'm,' murmured Miss Ley. 'It would be more to the purpose if they paid their rent.'

Miss Ley presently left the room, and Bertha looked at the prim dahlias with a heart full of emotion. She gave a laugh.

'It's no good trying to hide it from myself,' she thought, 'I suppose I'm in love.'

She kissed the flowers and felt very glad. She evidently was in that condition, since by the night Bertha had made up her mind to marry Edward Craddock or die. She lost no time, for less than a month had passed, and their wedding-day was certainly in sight.

Miss Ley loathed all manifestations of feeling; Christmas, when everybody is supposed to take his neighbour to his bosom and harbour towards him a number of sentimental emotions, caused her such discomfort that she habitually buried herself for the time in some continental city where she knew no one and could escape the overbrimming of other people's hearts, their compliments of the season, and their state of mind generally. Even in summer Miss Ley could not see a holly tree without a little shiver of disgust; her mind went immediately to the decorations of middle-class houses, the mistletoe hanging from a gas chandelier and the foolish old gentlemen who found amusement in kissing stray females. She was glad that Bertha had thought fit to refuse the display of enthusiasm from servants and impoverished tenants that, on the attainment of her majority, Dr Ramsay had wished to arrange; Miss Ley could imagine that the festivities possible on such an occasion, the hand-shaking, the making of good cheer and the obtrusive joviality of the country Englishman, might surpass even the tawdry celebrations of Yuletide. But Bertha fortunately detested such festivities as sincerely as did Miss Ley herself, and suggested to the persons concerned that they could not oblige her more than by taking no notice of an event that really did not seem to her very significant.

But her guardian's heartiness could not be entirely restrained; he had a fine old English sense of fitness of things. He insisted on solemnly meeting Bertha to offer congratulations, a blessing, and some statement of his stewardship. Bertha came downstairs when Miss Ley was already eating breakfast, a very feminine breakfast consisting of nothing more substantial than a square inch of bacon and some dry toast. Miss Ley was really somewhat nervous, she was bothered by the necessity of referring to her niece's birthday.

'That is one advantage of women,' she told herself, 'after twenty-five they gloss over their birthdays like improprieties. A man is so impressed with his cleverness in having entered the world at all that the anniversary always interests him; and the foolish creature thinks it interests other people as well.'

But Bertha came into the room and kissed her.

'Good morning, dear,' said Miss Ley, and then, pouring out her niece's coffee: 'Our estimable cook has burnt the milk in honour of your majority; I trust she will not celebrate the occasion by getting drunk – at all events, till after dinner.'

'I hope Dr Ramsay won't enthuse too vigorously,' replied Bertha, understanding Miss Ley's feeling.

'Oh, my dear, I tremble at the prospect of his jollity. He's a good man, I should think his principles were excellent, and I don't suppose he's more ignorant than most general practitioners, but his friendliness is sometimes painfully aggressive.'

But Bertha's calm was merely external, her brain was in a whirl and her heart beat madly. She was full of impatience to declare her news. Bertha had some sense of dramatic effect, and looked forward a little to the scene when, the keys of her kingdom being handed over to her, she made the announcement that she had already chosen a king to rule by her side. She felt also that between herself and Miss Ley alone the necessary explanations would be awkward. Dr Ramsay's outspoken bluffness made him easier to deal with; there is always a certain difficulty in conducting oneself with a person who ostentatiously believes that everyone should mind her own business, and who, whatever her thoughts, takes more pleasure in the concealment than in the expression of them. Bertha sent a note to Craddock, telling him to come at three o'clock to be introduced as the future lord and master of the Ley estate.

Dr Ramsay arrived and burst at once into a prodigious stream of congratulation, partly jocose, partly grave and sentimental, but entirely distasteful to the fastidiousness of Miss Ley. Bertha's guardian was a big, broad-shouldered man, with a mane of fair hair, now turning white, and Miss Ley vowed he was the last person upon this earth to wear mutton-chop whiskers; he was very red-cheeked, and by his size, joviality and florid complexion gave one an idea of unalterable health. With his shaven chin and his loud-voiced burliness he looked like a yeoman of the old school, before bad times and the spread of education had made the farmer a sort of cross between the city clerk and the Newmarket trainer. Dr Ramsay's frock-coat and top-hat, notwithstanding the habit of many years, sat uneasily upon him with the air of Sunday clothes upon an agricultural labourer. Miss Ley, who liked to find absurd descriptions of people or hit upon an apt comparison, had never been able exactly to suit him, and that somewhat irritated her. In her eyes the only link that connected him with humanity was a certain love of antiquities, which had filled his house with old snuff-boxes, china and other precious things. Humanity, Miss Ley took to be a small circle of persons, mostly feminine, middle-aged, unattached and of independent means, who travelled on the Continent, read good literature and abhorred the vast majority of their fellow-creatures, especially when these shrieked philan-thropically, thrust their religion in your face, or cultivated their muscle with aggressive ardour.

Dr Ramsay ate his luncheon with a voracity that Miss Ley thought must be a source of satisfaction to his butcher. She asked politely after his wife, to whom she secretly objected for her meek submission to the doctor. Miss Ley made a practice of avoiding those women who had turned themselves into mere shadows of their husbands, more especially when their conversation was of household affairs; and Mrs Ramsay, except on Sundays, when her mind was turned to the clothes of the congregation, thought of nothing beyond her husband's enormous appetite and the methods of subduing it.

They returned to the drawing-room, and Dr Ramsay began telling Bertha about the property; who this tenant was and the condition of that farm; winding up with the pitiful state of the times and the impossibility of getting any rents.

'And now, Bertha, what are you thinking of doing?' he asked.

This was the opportunity for which Bertha had been looking.

'I? Oh, I intend to get married.'

Dr Ramsay, opening his mouth, threw back his head and laughed immoderately.

'Very good indeed,' he cried.

Miss Ley looked at him with uplifted eyebrows.

'Girls are coming on nowadays,' he said, with much amuse-ment. 'Why, in my time, a young woman would have been all blushes and downcast glances. If anyone had talked of marriage she would have prayed Heaven to send an earthquake to swallow her up.'

'Fiddlesticks!' said Miss Ley.

28

Bertha was looking at Dr Ramsay with a smile that she difficultly repressed, and Miss Ley caught the expression.

'So you intend to be married, Bertha?' said the doctor, again laughing.

'Yes,' she replied.

'When?' asked Miss Ley, who did not take Bertha's remarks as merely playful and fantastic.

Bertha was looking out of the window, wondering when Edward would arrive.

'When?' she repeated, turning round. 'This day four weeks.'

'What!' cried Dr Ramsay, jumping up. 'You don't mean to say you've found someone! Are you engaged? Oh, I see, I see! You've been having a little joke with me. Why didn't you tell me that Bertha was engaged all the time, Miss Ley?'

'My good doctor,' answered Miss Ley, with great calmness, 'until this moment I knew nothing whatever about it. I suppose we ought to offer our congratulations; it's a blessing to get them all over on one day.'

Dr Ramsay looked from one to the other with perplexity.

'Well, upon my word,' he said, 'I don't understand.'

'Neither do I,' said Miss Ley, 'but I keep calm.'

'It's very simple,' said Bertha. 'I got engaged last night, and I mean to be married exactly four weeks from today – to Mr Craddock.'

This time Dr Ramsay was more surprised than ever.

'What!' he cried, jumping up in his astonishment and causing the floor to quake in the most dangerous way. 'Craddock! What d'you mean? Which Craddock?'

'Edward Craddock,' replied Bertha with perfect calm, 'of Bewlie's Farm.'

'Brrh!' Dr Ramsay's exclamation cannot be transcribed, but it sounded horrid. 'It's absurd. You'll do nothing of the sort.'

Bertha looked at him with a gentle smile, she did not trouble to answer.

'You're very emphatic, dear doctor,' said Miss Ley. 'Who is this gentleman?'

'He isn't a gentleman,' said Dr Ramsay, becoming purple with vexation.

'He's going to be my husband, Dr Ramsay,' said Bertha

compressing her lips in the manner which with Miss Ley had become habitual, and turned to that lady: 'I've known him all my life. Father was a great friend of his father's. He's a gentleman-farmer.'

'The definition of which,' said Dr Ramsay, 'is a man who's neither a farmer nor a gentleman.'

'I forget what your father was,' said Bertha, who remembered perfectly well.

'My father was a farmer,' replied Dr Ramsay with some heat, 'and, thank God! he made no pretence of being a gentleman. He worked with his own hands, and I've seen him often enough with a pitchfork turning over a heap of manure, when no one else was handy.'

'I see,' said Bertha.

'But my father can have nothing to do with it; you can't marry him because he's been dead these thirty years, and you can't marry me because I've got a wife already.'

Miss Ley concealed a smile; Bertha was too clever for it not to give the elder lady some slight pleasure to see her snubbed. Bertha was getting angry, she thought the doctor rude.

'And what have you against him?' she asked.

'If you want to make a fool of yourself, he's got no right to encourage you. He knows he's not a fit match for you.'

'Why not, if I love him?'

'Why not?' shouted Dr Ramsay. 'Because he's the son of a farmer – like I am – and you're Miss Ley of Court Leys. Because a man in that position, without fifty pounds to his back, doesn't make love on the sly to a girl with a fortune.'

'Five thousand acres that pay no rent,' murmured Miss Ley, who was always in opposition.

'You have nothing whatever against him,' retorted Bertha. 'You told me yourself that he had the very best reputation.'

'I didn't know you were asking me with a view to matrimony,' said the doctor.

'I wasn't. I care nothing for his reputation. If he were drunken and idle and dissolute, I'd marry him – because I love him.'

'My dear Bertha,' said Miss Ley, 'the doctor will have an apoplectic fit if you say such things.'

'You told me he was one of the best fellows you knew, Dr Ramsay,' said Bertha.

'I don't deny it,' shouted the doctor, and his red cheeks really had in them a purple tinge that was quite alarming. 'He knows his business and he works hard and he's straight and steady.'

'Good heavens, doctor,' cried Miss Ley, 'he must be a miracle of rural excellence. Bertha would surely never have fallen in love with him if he were faultless.'

'If Bertha wanted an agent,' Dr Ramsay proceeded, 'I could recommend no one better – but as for marrying him –'

'Does he pay his rent?' asked Miss Ley.

'He's one of the best tenants we've got,' growled the doctor. Miss Ley's frivolous interruptions annoyed him.

'Of course in these bad times,' added Miss Ley, who was determined not to allow the doctor to play the heavy father with too much seriousness, 'I suppose about the only resource of the respectable farmer is to marry his landlady.'

'Here he is!' interrupted Bertha.

'Good God, is he coming here?' cried her guardian.

'I sent for him. Remember he is going to be my husband.'

'I'm damned if he is!' said Dr Ramsay.

Miss Ley laughed gently; she rather liked an occasional oath, it relieved the commonplace of masculine conversation in the presence of ladies.

4

BERTHA threw off her troubled looks and the vexation that the argument had caused her. She blushed charmingly as the door opened, and with the entrance of the fairy prince her face was wreathed in smiles. She went towards him and took his hands.

'Aunt Polly,' she said, 'this is Mr Edward Craddock. Dr Ramsay you know.'

He shook hands with Miss Ley and looked at the doctor, who promptly turned his back on him. Craddock flushed a little and sat down by Miss Ley's side.

'We were talking about you, dearest,' said Bertha. The pause at his arrival had been disconcerting, and while Craddock was nervously thinking of something to say, Miss Ley made no effort to help him. 'I have told Aunt Polly and Dr Ramsay that we intend to be married four weeks from today.'

This was the first that Craddock had heard of the date, but he showed no astonishment. He was in fact trying to recall the speech that he had composed for the occasion.

'I will try to be a good husband to your niece, Miss Ley,' he began.

But that lady interrupted him; she had already come to the conclusion that he was a man likely to say on a given occasion the sort of thing that might be expected; and that in her eyes was a hideous crime.

'Oh, yes, I have no doubt,' she replied. 'Bertha, as you know, is her own mistress and responsible for her acts to no one.'

Craddock was a little embarrassed; he had meant to express his sense of unworthiness and his desire to do his duty, also to explain his own position; but Miss Ley's remark seemed to prohibit further explanation.

'Which is really very convenient,' said Bertha, coming to his rescue. 'Because I have a mind to manage my life in my own way without interference from anybody.'

Miss Ley wondered whether the young man looked upon Bertha's statement as auguring complete tranquillity in the future; but Craddock seemed to see in it nothing ominous, he looked at Bertha with a grateful smile, and the glance that she returned to him was full of the most passionate devotion. Since his arrival Miss Ley had been observing Craddock with great minuteness, and being a woman she could not help finding some pleasure in the knowledge that Bertha was trying with anxiety to discover her judgement. Craddock's appearance was pleasing. Miss Ley liked young men generally, and this was a very good-looking member of the species. His eyes were good, but otherwise there was nothing remarkable in his physiognomy; he looked healthy and good-tempered. Miss Ley noticed even that he did not bite his nails and that his hands were strong and firm. There was really nothing to distinguish him from the common run of healthy young Englishmen with good morals and fine physique; but the class is pleasant. Miss Ley's only wonder was that Bertha had chosen him rather than ten thousand others of the same variety; for that Bertha had chosen him rather actively there was in Miss Ley's mind not the shadow of a doubt.

Miss Ley turned to him.

'Has Bertha shown you our chickens?' she asked calmly.

'No,' he said, rather surprised at the question. 'I hope she will.'

'Oh, no doubt. You know I am quite ignorant of agriculture. Have you ever been abroad?'

'No, I stick to my own country,' he replied, 'it's good enough for me.'

'I daresay it is,' said Miss Ley, looking to the ground. 'Bertha must certainly show you our chickens. They interest me because they're very like human beings; they're so stupid.'

'I can't get mine to lay at all at this time of year,' said Craddock.

'Of course I'm not an agriculturist,' repeated Miss Ley. 'But chickens amuse me.'

Dr Ramsay began to smile, and Bertha flushed angrily.

'You have never shown any interest in the chickens before, Aunt Polly.'

'Haven't I, my dear? Don't you remember last night I remarked how tough was that one we had for dinner? How long have you known Bertha, Mr Craddock?'

'It seems all my life,' he replied. 'And I want to know her more.'

This time Bertha smiled, and Miss Ley, though she felt certain it was unintentional, was not displeased with the manner in which he had parried her question. Dr Ramsay sat in a peevish silence.

'I have never seen you sit so still before, Dr Ramsay,' said Bertha, not too pleased with him.

'I think what I have to say would scarcely please you, Miss Bertha,' he answered bluntly.

Miss Ley was anxious that no altercation should disturb the polite discomfort of the meeting.

'You're thinking about those rents again, doctor,' she said, and turning to Craddock: 'The poor doctor is unhappy because half our tenants say they cannot pay.'

The poor doctor grunted and sniffed, and Miss Ley thought it high time for the young man to take his leave. She looked at Bertha, who quickly understood, and getting up, said:

'Let us leave them alone, Eddie; I want to show you the house.'

He rose with great alacrity, evidently much relieved at the end of the ordeal. He shook Miss Ley's hand, and this time could not be restrained from making a little speech.

'I hope you're not angry with me for taking Bertha away from you. I hope I shall soon get to know you better and that we shall become great friends.'

Miss Ley was taken aback, but really she thought his effort not bad. It might have been much worse, and at all events he had kept out of it references to the Almighty and his Duty. Then Craddock turned to Dr Ramsay and went up to him with an outstretched hand that could not be refused.

'I should like to see you some time, Dr Ramsay,' he said, looking at him steadily. 'I fancy you want to have a talk with me, and I should like it too. When can you give me an appointment?'

Bertha flushed with pleasure at his frank words, and Miss Ley was pleased at the courage with which he had attacked the old curmudgeon.

'I think it would be a very good idea,' said the doctor. 'I can see you tonight at eight.'

'Good! Good-bye, Miss Ley.'

He went out with Bertha.

Miss Ley was not one of those persons who consider it indiscreet to form an opinion upon small evidence. Before knowing a person five minutes she made up her mind about him, and liked nothing better than to impart her impression to anyone who asked her.

'Upon my word, doctor,' she said as soon as the door was shut upon the young couple, 'he's not so terrible as I expected.'

'I never said he was not good-looking,' pointedly answered Dr Ramsay, who was convinced that any and every woman was willing to make herself a fool with a handsome man.

Miss Ley smiled. 'Good looks, my dear doctor, are three parts of the necessary equipment in the battle of life. You can't imagine the miserable existence of a really plain girl.'

'Do you approve of Bertha's ridiculous idea?'

'To tell you the truth, I think it makes very little difference if you and I approve or not; therefore we'd much better take the matter quietly.'

'You can do what you like, Miss Ley,' replied the doctor very bluntly, 'but I mean to stop this business.'

'You won't, my dear doctor,' said Miss Ley, smiling again. 'I know Bertha so much better than you. I've lived with her three years, and I've found constant entertainment in the study of her character. Let me tell you how I first knew her. Of course you know that her father and I hadn't been on speaking terms for years: having played ducks and drakes with his own money, he wanted to play the same silly game with mine; and as I strongly objected he flew into a violent passion, called me an ungrateful wretch, and nourished the grievance to the end of his days. Well, his health broke down after his wife's death, and he spent several years with Bertha wandering about the Continent. She was educated as best could be in half a dozen countries, and it's a marvel to me that she is not entirely ignorant or entirely vicious. She's a brilliant example in favour of the opinion that the human race is inclined to good rather than to evil.'

Miss Ley smiled, for she was herself none too certain of it.

'Well, one day,' she proceeded, 'I got a telegram, sent through my solicitors. "Father dead, please come if convenient, Bertha Ley." It was addressed from Naples, and I was in Florence. Of course I rushed down, taking nothing but a bag, a few yards of crape and some smelling-salts. I was met at the station by Bertha, whom I hadn't seen for ten years. I saw a tall and handsome young woman, self-possessed and admirably gowned in the very latest fashion. I kissed her in a subdued way, proper to the occasion, and as we drove back inquired when the funeral was to be, holding the smelling-salts in readiness for an outburst of weeping. "Oh, it's all over," she said. "I didn't send my wire till everything was settled. I thought it would only upset you. I've given notice to the landlord of the villa and to the servants. There was really no need for you to come at all, only the doctor and the English parson seemed to think it rather queer of me to be here alone." I used the smelling-salts myself! Imagine my emotion! I expected to find a hobblede-hoy of a girl in hysterics, everything topsy-turvy and all sorts of horrid things to do; instead of which I found everything arranged perfectly well and the hobbledehoy rather disposed to manage me, if I let her. At luncheon she looked at my travelling-dress. "I sup-pose you left Florence in rather a hurry," she remarked. "If you want to get anything black you'd better go to my dressmaker. She's not bad. I must go there this afternoon myself to try some things on."'

Miss Ley stopped and looked at the doctor to see the effect of her words. He said nothing.

'And the impression I gained then,' she added, 'has only been strengthened since. You'll be a very clever man if you prevent Bertha from doing a thing upon which she has set her mind.'

'D'you mean to tell me that you're going to sanction this marriage?' asked the doctor.

Miss Ley shrugged her shoulders: 'My dear Dr Ramsay, I tell you it won't make the least difference whether we either of us bless or curse. And he seems an average sort of young man. Let us be thankful that she's done no worse; he's not uneducated.'

'No, he's not that. He spent ten years at Regis School, Tercanbury; so he ought to know something.'

'What exactly was his father?'

'His father was the same as himself – a gentleman-farmer. He'd been educated at Regis School as his son was. He knew most of the gentry, but he wasn't quite one of them; he knew all the farmers and he wasn't quite one of them either. And that's what they've been for generations, neither flesh, fowl, nor good red-herring.'

'It's those people that the newspapers tell us are the backbone of the country, Dr Ramsay.'

'Let 'em remain in their proper place then, in the back,' said the doctor. 'You can do as you please, Miss Ley; I'm going to put a stop to this nonsense. After all, Mr Ley made me the girl's guardian, and though she is twenty-one I think it's my duty to see that she doesn't fall into the hands of the first penniless scamp who asks her to marry him.'

'You can do as you please,' retorted Miss Ley, who was somewhat bored with the good man. 'You'll do no good with Bertha.'

'I'm not going to Bertha, I'm going to Craddock direct, and I mean to give him a piece of my mind.'

Miss Ley shrugged her shoulders. Dr Ramsay evidently did not see who was the active party in the matter, and she did not feel it her duty to inform him. The doctor took his leave, and in a few minutes Bertha joined Miss Ley. The latter obviously intended to make no efforts to disturb the course of true love.

'You'll have to be thinking of ordering your trousseau, my dear,' she said with a dry smile.

'We're going to be married quite privately,' answered Bertha. 'We neither of us want to make a fuss.'

'I think you're very wise. Most people when they get married fancy they're doing a very original thing. It never occurs to them that quite a number of persons have committed matrimony since Adam and Eve.'

'I've asked Edward to come to luncheon tomorrow,' said Bertha.

5

NEXT day, after luncheon, Miss Ley retired to the drawing-room and unpacked the books that had just arrived from Mudie. She looked through them and read a page here and there to see what they were like, thinking meanwhile of the meal they had just finished. Edward Craddock had been rather nervous, sitting uncomfortably on his chair, and too officious perhaps in handing things to Miss Ley, salt and pepper and such like, as he saw she wanted them; he evidently wished to make himself amiable. At the same time he was subdued, and not gaily enthusiastic, as might be expected from a happy lover. Miss Ley could not help asking herself if he really loved her niece. Bertha was obviously without a doubt on the subject; she had been radiant, keeping her eyes all the while fixed upon the young man as if he were the most delightful and wonderful thing she had ever seen. Miss Ley was surprised at the girl's expansiveness, contrasting with her old reserve; she seemed now not to care a straw if all the world saw her emotions. She was not only happy to be in love, she was proud. Miss Ley laughed aloud at the doctor's idea that he could disturb the course of such passion. But if Miss Ley, well aware that the watering-pots of reason could not put out those raging fires, had no intention of hindering the match, neither had she a desire to witness the preliminaries thereof; and after luncheon, remarking that she felt tired and meant to lie down, she had gone into the drawing-room alone. It pleased her to think that she could at the same time suit the lovers' pleasure and her own convenience.

She chose the book from the bundle that seemed most promising and began to read. Presently the door was opened by a servant and Miss Glover was announced. A look of annoyance passed over Miss Ley's face, but it was immediately succeeded by one of mellifluous amiability.

'Oh, don't get up, dear Miss Ley,' said the visitor as her hostess slowly rose from the sofa upon which she had been so comfortably lying.

Miss Ley shook hands and began to talk. She said she was delighted to see Miss Glover, thinking meanwhile that this estimable person's sense of etiquette was very tiresome. The Glovers had dined at Court Leys during the previous week, and punctually seven days afterwards Miss Glover was paying a ceremonious call.

Miss Glover was a worthy person, but tedious; and that Miss Ley could not forgive. Better ten thousand times, in her opinion, was it to be Becky Sharp and a monster of wickedness than Amelia and a monster of stupidity.

Miss Glover was one of the best-natured and most charitable creatures upon the face of the earth, a miracle of abnegation and unselfishness; but a person to be amused by her could have been only an absolute lunatic.

'She's a dear kind thing,' said Miss Ley of her, 'and she does endless good in the parish; but she's really too dull, she's only fit for heaven.'

And the image passed through Miss Ley's mind, unsobered by advancing years, of Miss Glover, with her colourless hair hanging down her back, wings and a golden harp, singing hymns in a squeaky voice, morning, noon and night. Indeed, the general conception of paradisaical costume suited Miss Glover very ill. She was a woman of about eight and twenty, but might have been any age between one score and two; you felt that she had always been the same and that years would have no power over her strength of mind. She had no figure, and her clothes were so stiff and unyielding as to give an impression of armour. She was always dressed in a tight black jacket of ribbed cloth that was evidently most durable, the plainest of skirts, and strong, really strong, boots. Her hat was suited to wear in all weathers, and she had made it herself. She never wore a veil, and her skin was dry and hard, drawn so tightly over the bones as to give her face extraordinary angularity; over her prominent cheek-bones was a red flush, the colour of which was not uniformly suffused, but with the capillaries standing out distinctly forming a network. Her nose and mouth were what is politely termed of a determined character, her pale blue eyes slightly protruded; ten years of East Anglian winds had blown all the softness out of her face, and their bitter fury seemed to have bleached even her hair. One could not tell if this was brown and had lost its richness, or gold from which the shimmer had vanished; the roots sprang from the cranium with a curious apartness, so that Miss Ley always thought how easy in her case it would be to number the hairs. But notwithstanding the hard, uncompromising exterior which suggested extreme determination, she was so bashful, so absurdly self-conscious as to blush at every opportunity, and in the presence of a stranger to go through utter misery from inability to think of a single word to say. At the same time she had the tenderest of hearts, sympathetic, compassionate; she overflowed with love and pity for her fellow-creatures. She was excessively sentimental.

'And how is your brother?' asked Miss Ley.

Mr Glover was the Vicar of Leanham, which was about a mile from Court Leys on the Tercanbury Road, and Miss Glover had kept house for him since his appointment to the living.

'Oh, he's very well. Of course he's rather worried about the dissenters. You know they're putting up a new chapel in Leanham? It's perfectly dreadful.'

'Mr Craddock mentioned the fact at luncheon.'

'Oh, was he lunching with you? I didn't know you knew him well enough for that.'

'I suppose he's here now,' said Miss Ley, 'he's not been in to say good-bye.'

Miss Glover looked at her with some want of intelligence. But it was not to be expected that Miss Ley would explain before making the affair a good deal more complicated.

'And how is Bertha?' asked Miss Glover, whose conversation was chiefly concerned with inquiries about common acquaintances.

'Oh, of course, she's in the seventh heaven of delight.'

'Oh!' said Miss Glover, not understanding at all what Miss Ley meant. She was somewhat afraid of the elder lady: even though her brother Charles said he feared she was worldly, Miss Glover could not fail to respect a woman who had lived in London and on the Continent, who had met Dean Farrer and seen Miss Marie Corelli. 'Of course,' she said, 'Bertha is young, and naturally high-spirited.'

'Well, I'm sure I hope she'll be happy.'

'You must be very anxious about her future, Miss Ley.'

Miss Glover found her hostess's observations cryptic, and feeling foolish blushed a fiery red.

'Not at all,' said Miss Ley. 'She's her own mistress and as able-bodied and reasonable-minded as most young women. But, of course, it's a great risk.'

'I'm very sorry, Miss Ley,' said the vicar's sister, in such distress as to give Miss Ley certain qualms of conscience, 'but I really don't understand. What is a great risk?'

'Matrimony, my dear.'

'Is Bertha – going – to get married? Oh, dear Miss Ley, let me congratulate you. How happy and proud you must be!'

'My dear Miss Glover, please keep calm. And if you want to congratulate anybody congratulate Bertha – not me.'

'But I'm so glad, Miss Ley. To think of dear Bertha getting married! Charles will be so pleased.'

'It's to Mr Edward Craddock,' drily said Miss Ley, interrupting these transports.

'Oh!' Miss Glover's jaw dropped and she changed colour; then recovering herself: 'You don't say so!'

'You seem surprised, dear Miss Glover,' said the elder lady with a thin smile.

'I am surprised. I thought they scarcely knew one another; and besides – ' Miss Glover stopped with embarrassment.

'And besides what?' inquired Miss Ley sharply.

'Well, Miss Ley, of course Mr Craddock is a very good young man, and I like him; but I shouldn't have thought him a suitable match for Bertha.'

'It depends on what you mean by a suitable match,' answered Miss Ley.

'I was always hoping Bertha would marry young Mr Branderton of the Towers.'

'H'm!' said Miss Ley, who did not like the neighbouring squire's mother. 'I don't know what Mr Branderton has to recommend him beyond the possession of four or five generations of particularly stupid ancestors and two or three thousand acres that he can neither let nor sell.'

'Of course Mr Craddock is a very worthy young man,' added Miss Glover, who was afraid she had said too much. 'If you approve of the match no one else can complain.'

'I don't approve of the match, Miss Glover, but I'm not such a fool as to oppose it. Marriage is always a hopeless idiocy for a woman who has enough of her own to live upon.'

'It's an institution of the Church, Miss Ley,' replied Miss Glover.

'Is it?' retorted Miss Ley. 'I always thought it was an institution to provide work for the judges in the Divorce Court.'

To this Miss Glover very properly made no answer.

'Do you think they'll be happy together?' she asked finally.

'I think it very improbable,' said Miss Ley.

'Well, don't you think it's your duty – excuse my mentioning it, Miss Ley – to do something?'

'My dear Miss Glover, I don't think they'll be more unhappy than most married couples; and one's greatest duty in this world is to leave people alone.'

'There I cannot agree with you,' said Miss Glover, bridling. 'If duty was not more difficult than that, there would be no credit in doing it.'

'Ah, my dear, your idea of a happy life is always to do the disagreeable thing; mine is to gather the roses – with gloves on, so that the thorns should not prick me.'

'That's not the way to win the battle, Miss Ley. We must all fight.'

Miss Ley raised her eyebrows. She fancied it somewhat impertinent for a woman twenty years younger than herself to exhort her to lead a better life. But the picture of that poor, scraggy, ill-dressed creature fighting with a devil, cloven-footed, betailed and behorned, was as pitiful as it was comic; and with difficulty Miss Ley repressed an impulse to argue and startle a little her estimable friend. But at that moment Dr Ramsay came in. He shook hands with the two ladies.

'I thought I'd look in to see how Bertha was,' he said.

'Poor Mr Craddock has another adversary,' remarked Miss Ley. 'Miss Glover thinks I ought to take the affair – seriously.'

'I do indeed,' said Miss Glover.

'Ever since I was a young girl,' said Miss Ley, 'I've been trying not to take things seriously; and I'm afraid now I'm hopelessly frivolous.'

The contrast between this assertion and Miss Ley's prim manner was really funny; but Miss Glover saw only something quite incomprehensible.

'After all,' added Miss Ley, 'nine marriages out of ten are more or less unsatisfactory. You say young Branderton would have been more suitable; but really a string of ancestors is no particular assistance to matrimonial felicity, and otherwise I see no marked difference between him and Edward Craddock. Mr Branderton has been to Eton and Oxford, but he conceals the fact with very great success. Practically he's just as much a gentleman-farmer as Mr Craddock; but one family is working itself up and the other is working itself down. The Brandertons represent the past and the Craddocks the future; and though I detest reform and progress, so far as matrimony is concerned I myself prefer the man who founds a family to the man who ends it. But, good Heavens, you're making me sententious!'

Opposition was making Miss Ley almost a champion of Edward Craddock.

'Well,' said the doctor in his heavy way, 'I'm in favour of everyone sticking to his own class. Nowadays, whoever a man is he wants to be the next thing better; the labourer apes the tradesman, the tradesman apes the professional man.'

'And the professional man is worst of all, dear doctor,' said Miss Ley, 'for he apes the noble lord, who seldom affords a very admirable example. And the amusing thing is that each set thinks itself quite as good as the set above it and has a profound contempt for the set below it. In fact the only members of society who hold themselves in proper estimation are the servants. I always think that the domestics of gentlemen's houses in South Kensington are several degrees less odious than their masters.'

This was not a subject that Miss Glover and Dr Ramsay could discuss, and there was a momentary pause. 'What single point can you bring in favour of this marriage?' asked the doctor suddenly.

Miss Ley looked at him as if she were thinking, then with a dry smile: 'My dear doctor, Mr Craddock is so matter of fact – the moon will never arouse him to poetic ecstasies.'

'Miss Ley!' said the parson's sister in a tone of entreaty.

Miss Ley glanced from one to the other. 'Do you want my serious opinion?' she asked, rather more gravely than usual. 'The girl loves him, my dear doctor. Marriage, after all, is such a risk that only passion makes it worth while.'

Miss Glover looked up rather uneasily at the word.

'Yes, I know what you all think in England,' said Miss Ley, catching the glance and its meaning. 'You expect people to marry from every reason except the proper one – and that is the instinct of reproduction.'

'Miss Ley!' exclaimed Miss Glover, blushing.

'Oh, you're old enough to take a sensible view of the matter,' answered Miss Ley brutally. 'Bertha is merely the female attracted to the male, and that is the only decent foundation of marriage; the other way seems to me merely pornographic. And what does it matter if the man is not of the same station? The instinct has nothing to do with the walk in life. If I'd ever been in love I shouldn't have cared if it was a pot-boy, I'd have married him – if he asked me.'

'Well, upon my word!' said the doctor.

But Miss Ley was roused now, and interrupted him: 'The particular function of a woman is to propagate her species, and if she's wise she'll choose a strong and healthy man to be the father of her children. I have no patience with those women who marry a man because he's got brains. What is the good of a husband who can make abstruse mathematical calculations? A woman wants a man with strong arms and the digestion of an ox.'

'Miss Ley,' broke in Miss Glover, 'I'm not clever enough to argue with you, but I know you're wrong. I don't think I ought to listen to you; I'm sure Charles wouldn't like it.'

'My dear, you've been brought up like the majority of English girls, that is, like a fool.'

Poor Miss Glover blushed. 'At all events I've been brought up to regard marriage as a holy institution. We're here upon earth to mortify the flesh, not to indulge it. I hope I shall never be tempted to think of such matters in the way you've suggested. If ever I marry, I know that nothing will be further from me than carnal thoughts. I look upon marriage as a spiritual union in which it's my duty to love, honour and obey my husband, to assist and sustain him, to live with him such a life that when the end comes we may be prepared for it.'

'Fiddlesticks!' said Miss Ley.

'I should have thought you of all people,' said Dr Ramsay, 'would object to Bertha's marrying beneath her.'

'They can't be happy,' said Miss Glover.

'Why not? I used to know in Italy Lady Justitia Shawe, who married her footman. She made him take her name, and they drank like fishes. They lived for forty years in complete happiness, and when he drank himself to death, poor Lady Justitia was so grieved that her next attack of *delirium tremens* carried her off. It was most pathetic.'

43

'I can't think you look forward with pleasure to such a fate for your only niece, Miss Ley,' said Miss Glover, who took everything seriously.

'I have another niece, you know,' answered Miss Ley. 'My sister, who married Sir James Courte, has three children.'

But the doctor broke in: 'Well, I don't think you need trouble yourselves about the matter, for I have authority to announce to you that the marriage of Bertha and young Craddock is broken off.'

'What!' cried Miss Ley. 'I don't believe it.'

'You don't say so,' ejaculated Miss Glover at the same moment. 'Oh, I *am* relieved!'

Dr Ramsay rubbed his hands, beaming with delight. 'I knew I should stop it,' he said. 'What do you think now, Miss Ley?'

He was evidently rejoicing over her discomfiture. It made her cross.

'How can I think anything till you explain yourself?' she asked.

'He came to see me last night – you remember he asked for an interview of his own accord – and I put the case before him. I talked to him, I told him that the marriage was impossible, and I said the Leanham and Blackstable people would call him a fortune-hunter. I appealed to him for Bertha's sake. He's an honest, straightforward fellow. I always said he was. I made him see he wasn't doing the straight thing, and at last he promised to break it off.'

'He won't keep a promise of that sort,' said Miss Ley.

'Oh, won't he!' cried the doctor. 'I've known him all his life, and he'd rather die than break his word.'

'Poor fellow,' said Miss Glover, 'it must have pained him terribly.'

'He bore it like a man.'

Miss Ley pursed her lips till they practically disappeared. 'And when is he supposed to carry out your ridiculous suggestion, Dr Ramsay?' she asked.

'He told me he was lunching here today, and would take the opportunity to ask Bertha for his release.'

'The man's a fool!' muttered Miss Ley to herself, but quite audibly.

'I think it's very noble of him,' said Miss Glover, 'and I shall make a point of telling him so.'

'I wasn't thinking of Mr Craddock,' snapped Miss Ley, 'but of Dr Ramsay.'

Miss Glover looked at the worthy man to see how he took the rudeness; but at that moment the door opened and Bertha walked in. Miss Ley caught her mood at a glance. Bertha was evidently not at all distressed, there was no sign of tears, but her cheeks showed more colour than usual and her lips were firmly compressed; Miss Ley concluded that her niece was in a very pretty passion. She drove away the appearance of anger, and her face was full of smiles, however, as she greeted her visitors.

'Miss Glover, how kind of you to come! How d'you do, Dr Ramsay? By the way, I think I must ask you not to interfere in future with my private concerns.'

'Dearest,' broke in Miss Glover, 'it's all for the best.'

Bertha turned to her, and the flush on her face deepened. 'Ah, I see you've been discussing the matter. How good of you! Edward has been asking me to release him.'

Dr Ramsay nodded with satisfaction.

'But I refused!'

Dr Ramsay sprang up, and Miss Glover, lifting her hands, cried: 'Oh, dear! Oh, dear!'

This was one of the rare occasions in her life upon which Miss Ley was known to laugh outright. Bertha now was simply beaming with happiness. 'He pretended that he wanted to break the engagement, but I utterly declined.'

'You mean to say you wouldn't let him go when he asked you?' said the doctor.

'Did you think I was going to let my happiness be destroyed by you?' she asked contemptuously. 'I found out that you had been meddling, Dr Ramsay. Poor boy, he thought his honour required him not to take advantage of my inexperience. I told him, what I've told him a thousand times, that I love him and that I can't live without him. Oh, I think you ought to be ashamed of yourself, Dr Ramsay. What d'you mean by coming between me and Edward?'

Bertha said the last words passionately. She was breathing hard. Dr Ramsay was taken aback, and Miss Glover, thinking such a manner of speech unladylike, looked down. Miss Ley's sharp eyes played from one to the other.

'Do you think he really loves you?' said Miss Glover at last. 'It seems to me that if he had, he would not have been so ready to give you up.'

Miss Ley smiled; it was certainly curious that a creature of quite angelic goodness should make so machiavellian a suggestion.

'He offered to give me up because he loved me,' said Bertha proudly. 'I adore him ten thousand times more for the suggestion.'

'I have no patience with you,' cried the doctor, unable to contain himself. 'He's marrying you for your money.'

Bertha gave a little laugh. She was standing by the fire, and turned to the glass. She looked at her hands, resting on the edge of the chimney-piece, small and exquisitely modelled, the fingers tapering, the nails of the softest pink; they were the gentlest hands in the world, made for caresses; and, conscious of their beauty, she wore no rings. With them Bertha was well satisfied. Then, raising her glance, she saw herself in the mirror. For a while she gazed into her dark eyes, flashing sometimes and at others conveying the burning messages of love. She looked at her ears, small and pink like a shell; they made one feel that no materials were so grateful to the artist's hands as the materials that make up the body of man. Her hair was dark too, so abundant that she scarcely knew how to wear it, curling, and one wanted to pass one's hands through it, imagining that its touch must be delightful. She put her fingers to one side, to arrange a stray lock; they might say what they liked, she thought, but her hair was good. Bertha wondered why she was so dark; her olive skin suggested, indeed, the South with its burning passion; she had the complexion of the women of Umbria, clear and soft beyond description: a painter once had said that her skin had in it all the colours of the setting sun, of the setting sun at its borders, where the splendour mingles with the sky; it had a hundred mellow tints – cream and ivory, the palest yellow of the heart of roses and the faintest, the very faintest green, all flushed with radiant light. She looked at her full red lips, almost passionately sensual; it made the heart beat to imagine the kisses of that mouth. Bertha smiled at herself, and saw the even, glistening teeth. The scrutiny had made her blush, and the colour rendered still more exquisite the pallid, marvellous complexion. She turned slowly and faced the three persons looking at her.

'Do you think it impossible for a man to love me for myself? You are not flattering, dear doctor.'

Miss Ley thought Bertha certainly very bold thus to challenge

46

the criticism of two women, both unmarried; but she silenced it. Miss Ley's eyes went from the statuesque neck to the arms as finely formed, and to the shapely body.

'You're looking your best, my dear,' she said with a smile.

The doctor uttered an expression of annoyance: 'Can you do nothing to hinder this madness, Miss Ley?'

'My dear Dr Ramsay, I have trouble enough in arranging my own life; do not ask me to interfere with other people's.'

6

BERTHA gave herself over completely to the enjoyment of her love. Her sanguine temperament never allowed her to do anything half-heartedly, and she took no care now to conceal her feelings; love was a great sea into which she boldly plunged, uncaring whether she would swim or sink.

'I am such a fool,' she told Craddock. 'I can't realize that anyone has loved before. I feel that the world is only now beginning.'

She hated any separation from him. In the morning she existed for nothing but her lover's visit at luncheon time and the walk back with him to his farm; then the afternoon seemed endless, and she counted the hours that must pass before she saw him again. But what bliss it was when, after his work was over, he arrived and they sat side by side near the fire, talking! Bertha would have no other light than the fitful flaming of the coals: but for the little space where they sat the room was dark, and the redness of the fire threw on Edward's face a glow and weird shadows. She loved to look at him, at his clean-cut features and his curly hair, into his grey eyes. Then her passion knew no restraint.

'Shut your eyes,' she whispered, and kissed the closed lids; she passed her lips slowly over his lips, and the soft contact made her shudder and laugh. She buried her face in his clothes inhaling those masterful scents of the countryside that had always fascinated her. 'What have you been doing today, my dearest?'

'Oh, there's nothing much doing on the farm just now. We've just been ploughing and root-carting.'

It enchanted her to receive information on agricultural subjects, and she could have listened to him for hours. Every word that Edward spoke was charming and original. Bertha never took her eyes off him, she loved to hear him speak but often scarcely listened to what he said, merely watching the play of his expression. It puzzled him sometimes to catch her smile of intense happiness when he was discussing the bush-drainage of a field. However, she really took a deep interest in all his stock, and never failed to inquire after a bullock that was indisposed; it pleased her to think of the strong man among his beasts, and the thought gave a tautness to her own muscles. She determined to learn riding and tennis and golf, so that she might accompany him in all his amusements. Her own accomplishments seemed unnecessary and even humiliating. Looking at Edward Craddock she realized that Man was indeed the lord of creation. She saw him striding over his fields with long steps, ordering his labourers here and there, able to direct their operations, fearless, brave and free. It was astonishing how many excellent trait sshe derived from the examination of his profile.

He talked of the men he employed, and she could imagine no felicity greater than to have such a master.

'I should like to be a milkmaid on your farm,' she said.

'I don't keep milkmaids,' he replied. 'I have a milkman, it's more useful.'

'You dear old thing,' she cried. 'How matter-of-fact you are!'

She caught hold of his hands and looked at them.

'I'm rather frightened of you sometimes,' she said, laughing. 'You're so strong. I feel so utterly weak and helpless beside you.'

'Are you afraid I shall beat you?' he asked, with a smile.

She looked up at him and then down at the strong hands she was still holding.

'I don't think I should mind if you did,' she said. 'I think I should only love you more.'

He burst out laughing and kissed her.

'I'm not joking,' she said. 'I understand now those women who love beasts of men. It's a commonplace that some wives will stand anything from their husbands; it seems they love them all the more because they're brutal. I think I'm like that. But I've never seen you in a passion, Eddie. What are you like when you're angry?'

'I never am angry,' he answered.

'Miss Glover told me that you had the best temper in the world. I'm terrified of all these perfections.'

'Don't expect too much from me, Bertha. I'm not a model man, you know.'

'I'm pleased,' she answered. 'I don't want perfection. Of course you've got faults, though I can't see them yet. But when I do, I know I shall only love you better. When a woman loves an ugly man, they say his ugliness only makes him more attractive, and I shall love your faults as I love everything that is yours.'

They sat for a while without speaking, and the silence was even more entrancing than the speech. Bertha wished she could remain thus for ever, resting in his arms; she forgot that soon Craddock would develop a healthy appetite and demolish a substantial dinner.

'Let me look at your hands,' she said.

She loved them too. They were large and roughly made, hard with work and exposure, ten times nicer, she thought, than the soft hands of the townsman. She felt them firm and intensely masculine; they reminded her of a hand in an Italian museum, sculptured in porphyry, but for some reason left unfinished; the lack of detail gave the same impression of massive strength. His hands too might have been those of a demi-god or of a hero. She stretched out the long, strong fingers. Craddock looked at her with some wonder, mingled with amusement; he knew her really very little. She caught his glance, and with a smile bent down to kiss the upturned palms. She wanted to abase herself before the strong man, to be low and humble before him. She would have been his handmaiden, and nothing could have satisfied her so much as to perform for him menial services. She knew not how to show the immensity of her passion.

It pleased Bertha to walk into Blackstable with her lover and catch the people's glances, knowing how intensely the marriage interested them. What did she care if they were surprised at her choosing Edward Craddock, whom they had known all his life? She was proud of him, proud to be his wife.

One day, when it was very warm for the time of the year, she was resting on a stile, while Craddock stood by her side. They did not speak, but looked at one another in ecstatic happiness.

'Look,' said Craddock suddenly, 'there's Arthur Branderton.'

He glanced up at Bertha, then from side to side uneasily, as if he wished to avoid a meeting.

'He's been away, hasn't he?' asked Bertha. 'I wanted to meet him.' She was quite willing that all the world should see them. 'Good afternoon, Arthur,' she called out as the youth approached.

'Oh, is it you, Bertha? Hulloa, Craddock.'

He looked at Edward, wondering what he did there with Miss Ley.

'We've just been walking into Leanham and I was tired.'

'Oh!'

Young Branderton thought it queer that Bertha should take walks with Craddock.

Bertha burst out laughing. 'Oh, he doesn't know, Edward. He's the only person in the county who hasn't heard the news.'

'What news?' asked Branderton. 'I've been in Yorkshire for the last week at my brother-in-law's.'

'Edward and I are going to be married.'

'Are you, by Jove?'

He looked at Craddock, and then awkwardly offered his congratulations. They could not help seeing his astonishment, and Craddock flushed, knowing it was due to the fact that Bertha had consented to marry a penniless beggar like himself and a man of no family.

'I hope you'll invite me to the wedding,' said the young man to cover his confusion.

'Oh, it's going to be very quiet. There will only be ourselves, Dr Ramsay, my aunt and Edward's best man.'

'Then mayn't I come?' asked Branderton.

Bertha looked quickly at Edward. It had caused her some uneasiness to think that he might be supported by a person of no great consequence in the place. After all she was Miss Ley; and she had already discovered that some of her lover's friends were not too desirable. Chance offered her means of surmounting the difficulty.

'I'm afraid it's impossible,' she said, 'unless you can get Edward to offer you the important post of best man.'

She succeeded in making the two men very uncomfortable. Branderton had no great wish to perform that office for Edward. 'Of course, Craddock was a very good fellow and a fine sportsman, but not the sort of chap you'd expect a girl like Bertha Ley

50

to marry.' And Edward, understanding the young man's feelings, was silent. But Branderton had some knowledge of polite society, and broke the momentary silence.

'Who is going to be your best man, Craddock?' he asked. He could do nothing else.

'I don't know; I haven't thought of it.'

But Branderton, catching Bertha's eye, suddenly realized her desire and the reason of it.

'Won't you have me?' he said quickly. 'I daresay you'll find me intelligent enough to learn the duties.'

'I should like it very much,' answered Craddock. 'It's very good of you.'

Branderton looked at Bertha, and she smiled her thanks; he saw she was pleased.

'Where are you going for your honeymoon?' he asked now, to make conversation.

'I don't know,' answered Craddock. 'We've hardly had time to think of it yet.'

'You certainly are very vague in all your plans.'

He shook hands with them, receiving from Bertha a grateful pressure, and went off.

'Have you really not thought of our honeymoon, foolish boy?' asked Bertha.

'No.'

'Well, I have. I've made up my mind and settled it all. We're going to Italy, and I mean to show you Florence and Pisa and Sienna. It'll be simply heavenly. We won't go to Venice, because it's too sentimental; self-respecting people can't make love in gondolas at the end of the nineteenth century. Oh, I long to be with you in the South, beneath the blue sky and the countless stars of night.'

'I've never been abroad before,' he said, without much enthusiasm.

But her fire was quite enough for two: 'I know. I shall have the pleasure of unfolding it all to you. I shall enjoy it more than I ever have before; it'll all be so new to you. And we can stay six months if we like.'

'Oh, I couldn't possibly,' he cried. 'Think of the farm.'

'Oh, bother the farm. It's our honeymoon, *sposo mio*.'

'I don't think I could possibly stay away more than a fortnight.'

'What nonsense! We can't go to Italy for a fortnight. The farm can get on without you.'

'And in January and February, too, when all the lambing is coming on.'

He did not want to distress Bertha, but really half his lambs would die if he were not there to superintend their entrance into the world.

'But you must go,' said Bertha. 'I've set my heart upon it.'

He looked down for a while, looking rather unhappy.

'Wouldn't a month do?' he asked. 'I'll do anything you really want, Bertha.'

But his obvious dislike to the suggestion cut Bertha's heart. She was only inclined to be stubborn when she saw he might resist her; and his first word of surrender made her veer round penitently.

'What a selfish beast I am!' she said. 'I don't want to make you miserable, Eddie. I thought it would please you to go abroad, and I'd planned it all so well. But we won't go; I hate Italy. Let's just go up to town for a fortnight like two country bumpkins.'

'Oh, but you won't like that,' he said.

'Of course I shall. I like everything you like. D'you think I care where we go as long as I'm with you? You're not angry with me, darling, are you?'

Mr Craddock was good enough to intimate that he was not.

Miss Ley, much against her will, had been driven by Miss Glover into working for some charitable institution, and was knitting babies' socks (as the smallest garments she could make) when Bertha told her of the altered plans. She dropped a stitch. She was too wise to say anything, but she wondered if the world was coming to an end; Bertha's schemes were shattered like brittle glass and she really seemed delighted; a month ago opposition would have made Bertha traverse seas and scale precipices rather than abandon a notion that she had got into her head. Verily love is a prestidigitator who can change the lion into the lamb as easily as a handkerchief into a flower-pot! Miss Ley began to admire Edward Craddock.

He, on his way home after leaving Bertha, was met by the Vicar of Leanham. Mr Glover was a tall man, angular, fair, thin and red-cheeked, a somewhat feminine edition of his sister, but smell-

52

ing in the most remarkable fashion of antiseptics; Miss Ley vowed he peppered his clothes with iodoform and bathed daily in carbolic acid. He was strenuous and charitable, he hated a dissenter and was over forty.

'Ah, Craddock, I wanted to see you.'

'Not about the banns, vicar, is it? We're going to be married by special licence.'

Like many countrymen, Edward saw something funny in the clergy – one should not grudge it them, for it is the only jest in their lives – and he was given to treating the parson with more humour than he used in the other affairs of this world. The vicar laughed; it is one of the best traits of the country clergy that they are willing to be amused with their parishioners' jocosity.

'The marriage is all settled then? You're a very lucky young man.'

Craddock put his arm through Mr Glover's with the unconscious friendliness that had gained him a hundred friends.

'Yes, I am lucky,' he said. 'I know you people think it rather queer that Bertha and I should get married, but – we're very much attached to one another, and I mean to do my best by her. You know I've never racketted about, vicar, don't you?'

'Yes, my boy,' said the vicar, touched by Edward's confidence. 'Everyone knows you're steady enough.'

'Of course, she could have found men of much better social position than mine, but I'll try and make her happy. And I've got nothing to hide from her as some men have; I go to her almost as straight as she comes to me.'

'That is a very fortunate thing to be able to say,' replied the vicar.

'I have never loved another woman in my life, and as for the rest – well, of course, I'm young and I've been up to town sometimes; but I always hated and loathed it. And the country and the hard work keep one pretty clear of anything nasty.'

'I'm very glad to hear you say that,' answered Mr Glover. 'I hope you'll be happy, and I think you will.'

The vicar felt a slight pricking of conscience, for at first his sister and himself had called the match a *mésalliance* (they pronounced the word vilely), and not till they learned it was inevitable did they begin to see that their attitude was a little wanting in charity. The two men shook hands when they parted.

'I hope you don't mind me spitting out these things to you, vicar. I suppose it's your business in a sort of way. I wanted to tell Miss Ley something of the kind; but somehow or other I can never get an opportunity.'

7

EXACTLY one month after the attainment of her majority, as Bertha had announced, the marriage took place and the young couple started off to spend their honeymoon in London. Bertha, knowing she would not read, took with her nothwithstanding a book, to wit the *Meditations of Marcus Aurelius*, and Edward, thinking that railway journeys were always tedious, bought for the occasion *The Mystery of the Six-fingered Woman*, the title of which attracted him. He was determined not to be bored, for not content with his novel he purchased at the station a *Sporting Times*.

'Oh,' said Bertha when the train had started, heaving a great sigh of relief, 'I'm so glad to be alone with you at last. Now we shan't have anybody to worry us and no one can separate us, and we shall be together for the rest of our lives.'

Craddock put down the newspaper which, from force of habit, he had opened after settling himself down in his seat.

'I'm glad to have the ceremony over, too.'

'D'you know,' she said, 'I was terrified on the way to church; it occurred to me that you might not be there – that you might have changed your mind and fled.'

He laughed. 'Why on earth should I change my mind?'

'Oh, I can't sit solemnly opposite you as if we'd been married a century. Make room for me, boy.'

She came over to his side and nestled close to him.

'Tell me you love me,' she whispered.

'I love you very much.'

He bent down and kissed her, then putting his arm round her waist drew her closer to him. He was a little nervous, he would not really have been very sorry if some officious person had disregarded the *engaged* on the carriage and entered. He felt scarcely at home with his wife, and was still a little bewildered by his change of fortune; there was, indeed, a vast difference between Court Leys and Bewlie's Farm.

'I'm so happy,' said Bertha. 'Sometimes I'm afraid. D'you think it can last, d'you think we shall always be as happy? I've got everything I want in the world, I'm absolutely and completely content.' She was silent for a minute, caressing his hands. 'You will always love me, Eddie, won't you – even when I'm old and horrible?'

'I'm not the sort of chap to alter,' he said.

'Oh, you don't know how I adore you,' she cried, passionately. '*My* love will never alter, it is too strong. To the end of my days I shall always love you with all my heart. I wish I could tell you what I feel.'

Of late the English language had seemed quite incompetent for the expression of her manifold emotions.

They went to a far more expensive hotel than they could afford; Craddock had prudently suggested something less extravagant, but Bertha would not hear of it; as Miss Ley she had been unused to the second-rate, and she was too proud of her new name to take it to any but the best hotel in London.

The more Bertha saw of her husband's mind the more it delighted her. She loved the simplicity and the naturalness of the man; she cast off like a tattered silken cloak the sentiments with which for years she had lived, and robed herself in the sturdy homespun that so well suited her lord and master. It was charming to see his naïve enjoyment of everything; to him all was fresh and novel; he would explode with laughter at the comic papers and in the dailies continually find observations that struck him as extremely original. He was the unspoiled child of nature, his mind free from the million perversities of civilization. To know him was, in Bertha's opinion, an education in all the goodness and purity, the strength and virtue of the Englishman. They went often to the theatre, and it pleased Bertha to watch her husband's simple enjoyment; the pathetic passages of melodrama that made Bertha's lips curl with amused contempt moved him to facile tears, and in the darkness he held her hand to comfort her, imagining that she experienced the same emotions as himself. Ah, she wished she could; she hated the education in foreign countries that in the study of pictures and palaces and strange peoples had released her mind from its prison of darkness, yet had destroyed half her illusions; now she would far rather have retained the plain and unadorned illiteracy, the ingenuous ignorance of the typical and creamy English girl. What is the use of knowledge? Blessed are the poor in spirit; all that a woman really wants is purity and goodness and perhaps a certain acquaintance with plain cooking.

'Isn't it splendid?' he said, turning to his wife.

'You dear thing!' she whispered.

It touched her to see how deeply he felt it all. She loved him ten times more because his emotions were easily aroused; ah, yes, she abhorred the cold cynicism of the worldly-wise who sneer at the burning tears of the simple-minded.

But the lovers, the injured heroine and the wrongly suspected hero, had bidden one another a heart-rending good-bye, and the curtain descended to rapturous applause. Edward cleared his throat and blew his nose. The curtain rose on the next act, and in his eagerness to see what was going to happen Edward immediately ceased to listen to what Bertha was in the middle of saying, and gave himself over to the play. The feelings of the audience having been sufficiently harrowed, the comic relief was turned on; the funny man made jokes about various articles of clothing, tumbled over tables and chairs, and it charmed Bertha again to hear her husband's peals of unrestrained laughter; he put his head back and with his hands to his sides simply roared.

'He has a charming character,' she thought.

Craddock had the strictest notions of morality, and absolutely refused to take his wife to a music-hall; Bertha had seen abroad many sights the like of which Edward did not dream, but she respected his innocence. It pleased her to see the firmness with which he upheld his principles and it amused her to be treated like a little girl. They went to all the theatres; Edward on his rare visits to London had done his sight-seeing economically, and the purchase of stalls, the getting into evening clothes, were new sensations that caused him great pleasure. Bertha liked to see her husband in evening dress; the black suited his florid style, and the white shirt with a high collar threw up his sunburned, weather-beaten face. He looked strong above all things, and manly; and he was her husband, never to be parted from her except by death. She adored him.

Craddock's interest in the stage was unflagging, he always

wanted to know what was going to happen and he was able to follow with the closest attention, even the incomprehensible plot of a musical comedy. Nothing bored him. Even the most ingenuous find a little cloying the humours and the harmonies of a Gaiety burlesque; they are like toffee and butterscotch, delicacies for which we cannot understand our youthful craving. Bertha had learnt something of music in lands where it is cultivated as a pleasure rather than as a duty, and the popular melodies with obvious refrains sent cold shivers down her back. But they stirred Craddock to the depths of his soul; he beat time to the swinging, vulgar tunes, and his face was transfigured when the band played a patriotic march with a great braying of brass and beating of drums. He whistled and hummed it for days afterwards.

'I love music,' he told Bertha in the interval. 'Don't you?'

With a tender smile she confessed she did, and for fear of hurting his feelings did not suggest that the music in question made her almost vomit. What did it matter if his taste in that respect were not beyond reproach? After all there was something to be said for the honest, homely melodies that touched the people's heart.

'When we get home,' said Craddock, 'I want you to play to me, I'm so fond of it.'

'I shall love to,' she murmured.

She thought of the long winter evenings which they would spend at the piano, her husband by her side to turn the leaves, while to his astonished ears she unfolded the manifold riches of the great composers. She was convinced that his taste was really excellent.

'I have lots of music that my mother used to play,' he said. 'By Jove, I shall like to hear it again – some of those old tunes I can never hear often enough – "The Last Rose of Summer" and "Home, Sweet Home" and a lot more like that.'

'By Jove, that show was good,' said Craddock when they were having supper. 'I should like to see it again before we go back.'

'We'll do whatever you like, my dear.'

'I think an evening like that does you good. It bucks me up; doesn't it you?'

'It does me good to see you amused,' replied Bertha diplomatically.

The performance had appeared to her vulgar, but in the face of her husband's enthusiasm she could only accuse herself of a ridiculous squeamishness. Why should she set herself up as a judge of these things? Was it not rather vulgar of her to find vulgarity in what gave such pleasure to the unsophisticated? She was like the *nouveau riche* who is distressed at the universal lack of gentility. But she was tired of analysis and subtlety and all the accessories of a decadent civilization.

'For goodness' sake,' she thought, 'let us be simple and easily amused.'

She remembered the four young ladies who had appeared in skin tights and nothing else worth mentioning and danced a singularly ungraceful jig, which the audience in its delight had insisted on having twice repeated.

There is some difficulty in knowing how to spend one's time in London when one has no business to do and no friends to visit. Bertha would have been content to sit all day with Edward in their private sitting-room, contemplating him and her felicity. But Craddock had all the fine energy of the Anglo-Saxon race, that desire to be always doing something or other which has made the English athletes and missionaries and members of Parliament. After his first mouthful of breakfast, he invariably asked: 'What shall we do today?' And Bertha ransacked her brain and a Baedeker to find sights to visit, for to treat London as a foreign town and systematically explore it was their only resource. They went to the Tower of London and gaped at the crowns and sceptres, at the insignia of the various orders; to Westminster Abbey and, joining the party of Americans and country-folk who were being driven hither and thither by a black-robed verger, they visited the tombs of the kings and saw everything that it was their duty to see. Bertha developed a fine enthusiasm for the antiquities of London; she quite enjoyed the sensation of bovine ignorance with which the Cook's tourist surrenders himself into the hands of a custodian, looking as he is told and swallowing with open mouth the most unreliable information. Feeling herself more stupid, Bertha was conscious of a closer connexion with her fellow-men. Edward did not like all things in an equal degree; pictures bored him (they were the only things that really did), and their visit to the National Gallery was not a success. Neither did the British Museum meet with his approval; for one thing, he had great difficulty in directing Bertha's attention so that her eyes should not wander to various naked statues that are exhibited there with no regard at all for the susceptibilities of modest persons. Once she stopped in front of a group that some shields and swords quite inadequately clothed, and remarked on their beauty. Edward looked about uneasily to see whether anyone noticed them, and agreeing with her briefly that they were fine figures, moved her rapidly away to some less questionable object.

'I can't stand all this rot,' he said when they stood opposite the three goddesses of the Parthenon. 'I wouldn't give twopence to come to this place again.'

Bertha felt a little ashamed that she had a sneaking admiration for the statues in question.

'Now tell me,' he said, 'where is the beauty of those creatures without any heads?'

Bertha could not tell him, and he was triumphant. He was a dear, and she loved him with all her heart.

The Natural History Museum, on the other hand, aroused Craddock to enthusiasm. Here he was quite at home, no improprieties were there from which he must keep his wife, and animals were the sort of things that any man could understand. But they brought back to him strongly the country of East Kent and the life which it pleased him most to lead. London was all very well, but he did not feel at home, and it was beginning to pall upon him. Bertha also began talking of home and Court Leys; she had always lived more in the future than in the present, and even in this, the time of her greatest happiness, looked forward to the days to come at Leanham when complete bliss would indeed be hers.

She was contented enough now; it was only the eighth day of her married life, but she ardently wished to settle down and satisfy all her anticipations. They talked of the alterations they must make in the house. Craddock had already plans for putting the park in order, for taking over the Home Farm and working it himself.

'I wish we were home,' said Bertha. 'I'm sick of London.'

'I don't think I should mind much if we'd got to the end of our fortnight,' he replied.

Craddock had arranged with himself to stay in town fourteen days, and he could not change his mind. It made him uncomfortable to alter his plans and think out something new; he prided himself on always doing the thing he had determined.

But a letter came from Miss Ley announcing that she had packed her trunks and was starting for the Continent.

'Oughtn't we to ask her to stay on?' said Craddock. 'It seems rather rough on her to turn her out so quickly.'

'You don't want to have her to live with us, do you?' asked Bertha in dismay.

'No, rather not; but I don't see why you should pack her off like a servant with a month's notice.'

'Oh, I'll ask her to stay,' said Bertha anxious to obey her husband's smallest wish; and obedience was easy, for she knew that Miss Ley would never dream of accepting the offer.

Bertha wished to see no one just now, least of all her aunt, feeling confusedly that her happiness would be diminished by the intrusion of an actor in her old life; her emotions also were too intense for concealment, and she would have been ashamed to display them to Miss Ley's critical sense. Bertha saw only discomfort in meeting the elder lady, with her calm irony and polite contempt for the things which on her husband's account Bertha now sincerely cherished.

But Miss Ley's reply showed perhaps that she guessed her niece's thoughts better than Bertha had given her credit for.

My Dearest Bertha,

I am much obliged to your husband for his politeness in asking me to stay at Court Leys; but I flatter myself that you have too high an opinion of me to think me capable of accepting. Newly married people offer much matter for ridicule (which they say, is the noblest characteristic of man, being the only one that distinguishes him from the brutes), but since I am a peculiarly self-denying creature, I do not propose to avail myself of the opportunity you offer. Perhaps in a year you will have begun to see one another's imperfections, and then, though less amusing, you will be more interesting. No, I am going to Italy – to hurl myself once more into that sea of pensions and second-rate hotels wherein it is the fate of single women with moderate incomes to spend their lives; and I am taking with me a Baedeker so that if ever I am inclined to think myself less foolish than the average man I may look upon its red cover and remember that I am but human. By the way, I hope you do not show your correspondence to your husband, least of all mine; a man can never understand a woman's epistolary communications, for he reads them with his own simple alphabet of twenty-six letters, whereas he requires one of at least fifty-two; and even that is little. It is a bad system to allow a husband to read one's letters, and my observation of married couples has led me to the belief that there is no surer way to the divorce court; in fact it is madness for a happy pair to pretend to have no secrets from one another; it leads them into so much deception. If, however, as I suspect, you think it is your duty to show Edward this note of mine, he will perhaps find it not unuseful for the explanation of my character – on the study of which I myself have spent many entertaining years.

I give you no address, so that you may not be in want of an excuse to leave this missive unanswered.

Your affectionate aunt,
Mary Ley.

Bertha, a trifle impatiently, tossed the letter to Edward.

'What does she mean?' he asked when he had read it.

Bertha shrugged her shoulders: 'She believes in nothing but the stupidity of other people. Poor woman, she has never been in love. But we won't have any secrets from one another, Eddie. I know that you will never hide anything from me, and I – What can I do that is not at your telling?'

'It's a funny letter,' he replied, looking at it again.

'But we're free now, darling,' she said. 'The house is ready for us. Shall we go at once?'

'But we haven't been here a fortnight yet,' he objected.

'What does it matter? We're both sick of London; let us go home and start our life. We're going to lead it for the rest of our lives, so we'd better begin it quickly. Honeymoons are stupid things.'

'Well, I don't mind. By Jove, fancy if we'd gone to Italy for six weeks.'

'Oh, I didn't know what a honeymoon was like. I think I imagined something quite different.'

'You see I was right, wasn't I?'

'Of course you were right,' she answered, flinging her arms round his neck. 'You're always right, my darling. Ah, you can't think how I love you.'

8

THE Kentish coast is bleak and grey between Leanham and Blackstable; through the long winter months the winds of the North Sea sweep down upon it, bowing the trees before them, and from the murky waters perpetually arise the clouds, and roll up in heavy banks. It is a country that offers those who live there what they give: sometimes the sombre colours and the silent sea express only restfulness and peace, sometimes the chill breezes send the blood racing through the veins, and red cheeks and swinging stride tell the joy of life; but also the solitude can answer the deepest melancholy, or the cheerless sky a misery that is more terrible than death. One's mood seems always reproduced in the surrounding scenes, and in them may be found, as it were, a synthesis of one's emotions. Bertha stood upon the high road that ran past Court Leys, and from the height looked down upon the lands that were hers. Close at hand the only habitations were a pair of humble cottages, from which time and rough weather had almost effaced the obtrusiveness of human handiwork. They stood away from the road, among fruit trees, a part of nature, and not a blot upon it, as Court Leys had never ceased to be. All around were fields, great stretches of ploughed earth and meadows of coarse herbage. The trees were few, and stood out here and there in the distance, bent before the wind. Beyond was Blackstable, straggling grey houses with a border of new villas built for the Londoners who came in summer; it was a fishing town, and the sea was dotted with smacks.

Bertha looked at the scene with sensations that she had never known. The heavy clouds hung above her, shutting out the whole world, and she felt an invisible barrier between herself and all other things. This was the land of her birth, out of which she, and her fathers before her, had arisen. They had had their day, and one by one returned whence they came and become again united with the earth. She had withdrawn from the pomps and vanities of life to live as her ancestors had lived, ploughing the land, sowing and reaping; but her children, the sons of the future, would belong to a new stock, stronger and fairer than the old. The Leys had gone down into the darkness of death, and her children would bear another name. All these things she gathered out of the brown fields and the grey sea mist. She was a little tired, and the physical sensation caused a mental fatigue, so that she felt in herself suddenly the weariness of a family that had lived too long; she knew she was right to choose new blood to mix with the old blood of the Leys. It needed the freshness and youth, the massive strength of her husband, to bring life to the decayed race. Her thoughts wandered to her father, the dilettante who wandered in Italy in search of beautiful things and emotions that his native country could not give him; to Miss Ley, whose attitude towards life was a shrug of the shoulders and a well-bred smile of contempt. Was not she, the last of them, wise? Feeling herself too weak to stand alone, she had taken a mate whose will and vitality would be a pillar of strength to her frailty; her husband had still in his sinews the might of his mother, the Earth, a barbaric power that knew not the subtleties of weakness; he was the conqueror and she was his handmaiden.

But an umbrella was being waved at Mrs Craddock from the bottom of the hill, and she smiled, recognizing the masculine walk of Miss Glover. Even from a distance the maiden's determination was apparent; she approached, her face redder even than usual after the climb, encased in a braided jacket that fitted her as severely as sardines are fitted in their tin.

'I was coming to see you, Bertha,' she cried. 'I heard you were back.'

'We've been home several days, getting to rights.'

Miss Glover shook Bertha's hand with vigour, and together they walked back to the house, along the avenue bordered with leafless trees.

'Now, do tell me all about your honeymoon; I'm so anxious to hear everything.'

But Bertha was not communicative, she had an instinctive dislike to telling her private affairs, and never had any overpowering desire for sympathy.

'Oh, I don't think there's much to tell,' she answered, when they were in the drawing-room and she was pouring out tea for her guest. 'I suppose all honeymoons are more or less alike.'

'You funny girl,' said Miss Glover. 'Didn't you enjoy it?'

'Yes,' said Bertha, with a smile that was almost ecstatic; then

63

after a little pause: 'We had a very good time; we went to all the theatres.'

Miss Glover felt that marriage had caused a difference in Bertha, and it made her nervous to realize the change. She looked uneasily at the married woman and occasionally blushed.

'And are you really happy?' she blurted out suddenly.

Bertha smiled, and, reddening, looked more charming than ever.

'Yes, I think I'm perfectly happy.'

'Aren't you sure?' asked Miss Glover, who cultivated precision and strongly disapproved of persons who did not know their own minds.

Bertha looked at her for a moment, as if considering the question.

'You know,' she answered at last, 'happiness is never quite what one expected it to be. I hardly hoped for so much; but I didn't imagine it quite as it is.'

'Ah, well, I think it's better not to go into these things,' replied Miss Glover, a little severely, thinking the suggestion of self-analysis scarcely suitable in a young married woman. 'We ought to take things as they are and be thankful.'

'Ought we?' said Bertha lightly. 'I never do. I'm never satisfied with what I have.'

They heard the opening of the front door, and Bertha jumped up.

'There's Edward! I must go and see him. You don't mind, do you?'

She almost skipped out of the room; marriage, curiously enough, had dissipated the gravity of manner that had made people find so little girlishness in her. She seemed younger, lighter of heart.

'What a funny creature she is!' thought Miss Glover. 'When she was a girl she had all the ways of a married woman, and now that she's married she might be a schoolgirl.'

The parson's sister was not certain whether the irresponsibility of Bertha was fit to her responsible position, whether her unusual bursts of laughter were proper to a mystic state demanding gravity.

'I hope she'll turn out all right,' she sighed.

But Bertha impulsively rushed up to her husband and kissed him. She helped him off with his coat.

'I'm so glad to see you again,' she cried, laughing a little at her own eagerness, for it was only after luncheon that he had left her.

'Is anyone here?' he asked, noticing Miss Glover's umbrella.
He returned his wife's embrace somewhat mechanically.

'Come and see,' said his wife, taking his arm and dragging him along. 'You must be dying for tea, you poor thing.'

'Miss Glover!' he said, shaking the lady's hand as energetically as she shook his. 'How good of you to come and see us. I *am* glad to see you! You see, we came home sooner than we expected; there's no place like the country, is there?'

'You're right there, Mr Craddock; I can't bear London.'

'Oh, you don't know it,' said Bertha. 'For you it's Aerated Bread Shops, Exeter Hall and Church Congresses.'

'Bertha!' cried Edward in a tone of surprise; he could not understand frivolity with Miss Glover.

That good creature was far too kind-hearted to take offence at any remark of Bertha's, and smiled grimly; she could smile in no other way.

'Tell me what you did in London; I can't get anything out of Bertha.'

Craddock, on the other hand, was communicative; nothing pleased him more than to give people information, and he was always ready to share his knowledge with the world at large. He never picked up a fact without rushing to tell it to somebody else. Some persons when they know a thing immediately lose interest in it and it bores them to discuss it. Craddock was not of these. Nor could repetition exhaust his eagerness to enlighten his fellows; he would tell a hundred people the news of the day, and be as fresh as ever when it came to the hundred and first. Such a characteristic is undoubtedly a gift, useful in the highest degree to schoolmasters and politicians, but slightly tedious to their hearers. Craddock favoured his guest with a detailed account of all their adventures in London, the plays they had seen, their plots and the actors who played in them. He gave the complete list of the museums and churches and public buildings they had visited. Bertha looked at him the while, smiling happily at his enthusiasm; she cared little what he spoke of, the mere sound of his voice was music to her ears, and she would have listened delightedly while he read aloud from end to end *Whitaker's Almanack*; that was a thing, by the way, that he was quite capable of doing. Edward corresponded far more with Miss Glover's conception of the newly-married man than did Bertha with that of the newly-married woman.

'He is a nice fellow,' she said to her brother afterwards when they were eating their supper of cold mutton, solemnly seated at either end of a long table.

'Yes,' answered the vicar, in his tired, patient voice. 'I think he'll turn out a good husband.'

Mr Glover was patience itself, which a little irritated Miss Ley, who liked a man of spirit, and of that Mr Glover had never had a grain. He was resigned to everything: he was resigned to his food being badly cooked, to the perversity of human nature, to the existence of dissenters (almost), to his infinitesimal salary; he was resignation driven to death. Miss Ley said he was like those Spanish donkeys whom one sees plodding along in a long string, listlessly bearing over-heavy loads, patient, patient, patient. But not so patient as Mr Glover, the donkey sometimes kicked: the Vicar of Leanham never!

'I do hope it will turn out well, Charles,' said Miss Glover.

'I hope it will,' he answered; then, after a pause: 'Did you ask them if they were coming to church tomorrow?'

Helping himself to mashed potatoes, he noticed long-sufferingly that they were burnt again; the potatoes were always burnt; but he made no comment.

'Oh, I quite forgot to, but I think they're sure to. Edward Craddock was always a regular attendant.'

Mr Glover made no reply, and they kept silence for the rest of the meal. Immediately afterwards the parson went into his study to finish his sermon, and Miss Glover took out of her basket her brother's woollen socks and began to darn them. She worked for more than an hour, thinking meanwhile of the Craddocks; she liked Edward better and better each time she saw him, and she felt he was a man who could be trusted. She upbraided herself a little for her disapproval of the marriage; her action was un-christian, and she asked herself whether it was not her duty to apologize to Bertha or Craddock; the thought of doing something humiliating to her own self-respect attracted her wonderfully. But Bertha was different from other girls; Miss Glover, thinking of her, grew confused.

But a tick of the clock to announce an hour to strike made her look up. She saw it wanted but five minutes to ten.

'I had no idea it was so late.'

She got up and tidily put away her work, then taking from the

66

top of the harmonium the Bible and the big prayer-book that were upon it, placed them at the end of the table. She drew a chair for her brother and sat patiently to await his coming. As the clock struck she heard the study door open. The vicar walked in. Without a word he went to the books and, sitting down, found his place in the Bible.

'Are you ready,' she asked.

He looked up one moment: 'Yes.'

Miss Glover leant forward and rang the bell. The servant appeared with a basket of eggs, which she placed on the table. Mr Glover looked at her till she was settled on her chair and began the lesson. Afterwards the servant lit two candles and bade them good night. Miss Glover counted the eggs.

'How many are there today?' asked the parson.

'Seven,' she answered, dating them one by one, and entering the number in a book kept for the purpose.

'Are you ready?' asked Mr Glover.

'Yes, Charles,' she said, taking up one of the candles.

He put out the lamp and with the other candle followed her upstairs. She stopped outside her door and bade him good night, he kissed her coldly on the forehead and they went into their respective rooms.

There is always a certain flurry in a country-house on Sunday morning. There is in the air a feeling peculiar to the day, a state of alertness and expectation; even when they are repeated for years, week by week, the preparations for church cannot be taken coolly. The odour of clean linen is unmistakable, everyone is highly starched and somewhat ill at ease; there is a hunt for prayer-books and hymn-books; the ladies of the party are never ready in time and sally out at last buttoning their gloves; the men stamp and fume and take out their watches. Edward, of course, wore a tail-coat and a top-hat, which is quite the proper costume for the squire to go to church in, and no one gave more thought to the proprieties than Edward; he held himself very upright, cultivating the slightly self-conscious gravity thought fit for the occasion.

'We shall be late, Bertha,' he said. 'It will look so bad – the first time we come to church since our marriage, too.'

'My dear,' said Bertha, 'you may be quite certain that even if

67

Mr Glover is so indiscreet as to start, for the congregation the ceremony will not really begin till we appear.'

They drove up in an old-fashioned brougham used only for going to church and to dinner-parties and the word was immediately passed by the loungers at the porch to the devout within; there was a rustle of attention as Mr and Mrs Craddock walked up the aisle to the front pew that was theirs by right.

'He looks at home, don't he?' murmured the natives, for the behaviour of Edward interested them more than that of his wife, who was sufficiently above them to be almost a stranger.

Bertha sailed up with a royal unconsciousness of the eyes upon her; she was pleased with her personal appearance and intensely proud of her good-looking husband. Mrs Branderton, the mother of Craddock's best man, fixed her eye-glass upon her and stared as is the custom of great ladies. Mrs Branderton was a woman who cultivated the mode in the depths of the country, a little, giggling, grey-haired creature, who talked stupidly in a high, cracked voice and had her too juvenile bonnets straight from Paris. She was a gentlewoman, and this, of course, is a very fine thing to be; she was proud of it (in a quite gentlewomanly way), and in the habit of saying that gentlefolk were gentlefolk, which, if you come to think of it, is a profound remark.

'I mean to go and speak to the Craddocks afterwards,' she whispered to her son. 'It will have a good effect on the Leanham people; I wonder if poor Bertha feels it yet.'

Mrs Branderton had a self-importance that was almost sublime; it never occurred to her that there might be persons sufficiently ill-conditioned as to resent her patronage. She showered advice upon all and sundry, besides soups and jellies upon the poor, to whom when they were ill she even sent her cook to read the Bible. She would have gone herself, only she strongly disapproved of familiarity with the lower classes; it made them independent and often rude. Mrs Branderton knew without possibility of question that she and her equals were made of different clay from common people; but, being a gentlewoman did not throw this fact in their faces, unless, of course, they gave themselves airs, when she thought a straight talking to did them good. Without any striking advantages of birth, money or intelligence, Mrs Branderton never doubted her right to direct the affairs and fashions, even the modes of thought of her neighbours, and by sheer force of self-esteem had caused them to submit for thirty years to her tyranny, hating her and yet looking upon her invitations to a bad dinner as something quite desirable.

Mrs Branderton had debated with herself how she should treat the Craddocks.

'I wonder if it's my duty to cut them,' she said. 'Edward Craddock is not the sort of man a Miss Ley ought to marry. But there are so few gentlefolk in the neighbourhood, and of course people do make marriages which they wouldn't have dreamt of twenty years ago. Even the very best society is mixed nowadays. Perhaps I'd better err on the side of mercy.'

Mrs Branderton was a little pleased to think that the Leys required her support, as was proved by the request of her son's services at the wedding.

'The fact is, gentlefolk are gentlefolk, and they must stand by one another in these days of pork-butchers and furniture people.'

After the service, when the parishioners were standing about the churchyard, Mrs Branderton sailed up to the Craddocks, followed by Arthur, and in her high, cracked voice began to talk to Edward. She kept an eye on the Leanham people to see that her action was being duly noticed, and spoke to Craddock in the manner a gentlewoman should adopt with a man who, though possibly a gentleman, was not county. He was pleased and flattered.

9

SOME days later, after the due preliminaries which Mrs Branderton would on no account have neglected, the Craddocks received an invitation to dinner. Bertha read and silently passed it to her husband.

'I wonder who she'll ask to meet us,' he said.

'D'you want to go?' asked Bertha.

'Why, don't you? We've got no engagement, have we?'

'Have you ever dined there before?'

'No. I've been to tennis-parties and that sort of thing, but I've hardly set foot inside their house.'

'Well, I think it's an impertinence of her to ask you now.'

Edward opened his mouth wide: 'What on earth d'you mean?'

'Oh, don't you see?' cried his wife. 'They're merely asking you because you're my husband. It's humiliating.'

'Nonsense!' replied Edward, laughing. 'And if they are, what do I care? I'm not so thin-skinned as that. Mrs Branderton was very nice to me on Sunday; it would be funny if we didn't accept.'

'Did you think she was nice? Didn't you see that she was patronizing you as if you were a groom. It made me boil with rage. I could hardly hold my tongue.'

Edward laughed again. 'I never noticed anything. It's just your fancy, Bertha.'

'I'm not going to the horrid dinner-party.'

'Then I shall go by myself.'

Bertha started and turned white; it was as if she had received a sudden blow; but he was laughing. Of course he did not mean what he said. She hurriedly agreed to all he asked.

'Of course if you want to go, Eddie, I'll come too. It was only for your sake that I didn't wish to.'

'We must be neighbourly. I want to be friends with everybody.'

She sat on the arm of his chair, and put her arm round his neck. Edward patted her hand, and she looked at him with eyes full of eager love. She bent down and kissed his hair. How foolish had been her sudden thought that he did not love her!

But Bertha had another reason for not wishing to go to Mrs Branderton's. She knew Edward would be bitterly criticized, and the thought made her wretched; they would talk of his appearance and manner, and wonder how they got on together. Bertha understood well enough the position Edward had occupied in Leanham: the Branderton's and their like, knowing him all his life, had treated him as a mere acquaintance, for then he had been a person to whom you are civil and that is all. This was the first occasion upon which he had been dealt with as an equal; it was his introduction into what Mrs Branderton was pleased to call the upper ten of Leanham. It did indeed make Bertha's blood boil; and it cut her to the heart to think that for years he had been used in so infamous a fashion. He did not seem to mind.

'If I were he,' she said, 'I'd rather die than go. They've ignored him always, and now they take him up as a favour to me.'

But Edward appeared to have no pride. He neither resented the former neglect of the Brandertons nor their present impertinence.

Bertha was in a tremor of anxiety. She guessed who the other guests would be. Would they laugh at him? Of course, not openly; Mrs Branderton, the least charitable of them all, prided herself on her breeding; but Edward was shy and among strangers rather awkward. To Bertha this was a charm rather than a defect; his bashful candour touched her, and she compared it favourably with the foolish worldliness of the imaginary man about town whose dissipation she always opposed to her husband's virtues. But she knew that a spiteful tongue would find another name for what she called a delightful *naïveté*.

When at last the great day arrived and they trundled off in the old-fashioned brougham, Bertha was thoroughly prepared to take mortal offence at the merest shadow of a slight offered to her husband. The Lord Chief Justice himself could not have been more careful of a company promoter's fair name than was Mrs Craddock of her husband's susceptibilities; Edward, like the financier, treated the affair with indifference.

Mrs Branderton had routed out the whole countryside for her show of gentlefolk. They had come from Blackstable and Tercanbury and Faversley, and from the seats and mansions that surrounded those places. Mrs Mayston Ryle was there in a wonderful black wig and a voluminous dress of violet silk; Lady Waggett was there.

'Merely the widow of a city knight, my dear,' said the hostess to Bertha; 'but if she isn't distinguished, she's good, so one mustn't be too hard upon her.'

General Hancock arrived with two frizzle-haired daughters, who were dreadfully plain, but pretended not to know it. They had walked, and while the old soldier toddled in, blowing like a grampus, the girls (whose united ages made the respectable total of sixty-five years) stayed behind to remove their boots and put on the shoes that they had brought in a bag. Then in a little while came the Dean, meek and rather talkative; Mr Glover had been invited for his sake, and of course Charles's sister could not be omitted. She was looking almost festive in very shiny black satin.

'Poor dear,' said Mrs Branderton to another guest, 'it's her only dinner dress; I've seen it for years. I'd willingly give her one of my old ones, only I'm afraid I should offend her by offering it. People in that class are so ridiculously sensitive.'

Mr Atthill Bacot was announced. He had once contested the seat, and ever after been regarded as an authority upon the nation's affairs. Mr James Lycett and Mr Molson came next, both red-faced squires with dogmatic opinions. They were as alike as two peas, and it had been the local joke for thirty years that no one but their wives could tell them apart. Mrs Lycett was thin and quiet and staid, wearing two little strips of lace on her hair to represent a cap; Mrs Molson was so insignificant that no one had ever noticed what she was like. It was one of Mrs Branderton's representative gatherings; moral excellence was joined to perfect gentility, and the result could not fail to edify. She was herself in high spirits, and her cracked voice rang high and shrill. She was conscious of a successful frock; it was quite pretty, and would have looked charming on a woman half her age.

The dinner just missed being eatable. Mrs Branderton, a woman of fashion, disdained the solid fare of a country dinner-party – thick soup, fried soles, mutton cutlets, roast mutton, pheasant, charlotte russe and jellies – and saying she must be a little more 'distangay' than that, provided her guests with clear soup, *entreés* from the Stores, chicken *en casserole* and a fluffy sweet that looked pretty and tasted horrid. The feast was elegant, but it was not filling, which is unpleasant to elderly squires with large appetites.

'I never get enough to eat at the Brandertons',' said Mr Atthill Bacot indignantly.

'Well, I know the old woman,' replied Mr Molson. (Mrs Branderton was the same age as himself, but he was rather a dog, and thought himself quite young enough to flirt with the least plain of the two Miss Hancocks.) 'I know her well, and I make a point of drinking a glass of sherry with a couple of eggs beaten up in it before I come.'

'The wines are positively immoral,' said Mrs Mayston Ryle, who prided herself on her palate. 'I'm always inclined to bring with me a flask with a little good whisky in it.'

But if the food was not heavy, the conversation was. It is an axiom of narration that truth should coincide with probability, and the realist is perpetually hampered by the wild exaggeration of actual facts. A verbatim report of the conversation at Mrs Branderton's dinner-party would read like shrieking caricature. The anecdote reigned supreme. Mrs Mayston Ryle was a specialist in the clerical anecdote; she successively related the story of Bishop

Thorold and his white hands and the story of Bishop Wilberforce and the bloody shovel. (This somewhat shocked the ladies, but Mrs Mayston Ryle could not spoil her point by the omission of a swear word.) The Dean gave an anecdote about himself, to which Mrs Mayston Ryle retorted with one about the Archbishop of Canterbury and the tedious curate. Mr Atthill Bacot gave political anecdotes – Mr Gladstone and the table of the House of Commons, Dizzy and the agricultural labourer. The climax came when General Hancock gave his celebrated stories about the Duke of Wellington. Edward laughed heartily at them all.

Bertha's eyes were constantly upon her husband. She was horribly anxious. She felt it mean to think the thoughts that ran through her head; that they should ever come to her was disparaging to him and made her despise herself. Was he not perfect and handsome and adorable? Why should she tremble before the opinion of a dozen stupid people? She could not help it. However much she despised her neighbours, she could not prevent herself from being miserably affected by their judgement. And what did Edward feel? Was he as nervous as she? She could not bear the thought of him suffering pain. It was an immense relief when Mrs Branderton rose from the table. Bertha looked at Arthur holding open the door; she would have given anything to ask him to look after Edward, but dared not. She was terrified lest those horrid old men should leave him in the cold and he be humiliated. On reaching the drawing-room, Miss Glover found herself by Bertha's side, a little apart from the others, and the accident seemed to be designed by higher powers to give her an opportunity for the amends which she felt it her duty to make Mrs Craddock for her former disparagement of Edward. She had been thinking the matter over, and she thought an apology distinctly needful. But Miss Glover suffered terribly from nervousness, and the notion of broaching so delicate a subject caused her indescribable tortures. The very unpleasantness of it reassured her: if speech was so disagreeable it must obviously be her duty. But the words stuck in her throat, and she began talking of the weather; she reproached herself for cowardice, she set her teeth and grew scarlet.

'Bertha, I want to beg your pardon,' she blurted out suddenly.

'What on earth for?' Bertha opened her eyes wide and looked at the poor woman with astonishment.

'I feel I've been unjust to your husband. I thought he wasn't a

73

proper match for you, and I said things about him which I shouldn't even have thought. I'm very sorry. He's one of the best and kindest men I've ever seen, and I'm very glad you married him, and I'm sure you'll be very happy.'

Tears came to Bertha's eyes as she laughed; she felt inclined to throw her arms round the grim Miss Glover's neck, for such a speech at that moment was very comforting.

'Of course, I know you didn't mean what you said.'

'Oh, yes, I did, I'm sorry to say,' replied Miss Glover, who could allow no extenuation of her crime.

'I'd quite forgotten all about it, and I believe you'll soon be as madly in love with Edward as I am.'

'My dear Bertha,' replied Miss Glover, who never jested. 'With your husband? You must be joking.'

But Mrs Branderton interrupted them with her high voice.

'Bertha, dear, I want to talk to you.'

Bertha, smiling, sat down beside her, and Mrs Branderton proceeded in undertones:

'I must tell you. Everyone has been saying you're the handsomest couple in the county, and we all think your husband is so nice.'

'He laughed at all your jokes,' replied Bertha.

'Yes,' said Mrs Branderton, looking upwards and sideways like a canary, 'he has such a merry disposition. But I've always liked him, dear. I was telling Mrs Mayston Ryle that I've known him intimately ever since he was born. I thought it would please you to know that we all think your husband is nice.'

'I'm very much pleased. I hope Edward will be equally satisfied with all of you.'

The Craddocks' carriage came early, and Bertha offered to drive the Glovers home.

'I wonder if that lady has swallowed a poker,' said Mr Molson, as soon as the drawing-room door was closed upon them.

The two Miss Hancocks went into shrieks of laughter at this sally, and even the Dean smiled gently.

'Where did she get her diamonds from?' asked the elder Miss Hancock. 'I thought they were as poor as church mice.'

'The diamonds and the pictures are the only things they have left,' said Mrs Branderton. 'Her family always refused to sell them; though of course it's absurd for people in that position to have such jewels.'

'He's a remarkably nice fellow,' said Mrs Mayston Ryle in her deep, authoritative voice. 'But I agree with Mr Molson, she's distinctly inclined to give herself airs.'

'The Leys for generations have been as proud as turkey-cocks,' added Mrs Branderton.

'I shouldn't have thought Mrs Craddock had much to be proud of now, at all events,' said the elder Miss Hancock, who had no ancestors and thought people who had were snobs.

'Perhaps she was a little nervous,' said Lady Waggett, who, though not distinguished, was good. 'I know when I was a bride I used to be all of a tremble when I went to dinner-parties.'

'Nonsense,' said Mrs Mayston Ryle. 'She was extremely self-possessed. I don't think it looks well for a young woman to have so much assurance.'

'Well, what do you think she said to me?' said Mrs Branderton, waving her thin arms. 'I was telling her that we were all so pleased with her husband; I thought it would comfort her a little, poor thing; and she said she hoped he would be equally satisfied with us.'

Mrs Mayston Ryle for a moment was stupefied. 'How very amusing!' she cried, rising from her chair. 'Ha! Ha! She hopes Mr Edward Craddock will be satisfied with Mrs Mayston Ryle.'

The two Miss Hancocks said 'Ha! Ha!' in chorus. Then, the great lady's carriage being announced, she bade the assembly good night and swept out with a great rustling of her violet silk. The party might now really be looked upon as concluded, and the others obediently flocked off.

When they had put the Glovers down, Bertha nestled close to her husband.

'I'm so glad it's all over,' she whispered; 'I'm only happy when I'm alone with you.'

'It was a jolly evening, wasn't it?' he said. 'I thought they were all ripping.'

'I'm so glad you enjoyed it, dear; I was afraid you'd be bored.'

'Good Heavens, that's the last thing I should be. It does one good to hear conversation like that now and then; it brightens one up.'

Bertha started a little.

'Old Bacot is a very well-informed man, isn't he? I shouldn't wonder if he was right in thinking that the Government would go out at the end of their six years.'

'He always leads one to believe that he's in the Prime Minister's confidence,' said Bertha.

'And the General is a funny old chap,' added Edward. 'That was a good story he told about the Duke of Wellington.'

This remark had a curious effect upon Bertha; she could not restrain herself, but burst suddenly into shrieks of hysterical laughter. Her husband, thinking she was laughing at the anecdote, burst also into peal upon peal.

'And the story about the Bishop's gaiter!' cried Edward, shouting with merriment.

The more he laughed, the more hysterical became Bertha, and as they drove through the silent night they both screamed and yelled and shook with uncontrollable mirth.

10

AND so the Craddocks began their journey along the great road that is called the road of Holy Matrimony. The spring came and with it a hundred new delights. Bertha watched the lengthening days, the coloured crocus spring from the ground, the snowdrops; the warm damp days of February brought the primroses and then the violets. February is a month of languors; the world's heart is heavy, listless of the unrest of April and the vigorous life of May; throughout nature the seed is germinating and the pulse of all things throbs, like a woman when first she is with child. The sea mists arose from the North Sea and covered the Kentish land with a veil of moisture, white and almost transparent, so that through it the leafless trees were seen strangely distorted, their branches like long arms writhing to free themselves from the shackles of winter; the grass was very green in the marshes and the young lambs frisked and gambolled, bleating to their mothers. Already the thrushes and the blackbirds were singing in the hedgerows. March roared in boisterously, and the clouds, higher than usual, swept across the sky before the tearing winds, sometimes heaped up in heavy masses and then blown asunder, flying westwards, tripping over one another's heels in their hurry. Nature was resting, holding her breath, as it were, before the great effort of birth.

Gradually Bertha came to know her husband better. At her marriage she had really known nothing but that she loved him; the senses only had spoken, she and he were merely puppets that nature had thrown together and made attractive in one another's eyes that the race might be continued. Bertha, desire burning within her like a fire, had flung herself into her husband's arms, loving as the beasts love – and as the gods. He was the man and she was the woman, and the world was a garden of Eden conjured up by the power of passion. But greater knowledge brought only greater love. Little by little, reading in Edward's mind, Bertha discovered to her delight an unexpected purity; it was with a feeling of curious happiness that she recognized his extreme innocence. She saw that he had never loved before, that woman to him was a strange thing, a thing he had scarcely known. She was proud that her husband had come to her unsoiled by foreign embraces, the lips that kissed hers were clean: no speech on the subject had passed between them, and yet she felt certain of his extreme chastity. His soul was truly virginal.

And this being so how could she fail to adore him? Bertha was only happy in her husband's company, and it was an exquisite pleasure for her to think that their bonds could not be sundered, that as long as they lived they would always be together, always inseparable. She followed him like a dog, with a subjection that was really touching; her pride had vanished, and she desired to exist only in Edward, to fuse her character with his and be entirely one with him. She wanted him to be her only individuality, likening herself to ivy clinging to the oak tree, for he was an oak tree, a pillar of strength, and she was very weak. In the morning after breakfast she accompanied him on his walk round the farms, and only when her presence was impossible did she stay at home to look after her house. The attempt to read was hopeless, and she had thrown aside her books. Why should she read? Not for entertainment, since her husband was a perpetual occupation, and if she knew how to love what other knowledge was useful? Often, left alone, for a while, she would take up some volume, but her mind quickly wandered and she thought of Edward again, wishing to be with him.

Bertha's life was an exquisite dream, a dream that need never end, for her happiness was not of that boisterous sort that breeds excursions and alarums, but equable and smooth; she dwelt in a paradise of rosy tints, in which were neither violent shadows nor glaring lights. She was in heaven, and the only link attaching her to earth was the weekly service at Leanham. There was a delightful humanity about the bare church with its pitchpine, highly varnished pews, and the odours of hair-pomade and Reckitt's Blue. Edward was in his sabbath garments, the organist made horrid sounds and the village choir sang out of tune; Mr Glover's mechanical delivery of the prayers cleverly extracted all beauty from them and his sermon was matter-of-fact. Those two hours of church gave Bertha just the touch of earthliness that was necessary to make her realize that life was not entirely spiritual.

Now came April; the elm trees before Court Leys were beginning to burst into leaf, the green buds covered the branches like a delicate rain, like a verdant haze that was visible from a little distance and vanished when one came near. The brown fields clothed themselves with a summer garment, the clover sprang up green and luscious, and the crops showed good promise for the future. There were days when the air was almost balmy, when the sun was warm and the heart leapt, certain at last that spring was at hand. The warm and comfortable rain soaked into the ground, and from the branches continually hung the countless drops, glistening in the succeeding sun. The self-conscious tulip unfolded her petals and carpeted the ground with gaudy colour. The clouds above Leanham were lifted up and the world was stretched out in a greater circle. The birds now sang with no uncertain notes as in March, but from a full throat, filling the air; and in the hawthorn behind Court Leys the first nightingale poured out his richness. And the full scents of the earth arose, the fragrance of the mould and of the rain, the perfumes of the sun and of the soft breezes.

But sometimes, without ceasing, it rained from morning till night, and then Edward rubbed his hands.

'I wish this would keep on for a week: it's just what the country wants.'

One such day Bertha was lounging on a sofa while Edward stood at the window, looking at the pattering rain. She thought of the November afternoon when she had stood at the same window considering the dreariness of the winter, but her heart full of hope and love.

'Come and sit down beside me, Eddie dear,' she said. 'I've hardly seen you all day.'

'I've got to go out,' he said, without turning round.

'Oh, no, you haven't; come here and sit down.'

'I'll come for two minutes,' he said, 'while they're putting the trap in.'

He sat down and she put her arm round his neck.

'Kiss me.'

He kissed her, and she laughed.

'You funny boy, I don't believe you care about kissing me a bit.'

He could not answer this, for at that moment the trap came to the door and he sprang up.

'Where are you going?'

'I'm driving over to see old Potts at Herne about some sheep.'

'Is that all? Don't you think you might stay in for an afternoon when I ask you?'

'Why?' he replied. 'There's nothing to do in here. Nobody is coming, I suppose.'

'I want to be with you, Eddie,' she said, rather plaintively.

He laughed. 'I'm afraid I can't break an appointment just for that.'

'Shall I come with you then?'

'What on earth for?' he asked, with surprise.

'I want to be with you, I hate being always separated from you.'

'But we're not always separated,' said Edward. 'Hang it all, it seems to me that we're always together.'

'You don't notice my absence as I notice yours,' said Bertha in a low voice, looking down.

'But it's raining cats and dogs, and you'll get wet through if you come.'

'What do I care about that if I'm with you?'

'Then come by all means if you like.'

'You don't care if I come or not; it's nothing to you.'

'Well, I think it would be very silly of you to come in the rain. You bet I shouldn't go if I could help it.'

'Then go,' she said.

She kept back with difficulty the bitter words that were on the tip of her tongue.

'You're much better at home,' said her husband cheerfully. 'I shall be in for tea at five. Ta-ta!'

He might have said a thousand things. He might have said that nothing would please him more than that she should accompany him, that the appointment could go to the devil and he would stay with her. But he went off cheerfully, whistling. He didn't care. Bertha's cheeks grew red with the humiliation of his refusal.

'He doesn't love me,' she said, and suddenly burst into tears, the first tears of her married life, the first she had wept since her father's death; and they made her ashamed. She tried to control them, but could not, and wept on ungovernably. Edward's words seemed terribly cruel, she wondered how he could have said them.

'I might have expected it,' she said. 'He doesn't love me.'

She grew angry with him, remembering the little coldnesses that had often pained her. Often he almost pushed her away when she came to caress him, because he had at the moment something else to occupy him; often he had left unanswered her protestations of undying affection. Did he not know that he cut her to the quick? When she said she loved him with all her heart, he wondered if the clock was wound up! Bertha brooded for two hours over her unhappiness, and, ignorant of the time, was surprised to hear the trap again at the door; her first impulse was to run and let Edward in, but she restrained herself. She was very angry with him. He entered, and, shouting to her that he was wet and must change, pounded upstairs. Of course he had not noticed that for the first time since their marriage his wife had not met him in the hall when he came in: he never noticed anything.

Edward entered the room, his face glowing with the fresh air.

'By Jove, I'm glad you didn't come. The rain simply poured down. How about tea? I'm starving.'

He thought of his tea when Bertha wanted apologies, humble excuses, and a plea for pardon. He was as cheerful as usual, and quite unconscious that his wife had been crying herself into a towering passion.

'Did you buy your sheep?' she said in an indignant tone.

She was anxious for Edward to notice her discomposure, so that she might reproach him for his sins; but he noticed nothing.

'Not much,' he cried. 'I wouldn't have given a fiver for the lot.'

'You might as well have stayed with me, as I asked you,' said Bertha bitterly.

'As far as business goes, I really might. But I daresay the drive across country did me good.'

He was a man who always made the best of things. Bertha took up a book and began reading.

'Where's the paper?' asked Edward. 'I haven't read the leading articles yet.'

'I'm sure I don't know,' replied Bertha.

They sat till dinner, Edward methodically going through the *Standard*, column after column, Bertha turning over the pages of her book, trying to understand, but occupied the whole time only with her injuries. They ate dinner almost in silence, for Edward was not talkative and the conversation rested usually with Bertha. He merely remarked that soon they would be having new potatoes and that he had met Dr Ramsay. Bertha answered in monosyllables.

'You're very quiet, Bertha,' he remarked later in the evening. 'What's the matter?'

'Nothing.'

'Got a headache?'

'No.'

He made no more inquiries, satisfied that her quietness was due to natural causes. He did not seem to notice that she was in any way different from usual. She held herself in as long as she could, but finally burst out, referring to his remark of an hour before.

'Do you care if I have a headache or not?' she cried. It was hardly a question so much as a taunt.

He looked up with surprise: 'What's the matter?'

She looked at him, and then, with a gesture of impatience, turned away. But coming to her, he put his arm round her waist.

'Aren't you well, dear?' he asked with concern.

She looked at him again, but now her eyes were full of tears and she could not repress a sob.

'Oh, Eddie, be nice to me,' she said, suddenly weakening.

'Do tell me what's wrong.'

He put his arms round her and kissed her lips. The contact revived the passion that for an hour had been a-dying, and she burst into tears.

'Don't be angry with me, Eddie,' she sobbed; it was she who apologized and made excuses. 'I've been horrid to you. I couldn't help it. You're not angry, are you?'

'What on earth for?' he asked, completely mystified.

'I was so hurt this afternoon because you didn't seem to care

81

about me two straws. You must love me, Eddie. I can't live without it.'

'You are silly,' he said, laughing.

She dried her tears, smiling. His forgiveness greatly comforted her, and she felt now trebly happy.

11

BUT Edward was certainly not an ardent lover. Bertha could not tell when first she had noticed his unresponsiveness to her passionate outbursts; at the beginning she had known nothing but that she loved her husband with all her heart, and her ardour had lit up his slightly pallid attachment till it seemed to glow as fiercely as her own. Yet, little by little, she seemed to see very small return for the wealth of affection that she lavished upon him. The causes of her dissatisfaction were scarcely explicable, a slight motion of withdrawal, an indifference to her feelings – little nothings that had seemed almost comic. Bertha at first likened Edward to the Hippolytus of Phaedra; he was untamed and wild, the kisses of women frightened him, his phlegm, disguised as rustic savagery, pleased her, and she said her passion should thaw the icicles in his heart. But soon she ceased to consider his passiveness amusing, sometimes she upbraided him, and often, when alone, she wept.

'I wonder if you realize what pain you cause me at times,' said Bertha.

'Oh, I don't think I do anything of the kind.'

'You don't see it. When I come up and kiss you it's the most natural thing in the world for you to push me away, as if – almost as if you couldn't bear me.'

'Nonsense,' he replied.

To himself Edward was the same now as when they were first married.

'Of course after four months of married life you can't expect a man to be the same as on his honeymoon. One can't always be making love and canoodling. Everything in its proper time and season.'

After the day's work he liked to read his *Standard* in peace, so when Bertha came up to him he put her gently aside.

'Leave me alone for a bit, there's a good girl,' he said.

'Oh, you don't love me,' she cried then, feeling as if her heart would break.

He did not look up from his paper or make reply: he was in the middle of a leading article.

'Why don't you answer?' she cried.

'Because you're talking nonsense.'

He was the best-humoured of men, and Bertha's bad temper never disturbed his equilibrium. He knew that women felt a little irritable at times, but if a man gave 'em plenty of rope they'd calm down after a bit.

'Women are like chickens,' he told a friend. 'Give 'em a good run, properly closed in with stout wire-netting so that they can't get into mischief, and when they cluck and cackle just sit tight and take no notice.'

Marriage had made no great difference in Edward's life. He had always been a man of regular habits, and these he continued to cultivate. Of course he was more comfortable.

'There's no denying it, a fellow wants a woman to look after him,' he told Dr Ramsay, whom he sometimes met on the latter's rounds. 'Before I was married I used to find my shirts worn out in no time, but now when I see a cuff getting a bit groggy I just give it to the missus, and she makes it as good as new.'

'There's a good deal of extra work, isn't there, now you've taken on the Home Farm?'

'Oh, bless you, I enjoy it. Fact is, I can't get enough work to do. And it seems to me that if you want to make farming pay nowadays you must do it on a big scale.'

All day Edward was occupied, if not on the farms, then with business at Blackstable, Tercanbury or Faversley.

'I don't approve of idleness,' he said. 'They always say the devil finds work for idle hands to do, and upon my word I think there's a lot of truth in it.'

Miss Glover, to whom this sentiment was addressed, naturally approved, and when Edward immediately afterwards went out, leaving her with Bertha, she said: 'What a good fellow your husband is! You don't mind my saying so, do you?'

'Not if it pleases you,' said Bertha, drily.

'I hear praise of him from every side. Of course Charles has the highest opinion of him.'

Bertha did not answer, and Miss Glover added: 'You can't think how glad I am that you're so happy.'

Bertha smiled: 'You've got such a kind heart, Fanny.'

The conversation dragged, and after five minutes of heavy silence Miss Glover rose to go. When the door was closed upon her Bertha sank back in her chair, thinking. This was one of her unhappy days: Eddie had walked into Blackstable, and she had wished to accompany him.

'I don't think you'd better come with me,' he said. 'I'm in rather a hurry and I shall walk fast.'

'I can walk fast too,' she said, her face clouding over.

'No, you can't. I know what you call walking fast. If you like you can come and meet me on the way back.'

'Oh, you do everything you can to hurt me. It looks as if you welcomed an opportunity of being cruel.'

'How unreasonable you are, Bertha! Can't you see that I'm in a hurry, and I haven't got time to saunter along and chatter about the buttercups?'

'Well, let's drive in.'

'That's impossible. The mare isn't well and the pony had a hard day yesterday; he must rest today.'

'It's simply because you don't want me to come. It's always the same, day after day. You invent anything to get rid of me, you push me away even when I want to kiss you.'

She burst into tears, knowing that what she said was unjust, but feeling notwithstanding extremely ill-used. Edward smiled with irritating good-temper.

'You'll be sorry for what you've said when you've calmed down, and then you'll want me to forgive you.'

She looked up, flushing: 'You think I'm a child and a fool.'

'No I just think you're out of sorts today.'

Then he went out whistling, and she heard him give an order to the gardener in his usual manner, as cheerful as if nothing had happened. Bertha knew that he had already forgotten the little scene; nothing affected his good humour – she might weep, she might tear her heart out (metaphorically) and bang it on the floor. Edward would not be perturbed; he would still be placid, good-tempered and forbearing. Hard words, he said, broke nobody's bones. 'Women are like chickens, when they cluck and cackle sit tight and take no notice.'

On his return Edward appeared not to see that his wife was out of temper. His spirits were always equable, and he was an observant person; she answered him in monosyllables, but he chattered away, delighted at having driven a good bargain with a man in Blackstable. Bertha longed for him to remark upon her condition, so that she might burst into reproaches, but Edward was hopelessly dense – or else he saw and was unwilling to give her an opportunity to speak. Bertha, almost for the first time, was seriously angry with her husband, and it frightened her: suddenly Edward seemed an enemy, and she wished to inflict some hurt upon him. She did not understand herself. What was going to happen next? Why wouldn't he say something so that she might pour forth her woes and then be reconciled? The day wore on and she preserved a sullen silence; her heart was beginning to ache terribly. The night came, and still Edward made no sign; she looked about for a chance of beginning the quarrel, but nothing offered. They went to bed, and, turning her back on him, Bertha pretended to go to sleep; she did not give him the kiss, the never-ending kiss of lovers, that they always exchanged at night. Surely he would notice it, surely he would ask what troubled her, and then she could at last bring him to his knees. But he said nothing, he was dog-tired after a hard day's work, and without a word went to sleep. In five minutes Bertha heard his heavy, regular breathing.

Then she broke down; she could never sleep without saying good night to him, without the kiss of his lips.

'He's stronger than I,' she said, 'because he doesn't love me.'

Bertha sobbed silently; she couldn't bear to be angry with her husband. She would submit to anything rather than pass the night in wrath and the next day as unhappily as this. She was entirely humbled. At last, unable any longer to bear the agony, she awoke him.

'Eddie, you've not said good night to me.'

'By Jove, I forgot all about it,' he answered sleepily.

Bertha stifled a sob.

'Hulloa, what's the matter? You're not crying just because I forgot to kiss you? I was awfully fagged, you know.'

He really had noticed nothing. While she was passing through utter distress he had been as happily self-satisfied as usual. But the momentary recurrence of Bertha's anger was quickly stifled. She could not afford now to be proud.

'You're not angry with me?' she said. 'I can't sleep unless you kiss me.'

'Silly girl!' he whispered.

'You do love me, don't you?'

'Yes.'

He kissed her as she loved to be kissed, and in the delight of it her anger was entirely forgotten.

'I can't live unless you love me.' She nestled against his bosom, sobbing. 'Oh, I wish I could make you understand how I love you. We're friends again now, aren't we?'

'We haven't been ever otherwise.'

Bertha gave a sigh of relief, and lay in his arms completely happy. A minute more and Edward's breathing told her that he had already fallen asleep; she dared not move for fear of waking him.

The summer brought Bertha new pleasures, and she set herself to enjoy the pastoral life that she had looked forward to. The elms of Court Leys now were dark with leaves, and the heavy, close-fitting verdure gave quite a stately look to the house. The elm is the most respectable of trees, over-pompous if anything, but perfectly well-bred, and the shade it casts is no ordinary shade, but solid and self-assured as befits the estate of a county family. The fallen trunk had been removed, and in the autumn young trees were to be placed in the vacant spaces. Edward had set himself with a will to put the place to rights. The spring had seen a new coat of paint on Court Leys, so that it looked as spick and span as the suburban mansion of a stockbroker; the beds, which for years had been neglected, now were trim with the abominations of carpet bedding; squares of red geraniums contrasted with circles of yellow calceolarias; the overgrown boxwood was cut down to a just height; the hawthorn hedge was doomed, and Edward had arranged to enclose the grounds with a wooden palisade and laurel bushes. The drive was decorated with several loads of gravel, so that it became a thing of pride to the successor of an ancient and lackadaisical race. Craddock had not reigned in their stead a fortnight before the grimy sheep were expelled from the lawns on either side of the avenue, and since then the grass had been industriously mown and rolled. Now a tennis-court had been marked out, which, as Edward said, made things look homely.

Finally, the iron gates were gorgeous in black and gold, as suited the entrance to a gentleman's mansion, and the renovated lodge proved to all and sundry that Court Leys was in the hands of a man who knew what was what and delighted in the proprieties.

Though Bertha abhorred all innovations, she had meekly accepted Edward's improvements; they formed an inexhaustible topic of conversation, and his enthusiasm delighted her.

'By Jove,' he said, rubbing his hands, 'the changes will make your aunt simply jump, won't they?'

'They will indeed,' said Bertha, smiling, but with a shudder at the prospect of Miss Ley's sarcastic praise.

'She'll hardly recognize the place; the house looks as good as new, and the grounds might have been laid out only half a dozen years ago. Give me five years more, and even you won't know your old home.'

Miss Ley had at last accepted one of the invitations that Edward had insisted should be showered upon her, and wrote to say she was coming down for a week. Edward was, of course, much pleased; as he said, he wanted to be friends with everybody, and it didn't seem natural that Bertha's only relative should make a point of avoiding them.

'It looks as if she didn't approve of our marriage, and it makes people talk.'

He met the good lady at the station, and, somewhat to her dismay, greeted her with effusion.

'Ah, here you are at last!' he bellowed in his jovial way. 'We thought you were never coming. Here, porter!'

He raised his voice so that the platform shook and rumbled. He seized both Miss Ley's hands, and the terrifying thought flashed through her head that he would kiss her before the assembled multitude. Six people.

'He's cultivating the airs of the country squire,' she thought. 'I wish he wouldn't.'

He took the innumerable bags with which she travelled and scattered them among the attendants. He even tried to induce her to take his arm to the dog-cart, but this honour she stoutly refused.

'Now, will you come round to this side, and I'll help you up. Your luggage will come on afterwards with the pony.'

He was managing everything in a self-confident and masterful fashion. Miss Ley noticed that marriage had dispelled the shyness that had been in him rather an attractive feature. He was becoming bluff and hearty. Also he was filling out; prosperity and a consciousness of his greater importance had broadened his back and straightened his shoulders; he was quite three inches more round the chest than when she had first known him, and his waist had proportionately increased.

'If he goes on developing in this way,' she thought, 'the good man will be colossal by the time he's forty.'

'Of course, Aunt Polly,' he said, boldly dropping the respectful *Miss Ley* that hitherto he had invariably used, though his new relative was not a woman whom most men would have ventured to treat familiarly, 'of course, it's all rot about your leaving us in a week; you must stay a couple of months at least.'

'It's very good of you, dear Edward,' replied Miss Ley drily. 'But I have other engagements.'

'Then you must break them. I can't have people leave my house immediately they come.'

Miss Ley raised her eyebrows and smiled. Was it *his* house already? Dear me!

'My dear Edward,' she answered, 'I never stay anywhere longer than two days – the first day I talk to people, the second I let them talk to me and the third I go. I stay a week at hotels so as to go *en pension* and get my washing properly aired.'

'You're treating us like a hotel,' said Edward, laughing.

'It's a great compliment; in private houses one gets so abominably waited on.'

'Ah, well, we'll say no more about it. But I shall have your boxes taken to the box-room, and I keep the key of it.'

Miss Ley gave the short dry laugh that denoted that the remark of the person she was with had not amused her, but something in her own mind. They arrived at Court Leys.

'D'you see all the differences since you were last here?' asked Edward jovially.

Miss Ley looked round and pursed her lips.

'It's charming,' she said.

'I knew it would make you sit up,' he cried, laughing.

Bertha received her aunt in the hall, and embraced her with the grave decorum that had always characterized their relations.

'How clever you are, Bertha,' said Miss Ley. 'You manage to preserve your beautiful figure.'

Then she set herself solemnly to investigate the connubial bliss of the youthful couple.

12

THE passion to analyse the casual fellow-creature was the most absorbing vice that Miss Ley possessed, and no ties of relationship or affection prevented her from exercising her talents in this direction. She observed Bertha and Edward during luncheon. Bertha was talkative, chattering with a vivacity that seemed suspicious about the neighbours – Mrs Branderton's new bonnets and new hair, Miss Glover's good works and Mr Glover's visit to London. Edward was silent, except when he pressed Miss Ley to take a second helping. He ate largely, and the maiden lady noticed the enormous mouthfuls he took and the heartiness with which he drank his beer. Of course she drew conclusions; and she drew further conclusions when, having devoured half a pound of cheese and taken a last drink of all, he pushed back his chair with a sort of low roar reminding one of a beast of prey gorged with food, and said:

'Ah, well, I suppose I must set about my work. There's no rest for the weary.'

He pulled a new briarwood pipe out of his pocket, filled and lit it.

'I feel better now. Well, good-bye, I shall be in to tea.'

Conclusions buzzed about Miss Ley like midges on a summer's day. She drew them all the afternoon and again at dinner. Bertha was effusive too, unusually so; and Miss Ley asked herself a dozen times if this stream of chatter, these peals of laughter, proceeded from a light heart or from a base desire to deceive a middle-aged and inquiring aunt. After dinner, Edward, telling her that of course she was one of the family, so he hoped she did not wish him to stand on ceremony, began reading the paper. When Bertha at Miss Ley's request played the piano, good manners made him put it aside, and he yawned a dozen times in a quarter of an hour.

'I mustn't play any more,' said Bertha, 'or Eddie will go to sleep. Won't you, darling?'

'I shouldn't wonder,' he replied, laughing. 'The fact is that the things Bertha plays when we've got company give me the fair hump.'

'Edward only consents to listen when I play "The Blue Bells of Scotland" or "Yankee Doodle".'

Bertha made the remark, smiling good-naturedly at her husband, but Miss Ley drew conclusions.

'I don't mind confessing that I can't stand all this foreign music. What I say to Bertha is, Why can't you play English stuff?'

'If you must play at all,' interposed his wife.

'After all's said and done, "The Blue Bells of Scotland" has got a tune about it that a fellow can get his teeth into.'

'You see, there's the difference,' said Bertha, strumming a few bars of 'Rule, Britannia,' 'it sets mine on edge.'

'Well, I'm patriotic,' retorted Edward. 'I like the good, honest, homely English airs. I like 'em because they're English. I'm not ashamed to say that for me the best piece of music that's ever been written is "God Save the Queen".'

'Which was written by a German, dear Edward,' said Miss Ley, smiling.

'That's as it may be,' said Edward, unabashed, 'but the sentiment's English, and that's all I care about.'

'Hear! Hear!' cried Bertha. 'I believe Edward has aspirations towards a political career. I know I shall finish up as the wife of the local M.P.'

'I'm patriotic,' said Edward, 'and I'm not ashamed to confess it.'

'Rule, Britannia,' sang Bertha, 'Britannia rules the waves, Britons never, never shall be slaves. Ta-ra-ra-boom-de-ay! Ta-ra-ra-boom-de-ay!'

'It's the same everywhere now,' proceeded the orator. 'We're chock full of foreigners and their goods. I think it's scandalous. English music isn't good enough for you; you get it from France and Germany. Where do you get your butter from? Brittany! Where d'you get your meat from? New Zealand!' This he said with great scorn, and Bertha punctuated it with a resounding chord. 'And as far as the butter goes, it isn't butter – it's margarine.

Where does your bread come from? America. Your vegetables from Jersey.'

'Your fish from the sea,' interposed Bertha.

'And so it is all along the line; the British farmer hasn't got a chance.'

To this speech Bertha played a burlesque accompaniment that would have irritated a more sensitive man than Craddock; but he merely laughed good-naturedly.

'Bertha won't take these things seriously,' he said, passing his hand affectionately over her hair.

She suddenly stopped playing, and his good humour, joined with the loving gesture, filled her with remorse. Her eyes filled with tears.

'You are a dear good thing,' she faltered, 'and I'm utterly horrid.'

'Now don't talk stuff before Aunt Polly. You know she'll laugh at us.'

'Oh, I don't care,' said Bertha, smiling happily. She stood up and linked her arm with his. 'Eddie's the best-tempered person in the world; he's perfectly wonderful.'

'He must be indeed,' said Miss Ley, 'if you have preserved your faith in him after six months of marriage.'

But the maiden lady had stored so many observations, her impressions were so multitudinous, that she felt an urgent need to retire to the privacy of her bed-chamber and sort them. She kissed Bertha and held out her hand to Edward.

'Oh, if you kiss Bertha, you must kiss me too,' said he, bending forward with a laugh.

'Upon my word!' said Miss Ley, somewhat taken aback, then, as he was evidently insisting, she embraced him on the cheek. She positively blushed.

The upshot of Miss Ley's investigation was that once again the hymeneal path had not been found strewn with roses; and the notion crossed her head, as she laid it on the pillow, that Dr Ramsay would certainly come and crow over her; it was not in masculine human nature, she thought, to miss an opportunity of exulting over a vanquished foe.

'He'll vow that I was the direct cause of the marriage. The dear man, he'll be so pleased with my discomfiture that I shall never hear the last of it. He's sure to call tomorrow.'

Indeed the news of Miss Ley's arrival had been by Edward industriously spread abroad, and promptly Mrs Ramsay put on her blue velvet calling dress and in the doctor's brougham drove with him to Court Leys. The Ramsays found Miss Glover and the Vicar of Leanham already in possession of the field. Mr Glover looked thinner and older than when Miss Ley had last seen him; he was more weary, meek and brow-beaten. Miss Glover never altered.

'The parish?' said the parson, in answer to Miss Ley's polite inquiry, 'I'm afraid it's in a bad way. The dissenters have got a new chapel, you know; and they say the Salvation Army is going to set up "barracks", as they call them. It's a great pity the Government doesn't step in; after all, we are established by law, and the law ought to protect us from encroachment.'

'You don't believe in liberty of conscience?' asked Miss Ley.

'My dear Miss Ley,' said the vicar in his tired voice, 'everything has its limits. I should have thought there was in the Established Church enough liberty of conscience for anyone.'

'Things are becoming dreadful in Leanham,' said Miss Glover. 'Practically all the tradesmen go to chapel now, and it makes it so difficult for us.'

'Yes,' replied the vicar with a weary sigh, 'and as if we hadn't enough to put up with, I hear that Walker has ceased coming to church.'

'Oh, dear! oh, dear!' said Miss Glover.

'Walker, the baker?' asked Edward.

'Yes, and now the only baker in Leanham who goes to church is Andrews.'

'Well, we can't possibly deal with him, Charles,' said Miss Glover. 'His bread is too bad.'

'My dear, we must,' groaned her brother. 'It would be against all my principles to deal with a tradesman who goes to chapel. You must tell Walker to send his book in, unless he will give an assurance that he'll come to church regularly.'

'But Andrews's bread always gives you indigestion, Charles,' cried Miss Glover.

'I must put up with it. If none of our martyrdoms were more serious than that we should have no cause to complain.'

'Well, it's quite easy to get your bread from Tercanbury,' said Mrs Ramsay, who was severely practical.

Both Mr and Miss Glover threw up their hands in dismay.

'Then Andrews would go to chapel too. The only thing that keeps them at church, I'm sorry to say, is the vicarage custom, or the hope of getting it.'

Presently Miss Ley found herself alone with the parson's sister.

'You must be very glad to see Bertha again, Miss Ley.'

'Now she's going to crow,' thought the good lady. 'Of course I am,' she said aloud.

'And it must be such a relief to you to see how well it's all turned out.'

Miss Ley looked sharply at Miss Glover, but saw no trace of irony.

'Oh, I think it's beautiful to see a married couple so thoroughly happy. It really makes me feel a better woman when I come here and see how those two worship one another.'

'Of course the poor thing's a perfect idiot,' thought Miss Ley. 'Yes, it's very satisfactory,' she said, drily.

She glanced round for Dr Ramsay, looking forward, notwithstanding that she was on the losing side, to the tussle she foresaw. She had the instinct of the fighting woman, and even though defeat was inevitable, never avoided an encounter. The doctor approached.

'Well, Miss Ley, so you have come back to us. We're all delighted to see you.'

'How cordial these people are,' thought Miss Ley, rather crossly, thinking Dr Ramsay's remark preliminary to coarse banter or reproach. 'Shall we take a turn in the garden? I'm sure you wish to quarrel with me.'

'There's nothing I should like better. To walk in the garden, I mean; of course no one could quarrel with so charming a lady as yourself.'

'He would never be so polite if he did not mean afterwards to be very rude,' thought Miss Ley. 'I'm glad you like the garden.'

'Craddock has improved it so wonderfully. It's a perfect pleasure to look at all he's done.'

This Miss Ley considered a gibe, and she looked for a repartee, but, finding none, was silent; Miss Ley was a wise woman. They walked a few steps without a word, and then Dr Ramsay suddenly burst out:

'Well, Miss Ley, you were right after all.'

She stopped and looked at the speaker. He seemed quite serious.

'Yes,' he said, 'I don't mind acknowledging it. I was wrong. It's a great triumph for you, isn't it?'

He looked at her and shook with good-tempered laughter.

'Is he making fun of me?' Miss Ley asked herself, with something not very far removed from dismay; this was the first occasion upon which she had been unable to understand, not only the good doctor, but his inmost thoughts as well. 'So you think the estate has been improved?'

'I can't make out how the man's done so much in so short a time. Why, just look at it!'

Miss Ley pursed her lips. 'Even in its most dilapidated days, Court Leys looked gentlemanly; now all this,' she glanced round with upturned nose, 'might be the country mansion of a pork-butcher.'

'My dear Miss Ley, you must pardon my saying so, but the place wasn't even respectable.'

'But it is now; that is my complaint. My dear doctor, in the old days the passer-by could see that the owners of Court Leys were decent people; that they could not make both ends meet was a detail; it was possibly because they burnt one end too rapidly, which is the sign of a rather delicate mind,' – Miss Ley was mixing her metaphors – 'And he moralized accordingly. For a gentleman there are only two decorous states, absolute poverty or over-powering wealth; the middle condition is vulgar. Now the passer-by sees thrift and careful management, the ends meet, but they do it aggressively, as if it were something to be proud of. Pennies are looked at before they are spent; and, good Heavens, the Leys serve to point a moral and adorn a tale. The Leys who gambled and squandered their sustenance, who bought diamonds when they hadn't got bread, and pawned the diamonds to give the king a garden-party, now form the heading of a copy-book and the ideal of a market-gardener.'

Miss Ley had the characteristics of the true phrase-maker, for so long as her period was well rounded off she did not mind how much nonsense it contained. Coming to the end of her tirade, she looked at the doctor for the signs of disapproval which she thought her right; but he merely laughed.

'I see you want to rub it in,' he said.

'What on earth does the creature mean?' Miss Ley asked herself.

'I confess I did believe things would turn out badly,' the doctor proceeded. 'And I couldn't help thinking he'd be tempted to play ducks and drakes with the whole property. Well, I don't mind frankly acknowledging that Bertha couldn't have chosen a better husband; he's a thoroughly good fellow, no one realized what he had in him, and there's no knowing how far he'll go.'

A man would have expressed Miss Ley's feeling with a little whistle, but that lady merely raised her eyebrows. Then Dr Ramsay shared the opinion of Miss Glover?

'And what precisely is the opinion of the county?' she asked. 'Of that odious Mrs Branderton, of Mrs Ryle (she has no right to the *Mayston* at all), of the Hancocks and the rest?'

'Edward Craddock has won golden opinions all round. Everyone likes him and thinks well of him. He's not conceited – he never had an ounce of conceit and he's not a bit changed. No, I assure you, although I'm not so fond as all that of confessing I was wrong, he's the right man in the right place. It's extraordinary how people look up to him and respect him already. I give you my word for it, Bertha has reason to congratulate herself; a girl doesn't pick up a husband like that every day of the week.'

Miss Ley smiled; it was a great relief to find that she really was no more foolish than most people (so she modestly put it), for a doubt on the subject had for a short while given her some uneasiness.

'So everyone thinks they're as happy as turtle-doves?'

'Why, so they are,' cried the doctor. 'Surely you don't think otherwise?'

Miss Ley never considered it a duty to dispel the error of her fellow-creatures, and whenever she had a little piece of knowledge, vastly preferred keeping it to herself.

'I?' she answered. 'I make a point of thinking with the majority; it's the only way to get a reputation for wisdom.' But Miss Ley, after all, was only human. 'Which do you think is the predominant partner?' she asked, smiling drily.

'The man, as he should be,' gruffly replied the doctor.

'Do you think he has more brains?'

'Ah, you're a feminist,' said Dr Ramsay, with great scorn.

'My dear doctor, my gloves are sixes, and perceive my shoes.'

She put out for the old gentleman's inspection a very pointed, high-heeled shoe, displaying at the same time the elaborate open-work of a silk stocking.

'Do you intend me to take that as an acknowledgement of the superiority of man?'

'Heavens, how argumentative you are!' Miss Ley laughed, for she was getting into her own particular element. 'I knew you wished to quarrel with me. Do you really want my opinion?'

'Yes.'

'Well, it seems to me that if you take the very clever woman and set her beside an ordinary man, you prove nothing. That is how we women mostly argue. We place George Eliot (who, by the way, had nothing of the woman but petticoats, and those not always) beside plain John Smith and ask tragically if such a woman can be considered inferior to such a man. But that's silly. The question I've been asking myself for the last five-and-twenty years is whether the average fool of a woman is a greater fool than the average fool of a man.'

'And the answer?'

'Well, upon my word, I don't think there's much to choose between them.'

'Then you haven't really an opinion on the subject at all?' cried the doctor.

'That is why I give it to you,' said Miss Ley.

'H'm!' grunted Dr Ramsay. 'And how does that apply to the Craddocks?'

'It doesn't apply to them. I don't think Bertha is a fool.'

'She couldn't be, having had the discretion to be born your niece, eh?'

'Why, doctor, you are growing quite pert,' answered Miss Ley, with a smile.

They had finished the tour of the garden, and Mrs Ramsay was seen in the drawing-room bidding Bertha good-bye.

'Now, seriously, Miss Ley,' said the doctor, 'they're quite happy, aren't they? Everyone thinks so.'

'Everyone is always right,' said Miss Ley.

'And what is your opinion?'

'Good Heavens, what an insistent man it is! Well, Dr Ramsay, all I would suggest is that for Bertha, you know, the book of life is written throughout in italics; for Edward it is all in the big round hand of the copy-book heading. Don't you think it will make the reading of the book somewhat difficult?'

13

RURAL pastimes had been one of the pleasures to which Bertha had chiefly looked forward, and with the summer Edward began to teach her the noble game of lawn tennis.

In the long evenings, when Craddock had finished his work and changed into the flannels that suited him so well, they played set after set. He prided himself upon his skill in this pursuit, and naturally found it trying to play with a beginner; but on the whole he was very patient, hoping that eventually Bertha would acquire sufficient skill to give him a good game. She did not find the sport so exhilarating as she had expected; it was difficult and she was slow at learning. However, to be doing something with her husband sufficiently amused her; she liked him to correct her mistakes, to show her this stroke and that, she admired his good-nature and inexhaustible spirits; with him she would have found endless entertainment even in such dull games as Beggar-my-Neighbour and Bagatelle. And now she looked for fine days so that their amusement might not be hindered. Those evenings were always pleasant; but the greatest delight for Bertha was to lie on the long chair by the lawn when the game was over and enjoy her fatigue, gossiping of the little nothings that love made absorbingly interesting.

Miss Ley had been persuaded to prolong her stay; she had vowed to go at the end of her week, but Edward, in his high-handed fashion, had ordered the key of the box-room to be given him, and refused to surrender it.

'Oh, no,' he said, 'I can't make people come here, but I can prevent them from going away. In this house everyone has to do as I tell them. Isn't that so, Bertha?'

'If you say it, my dear,' replied his wife.

Miss Ley gracefully acceded to her nephew's desire, which was the more easy since the house was comfortable; she had really no pressing engagements and her mind was set upon making further examination into the married life of her relatives. It would have been weakness, unworthy of her, to maintain her intention for consistence' sake. Why, for days and days, were Edward and Bertha the happiest lovers, and then suddenly why did Bertha behave almost brutally towards her husband, while he remained invariably good-tempered and amiable? The obvious reason was that some little quarrel had arisen, such as, since Adam and Eve, has troubled every married couple in the world; but the obvious reason was that which Miss Ley was least likely to credit. She never saw anything in the way of a disagreement; Bertha acceded to all her husband's proposals; and with such docility on the one hand, such good humour on the other, what on earth could form a bone of contention?

Miss Ley had discovered that when the green leaves of life are turning red and golden with approaching autumn more pleasure can be obtained by a judicious mingling in simplicity of the gifts of nature and the resources of civilization; she was satisfied to come in the evenings to the tennis lawn and sit on a comfortable chair, shaded by trees and protected by a red parasol from the rays of the setting sun. She was not a woman to find distraction in needle-work, and brought with her, therefore, a volume of Montaigne, who was her favourite writer. She read a page and then lifted her sharp eyes to the players. Edward was certainly very handsome; he looked very clean; he was one of those men who carry the morning tub stamped on every line of their faces. You felt that Pears' Soap was as essential to him as his belief in the Conservative Party, Derby Day and the Depression of Agriculture.

As Bertha often said, his energy was superabundant; notwith-standing his increasing size he was most agile; he was perpetually doing unnecessary feats of strength, such as jumping and hopping over the net, and holding chairs with outstretched arm.

'If health and a good digestion are all that is necessary in a husband, Bertha certainly ought to be the most contented woman alive.'

Miss Ley never believed so implicitly in her own theories that she was prevented from laughing at them; she had an impartial mind, and saw the two sides of a question clearly enough to find little to choose between them; consequently she was able and willing to argue with equal force from either point of view.

The set was finished, and Bertha threw herself on a chair, panting.

'Find the balls, there's a dear,' she cried.

Edward went off on the search, and Bertha looked at him with a delighted smile.

'He is such a good-tempered person,' she said to Miss Ley. 'Sometimes he makes me feel positively ashamed.'

'He has all the virtues. Dr Ramsay, Miss Glover, even Mrs Branderton have been drumming his praise into my ears.'

'Yes, they all like him. Arthur Branderton is always here, asking his advice about something or other. He's a dear good thing.'

'Who? Arthur Branderton?'

'No, of course not. Eddie.'

Bertha took off her hat and stretched herself more comfortably in the long chair; her hair was somewhat disarranged, and the rich locks wandered about her forehead and the nape of her neck in a way that would have distracted any minor poet under seventy. Miss Ley looked at her niece's fine profile, and wondered again at the complexion made of the softest colours in the setting sun. Her eyes now were liquid with love, languorous with the shade of long lashes, and her full, sensual mouth was half-open with a smile.

'Is my hair very untidy?' asked Bertha, catching Miss Ley's look and its meaning.

'No, I think it suits you when it is not done too severely.'

'Edward hates it; he likes me to be trim. And of course I don't care how I look as long as he's pleased. Don't you think he's very good-looking?'

Then, without waiting for an answer, she asked a second question.

'Do you think me a great fool for being so much in love, Aunt Polly?'

'My dear, it's surely the proper behaviour with one's lord and master.'

Bertha's smile became a little sad as she replied:

'Edward seems to think it unusual.' She followed him with her eyes, picking up the balls one by one, hunting among bushes; she was in the mood for confidences that afternoon. 'You don't know how different everything has been since I fell in love. The world is fuller. It's the only state worth living in.' Edward advanced with the eight balls on his racket. 'Come here and be kissed, Eddie,' she cried.

'Not if I know it,' he replied, laughing. 'Bertha's a perfect terror.

She wants me to spend my whole life in kissing her. Don't you think it's unreasonable, Aunt Polly? My motto is: everything in its place and season.'

'One kiss in the morning,' said Bertha, 'one kiss at night will do to keep your wife quiet, and the rest of the time you can attend to your work and read your paper.'

Again Bertha smiled charmingly, but Miss Ley saw no amusement in her eyes.

'Well, one can have too much of a good thing,' said Edward, balancing his racket on the tip of his nose.

'Even of proverbial philosophy,' remarked Bertha.

A few days later, his guest having definitely announced that she must go, Edward proposed a tennis-party as a parting honour. Miss Ley would gladly have escaped an afternoon of small-talk with the notabilities of Leanham, but Edward was determined to pay his aunt every attention, and his inner consciousness assured him that at least a small party was necessary to the occasion. They came, Mr and Miss Glover, the Brandertons, Mr Atthill Bacot, the great politician (of the district), and the Hancocks. But Mr Atthill Bacot was more than political, he was gallant; he devoted himself to the entertainment of Miss Ley. He discussed with her the sins of the Government and the incapacity of the army.

'More men, more guns,' he said. 'An elementary education in common sense for the officers, and the rudiments of grammar if there's time.'

'Good Heavens, Mr Bacot, you mustn't say such things. I thought you were a Conservative.'

'Madam, I stood for the constituency in '85. I may say that if a Conservative member could have got in, I should have. But there are limits. Even the staunch Conservative will turn. Now look at General Hancock.'

'Please don't talk so loud,' said Miss Ley with alarm; for Mr Bacot had instinctively adopted his platform manner, and his voice could be heard through the whole garden.

'Look at General Hancock, I say,' he repeated, taking no notice of the interruption. 'Is that the sort of man whom you would wish to have the handling of ten thousand of your sons?'

'Oh, but be fair,' cried Miss Ley, laughing, 'they're not all such fools as poor General Hancock.'

'I give you my word, madam, I think they are. As far as I can

make out, when a man has shown himself incapable of doing anything else they make him a general, just to encourage the others. I
understand the reason. It's a great thing, of course, for parents
sending their sons into the army to be able to say: "Well, he may
be a fool, but there's no reason why he shouldn't become a general".'

'You wouldn't rob us of our generals,' said Miss Ley; 'they're
so useful at tea-parties.'

Mr Bacot was about to make a heated retort, when Edward
called to him: 'We want you to make up a set at tennis. Will you
play with Miss Hancock against my wife and the General? Come
on, Bertha.'

'Oh, no, I mean to sit out, Eddie,' said Bertha quickly. She saw
that Edward was putting all the bad players into one set, so that
they might be got rid of. 'I'm not going to play.'

'You must, or you'll disarrange the next lot,' said her husband.
'It's all settled; Miss Glover and I are going to take on Miss Jane
Hancock and Arthur Branderton.'

Bertha looked at him with eyes flashing angrily; of course he did
not notice her vexation. He preferred playing with Miss Glover.
The parson's sister played well, and for a good game he would
never hesitate to sacrifice his wife's feelings. Didn't he know that
she cared nothing for the game, but merely for the pleasure of
playing with him? Only Miss Glover and young Branderton were
within earshot, and in his jovial, pleasant manner, Edward
laughingly said:

'Bertha's such a duffer. Of course she's only just beginning. You
don't mind playing with the General, do you, dear?'

Arthur Branderton laughed, and Bertha smiled at the sally, but
she flushed.

'I'm not going to play at all; I must see to the tea, and I daresay
some more people will be coming in presently.'

'Oh, I forgot that,' said Edward. 'No, perhaps you oughtn't
to.' And then, putting his wife out of his thoughts and linking
his arm with young Branderton's, he sauntered off: 'Come
along, old chap, we must find someone else to make up the
pat-ball set.'

Edward had such a charming, frank manner, one could not
help liking him. Bertha watched the two men go, and turned very
white.

'I must just go into the house a moment,' she said to Miss Glover. 'Go and entertain Mrs Branderton, there's a dear.'

And precipitately she fled. She ran to her bedroom and, flinging herself on the bed, burst into a flood of tears. To her the humiliation seemed dreadful. She wondered how Eddie, whom she loved above all else in the world, could treat her so cruelly. What had she done? He knew – ah, yes, he knew well enough the happiness he could cause her – and he went out of his way to be brutal. She wept bitterly, and jealousy of Miss Glover (Miss Glover, of all people!) stabbed her to the heart with sudden pain.

'He doesn't love me,' she moaned, her tears redoubling.

Presently there was a knock at the door.

'Who is it?' she cried.

The handle was turned and Miss Glover came in, red-faced with nervousness.

'Forgive me for coming in, Bertha. But I thought you seemed unwell. Can't I do something for you?'

'Oh, I'm all right,' said Bertha, drying her tears. 'Only the heat upset me, and I've got a headache.'

'Shall I send Edward up to you?' asked Miss Glover, compassionately.

'What do I want with Edward?' replied Bertha, petulantly. 'I shall be all right in five minutes; I often have attacks like this.'

'I'm sure he didn't mean to say anything unkind. He's kindness itself, I know.'

Bertha flushed: 'What on earth d'you mean, Fanny? Who didn't say anything unkind?'

'I thought you were hurt by Edward's saying you were a duffer and a beginner.'

'Oh, my dear, you must think me a fool,' Bertha laughed hysterically. 'It's quite true that I'm a duffer. I tell you it's only the weather. Why, if my feelings were hurt each time Eddie said a thing like that I should lead a miserable life.'

'I wish you'd let me send him up to you,' said Miss Glover, unconvinced.

'Good Heavens, why? See, I'm all right now.' She washed her eyes and passed the powder-puff over her face. 'My dear, it was only the sun.'

With an effort she braced herself, and burst into a laugh joyful enough almost to deceive the vicar's sister.

'Now, we must go down, or Mrs Branderton will complain more than ever of my bad manners.'

She put her arm round Miss Glover's waist and ran her down the stairs, to the mingled terror and amazement of that good lady. For the rest of the afternoon, though her eyes never rested on Edward, she was perfectly charming, in the highest spirits, chattering incessantly, and laughing; everyone noticed her high spirits and commented upon her happiness.

'It does one good to see a couple like that,' said General Hancock. 'Just as happy as the day is long.'

But the little scene had not escaped Miss Ley's sharp eyes, and she noticed with agony that Miss Glover had gone to Bertha; she could not stop her, being at the moment in the toils of Mrs Branderton.

'Oh, these good people are too officious. Why can't she leave the girl alone to have it out with herself?'

But the explanation of everything now flashed across Miss Ley.

'What a fool I am!' she thought, and she was able to cogitate quite clearly while exchanging honeyed impertinences with Mrs Branderton. 'I noticed it the first day I saw them together. How could I ever forget?'

She shrugged her shoulders and murmured the maxim of La Rochefoucauld:

'*Entre deux amants il y a toujours un qui aime et un qui se laisse aimer.*'

And to this she added another, in the same language, which, knowing no original, she ventured to claim as her own; it seemed to summarize the situation.

'*Celui qui aime a toujours tort.*'

14

BERTHA and Miss Ley passed a troubled night, while Edward, of course, after much exercise and a hearty dinner slept the sleep of the just and of the pure at heart. Bertha was nursing her wrath; she had with difficulty brought herself to kiss her husband before, according to his habit, he turned his back upon her and began to snore. She had never felt so angry; she could hardly bear his touch, and withdrew as far from him as possible. Miss Ley, with her knowledge of the difficulties in store for the couple, asked herself if she could do anything. But what could she do? They were reading the book of life in their separate ways, one in italics, the other in the big round letters of the copy-book; and how could she help them to find a common character? Of course the first year of married life is difficult, and the weariness of the flesh adds to the inevitable disillusionment. Every marriage has its moments of despair. The great danger is in the onlooker, who may pay them too much attention, and by stepping in render the difficulty permanent. Miss Ley's cogitations brought her not unnaturally to the course that most suited her temperament; she concluded that far and away the best plan was to attempt nothing and let things right themselves as best they could. She did not postpone her departure but according to arrangement went on the following day.

'Well, you see,' said Edward, bidding her good-bye, 'I told you that I should make you stay longer than a week.'

'You're a wonderful person, Edward,' said Miss Ley, drily. 'I have never doubted it for an instant.'

He was pleased, seeing no irony in the compliment. Miss Ley took leave of Bertha with a suspicion of awkward tenderness that was quite unusual; she hated to show her feelings, and found it difficult, yet wanted to tell Bertha that if she were ever in difficulties she would always find in her an old friend and a true one. All she said was:

'If you want to do any shopping in London, I can always put you up, you know. And for the matter of that, I don't see why you shouldn't come and stay a month or so with me – if Edward can spare you. It will be a change.'

When Miss Ley drove off with him to the station, Bertha felt suddenly a terrible loneliness. Her aunt had been a barrier between herself and her husband, coming opportunely just when, after the first months of mad passion, she was beginning to see herself linked to a man she did not know. A third person in the house had been a restraint, and the moments alone with her husband had gained a sweetness by their comparative rarity. She looked forward already to the future with something like terror. Her love for Edward was a bitter heart-ache. Oh, yes, she loved him well, she loved him passionately; but he – he was fond of her in his placid, calm way; it made her furious to think of it.

The weather was rainy, and for two days there was no question of tennis. On the third, however, the sun came out, and the lawn was soon dry. Edward had driven over to Tercanbury, but returned towards the evening.

'Hulloa!' he said, 'you haven't got your tennis things on. You'd better hurry up.'

This was the opportunity for which Bertha had been looking. She was tired of always giving way, of humbling herself; she wanted an explanation.

'You're very good,' she said, 'but I don't want to play tennis with you any more.'

'Why on earth not?'

She burst out furiously: 'Because I'm sick and tired of being made a convenience by you. I'm too proud to be treated like that. Oh, don't look as if you didn't understand. You play with me because you've got no one else to play with. Isn't that so? That is how you are always with me. You prefer the company of the veriest fool in the world to mine. You seem to do everything you can to show your contempt for me.'

'Why, what have I done now?'

'Oh, of course, you forget. You never dream that you are making me frightfully unhappy. Do you think I like to be treated before people as a sort of poor idiot that you can laugh and sneer at?'

Edward had never seen his wife so angry, and this time he was forced to pay her attention. She stood before him, at the end of her speech, with her teeth clenched, her cheeks flaming.

'It's about the other day, I suppose. I saw at the time you were in a passion.'

'And didn't care two straws,' she cried. 'You knew I wanted to play with you, but what was that to you so long as you had a good game.'

'You're too silly,' he said, with a laugh. 'We couldn't play together the whole afternoon when we had a lot of people here. They laugh at us as it is for being so devoted to one another.'

'If only they knew how little you cared for me!'

'I might have managed a set with you later on, if you hadn't sulked and refused to play at all.'

'Why didn't you suggest it? I should have been so pleased. I'm satisfied with the smallest crumbs you let fall for me. But it would

105

never have occurred to you; I know you better than that. You're absolutely selfish.'

'Come, come, Bertha,' he cried, good-humouredly. 'That's a thing I've not been accused of before. No one has ever called me selfish.'

'Oh, no. They think you charming. They think because you're cheerful and even-tempered, because you're hail-fellow-well-met with everyone you meet, that you've got such a nice character. If they knew you as well as I do they'd understand it was merely because you're perfectly indifferent to them. You treat people as if they were your bosom friends, and then, five minutes after they've gone, you've forgotten all about them. And the worst of it is that I'm no more to you than anybody else.'

'Oh, come, I don't think you can really find such awful things wrong with me.'

'I've never known you sacrifice your slightest whim to gratify my most earnest desire.'

'You can't expect me to do things that I think unreasonable.'

'If you loved me you'd not always be asking if the things I want are reasonable. I didn't think of reason when I married you.'

Edward made no answer, which naturally added to Bertha's irritation. She was arranging flowers for the table, and broke off the stalks savagely. Edward after a pause went to the door.

'Where are you going?' she asked.

'Since you won't play, I'm just going to do a few serves for practice.'

'Why don't you send for Miss Glover to come and play with you?'

A new idea suddenly came to him (they came at sufficiently rare intervals not to spoil his equanimity), but the absurdity of it made him laugh: 'Surely you're not jealous of her, Bertha?'

'I?' began Bertha with tremendous scorn, and then, changing her mind: 'You prefered to play with her than to play with me.'

He wisely ignored part of the charge: 'Look at her and look at yourself. Do you think I could prefer her to you?'

'I think you're fool enough.'

The words slipped out of Bertha's mouth almost before she knew she had said them, and the bitter, scornful tone added to their violence. They rather frightened her, and going very white, she turned to look at her husband.

'Oh, I didn't mean to say that, Eddie.'

Fearing now that she had really wounded him, Bertha was entirely sorry; she would have given anything for the words to be unsaid. Was he very angry? Edward was turning over the pages of a book, looking at it listlessly. She went up to him gently.

'I haven't offended you, have I, Eddie? I didn't mean to say that.'

She put her arm in his; he didn't answer.

'Don't be angry with me,' she faltered again, and then, breaking down, buried face in his bosom. 'I didn't mean what I said. I lost command over myself. You don't know how you humiliated me the other day. I haven't been able to sleep at night, thinking of it. Kiss me.'

He turned his face away, but she would not let him go; at last she found his lips.

'Say you're not angry with me.'

'I'm not angry with you,' he said, smiling.

'Oh, I want your love so much, Eddie,' she murmured. 'Now more than ever. I'm going to have a child.' Then, in reply to his astonished exclamation: 'I wasn't certain till today. Oh, Eddie, I'm so glad. I think it's what I wanted to make me happy.'

'I'm glad too,' he said.

'But you will be kind to me, Eddie, and not mind if I'm fretful and bad-tempered? You know I can't help it, and I'm always sorry afterwards.'

He kissed her as passionately as his cold nature allowed, and peace returned to Bertha's tormented heart.

Bertha had intended as long as possible to make a secret of her news; it was a comfort in her distress and a bulwark against her increasing disillusionment. The knowledge that she was at last with child came as a great joy and as an even greater relief. She was unable to reconcile herself to the discovery, seen as yet dimly, that Edward's cold temperament could not satisfy her burning desires. Love to her was a fire, a flame that absorbed the rest of life; love to him was a convenient and necessary institution of Providence, a matter about which there was as little need for excitement as about the ordering of a suit of clothes. Bertha's passion for a while had masked her husband's want of ardour, and she would not see that his temperament was to blame. She accused him of not loving her, and asked herself distractedly how to gain his affection. Her pride found cause for humiliation in the circumstance that her own love was so much greater than his. For six months she had loved him blindly; and now, opening her eyes, she refused to look upon the naked fact, but insisted on seeing only what she wished.

But the truth, elbowing itself through the crowd of her illusions, tormented her. A cold fear seized her that Edward neither loved her nor had ever loved her, and she wavered uncertainly between the old passionate devotion and a new equally passionate hatred. She told herself that she could not do things by halves; she must love or detest, but in either case fiercely. And now the child made up for everything. Now it did not matter if Edward loved her or not; it no longer gave her terrible pain to realize how foolish had been her hopes, how quickly her ideal had been shattered; she felt that the infantine hands of her son were already breaking, one by one, the links that bound her to her husband. When she guessed her pregnancy, she gave a cry, not only of joy and pride, but also of exultation in her approaching freedom.

But when the suspicion was changed into a certainty, and Bertha knew finally that she would bear a child, her feelings veered round. Her emotions were always as unstable as the light winds of April. An extreme weakness made her long for the support and sympathy of her husband; she could not help telling him. In the hateful dispute of that very day she had forced herself to say bitter things, but all the time she wished him to take her in his arms, saying he loved her. It wanted so little to rekindle her dying affection, she wanted his help and she could not live without his love.

The weeks went on, and Bertha was touched to see a change in Edward's behaviour, more noticeable after his past indifference. He looked upon her now as an invalid, and, as such, entitled to consideration. He was really kind-hearted, and during this time did everything for his wife that did not involve a sacrifice of his own convenience. When the doctor suggested some dainty to tempt her appetite, Edward was delighted to ride over to Tercanbury to fetch it, and in her presence he trod more softly and spoke in a gentler voice. After a while he used to insist on carrying her up and downstairs, and though Dr Ramsay assured them it was a quite unnecessary proceeding, Bertha would not allow Edward to give it up. It amused her to feel a little child in his strong arms, and she loved to nestle against his breast. Then with the winter, when it was too cold to drive out, Bertha would lie for long hours on a couch by the window, looking at the line of elm trees, now leafless again and melancholy, and watch the heavy clouds that drove over from the sea; her heart was full of peace.

One day of the new year she was sitting as usual at her window when Edward came prancing up the drive on horseback. He stopped in front of her and waved his whip.

'What d'you think of my new horse?' he cried.

At that moment the animal began to cavort, and backed almost into a flower-bed.

'Quiet, old fellow,' cried Edward. 'Now then, don't make a fuss, quiet!'

The horse stood on its hind legs and laid its ears back viciously. Presently Edward dismounted and led him up to Bertha.

'Isn't he a stunner? Just look at him.'

He passed his hand down the beast's forelegs and stroked its sleek coat.

'I only gave thirty-five guineas for him,' he remarked. 'I must just take him round to the stable, and then I'll come in.'

In a few minutes Edward joined his wife. The riding-clothes suited him well, and in his top-boots he looked more than ever the fox-hunting country squire, which had always been his ideal. He was in high spirits over the new purchase.

'It's the beast that threw Arthur Branderton when we were out last week. Arthur's limping about now with a sprained ankle and a smashed collar-bone. He says the horse is the greatest devil he's ever ridden; he's frightened to try him again.'

Edward laughed scornfully.

'But you haven't bought him?' asked Bertha, with alarm.

'Of course I have,' said Edward; 'I couldn't miss a chance like that. Why, he's a perfect beauty – only he's got a temper, like we all have.'

'But is he dangerous?'

'A bit. That's why I got him cheap. Arthur gave a hundred guineas for him, and he told me I could have him for seventy. "No," I said, "I'll give you thirty-five – and take the risk of break-ing my neck." Well, he just had to accept my offer. The horse has got a bad name in the county, and he wouldn't get anyone to buy him in a hurry. A man has to get up early if he wants to do me over a gee.'

By this time Bertha was frightened out of her wits.

'But, Eddie, you're not going to ride him? Supposing something should happen? Oh, I wish you hadn't bought him.'

'He's all right,' said Craddock. 'If anyone can ride him, I can – and, by Jove, I'm going to risk it. Why, if I bought him and then didn't use him, I'd never hear the last of it.'

'To please me, Eddie, don't. What does it matter what people say? I'm so frightened. And now, of all times, you might do something to please me. It isn't often I ask you to do me a favour.'

'Well, when you ask for something reasonable, I always try my best to do it; but really, after I've paid thirty-five guineas for a horse, I can't cut him up for cat's-meat.'

'That means you'll always do anything for me as long as it doesn't interfere with your own likes and dislikes.'

'Ah, well, we're all like that, aren't we? Come, come, don't be nasty about it, Bertha.' He pinched her cheek good-naturedly. Women, we all know, would like the moon if they could get it; and the fact that they can't doesn't prevent them from persistently asking for it. Edward sat down beside his wife, holding her hand. 'Now, tell us what you've been up to today. Has anyone been?'

Bertha sighed deeply: she had absolutely no influence over her husband. Neither prayers nor tears would stop him from doing a thing he had set his mind on. However much she argued, he always managed to make her seem in the wrong, and then went his way rejoicing. But she had her child now.

'Thank God for that!' she murmured.

15

CRADDOCK went out on his new horse, and returned triumphant.

'He was as quiet as a lamb,' he said. 'I could ride him with my arms tied behind my back; and as to jumping – he takes a five-barred gate in his stride.'

Bertha was rather angry with him for having caused her such terror, angry with herself also for troubling so much.

'And it was rather lucky I had him today. Old Lord Philip Dirk was there, and he asked Branderton who I was. "You tell him," says he, "that it isn't often I've seen a man ride as well as he does." You should see Branderton; he isn't half glad at having let me take the beast for thirty-five guineas. And Mr Molson came up to me and said: "I knew that horse would get into your hands before long, you're the only man in this part who can ride it; but if it don't break your neck, you'll be lucky".'

He recounted with satisfaction the compliments paid to him.

'We had a good run today. And how are you, dear? Feeling comfy? Oh, I forgot to tell you: you know Rodgers, the huntsman? Well, he said to me: "That's a mighty fine hack you've got there, governor; but he takes some riding." "I know he does," I said, "but I flatter myself I know a thing or two more than most horses." They all thought I should get rolled over before the day was out, but I just went slick at everything, just to show I wasn't frightened.'

Then he gave details of the affair, and he had as great a passion for the meticulous as a German historian; he was one of those men who take infinite pains over trifles, flattering themselves that they never do things by halves. Bertha had a headache, and her husband bored her; she thought herself a great fool to be so concerned about his safety.

As the months wore on Miss Glover became dreadfully solicitous. The parson's sister looked upon birth as a mysteriously heart-fluttering business which, however, modesty required decent people to ignore. She treated her friend in an absurdly self-conscious manner, and blushed like a peony when Bertha, with the frankness usual in her, referred to the coming event. The greatest torment of Miss Glover's life was that, as lady of the vicarage, she had to manage the Maternity Bag, an institution to provide the infants of the needy with articles of raiment and their mothers with flannel petticoats. Miss Glover could never without much blushing ask the necessary questions of the recipients of her charity: and feeling that the whole thing ought not to be discussed at all, when she did so kept her eyes averted. Her manner caused great indignation among the virtuous poor.

'Well,' said one good lady, 'I'd rather not 'ave her bag at all than be treated like that. Why, she treats you as if – well, as if you wasn't married.'

'Yes,' said another, 'that's just what I complain of. I promise you I 'ad 'alf a mind to take me marriage lines out of me pocket an' show 'er. It ain't nothin' to be ashamed about. Nice thing it would be after 'aving sixteen if I was bashful.'

But of course the more unpleasant a duty was, the more zealously Miss Glover performed it; she felt it right to visit Bertha with frequency, and manfully bore the young wife's persistence in referring to an unpleasant subject. She carried her herosim to the pitch of knitting socks for the forthcoming baby, although to do so made her heart palpitate uncomfortably, and when she was surprised at the work by her brother her cheeks burned like two fires.

'Now, Bertha dear,' she said one day, pulling herself together and straightening her back as she always did when she was mortifying her flesh, 'now, Bertha dear, I want to talk to you seriously.'

Bertha smiled: 'Oh, don't, Fanny, you know how uncomfortable it makes you.'

'I must,' answered the good creature gravely. 'I know you'll think me ridiculous; but it's my duty.'

'I shan't think anything of the kind,' said Bertha, touched by her friend's humility.

'Well, you talk a great deal of – of what's going to happen.' Miss Glover blushed. 'But I'm not sure if you are really prepared for it.'

'Oh, is that all?' cried Bertha. 'The nurse will be here in a fortnight, and Dr Ramsay says she's a most reliable woman.'

'I wasn't thinking of earthly preparations,' said Miss Glover. 'I was thinking of the other. Are you quite sure you're approaching the – the *thing* in the right spirit?'

'What do you want me to do?' asked Bertha.

'It isn't what I want you to do. It's what you ought to do. I'm nobody. But have you thought at all of the spiritual side of it?'

Bertha gave a sigh that was chiefly voluptuous.

'I've thought that I'm going to have a son that's mine and Eddie's, and I'm awfully thankful.'

'Wouldn't you like me to read the Bible to you sometimes?'

'Good Heavens, you talk as if I were going to die.'

'One can never tell, dear Bertha,' replied Miss Glover, gloomily. 'I think you ought to be prepared. In the midst of life we are in death, and one can never tell what may happen.'

Bertha looked at her a trifle anxiously. She had been forcing herself of late to be cheerful, and had found it necessary to stifle a recurring presentiment of evil fortune. The vicar's sister never realized that she was doing everything possible to make Bertha thoroughly unhappy.

'I brought my own Bible with me,' she said. 'Do you mind if I read you a chapter?'

'I should like it,' said Bertha, and a cold shiver went through her.

'Have you got any preference for some particular part?' asked Miss Glover, on extracting the book from a little black bag that she always carried.

On Bertha's answer that she had no preference, she suggested opening the Bible at random and reading on from the first line that crossed her eyes.

'Charles doesn't quite approve of it,' she said. 'He thinks it smacks of superstition. But I can't help doing it, and the early Protestants constantly did the same.'

Miss Glover, having opened the book with closed eyes, began to read: 'The sons of Pharez; Hezron, and Hamul. And the sons of Zerah; Zimri, and Ethan, and Heman, and Calcol, and Dara: five of them in all.' Miss Glover cleared her throat: 'And the sons of Ethan: Azariah. The sons also of Hezron, that were born unto him; Jerahmeel, and Ram, and Chelubai. And Ram begat Amminadab; and Amminadab begat Nahshon, prince of the children of Judah.'

She had fallen upon the genealogical table at the beginning of the Book of Chronicles. The chapter was very long, and consisted entirely of names, uncouth and difficult to pronounce; but Miss Glover shirked not one of them. With grave and rather high-pitched delivery, modelled upon her brother's, she read out the endless list. Bertha looked at her in amazement, but Miss Glover went steadily on.

'That's the end of the chapter,' she said at last. 'Would you like me to read you another one?'

'Yes, I should like it very much; but I don't think the part you've hit on is quite to the point.'

'My dear, I don't want to reprove you – that's not my duty – but all the Bible is to the point.'

And as the time of her delivery approached, Bertha quite lost her courage, and was often seized by a panic fear; suddenly, without obvious cause, her heart sank, and she asked herself frantically how she could possibly get through her confinement. She thought she was going to die, and wondered what would happen if she did. What would Edward do without her? The tears came to her eyes thinking of his bitter grief; but her lips trembled with pity for herself when the suspicion came to her that he would not be heart-broken; he was not a man to feel either grief or joy very poignantly. He would not weep; at the most his gaiety for a couple of days would be obscured, and then he would go about as before. She imagined him relishing the sympathy of his friends. In six months he would almost have forgotten her, and such memory as remained would not be extraordinarily pleasing. He would marry again, she thought bitterly; Edward loathed solitude, and next time doubtless he would choose a different sort of woman, one less remote than she from his ideal. Edward cared nothing for appearance, and Bertha imagined her successor plain as Miss Hancock or dowdy as Miss Glover; and the irony of it lay in the knowledge that either of those two would make a wife more suitable than she to his character, answering better to his conception of a helpmate.

Bertha fancied that Edward would willingly have given her beauty for some solid advantage, such as a knowledge of dressmaking; her taste, her arts and accomplishments were nothing to him, and her impulsive passion was a positive defect. Handsome is as handsome does, said he; he was a plain, simple man, and he wanted a plain, simple wife.

She wondered if her death would really cause him much sorrow. Bertha's will gave him everything of which she was possessed, and he would spend it with a second wife. She was seized with insane jealousy.

'No, I won't die,' she cried between her teeth. 'I won't!'

But one day, while Edward was out hunting, her morbid thoughts took another turn; supposing he should die! The thought was unendurable, but the very horror of it fascinated her; she could not drive away the scenes which, with strange distinctness, her imagination set before her. She was sitting at the piano and heard suddenly a horse stop at the front door – Edward was back. But the bell rang. Why should Edward ring? There was a murmur of voices without, and then Arthur Branderton came in. In her

114

mind's eye she saw every detail most clearly. He was in his hunting things! Something had happened, and, knowing what it was, Bertha was yet able to realize her terrified wonder as one possibility and another rushed through her brain. He was uneasy; he had something to tell, but dared not say it; she looked at him, horror-stricken, and a faintness came over her so that she could hardly stand.

Bertha's heart beat fast; she told herself it was absurd to allow her imagination to run away with her; but while she was arguing with herself the pictures went on developing themselves in her mind: she seemed to be assisting at a ghastly play in which she was the principal actor.

And what would she do when the fact was finally told her that Edward was dead? She would faint or cry out.

'There's been an accident,' said Branderton. 'Your husband is rather hurt.'

Bertha put her hands to her eyes, the agony was dreadful.

'You musn't upset yourself,' he went on, trying to break it to her.

Then, rapidly passing over the intermediate details, she found herself with her husband. He was dead, lying on the floor, and she pictured him to herself; she knew exactly how he would look; sometimes he slept so soundly, so quietly, that she was nervous, and put her ear to his heart to hear if it was beating. Now he was dead. Despair suddenly swept down upon her, overpoweringly. Bertha tried again to shake off her fancies, she even went to the piano and played a few notes; but the morbid attraction was too strong for her, and the scene went on. Now that he was dead he could not repulse her passion; now he was helpless and she kissed him with all her love; she passed her hands through his hair, and stroked his face (he had hated this in life), she kissed his lips and his closed eyes.

The imagined grief was so poignant that Bertha burst into tears. She remained with the body, refusing to be separated from it, and Bertha buried her face in cushions so that nothing might disturb her illusion; she had ceased trying to drive it away. Ah, she loved him passionately, she had always loved him and could not live without him. She knew that she would shortly die – and she had been afraid of death. Ah, now it was welcome! She kissed his hands – he could not prevent her now – and with a little shudder opened one of his eyes; it was glassy, expressionless, immobile. She burst into tears and, clinging to him, sobbed in love and anguish. She would let no one touch him but herself; it was a relief to perform the last offices for him who had been her whole life. She did not know that her love was so great.

She undressed the body and washed it; she washed the limbs one by one and sponged them; then very gently dried them with a towel. The touch of the cold flesh made her shudder voluptuously: she thought of him taking her in his strong arms, kissing her on the mouth. She wrapped him in the white shroud and surrounded him with flowers. They placed him in the coffin, and her heart stood still. She could not leave him, she passed with him all day and all night, looking ever at the quiet, restful face. Dr Ramsay came and Miss Glover came, urging her to go away, but she refused. What was the care of her own health now? She had only wanted to live for him. The coffin was closed, and she saw the faces of the undertakers; she had seen her husband's face for the last time, her beloved; her heart was like a stone, and she clutched at her breast in the pain of the oppression.

Hurriedly now the pictures thronged upon her, the drive to the churchyard, the service, the coffin covered with flowers and finally the graveside. They tried to keep her at home. What cared she for the silly, the abominable convention that sought to prevent her from going to the funeral? Was it not her husband, the only light of her life, whom they were burying? They could not realize the horror of it, the utter despair. And distinctly, by the dimness of the winter day, in the drawing-room of Court Leys, Bertha saw the lowering of the coffin, heard the rattle of earth thrown upon it.

What would her life be afterwards? She would try to live, she would surround herself with Edward's things, so that his memory might be always with her. The loneliness of life was appalling. Court Leys was empty and bare. She saw the endless succession of grey days; the seasons brought no change, and continually the clouds hung heavily above her; the trees were always leafless, and it was desolate. She could not imagine that travel would bring solace; the whole of life was blank, and what to her now were the pictures and churches, the blue skies of Italy? Her only happiness was to weep.

Then distractedly Bertha thought she would kill herself; her life was impossible to endure. No life at all, the blankness of the grave was preferable to the pangs gnawing continually at her heart. It would be so easy to finish, with a little morphia to close the book of trouble; despair would give her courage, and the prick of the needle was the only pain. But her vision became dim, and she had to make an effort to retain it. Her thoughts, growing less coherent, travelled back to previous incidents, to the scene at the grave and to the voluptuous pleasure of washing the body.

It was all so vivid that the entrance of Edward came upon her as a surprise. But the relief was almost too great for words, it was the awakening from a horrible nightmare. When he came forward to kiss her, she flung her arms round his neck and pressed him passionately to her heart.

'Oh, thank God!' she cried.

'Hulloa, what's up now?'

'I don't know what's been the matter with me. I've been so miserable, Eddie. I thought you were dead.'

'You've been crying.'

'It was so awful, I couldn't get the idea out of my head. Oh, I should die also.'

Bertha could hardly realize that her husband was by her side in the flesh, alive and well.

'Would you be sorry if *I* died?' she asked him.

'But you're not going to do anything of the sort,' he said, cheerily.

'Sometimes I'm so frightened, I don't believe I'll get over it.'

He laughed at her, and his joyous tones were peculiarly comforting. She made him sit by her side, and held his strong hands, the hands that to her were the visible signs of his powerful manhood. She stroked them and kissed the palms. She was quite broken with the past emotions; her limbs trembled and her eyes glistened with tears.

16

THE nurse arrived, bringing new apprehensions. She was an old woman who for twenty years had brought the neighbouring gentry into the world, and she had a copious store of ghastly anecdotes. In her mouth the terrors of birth were innumerable, and she told her stories with a cumulative art that was appalling. Of course, in her own mind she acted for the best. Bertha was nervous, and the nurse could imagine no better way of reassuring her than to give detailed accounts of patients who for days had been at death's door, given up by all the doctors, and yet had finally recovered and lived happily ever afterwards.

Bertha's quick invention magnified the coming anguish till, for thinking of it, she could hardly sleep at night. The impossibility of even conceiving it rendered it more formidable; she saw before her a long, long agony and then death. She could not bear Eddie to be out of her sight.

'Why, of course you'll get over it,' he said. 'I promise you it's nothing to make a fuss about.'

He had bred animals for years, and was quite used to the process that supplied him with veal, mutton and beef for the local butchers. It was a ridiculous fuss that human beings made over a natural and ordinary phenomenon.

'Why, Dinah, the Irish terrier I used to have, had litters as regular as clockwork, and she was running about ten minutes afterwards.'

Bertha lay with her face to the wall, holding Edward's fingers with a feverish hand.

'Oh, I'm so afraid of the pain. I feel certain that I shan't get over it – it's awful. I wish I hadn't got to go through it.'

Then as the days passed she looked upon Dr Ramsay as her very stay.

'You won't hurt me,' she begged. 'I can't bear pain a bit. You'll give me chloroform all the time, won't you?'

'Good Heavens,' cried the doctor, 'one would think no one had ever had a baby before you.'

'Oh, don't laugh at me. Can't you see how frightened I am?'

She asked the nurse how long her agony must last. She lay in bed, white, with terror-filled eyes, her lips set and a little vertical line between the brows.

'I shall never get through it,' she whispered. 'I have a presentiment that I shall die.'

'I never knew a woman yet,' said Dr Ramsay, 'who hadn't a presentiment that she would die, even if she had nothing worse than a finger-ache the matter with her.'

'Oh, you can laugh,' said Bertha. 'I've got to go through it.'

And the thought recurred persistently that she would die.

Another day passed, and the nurse said the doctor must be immediately sent for. Bertha had made Edward promise to remain with her all the time.

'I think I shall have courage if I can hold your hand,' she said.

'Nonsense,' said Dr Ramsay, when Edward told him this. 'I'm not going to have a man meddling about.'

'I thought not,' said Edward, 'but I just promised to keep her quiet.'

'If you'll keep yourself quiet,' answered the doctor, 'that's all I shall expect.'

'Oh, you needn't fear about me. I know all about these things. Why, my dear doctor, I've brought a good sight more living things into the world than you have, I bet.'

Edward was an eminently sensible man, whom any woman might admire. He was neither hysterical nor nervous; calm, self-possessed and unimaginative, he was the ideal person for an emergency.

'There's no good my knocking about the house all the afternoon,' he said. 'I should only mope, and if I'm wanted I can always be sent for.'

He left word that he was going to Bewlie's Farm to see a cow that was sick. He was anxious about her.

'She's the best milker I've ever had. I don't know what I should do if something went wrong with her. She gives her so many pints a day as regular as possible. She's brought in over and over again the money I gave for her.'

He walked along with the free-and-easy stride that Bertha so much admired, glancing now and then at the fields that bordered the highway. He stopped to examine the beans of a rival farmer.

'That soil's no good,' he said, shaking his head. 'It don't pay to grow beans on a patch like that.'

Then, arriving at Bewlie's Farm, he called for the labourer in charge of the sick cow.

'Well, how's she going?'

'She ain't no better, squire.'

'Bad job! Has Thompson been to see her today?'

Thompson was the vet.

''E can't make nothin' of it. 'E thinks it's a habscess she's got, but I don't put much faith in Mister Thompson: 'is father was a

labourer same as me, only 'e didn't 'ave to do with farming, bein'
a bricklayer; and wot 'is son can know about cattle I don't know.'

'Well, let's go and look at her,' said Edward.

He strode over to the barn, followed by the labourer. The poor
beast was standing in one corner, looking even more meditative
than is usual with cows, hanging her head and humping her back;
she looked profoundly pessimistic.

'I should have thought Thompson could do something,' said
Edward.

''E says the butcher's the only thing for 'er,' said the other, with
great contempt.

Edward snorted indignantly. 'Butcher indeed! I'd like to
butcher him if I got the chance.'

He went into the farmhouse, which for years had been his home,
but he was a practical, sensible fellow, and it brought him no
memories, no particular emotion.

'Well, Mrs Jones,' he said to the tenant's wife, 'how's yourself?'

'Middlin', sir. And 'ow are you and Mrs Craddock?'

'I'm all right. The missus is having a baby, you know.'

He spoke in the jovial, careless way that endeared him to all and
sundry.

'Bless my soul, is she indeed, sir? And I knew you when you was
a boy. When d'you expect it?'

'I expect it every minute. Why, for all I know I may be a happy
father when I get back to tea.'

'Oh, I didn't know it was so soon as all that.'

'Well, it was about time, Mrs Jones. We've been married sixteen
months, and chance it.'

'Ah, well, sir, it's a thing as 'appens to everybody. I 'ope she's
takin' it well.'

'As well as can be expected, you know. Of course she's very
fanciful. Women are full of ideas; I never saw anything like 'em.
Now as I was saying to Dr Ramsay only today, a bitch'll have
half a dozen pups and be running about before you can say Jack
Robinson. What I want to know is, why aren't women the same?
All this fuss and bother; it's enough to turn a man's hair grey.'

'You take it pretty cool, governor,' said Farmer Jones, who had
known Edward in the days of his poverty.

'Me?' cried Edward, laughing. 'I know all about this sort of
thing, you see. Why, look at all the calves I've had; and, mind you,

120

I've not had an accident with a cow above twice all the time I've gone in for breeding. But I'd better be going to see how the missus is getting on. Good afternoon to you, Mrs Jones.'

'Now what I like about the squire,' said Mrs Jones, 'is that there's no 'aughtiness in 'im. 'E ain't too proud to take a cup of tea with you, although 'e is the squire now.'

''E's the best squire we've 'ad for thirty years,' said Farmer Jones. 'And as you say, my dear, there's not a drop of 'aughtiness in 'im – which is more than you can say for his missus.'

'Oh, well, she's young-like,' replied his wife. 'They do say as 'ow 'e's the master, and I daresay 'e'll teach 'er better.'

'Trust 'im for makin' 'is wife buckle under; 'e's not a man to stand nonsense from anybody.'

Edward swung along the road, whirling his stick round, whistling and talking to the dogs that accompanied him. He was of a hopeful disposition, and did not think it would be necessary to slaughter his best cow. He didn't believe in the vet half so much as in himself, and his private opinion was that she would recover. He walked up the avenue of Court Leys, looking at the young elms he had planted to fill up the gaps; they were pretty healthy on the whole, and he was pleased with his success. He entered, and as he was hanging up his hat a piercing scream reached his ears.

'Hulloa!' he said, 'things are beginning to get a bit lively.'

He went up to the bedroom and knocked at the door. Dr Ramsay opened it, but with his burly frame barred the passage.

'Oh, don't be afraid,' said Edward. 'I don't want to come in. I know when I'm best out of the way. How is she getting on?'

'Well, I'm afraid it won't be such an easy job as I thought,' whispered the doctor. 'But there's no reason to get alarmed. It's only a bit slow.'

'I shall be downstairs if you want me for anything.'

'She was asking for you a good deal just now, but Nurse told her it would upset you if you were there; so then she said: "Don't let him come. I'll bear it alone."'

'Oh, that's all right. In a time like this the husband is much better out of the way, I think.'

Dr Ramsay shut the door upon him. 'Sensible chap that!' he ˙aid. 'I like him better and better. Why, most men would be fussing about and getting hysterical and Lord knows what.'

'Was that Eddie?' asked Bertha, her voice trembling with recent agony.

'Yes, he came to see how you were.'

'Oh, the darling!' she groaned. 'He isn't very much upset, is he? Don't tell him I'm very bad. It'll make him wretched. I'll bear it alone.'

Edward, downstairs, told himself it was no use getting into a state, which was quite true, and taking the most comfortable chair in the room, settled down to read his paper. Before dinner he went upstairs to make more inquiries. Dr Ramsay came out saying he had given Bertha opium and for a while she was quiet.

'It's lucky you did it just at dinner-time,' said Edward, with a laugh. 'We'll be able to have a snack together.'

They sat down and began to eat; they rivalled one another in their appetites, and the doctor, liking Edward more and more said it did him good to see a man who could eat well. But before they had reached the pudding a message came from the nurse to say that Bertha was awake, and Dr Ramsay regretfully left the table. Edward went on eating steadily. At last, with the happy sigh of a man conscious of virtue and a distended stomach, he lit his pipe and again settling himself in the armchair in a little while began to nod. The evening was long and he felt bored.

'It ought to be all over by now,' he said. 'I wonder if I need stay up.'

Dr Ramsay was looking worried when Edward went up to him a third time.

'I'm afraid it's a difficult case,' he said. 'It's most unfortunate. She's been suffering a good deal, poor thing.'

'Well, is there anything I can do?' asked Edward.

'No, except to keep calm and not make a fuss.'

'Oh, I shan't do that, you needn't fear. I will say that for myself, I have got nerve.'

'You're splendid,' said Dr Ramsay. 'I tell you I like to see a man keep his head so well through a job like this.'

'Well, what I came to ask you was, is there any good in my sitting up? Of course I'll do it if anything can be done; but if not I may as well go to bed.'

'Yes, I think you'd much better. I'll call you if you're wanted. I think you might come in and say a word or two to Bertha; it will encourage her.'

122

Edward entered. Bertha was lying with staring, terrified eyes, eyes that seemed to have lately seen entirely new things; they shone glassily. Her face was whiter than ever, the blood had fled from her lips, and the cheeks were sunken: she looked as if she were dying. She greeted Edward with the faintest smile.

'How are you, little woman?' he asked.

His presence seemed to call her back to life, and a faint colour lit up her cheeks.

'I'm all right,' she groaned, making an effort. 'You musn't worry yourself, dear.'

'Been having a bad time?'

'No,' she said, bravely. 'I've not really suffered much. There's nothing for you to upset yourself about.'

He went out, and she called Dr Ramsay.

'You haven't told him what I've gone through, have you? I don't want him to know.'

'No, that's all right. I've told him to go to bed.'

'Oh, I'm glad. He can't bear not to get his proper night's rest. How long d'you think it will last? Already I feel as if I'd been tortured for ever, and it seems endless.'

'Oh, it'll soon be over now, I hope.'

'I'm sure I'm going to die,' she whispered. 'I feel that life is being gradually drawn out of me. I shouldn't mind if it weren't for Eddie. He'll be so cut up.'

'What nonsense!' said the nurse. 'You all say you're going to die. You'll be all right in a couple of hours.'

'D'you think it will last a couple of hours longer? I can't stand it. Oh, doctor, don't let me suffer any more.'

Edward went to bed quietly and soon was fast asleep. But his slumbers were somewhat troubled; generally he enjoyed the heavy, dreamless sleep of the man who has no nerves and takes plenty of exercise; tonight he dreamt. He dreamt not only that one cow was sick, but that all his cattle had fallen ill: the cows stood about with gloomy eyes and hump-backs, surly and dangerous, evidently with their livers totally deranged; the oxen were 'blown' and lay on their backs with legs kicking feebly in the air, and swollen to double their normal size.

'You must send them all to the butcher's,' said the vet. 'There's nothing to be done with them.'

'Good Lord deliver us,' said Edward. 'I shan't get four bob a stone for them.'

But his dream was disturbed by a knock at the door, and Edward awoke to find Dr Ramsay shaking him.

'Wake up, man. Get up and dress quickly.'

'What's the matter?' cried Edward, jumping out of bed and seizing his clothes. 'What's the time?'

'It's half-past four. I want you to go into Tercanbury for Dr Spencer. Bertha is very bad.'

'All right, I'll bring him back with me.'

Edward rapidly dressed.

'I'll go round and wake up the man to put the horse in.'

'No, I'll do that myself; it'll take me half the time.'

He methodically laced his boots.

'Bertha is in no immediate danger. But I must have a consultation. I still hope we shall bring her through it.'

'By Jove,' said Edward, 'I didn't know it was so bad as that.'

'You need not get alarmed yet. The great thing is for you to keep calm and bring Spencer along as quickly as possible. It's not hopeless yet.'

Edward with all his wits about him, was soon ready, and with equal rapidity set to harnessing the horse. He carefully lit the lamps as the proverb 'more haste less speed' passed through his mind. In two minutes he was on the main road, and whipped up the horse. He went with a quick, steady trot through the silent night.

Dr Ramsay, returning to the sick-room, thought what a splendid object a man was who could be relied upon to do anything, who never lost his head or got excited. His admiration for Edward was growing by leaps and bounds.

17

EDWARD CRADDOCK was a strong man and unimaginative. Driving through the night to Tercanbury he did not give way to distressing thoughts, but easily kept his anxiety within proper bounds, and gave his whole attention to conducting the horse. He kept his eyes on the road in front of him. The horse stepped out with swift, regular stride, rapidly passing the milestones. Edward rang Dr Spencer up and gave him the note he carried. The doctor presently came down, an undersized man with a squeaky voice and a gesticulative manner. He looked upon Edward with suspicion.

'I suppose you're the husband?' he said, as they clattered down the street. 'Would you like me to drive? I daresay you're rather upset.'

'No, and don't want to be,' answered Edward with a laugh. He looked down a little upon people who lived in towns, and never trusted a man who was less than six feet high and burly in proportion.

'I'm rather nervous of anxious husbands who drive me at breakneck pace in the middle of the night,' said the doctor. 'The ditches have an almost irresistible attraction for them.'

'Well, I'm not nervous, doctor, so it doesn't matter twopence if you are.'

When they reached the open country, Edward set the horse going at its fastest; he was amused at the doctor's desire to drive. Absurd little man!

'Are you holding on tight?' he asked, with good-natured scorn.

'I can see you can drive,' said the doctor.

'It is not the first time I've had reins in my hands,' replied Edward modestly. 'Here we are.'

He showed the specialist to the bedroom and asked whether Dr Ramsay required him further.

'No, I don't want you just now; but you'd better stay up to be ready, if anything happens. I'm afraid Bertha is very bad indeed. You must be prepared for everything.'

Edward retired to the next room and sat down. He was genuinely disturbed, but even now he could not realize that Bertha was dying; his mind was sluggish and he was unable to imagine the future. A more emotional man would have been white with fear, his heart beating painfully, and his nerves quivering with a hundred anticipated terrors. He would have been quite useless, while Edward was fit for any emergency; he could have been trusted to drive another ten miles in search of some appliance, and with perfect steadiness to help in any necessary operation.

'You know,' he said to Dr Ramsay, 'I don't want to get in your way; but if I should be any use in the room you can trust me not to get flurried.'

'I don't think there's anything you can do; the nurse is very trustworthy and capable.'

'Women,' said Edward, 'get so excited; they always make fools of themselves if they possibly can.'

But the night air had made Craddock sleepy, and after half an hour in the chair, trying to read a book, he dozed off. Presently, however, he awoke, and the first light of day filled the room with a grey coldness. He looked at his watch.

'By Jove, it's a long job,' he said.

There was a knock at the door, and the nurse came in.

'Will you please come?'

Dr Ramsay met him in the passage.

'Thank God, it's over. She's had a terrible time.'

'Is she all right?'

'I think she's in no danger now, but I'm sorry to say we couldn't save the child.'

A pang went through Edward's heart. 'Is it dead?'

'It was still-born. I was afraid it was hopeless. You'd better go to Bertha now, she wants you. She doesn't know about the child.'

Bertha was lying in an attitude of extreme exhaustion: she lay on her back, with arms stretched in utter weakness by her sides. Her face was grey with past anguish, her eyes now were dull and lifeless, half closed, and her jaw hung almost as hangs the jaw of a dead man. She tried to form a smile as she saw Edward, but in her feebleness the lips scarcely moved.

'Don't try to speak, dear,' said the nurse, seeing that Bertha was attempting words.

Edward bent down and kissed her; the faintest blush coloured her cheeks, and then she began to cry; the tears stealthily glided down her cheeks.

'Come nearer to me, Eddie,' she whispered.

He knelt down beside her, suddenly touched. He took her hand, and the contact had a vivifying effect; she drew a long breath and her lips formed a weary, weary smile.

'Thank God, it's over,' she groaned. 'Oh, Eddie darling, you can't think what I've gone through. It hurt so awfully.'

'Well, it's all over now,' said Edward.

'And you've been worrying too, Eddie. It encouraged me to think that you shared my trouble. You must go to sleep now. It was good of you to drive to Tercanbury for me.'

'You musn't talk,' said Dr Ramsay, coming back into the room after seeing the specialist sent off.

'I'm better now,' said Bertha, 'since I've seen Eddie.'

'Well, you must go to sleep.'

'You've not told me yet if it's a boy or a girl; tell me, Eddie, you know.'

Edward looked uneasily at the doctor.

'It's a boy,' said Dr Ramsay.

'I knew it would be,' she murmured. An expression of ecstatic pleasure came into her face, chasing away the greyness of death. 'I'm so glad. Have you seen it, Eddie?'

'Not yet.'

'It's our child, isn't it? It's worth going through the pain to have a baby. I'm so happy.'

'You must go to sleep now.'

'I'm not a bit sleepy, and I want to see my son.'

'No, you can't see him now,' said Dr Ramsay, 'he's asleep, and you mustn't disturb him.'

'Oh, I should like to see him – just for one minute. You needn't wake him.'

'You shall see him after you've been asleep,' said the doctor soothingly. 'It'll excite you too much.'

'Well, you go and see him, Eddie, and kiss him; and then I'll go to sleep.'

She seemed so anxious that at least its father should see his child that the nurse led Edward into the next room. On a chest of drawers was lying something covered with a towel. This the nurse lifted, and Edward saw his child; it was naked and very small, hardly human, repulsive, yet very pitiful. The eyes were closed, the eyes that had never opened. Edward looked at it for a minute.

'I promised I'd kiss it,' he whispered.

He bent down and touched with his lips the cold forehead; the nurse drew the towel over the body and they went back to Bertha.

'Is he sleeping?' she asked.

'Yes.'

'Did you kiss him?'

'Yes.'

Bertha smiled: 'Fancy your kissing my baby before me.'

But the soporific that Dr Ramsay had administered was taking its effect, and almost immediately Bertha fell into a happy sleep.

'Let's take a turn in the garden,' said Dr Ramsay, 'I think I ought to be here when she wakes.'

The air was fresh, scented with the spring flowers and the odour of the earth. Both men inspired it with relief after the close atmosphere of the sick-room. Dr Ramsay put his arm in Edward's.

'Cheer up, my boy,' he said. 'You've borne it all magnificently. I've never seen a man go through a night like this better than you; and upon my word you're as fresh as paint this morning.'

'Oh, I'm all right,' said Edward. 'What's to be done about – about the baby?'

'I think she'll be able to bear it better after she's had a sleep. I really didn't dare say it was still-born; I thought the shock would be too much for her.'

They went in and washed and ate, then waited for Bertha to wake. At last the nurse called them.

'You poor things,' cried Bertha as they entered the room. 'Have you had no sleep at all? I feel quite well now, and I want my baby. Nurse says it's sleeping and I can't have it, but I will. I want it to sleep with me, I want to look at my son.'

Edward and the nurse looked at Dr Ramsay, who for once was disconcerted.

'I don't think you'd better have him today, Bertha,' he said. 'It would upset you.'

'Oh, but I must have my baby. Nurse, bring him to me at once.'

Edward knelt down again by the bedside and took her hands. 'Now, Bertha, you musn't be alarmed, but the baby's not well and –'

'What d'you mean?'

Bertha suddenly sprang up in bed.

'Lie down. Lie down,' cried both Dr Ramsay and the nurse, forcing her back on the pillow.

'What's the matter with him, doctor?' she cried, in sudden terror.

'It's as Edward says, he's not well.'

'Oh, he isn't going to die – after all I've gone through.'

She looked from one to the other.

'Oh, tell me, don't keep me in suspense. I can bear it, whatever it is.'

Dr Ramsay touched Edward, encouraging him.

'You must prepare yourself for bad news, darling. You know –'

'He isn't dead?' she shrieked.

'I'm awfully sorry, dear. He was still-born.'

'Oh, God!' groaned Bertha.

It was a cry of despair. And then she burst into passionate weeping. Her sobs were terrible, unbridled, it was her life that she was weeping away, her hope of happiness, all her desires and dreams. Her heart seemed breaking. She put her hands to her eyes in agony.

'Then I went through it all for nothing? Oh, Eddie, you don't know the frightful pain of it. All night I thought I should die. I would have given anything to be put out of my suffering. And it was all useless.'

She sobbed uncontrollably. She was crushed by the recollection of what she had gone through and its futility.

'Oh, I wish I could die.'

The tears were in Edward's eyes, and he kissed her hands.

'Don't give way, darling,' he said, searching in vain for words to console her. His voice faltered and broke.

'Oh, Eddie,' she said, 'you're suffering just as much as I am. I forgot. Let me see him now.'

Dr Ramsay made a sign to the nurse, and she fetched the dead child. She carried it to the bedside, and uncovering its head showed the face to Bertha. She looked a moment, and then asked:

'Let me see the whole body.'

The nurse removed the cloth, and Bertha looked again. She said nothing, but finally turned away, and the nurse withdrew.

Bertha's tears now had ceased, but her mouth was set to a hopeless woe.

'Oh, I loved him already so much,' she murmured.

Edward bent over: 'Don't grieve, darling.'

She put her arms round his neck as she had delighted to do.

'Oh, Eddie, love me with all your heart. I want your love so badly.'

18

FOR days Bertha was overwhelmed with grief. She thought always of the dead child that had never lived, and her heart ached. But above all she was tormented by the idea that all her pain had been futile; she had gone through so much, her sleep still was full of the past agony, and it had been useless, utterly useless. Her body was mutilated so that she wondered it was possible for her to recover, she had lost her old buoyancy, that vitality that had been so enjoyable, and she felt like an old woman. Her weariness was unendurable; she felt so tired that it seemed to her impossible to rest. She lay in bed, day after day, in a posture of hopeless fatigue, on her back, with arms stretched out alongside of her, the pillows supporting her head; and all her limbs were powerless.

Recovery was very slow, and Edward suggested sending for Miss Ley; but Bertha refused.

'I don't want to see anybody,' she said. 'I merely want to lie still and be quiet.'

It bored her to speak with people, and even her affections for the time were dormant; she looked upon Edward as someone apart from her, his presence and absence gave her no particular emotion. She was tired and desired only to be left alone. Sympathy was unnecessary and useless; she knew that no one could enter into the bitterness of her sorrow, and she preferred to bear it alone.

Little by little, however, Bertha regained strength and consented to see the friends who called, some genuinely sorry, others impelled merely by a sense of duty or a ghoul-like curiosity. Miss Glover was a great trial; she felt the sincerest sympathy for Bertha, but her feelings were one thing and her sense of right and wrong was another. She did not think the young wife took her affliction with proper humility. Gradually a rebellious feeling had replaced the extreme prostration of the beginning, and Bertha raged at the injustice of her lot. Miss Glover came every day, bringing flowers and good advice; but Bertha was not docile, and refused to be satisfied with Miss Glover's pious consolations. When the good creature read the Bible, Bertha listened with a firmer closing of her lips, sullenly.

'Do you like me to read the Bible to you, dear?' asked the parson's sister sometimes.

But one day, Bertha, driven beyond her patience, could not as usual command her tongue.

'It amuses you, dear,' she answered bitterly.

'Oh, Bertha, you're not taking it in the proper spirit. You're so rebellious, and it's wrong, it's utterly wrong.'

'I can only think of my baby,' said Bertha, hoarsely.

'Why don't you pray to God, dear? Shall I offer a short prayer now, Bertha?'

'No, I don't want to pray to God. He's either impotent or cruel.'

'Bertha,' cried Miss Glover, 'you don't know what you're saying. Oh, pray to God, to melt your stubbornness, pray to God to forgive you.'

'I don't want to be forgiven. I've done nothing that needs it. It's God who needs my forgiveness – not I His.'

'You don't know what you're saying, Bertha,' said Miss Glover, very gravely and sorrowfully.

Bertha was still so ill that Miss Glover dared not press the subject, but she was grievously troubled. She asked herself whether she should consult her brother, to whom an absurd shyness prevented her from mentioning spiritual matters unless necessity compelled. But she had immense faith in him, and to her he was a type of all that the Christian clergyman should be: although her character was much stronger than his, Mr Glover seemed to his sister a pillar of strength, and often in past times, when the flesh was more stubborn, had she found strength and consolation in his very mediocre sermons. Finally, however, Miss Glover decided to speak with him on the subject that distressed her, with the result that for a week she avoided spiritual topics in her daily conversations with the invalid; then, Bertha having grown a little stronger, without previously mentioning her intention she brought her brother to Court Leys.

Miss Glover went alone to Bertha's room, her ardent sense of propriety fearing that Bertha, in bed, might not be costumed decorously enough for the visit of a clerical gentleman.

'Oh,' she said, 'Charles is downstairs, and would like to see you so much. I thought I'd better come up first to see if you were presentable.'

Bertha was sitting up in bed, with a mass of cushions and pillows behind her; a bright red jacket contrasted with her dark hair and the pallor of her skin. She drew her lips together when she heard that the vicar was below, and a slight frown darkened her forehead. Miss Glover caught sight of it.

'I don't think she likes your coming,' said Miss Glover – to encourage him – when she went to fetch her brother, 'but I think it's your duty.'

'Yes, I think it's my duty,' replied Mr Glover, who liked the approaching interview as little as Bertha.

He was an honest man, oppressed by the inroads of dissent, but his ministrations were confined to the services in church, the collecting of subscriptions, and the visiting of the church-going poor. It was something new to be brought before a rebellious gentlewoman, and he did not quite know how to treat her.

Miss Glover opened the bedroom door for her brother, and he entered, a cold wind laden with carbolic acid; she solemnly put a chair for him by the bedside and another for herself at a little distance.

'Ring for the tea before you sit down, Fanny,' said Bertha.

'I think, if you don't mind, Charles would like to speak to you first,' said Miss Glover. 'Am I not right, Charles?'

'Yes, dear.'

'I took the liberty of telling him what you had said to me the other day, Bertha.'

Mrs Craddock pursed her lips, but made no reply.

'I hope you're not angry with me for doing so, but I thought it my duty. Now, Charles.'

The Vicar of Leanham coughed.

'I can quite understand,' he said, 'that you must be most distressed at your affliction. It's a most unfortunate occurrence. I need not say that Fanny and I sympathize with you from the bottom of our hearts.'

'We do indeed,' said his sister.

Still Bertha did not answer, and Miss Glover looked at her uneasily. The vicar coughed again.

'But I always think that we should be thankful for the cross we have to bear. It is, as it were, a measure of the confidence that God places in us.'

Bertha remained silent, and the parson inquiringly looked at his sister. Miss Glover saw that no good would come by beating about the bush.

'The fact is, Bertha,' she said, breaking the awkward silence, 'that Charles and I are very anxious that you should be churched. You don't mind our saying so, but we're both a great deal older than you are, and we think it will do you good. We do hope you'll consent to it; but, more than that, Charles is here as the clergyman of your parish to tell you that it is your duty.'

'I hope it won't be necessary for me to put it in that way, Mrs Craddock.'

Bertha paused a moment longer, and then asked for a prayer-book. Miss Glover gave a smile which for her was radiant.

'I've been wanting for a long time to make you a little present, Bertha,' she said. 'And it occurred to me that you might like a prayer-book with good large print. I've noticed in church that the book you generally use is so small that it must try your eyes and be a temptation to you not to follow the service. So I've brought you one today, which it will give me very much pleasure if you will accept.'

She produced a large volume, bound in gloomy black cloth and redolent of the antiseptic odours that pervaded the Vicarage. The print was indeed large, but since the society that arranged the publication insisted on the combination of cheapness with utility, the paper was abominable.

'Thank you very much,' said Bertha, holding out her hand for the gift. 'It's awfully kind of you.'

'Shall I find you the "Churching of Women"?' asked Miss Glover.

Bertha nodded, and presently the vicar's sister handed her the book open. She read a few lines and dropped the volume.

'I have no wish to "give hearty thanks unto God,"' she said, looking almost fiercely at the worthy couple. 'I'm very sorry to offend your prejudices, but it seems to me absurd that I should prostrate myself in gratitude to God.'

'Oh, Mrs Craddock, I trust you don't mean what you say,' said the vicar.

'This is what I told you, Charles,' said Miss Glover. 'I don't think Bertha is well; but still this seems to me dreadfully wicked.'

Bertha frowned, finding it difficult to repress the sarcasms that rose to her lips; her forbearance was sorely tried. But Mr Glover was a little undecided.

'We must be as thankful to God for the afflictions that He sends us as for the benefits,' he said at last.

'I am not a worm to crawl along the ground and give thanks to the Foot that crushes me.'

'I think that is blasphemous, Bertha,' said Miss Glover.

'Oh, I have no patience with you, Fanny,' said Bertha, a flush lighting up her face. 'Can you realize what I've gone through, the terrible pain of it? Oh, it was too awful. Even now when I think of it I almost scream. Don't you know what it is? It feels as if your flesh were being torn, it's like sharp hooks dragged through your entrails. You try to be brave, you clench your teeth to stop crying out, but the pain is so awful that you're powerless. You shriek in your agony.'

'Bertha, Bertha,' said Miss Glover, horrified that such details should assail the chaste ears of the Vicar of Leanham.

'And the endlessness of it – they stand round you like ghouls, and do nothing. They say you must have patience, that it'll soon be over; and it lasts on. And time after time the awful agony comes, you feel it coming and you think you can't endure it. Oh, I wanted to die, it was too awful.'

'It is by suffering that we rise to our higher selves,' said Miss Glover. 'Suffering is a fire that burns away the grossness of our material natures.'

'What rubbish you talk,' cried Bertha passionately. 'You say that because you've never suffered. People say that suffering ennobles one; it's a lie, it only makes one brutal. But I would have borne it for the sake of my child. It was all useless – utterly useless. Dr Ramsay told me the child had been dead the whole time. Oh, if God made me suffer like that it's infamous. I wonder you're not ashamed to put it down to your God. How can you imagine Him to be so stupid, so cruel? Why, even the vilest, most brutal man on the earth wouldn't cause a woman such frightful and useless agony for the mere pleasure of it. Your God is a ruffian at a cock-fight, drinking in the bloodiness, laughing because the wretched birds, in their faintness, stagger ridiculously.'

Miss Glover sprang to her feet.

'Bertha, your illness is no excuse for this. You must either be mad or utterly depraved and wicked.'

'No, I'm more charitable than you,' cried Bertha. 'I know there is no God.'

'Then I for one can have nothing more to do with you.'

Miss Glover's cheeks were flaming, and a sudden indignation dispelled her habitual shyness.

'Fanny, Fanny,' cried her brother, 'restrain yourself!'

'Oh, this isn't the time to restrain oneself, Charles. It's one's duty to speak out sometimes. No, Bertha, if you're an atheist I can have nothing more to do with you.'

'She spoke in anger,' said the vicar. 'It is not our duty to judge her.'

'It's our duty to protest when the name of God is taken in vain. Charles, if you think Bertha's position excuses her blasphemies, then I think you ought to be ashamed of yourself. But I'm not afraid to speak out. Yes, Bertha, I've known for a long time that you were proud and headstrong, but I thought time would change you. I have always had confidence in you, because I thought at the bottom you were good. But if you deny your Maker, Bertha, there can be no hope for you.'

'Fanny, Fanny,' murmured the vicar.

'Let me speak, Charles. I think you're a bad and wicked woman, and I can no longer feel sorry for you, because everything that you have suffered I think you have thoroughly deserved. Your heart is absolutely hard, and I know nothing so thoroughly wicked as a hard-hearted woman.'

'My dear Fanny,' said Bertha, smiling, 'we've both been absurdly melodramatic.'

'I refuse to laugh at the subject. I see nothing ridiculous in it. Come, Charles, let us go and leave her to her own thoughts.'

But as Miss Glover bounded to the door, the handle was turned from the outside and Mrs Branderton came in. The position was awkward, and her appearance seemed almost providential to the vicar, who could not fling out of the room like his sister, but also could not make up his mind to shake hands with Bertha as if nothing had happened. Mrs Branderton came in, all airs and graces, smirking and ogling, and the gewgaws on her brand-new bonnet quivered with every movement.

'I told the servant I could find my way up alone, Bertha,' she said. 'I wanted so much to see you.'

'Mr and Miss Glover were just going,' said Bertha. 'How kind of you to come!'

Miss Glover bounced out of the room with a smile at Mrs Branderton that was almost ghastly; and Mr Glover, meek, polite and antiseptic as ever, shaking hands with Mrs Branderton, followed his sister.

'What queer people they are!' said Mrs Branderton, standing at the window to see them go out of the front door. 'I really don't think they're quite human. Why, she's walking on in front – she might wait for him – taking such long steps; and he's trying to catch her up. I believe they're having a race. What ridiculous people! Isn't it a pity she will wear short skirts? My dear, her great ankles are positively pornographic. I believe they wear one another's boots indiscriminately. And how are you, dear? I think you're looking much better.'

Mrs Branderton sat in such a position as to have a full view of herself in a mirror.

'What nice looking-glasses you have in your room, my dear. No woman can dress properly without them. Now you've only got to look at poor Fanny Glover to know that she's so modest as never even to look at herself in the glass to put her hat on.'

Mrs Branderton chattered on, thinking that she was doing Bertha good.

'A woman doesn't want to be solemn when she's ill. I know, when I have anything the matter, I like someone to talk to me about the fashions. I remember in my young days when I was ill I used to get old Mr Crowhurst, the former vicar, to come and read the ladies' papers to me. He was such a nice old man, not a bit like a clergyman, and he used to say I was his only parishioner whom he really liked visiting. I'm not tiring you, am I, dear?'

'Oh, dear, no,' said Bertha.

'Now, I suppose the Glovers have been talking all sorts of stuff to you. Of course, one has to put up with it, I suppose, because it sets a good example to the lower classes; but I must say, I think the clergy nowadays sometimes forget their place. I consider it most objectionable when they insist on talking religion with you as if you were a common person. But they're not nearly so nice as they used to be. In my young days the clergy were always gentlemen's sons – but then they weren't expected to trouble about the poor. I can quite understand that now a gentleman shouldn't like to become a clergyman; he has to mix with the lower classes, and they're growing more familiar every day.'

But suddenly, Bertha without warning burst into tears. Mrs Branderton was flabbergasted.

'My dear, what is the matter? Where are your salts? Shall I ring the bell?'

Bertha, sobbing violently, begged Mrs Branderton to take no notice of her. That fashionable creature had a sentimental heart, and would have been delighted to weep with Bertha, but she had several calls to make and therefore could not risk a disarrangement of her person; she was also curious, and would have given much to find out the cause of Bertha's outburst. She comforted herself, however, by giving the Hancocks, whose At Home day it was, a detailed account of the affair; and they shortly afterwards recounted it with sundry embellishments to Mrs Mayston Ryle.

Mrs Mayston Ryle, magnificently imposing as ever, snorted like a charger, eager for battle.

'Mrs Branderton sends *me* to sleep, frequently,' she said, 'but I can quite understand that if the poor thing isn't well, Mrs Branderton would make her cry. I never see her myself unless I'm in the most robust health, otherwise I know she'd simply make me howl.'

'But I wonder what was the matter with poor Mrs Craddock,' said Miss Hancock.

'I don't know,' answered Mrs Mayston Ryle, in her majestic manner. 'But I'll find out. I daresay she only wants a little good society. *I* shall go and see her.'

And she did!

19

BUT the apathy with which for weeks Bertha had looked upon all terrestrial concerns was passing away before her increasing strength; it had been due only to an utter physical weakness, of the same order as that merciful indifference to all earthly sympathies that gives ease to the final passage into the Unknown. The prospect of death would be unendurable if one did not know that the enfeebled body brought a like enfeeblement of spirit, dissolving the ties of the world: when the traveller must leave the hostel with the double gate, the wine he loved has lost its savour and the bread turned bitter in his mouth. Like useless gauds, Bertha had let fall the interest of life and her soul lay dying. Her spirit was a lighted candle in a lantern, flickering in the wind so that its flame was hardly seen, and the lantern was useless; but presently the wind of Death was stilled, and the light shone out and filled the darkness.

With the increasing strength the old passion returned; Love came back like a conqueror, and Bertha knew that she had not done with life. In her loneliness she yearned for Edward's affection; he now was all she had, and she stretched out her arms to him with a great desire. She blamed herself bitterly for her coldness, she wept at the idea of what he must have suffered. And she was ashamed that the love that she had thought eternal should have been for a while destroyed. But a change had come over her, she did not now love her husband with the old blind passion, but with a new feeling added to it; for to him were transferred the tenderness that she had lavished on her dead child and all the yearning that must now, to her life's end, go unsatisfied. Her heart was like a house with empty chambers, and the fires of love raged through them triumphantly.

Bertha thought a little painfully of Miss Glover, but dismissed her with a shrug of the shoulders. The good creature had kept her resolve never again to come near Court Leys, and for three days nothing had been heard of her.

'What does it matter?' cried Bertha. 'So long as Eddie loves me, the rest of the world is nothing.'

But her bedroom now had the aspect of a prison; she felt it impossible much longer to endure its dreadful monotony. Her bed was a bed of torture, and she fancied that so long as she remained stretched upon it she would never regain her health. She begged Dr Ramsay to allow her to get up, but was always met with the same refusal; and this was backed up by her husband's common sense. All she obtained was the dismissal of the nurse, to whom she had taken a sudden and violent dislike. From no reasonable cause Bertha found the mere presence of the poor woman unendurable; her officious loquacity irritated her beyond measure. If she must remain in bed, Bertha preferred absolute solitude; the turn of her mind was becoming almost misanthropic.

The hours passed endlessly. From her pillow Bertha could see only the sky, now a metallic blue with dazzling clouds swaying heavily across the line of sight, now grey, darkening the room; the furniture and the wallpaper forced themselves distastefully on her mind. Every detail was impressed on her consciousness as indelibly as the potter's mark on the clay.

Finally she made up her mind to get up, come what might. It was the Sunday after the quarrel with Miss Glover; Edward would be indoors, and doubtless intended to spend most of the afternoon in her bedroom, but she knew he disliked sitting there; the closeness, the odours of medicines and perfume, made his head ache. Her appearance in the drawing-room would be a pleasant surprise; she would not tell him that she was getting up, but go downstairs and take him unawares. She got out of bed, but as she put her feet to the ground had to cling to a chair; her legs were so weak that they hardly supported her, and her head reeled. But in a little while she gathered strength and dressed herself, slowly and very painfully; her weakness was almost pain. She had to sit down, and her hair was so wearisome to do that she was afraid she must give up the attempt and return to bed. But the thought of Edward's surprise upheld her; he had said how pleased he would be to have her downstairs with him. At last she was ready, and went to the door, supporting herself on every object at hand. But what a delight it was to be up again, to feel herself once more among the living, away from the grave of her bed!

She came to the top of the stairs and went down, leaning heavily on the banisters; she went one step at a time, as little children do, and she laughed at herself. But the laugh changed into a groan as in exhaustion she sank down and felt it impossible to go further. Then the thought of Edward urged her on. She struggled up and persevered till she reached the bottom. Now she was outside the drawing-room; she heard Edward whistling within. She crept along, eager to make no sound; noiselessly she turned the handle and flung the door open.

'Eddie!'

He turned round with a cry: 'Hulloa, what are you doing here?'

He came towards her, but did not show the great joy that she had expected.

'I wanted to surprise you. Aren't you glad to see me?'

'Yes, of course I am. But you oughtn't to have come without Dr Ramsay's leave. And I didn't expect you today.'

He led her to the sofa and she lay down.

'I thought you'd be so pleased.'

'Of course I am!'

He placed pillows under her and covered her with a rug.

'You don't know how I struggled,' she said. 'I thought I should never get my things on, and then I almost tumbled down the stairs, I was so weak. But I knew you must be lonely here, and you hate sitting in the bedroom.'

'You oughtn't to have risked it. It may throw you back,' he replied, gently. He looked at his watch. 'You must only stay half-an-hour, and then I shall carry you up to bed.'

Bertha gave a laugh, intending to permit nothing of the sort. It was so comfortable to lie on the sofa with Edward by her side. She held his hands.

'I simply couldn't stay in the room any longer. It was so gloomy with the rain pattering all day on the windows.'

It was one of those days of early autumn when the rain seems never ceasing and the air is filled with the melancholy of Nature conscious of the near decay.

'I was meaning to come up to you as soon as I'd finished my pipe.'

Bertha was exhausted, and, keeping silence, pressed Edward's hand in acknowledgement of his kind intention. It was delightful merely to be there with him, her heart was very full. Presently he looked at his watch again.

'Your half-hour's nearly up,' said he. 'In five minutes I'm going to carry you to your room.'

'Oh, no, you're not,' she replied, playfully, treating his remark as humorous. 'I'm going to stay till dinner.'

'No, you can't possibly. It will be very bad for you. To please me, go back to bed now.'

'Well, we'll split the difference and I'll go after tea.'

'No, you must go now.'

'Why, one would think you wanted to get rid of me!'

'I have to go out,' said Edward.

'Oh, no, you haven't; you're merely saying that to induce me to go upstairs. You fibber!'

'Let me carry you up now, there's a good girl.'

'I won't, I won't, I won't.'

'I shall have to leave you alone, Bertha. I didn't know you meant to get up today, and I have an engagement.'

140

'Oh, but you can't leave me the first time I get up. What is it? You can write a note and break it.'

'I'm awfully sorry,' he replied. 'But I'm afraid I can't do that. The fact is, I saw the Miss Hancocks after church; and they said they had to walk into Tercanbury this afternoon, and as it was so wet I offered to drive them in. I've promised to fetch them at three.'

'You're joking,' said Bertha.

Her eyes had suddenly become hard, and she was breathing fast. Edward looked at her uneasily.

'I didn't know you were going to get up, or I shouldn't have arranged to go out.'

'Oh, well, it doesn't matter,' said Bertha, throwing off the momentary anger. 'You can just write and say you can't come.'

'I'm afraid I can't do that,' he answered, gravely. 'I've given my word, and I can't break it.'

'Oh, but it's infamous!' Her wrath blazed out. 'Even you can't be so cruel as to leave me at such a time. I deserve some considera- tion after all I've suffered. For weeks I lay at death's door, and at last when I'm a little better and come down, thinking to give you pleasure, you're engaged to drive the Miss Hancocks into Tercan- bury.'

'Come, Bertha, be reasonable.' Edward condescended to ex- postulate with his wife, though it was not his habit to humour her extravagances. 'You see it's not my fault. Isn't it enough for you that I'm very sorry? I shall be back in an hour. Stay here, and then we'll spend the evening together.'

'Why did you lie to me?'

'I haven't lied: I'm not given to that,' said Edward, with natural satisfaction.

'You pretended it was for my health's sake that I must go upstairs. Isn't that a lie?'

'It was for your health's sake.'

'You lie again. You wanted to get me out of the way, so that you might go to the Miss Hancocks without telling me.'

'You ought to know me better than that by now.'

'Why did you say nothing about them till you found it impos- sible to avoid?'

Edward shrugged his shoulders good-humouredly. 'Because I know how touchy you are.'

'And yet you made them the offer.'

141

'It came out almost unawares. They were grumbling about the weather, and without thinking, I said, "I'll drive you over, if you like." And they jumped at it.'

'You're so good-natured if anyone but your wife is concerned.'

'Well, dear, I can't stay arguing, I shall be late already.'

'You're not really going?'

It had been impossible for Bertha to realize that Edward would carry out his intention.

'I must, my dear, it's my duty.'

'You have more duty to me than to anyone else. Oh, Eddie, don't go. You can't realize all it means to me.'

'I must; I'm not going because I want to. I shall be back in an hour.'

He bent down to kiss her, and she flung her arms round his neck, bursting into tears.

'Oh, please don't go – if you love me at all, if you've ever loved me. Don't you see that you're destroying my love for you?'

'Now, don't be silly, there's a good girl.'

He loosened her arms and moved away; but rising from the sofa, she followed him and took his arm, beseeching him to stay.

'You see how unhappy I am, and you are all I have in the world now. For God's sake stay, Eddie. It means more to me than you know.'

She sank on to the floor, still holding his hand; she was kneeling before him.

'Come, get on to the sofa. All this is very bad for you.'

He carried her to the couch, and then, to finish the scene, hurriedly left the room.

Bertha sprang up to follow him, but sank back as the door slammed, and burying her face in her hands surrendered herself to a passion of sobs. But humiliation and rage almost drove away her grief. She had knelt before her husband for a favour, and he had not granted it.

Suddenly she abhorred him; the love that had been a tower of brass fell like a house of cards. She would not try now to conceal from herself the faults that stared her in the face. He cared only for himself: with him it was only self, self, self. Bertha found a bitter fascination in stripping her idol of the finery with which her madness had bedizened him; she saw him naked now, and he was

142

utterly selfish. But most unbearable of all was her own extreme humiliation.

The rain poured down, unceasing, and the despair of Nature ate into her soul. At last she was exhausted, and, losing thought of time, lay half-unconscious, feeling at least no pain, her brain vacant and weary. When a servant came to ask if Miss Glover might see her, she hardly understood.

'Miss Glover doesn't usually stand on such ceremony,' she said, ill-temperedly, forgetting the incident of the previous week. 'Ask her to come in.'

The parson's sister came to the door and hesitated, growing red; the expression in her eyes was pained and even frightened.

'May I come in, Bertha?'

'Yes.'

She walked straight up to the sofa, and suddenly fell on her knees.

'Oh, Bertha, please forgive me. I was wrong and I've behaved wickedly to you.'

'My dear Fanny,' murmured Bertha, a smile breaking through her misery.

'I withdraw every word I said to you, Bertha; I can't understand how I said it. I humbly beg your forgiveness.'

'There is nothing to forgive.'

'Oh, yes, there is. Good Heavens, I know! My conscience has been reproaching me ever since I was here, but I hardened my heart and would not listen.'

Poor Miss Glover could not have really hardened her heart, however much she tried.

'I knew I ought to come to you and beg your forgiveness, but I wouldn't. I've not slept a wink at night. I was afraid of dying, and if I'd been cut off in the midst of my wickedness I should have been lost.'

She spoke very quickly, finding it a relief to express her trouble.

'I thought Charles would upbraid me, but he's never said a word. Oh, I wish he had; it would have been easier to bear than his sorrowful look. I know he's been worrying dreadfully, and I'm so sorry for him. I kept on saying I'd only done my duty, but in my heart I knew I had done wrong. Oh, Bertha, and this morning I dared not take Communion; I thought God would strike me for blasphemy. And I was afraid Charles would refuse me in front of

143

the whole congregation. It's the first Sunday since I was confirmed that I've missed taking Holy Communion.'

She buried her face in her hands and burst into tears. Bertha heard her almost listlessly; her own trouble was overwhelming her and she could not think of any other. Miss Glover raised her face, tear-stained and red; it was positively hideous; but, notwithstanding, pathetic.

'Then I couldn't bear it any longer. I thought if I begged your pardon I might be able to forgive myself. Oh, Bertha, please forget what I said and forgive me. And I fancied that Edward would be here today, and the thought of exposing myself before him too was almost more than I could bear. But I knew the humiliation would be good for me. Oh, I was so thankful when Jane said he was out. What can I do to earn your forgiveness?'

In her heart of hearts Miss Glover desired some horrible penance that would thoroughly mortify the flesh.

'I have already forgotten all about it,' said Bertha, smiling wearily. 'If my forgiveness is worth anything, I forgive you entirely.'

Miss Glover was pained at Bertha's manifest indifference, yet took it as a just punishment.

'And Bertha, let me say that I love you and admire you more than anyone after Charles. If you really think what you said the other day, I still love you and hope God will turn your heart. Charles and I will pray for you night and day, and soon I hope the Almighty will send you another child to take the place of the one you lost. Believe me, God is very good and merciful, and He will grant you what you wish.'

Bertha gave a low cry of pain. 'I can never have another child. Dr Ramsay told me it was impossible.'

'Oh, Bertha, I didn't know.'

Miss Glover took Bertha protectingly in her arms, crying, and kissed her like a little child.

But Bertha dried her eyes.

'Leave me now, Fanny, please. I'd rather be alone. But come and see me soon, and forgive me if I'm horrid. I'm very unhappy, and I shall never be happy again.'

A few minutes later Edward returned, cheery, jovial, red-faced, and in the best of humours.

'Here we are again!' he shouted. 'You see I've not been gone long, and you haven't missed me a rap. Now we'll have tea.'

He kissed her and put her cushions right.

'By Jove, it does me good to see you down again. You must pour out the tea for me. Now, confess, weren't you unreasonable to make such a fuss about my going away? And I couldn't help it, could I?'

20

BUT the love that had taken such despotic possession of Bertha's heart could not be overthrown by any sudden means. When she recovered her health and was able to resume her habits it blazed out again like a fire that has been momentarily subdued, but has gained new strength in its coercion. It dismayed her to think of her extreme loneliness; Edward was now her mainstay and her only hope. She no longer sought to deny that his love was very unlike hers; but his coldness was not always apparent, and she so vehemently wished to find a response to her own ardour that she closed her eyes to all that did not too readily obtrude itself. She had such a consuming desire to find in Edward the lover of her dreams, that for certain periods she was indeed able to live in a fool's paradise, which was none the less grateful because at the bottom of her heart she had an aching suspicion of its true character.

But it seemed that the more passionately Bertha yearned for her husband's love, the more frequent became their differences. As time went on the calm between the storms was shorter, and every quarrel left its mark and made Bertha more susceptible to affront. Realizing finally that Edward could not answer her demonstrations of affection, she became ten times more exacting: even the little tenderness that at the beginning of her married life would have overjoyed her, now too much resembled alms thrown to an importunate beggar to be received with anything but irritation. Their altercations proved conclusively that it does not require two to make a quarrel. Edward was a model of good temper and his equanimity imperturbable. However cross Bertha was, Edward never lost his serenity; he imagined that she was troubled over the loss of her child and that her health was not entirely restored: it had been his experience, especially with cows, that a difficult confinement frequently gave rise to a temporary change in disposition, so that the most docile animal in the world would suddenly develop an unexpected viciousness. He never tried to understand Bertha's varied moods; her passionate desire for love was to him as unreasonable as her outbursts of temper and the succeeding contrition. Now Edward was always the same, contented equally with the world at large and with himself: there was no shadow of doubt about the fact that the world he lived in, the particular spot and period, were the very best possible, and that no existence could be more satisfactory than happily to cultivate one's garden. Not being analytic, he forbore to think about the matter; and, if he had, would not have borrowed the phrases of M. de Voltaire, of whom he had never heard, and whom he would have utterly abhorred as a Frenchman, a philosopher and a wit. But the fact that Edward ate, drank, slept, and ate again as regularly as the oxen on his farm sufficiently proves that he enjoyed a happiness equal to theirs; and what more a decent man can want I certainly have not the faintest notion.

Edward had moreover that magnificent faculty of always doing right and knowing it which is said to be the most inestimable gift of the true Christian; but if his infallibility satisfied himself and edified his neighbours, it did not fail to cause his wife annoyance. She would clench her hands and from her eyes shoot arrows of fire when he stood in front of her smilingly conscious of the justice of his own standpoint and the unreason of hers. And the worst of it was that in her saner moments Bertha had to confess that Edward's view was invariably right and she completely in the wrong. Her injustice appalled her, and she took upon her own shoulders the blame of all their unhappiness. Always, after a quarrel from which Edward had come with his usual triumph, Bertha's rage would be succeeded by a passion of remorse, and she could not find sufficient reproaches with which to castigate herself. She asked frantically how her husband could be expected to love her, and in a transport of agony and fear would take the first opportunity of throwing her arms round his neck and making the most abject apology. Then, having eaten the dust before him, having wept and humiliated herself, she would be for a week absurdly happy, under the impression that henceforward nothing short of an earthquake could disturb their blissful equilibrium. Edward was again the golden idol, clothed in the diaphanous garments of true love; his word was law and his deeds were perfect; Bertha was a humble worshipper offering incense and devoutly grateful to the deity that forbore to crush her. It required very little for her to forget the slights and the coldness of her husband's affection; her love was like the tide covering a barren rock; the sea breaks into waves and is dispersed in foam, and the rock remains ever unchanged. This simile, by the way, would not have displeased Edward; when he thought at all he liked to think how firm and steadfast he was.

At night, before going to sleep, it was Bertha's greatest pleasure to kiss her husband on the lips, and it mortified her to see how mechanically he replied to this embrace. It was always she who had to make the advance, and when, to try him, she omitted to do so, he promptly went off to sleep without even bidding her good night. Then she told herself that he must utterly despise her.

'Oh, it drives me mad to think of the devotion I waste on you,' she cried. 'I'm a fool! You are all in the world to me, and I, to you, am a sort of accident: you might have married anyone but me. If I hadn't come across your path you would infallibly have married somebody else.'

'Well, so would you,' he answered, laughing.

'I? Never! If I had not met you, I should have married no one. My love isn't a bauble that I am willing to give to whomever chance throws in my way. My heart is one and indivisible, it would be impossible for me to love anyone but you. When I think that to you, I'm nothing more than any other woman might be, I'm ashamed.'

'You do talk the most awful rot sometimes.'

'Ah, that summarizes your whole opinion. To you I'm merely a fool of a woman. I'm a domestic animal, a little more companionable than a dog, but on the whole not so useful as a cow.'

'I don't know what you want me to do more than I actually do. You can't expect me to be kissing and cuddling all the time; the honeymoon is meant for that, and a man who goes on honeymooning all his life is a fool.'

'Ah, yes, with you love is kept out of sight all day, while you are occupied with the serious affairs of life, such as shearing sheep and hunting foxes; and after dinner it arises in your bosom, especially if you've had good things to eat, and is indistinguishable from the

147

process of digestion. But for me love is everything, the cause and reason of life. Without love I should be non-existent.'

'Well, you may love me,' said Edward, 'but, by Jove, you've got a jolly funny way of showing it. But as far as I'm concerned, if you'll tell me what you want me to do, I'll try to do it.'

'Oh, how can I tell you?' she cried, impatiently. 'I do everything I can to make you love me, and I can't. If you're a stock and a stone, how can I teach you to be the passionate lover? I want you to love me as I love you.'

'Well, if you ask me for my opinion I should say it was rather a good job I don't. Why, the furniture would be smashed up in a week if I were as violent as you.'

'I shouldn't mind if you were violent if you loved me,' replied Bertha, taking his remark with passionate seriousness. 'I shouldn't care if you beat me. I shouldn't mind how much you hurt me, if you did it because you loved me.'

'I think a week of it would about sicken you of that sort of love, my dear.'

'Anything would be preferable to your indifference.'

'But, God bless my soul, I'm not indifferent. Anyone would think I didn't care for you, or was gone on some other woman.'

'I almost wish you were,' answered Bertha. 'If you loved anyone at all, I might have some hope of gaining your affection. But you're incapable of love.'

'I don't know about that. I can say truly that after God and my honour I treasure nothing in the world so much as you.'

'You've forgotten your hunter.'

'No, I haven't,' answered Edward, gravely.

'What do you think I care for a position like that? You acknowledge that I am third; I would as soon be nowhere.'

'"I could not love you half so much, loved I not honour more,"' misquoted Edward.

'The man was a prig who wrote that. I want to be placed above your God and above your honour. The love I want is the love of the man who will lose everything, even his own soul, for the sake of a woman.'

Edward shrugged his shoulders: 'I don't know where you'll get that. My idea of love is that it's a very good thing in its place, but there's a limit to everything. There are other things in life.'

'Oh, yes, I know: there are duty and honour, and the farm and

148

fox-hunting, and the opinion of one's neighbours, and the dogs and the cat, and the new brougham and a million other things. What do you suppose you'd do if I had committed some crime and were likely to be imprisoned?'

'I don't want to suppose anything of the sort. You may be sure I'd do my duty.'

'Oh, I'm sick of your duty. You din it into my ear morning, noon and night. I wish to God you weren't so virtuous, you might be more human.'

Edward found his wife's behaviour so extraordinary that he consulted Dr Ramsay. The general practitioner had been for thirty years the recipient of marital confidences and was sceptical of the value of medicine in the cure of jealousy, talkativeness, incompatibility of temper and the like diseases. He assured Edward that time was the only remedy, by which all differences were reconciled; but after further pressing, consented to send Bertha a bottle of harmless tonic, which it was his habit to give to all and sundry for most of the ills to which the flesh is heir. It would doubtless do Bertha no harm, and that is an important consideration to a medical man. Dr Ramsay advised Edward to keep calm and be confident that Bertha would eventually become the dutiful and submissive spouse whom it is every man's ideal to see by his fireside when he wakes up from his after-dinner snooze.

Bertha's moods were trying. No one could tell one day how she would be the next, and this was peculiarly uncomfortable to a man who was willing to make the best of everything, but on the condition that he had time to get used to it. Sometimes in the twilight of winter afternoons, when the mind was naturally led to a contemplation of the vanity of existence and the futility of all human endeavour, she would be seized with melancholy. Edward, noticing she was pensive, a state which he detested, asked what were her thoughts, and half-dreamily she tried to express them.

'Good Lord deliver us!' he said cheerily. 'What rum things you do get into your little noddle! You must be out of sorts.'

'It isn't that,' she answered, smiling sadly.

'It's not natural for a woman to brood in that way. I think you ought to start taking that tonic again; but I daresay you're only tired and you'll think quite different in the morning.'

Bertha made no answer. She suffered from the nameless pain of existence, and he offered her – iron and quinine: when she required sympathy because her heart ached for the woes of her fellow-men, he poured tincture of nux vomica down her throat. He could not understand, it was no good explaining that she found a savour in the tender contemplation of the evils of mankind. But the worst of it was that Edward was quite right – the brute, he always was! When the morning came, the melancholy had vanished, Bertha was left without a care, and the world did not even need rose-coloured spectacles to seem attractive. It was humiliating to find that her most beautiful thoughts, the ennobling emotions that brought home to her the charming fiction that all men are brothers, were due to mere physical exhaustion.

Some people have extraordinarily literal minds, they never allow for the play of imagination: life for them has no beer and skittles, and, far from being an empty dream, is a matter of the deadly-dullest seriousness. Of such is the man who, when a woman tells him she feels dreadfully old, instead of answering that she looks absurdly young, replies that youth has its drawbacks and age its compensations. And of such was Edward; he could never realize that people did not mean exactly what they said. At first he had always consulted Bertha on the conduct of the estate; but she, pleased to be a nonentity in her own house, had consented to everything he suggested, and even begged him not to ask her. When she informed him that he was absolute lord not only of herself, but of all her worldly goods, it was not surprising that he should at last take her at her word.

'Women know nothing about farming,' he said, 'and it's best that I should have a free hand.'

The result of his stewardship was all that could be desired; the estate was put into apple-pie order and the farms paid rent for the first time for twenty years. The wandering winds, even the sun and rain, seemed to conspire in favour of so clever and hard-working a man; and fortune for once went hand in hand with virtue: Bertha constantly received congratulations from the surrounding squires on the admirable way in which Edward managed the place; and he on his side never failed to tell her his triumphs and the compliments they had occasioned. But not only was Edward looked upon as the master by his farm-hands and labourers; even the servants of Court Leys treated Bertha as a minor personage whose orders were only to be conditionally obeyed. Long generations of servitude have made the countryman peculiarly subtle in hierarchical distinctions, and there was a marked difference between his manner with Edward, on whom his livelihood depended, and his manner with Bertha, who shone only with a reflected light as the squire's missus.

At first it had only amused her, but the most subtle jest may lose its savour after three years. More than once she had to speak sharply to a gardener who hesitated to do as he was bid, because his orders were not from the master. Her pride reviving with the decline of love, Bertha began to find the position intolerable; her mind was now very susceptible to affront, and she was desirous of an opportunity to show that after all she was still the mistress of Court Leys.

It soon came. For it chanced that some ancient lover of trees, unpractical as the Leys had ever been, had planted six beeches in a hedgerow, and these in course of time had grown into stately trees, the admiration of all beholders. But one day as Bertha walked along a hideous gap caught her eyes: one of the six beeches had disappeared. There had been no storm, it could not have fallen of itself. She went up, and found it cut down; the men who had done the deed were already starting on another. A ladder was leaning against it, upon which stood a labourer attaching a line. No sight is more pathetic than an old tree levelled with the ground: the space which it filled suddenly stands out with an unsightly emptiness. But Bertha was more angry than pained.

'What are you doing, Hodgkins?' she angrily asked the foreman. 'Who gave you orders to cut down this tree?'

'The squire, Mum.'

'Oh, it must be a mistake. Mr Craddock never meant anything of the sort.'

''E told us positive to take down this one and them others yonder. You can see his mark, Mum.'

'Nonsense. I'll talk to Mr Craddock about it. Take that rope off and come down from the ladder. I forbid you to touch another tree.'

The man on the ladder looked at her, but made no attempt to do as he was bid.

'The squire said most particular that we was to cut that tree down today.'

'Will you have the goodness to do as I tell you?' said Bertha growing cold with anger. 'Tell that man to unfasten the rope and come down. I forbid you to touch the tree.'

The foreman repeated Bertha's order in a surly voice, and they all looked at her suspiciously, wishing to disobey but not daring to in case the squire should be angry.

'Well, I'll take no responsibility for it,' said Hodgkins.

'Please hold your tongue and do what I tell you as quickly as possible.'

She waited while the men gathered up their various belongings and finally trooped off.

21

BERTHA went home fuming, knowing perfectly well that Edward had given the order that she had countermanded, but glad of the chance to have a final settlement of rights. She did not see him for several hours.

'I say, Bertha,' he said, when he came in, 'why on earth did you stop those men cutting down the beeches on Carter's field? You've lost a whole half-day's work. I wanted to set them on something else tomorrow. Now I shall have to leave it over till Thursday.'

'I stopped them because I refuse to have the beeches cut down. They're the only ones in the place. I'm very annoyed that even one should have gone without my knowing about it. You should have asked me before you did a thing like that.'

'My good girl, I can't come and ask you each time I want a thing done.'

'Is the land mine or yours?'

'It's yours,' answered Edward, laughing, 'but I know better than you what ought to be done, and it's silly of you to interfere.'

Bertha flushed: 'In future, I wish to be consulted.'

'You've told me fifty thousands times to do always as I think fit.'

'Well, I've changed my mind.'

'It's too late now,' he laughed. 'You made me take the reins in my own hands, and I'm going to keep them.'

Bertha in her anger hardly restrained herself from telling him she could send him away like a hired servant.

'I want you to understand, Edward, that I'm not going to have those trees cut down. You must tell the men you've made a mistake.'

'I shall tell them nothing of the sort. I'm not going to cut them all down – only three. We don't want them there. For one thing the shade damages the crops, and otherwise Carter's is one of our best fields. And then I want the wood.'

'I care nothing about the crops, and if you want wood you can buy it. These trees were planted nearly a hundred years ago, and I would sooner die than cut them down.'

'The man who planted beeches in a hedgerow was about the silliest jackass I've ever heard of. Any tree's bad enough, but a beech of all things – why, it's drip, drip, drip, all the time, and not a thing will grow under them. That's the sort of thing that has been done all over the estate for years. It'll take me a life-time to repair the blunders of your – of the former owners.'

It is one of the curiosities of sentiment that its most abject slave rarely permits it to interfere with his temporal concerns; it appears as unusual for a man to sentimentalize in his own walk in life as for him to pick his own pocket. Edward, having passed his whole life in contact with the earth, might have been expected to cherish a certain love of Nature: the pathos of transpontine melodrama made him cough and blow his nose, and in literature he affected the titled and consumptive heroine and the soft-hearted, burly hero. But when it came to business, it was another matter: the sort of sentiment that asks a farmer to spare a sylvan glade for aesthetic reasons is absurd. Edward would have willingly allowed advertisement-mongers to put up boards on the most beautiful part of his estate if thereby he could have surreptitiously increased the profits on his farm.

'Whatever you may think of my ancestors,' said Bertha, 'you will kindly pay attention to me. The land is mine, and I refuse to let you spoil it.'

'It isn't spoiling it. It's the proper thing to do. You'll soon get used to not seeing the wretched trees, and I tell you I'm only going to take three down. I've given orders to cut the others tomorrow.'

'D'you mean to say you're going to ignore me absolutely?'

'I'm going to do what's right, and if you don't approve of it, I'm very sorry, but I shall do it all the same.'

'I shall give the men orders to do nothing of the kind.'

Edward laughed: 'Then you'll make an ass of yourself. You try giving them orders contrary to mine and see what they do.'

Bertha gave a cry. In her fury she looked round for something to throw, she would have liked to hit him; but he stood there, calm and self-possessed, very much amused.

'I think you must be mad,' she said. 'You do all you can to destroy my love for you.'

She was in too great a passion for words. This was the measure of his affection, he must indeed utterly despise her; and this was the only result of the love she had humbly laid at his feet. She asked herself what she could do: she could do nothing – but submit. She knew as well as he that her orders would be disobeyed if they did not agree with his; and that he would keep his word she did not for a moment doubt. To do so was his pride. She did not speak for the rest of the day, but next morning, when he was going out, asked what was his intention with regard to the trees.

'Oh, I thought you'd forgotten all about them,' he replied. 'I mean to do as I said.'

'If you have the trees cut down, I shall leave you. I shall go to Aunt Polly's.'

'And tell her that you wanted the moon and I was so unkind as not to give it you?' he replied, smiling. 'She'll laugh at you.'

'You will find me as careful to keep my word as you.'

Before luncheon she went out and walked to Carter's field: the men were still at work, but a second tree had gone; the third would doubtless fall in the afternoon. The men looked at her, and she thought they laughed. She stood looking at them for some while, so that she might thoroughly digest the humiliation. Then she went home and wrote her aunt the following letter.

My dear Aunt Polly,

I have been so seedy these last few weeks that Edward, poor dear, has been quite alarmed, and has been bothering me to come up to town to see a specialist. He's as urgent as if he wanted to get me out of the way, and I'm already half-jealous of my new parlour-maid, who has pink cheeks and golden hair, which is just the type that Edward really admires. I also think that Dr Ramsay hasn't the ghost of an idea what is the matter with me, and not being particularly desirous to depart this life just yet, I think it would be discreet to see somebody who will at least change my medicine. I have taken gallons of iron and quinine, and I'm frightfully afraid that my teeth will go black. My own opinion coinciding so exactly with Edward's, (that horrid Mrs Ryle calls us the humming-birds, meaning the turtle-doves, her knowledge of natural history arouses dear Edward's contempt,) I have gracefully acceded to his desire, and if you can put me up, will come at your earliest convenience.

Yours affectionately,

B.C.

P.S. I shall take the opportunity of getting clothes, (I am positively in rags,) so you will have to keep me some little time.

Edward came in shortly afterwards, looking much pleased with himself, and glanced slily at Bertha, thinking himself so clever that he could scarcely help laughing: had he not the habit of being most particular in his behaviour, he would undoubtedly have put his tongue in his cheek.

'With women, my dear sir, you must be firm. When you're putting them to a fence, close your legs and don't check 'em; but mind you keep 'em under control, or they'll lose their little heads. A man should always let a woman see that he's got her well in hand.'

Bertha was silent, able to eat nothing for luncheon; she sat opposite her husband, wondering how he could gorge so disgracefully when she was angry and unhappy. But in the afternoon her appetite returned and, going to the kitchen, she ate so many sandwiches that at dinner she could again touch nothing. She hoped Edward would notice that she refused all food, and be properly alarmed and sorry. But he demolished enough for two, and never saw that his wife fasted.

At night Bertha went to bed and bolted herself in their room. Presently Edward came up and tried the door. Finding it locked, he knocked and cried to her to open it. She did not answer. He knocked again more loudly and shook the handle.

'I want to have my room to myself,' she cried out. 'I'm ill. Please don't try to come in.'

'What? Where am I to sleep?'

'Oh, you can sleep in one of the spare rooms.'

'Nonsense!' he said, and without further ado put his shoulder

155

to the door. He was a strong man; one heave and the old hinges cracked. He entered laughing.

'If you wanted to keep me out, you ought to have barricaded yourself up with the furniture.'

Bertha was disinclined to treat the matter lightly. 'I'm not going to sleep with you,' she said. 'If you come in here I shall go out.'

'Oh, no, you won't,' he said.

Bertha got up and put on a dressing-gown.

'I'll spend the night on the sofa then,' she said. 'I don't want to quarrel with you any more or to make a scene. I have written to Aunt Polly, and the day after tomorrow I shall go to London.'

'I was going to suggest that a change of air would do you good,' he replied. 'I think your nerves are a bit groggy.'

'It's very good of you to take an interest in my nerves,' she replied, with a scornful glance, settling herself on the sofa.

'Are you really going to sleep there?' he said, getting into bed.

'It looks like it.'

'You'll find it awfully cold.'

'I'd rather freeze than sleep with you.'

'You'll have the snuffles in the morning; but I daresay you'll think better of it in an hour. I'm going to turn the light out. Good night!'

Bertha did not answer, and in a few minutes she was angrily listening to his snores. Could he really be asleep? Did it mean nothing to him that she should refuse to share her bed, that she should arrange to go away? It was infamous that he slept so calmly.

'Edward,' she called.

There was no answer, but she could not bring herself to believe that he was sleeping. She could never even close her eyes. He must be pretending – to annoy her. She wanted to touch him, but feared that he would burst out laughing. She felt indeed horribly cold, and piled rugs and dresses over her. It required great fortitude not to sneak back to bed. She was extremely unhappy, and soon became very thirsty. Nothing is so horrid as the water in toilet-bottles, with the glass tasting of tooth-wash; she gulped some down, though it almost made her sick, and then walked about the room, turning over her manifold wrongs. Edward slept on insufferably. She made a noise to wake him, but he did not stir; she knocked down a table which made a clatter sufficient to disturb the dead, but her husband was insensible. Then she looked at the bed, wondering whether she dared lie down for an hour and trust to waking up before him. She was so cold that she determined to risk it, feeling certain that she would not sleep long; she walked to the bed.

'Coming to bed after all?' said Edward in a sleepy voice.

She stopped and her heart rose to her mouth.

'I was coming for my pillow,' she replied, indignantly, thanking her stars that he had not spoken a moment later.

She returned to the sofa, and eventually making herself very comfortable fell asleep. In this blissful condition she continued till the morning, and when she awoke Edward was drawing up the blinds.

'Slept well?' he asked.

'I haven't slept a wink.'

'Oh, what a crammer. I've been looking at you for the last hour.'

'I've had my eyes closed for about ten minutes, if that's what you mean.'

Bertha was quite justly annoyed that her husband should have caught her napping soundly; it robbed her proceeding of half its effect. Moreover, Edward was as fresh as a bird, while she felt old and haggard, and hardly dared look at herself in the glass.

In the middle of the morning came a telegram from Miss Ley, telling Bertha to come whenever she liked and hoping Edward would come too. Bertha left it in a conspicuous place, so that he could not fail to see it.

'So you're really going?' he said.

'I told you I was as able to keep my word as you.'

'Well, I think it'll do you no end of good. How long will you stay?'

'How do I know! Perhaps for ever.'

'That's a big word, though it has only two syllables.'

It cut Bertha to the heart that Edward should be so indifferent. He could not care for her at all. He seemed to think it natural that she should leave him. He pretended it was good for her health. Oh, what did she care about her health? As she made the needful preparations her courage failed her; she felt it impossible to leave him, and her tears came rapidly as she thought of the difference between their present state and the ardent love of a year ago. She would have welcomed the poorest excuse that forced her to stay and yet saved her self-respect. If Edward would only express grief at the parting it might not be too late. But her boxes were packed and her train was fixed; he told Miss Glover that his wife was going away for change of air, and regretted that his farm prevented him from accompanying her. The trap was brought to the door, and Edward jumped up, taking his seat. Now there was no hope, and go she must. She wished she had the courage to tell Edward that she could not leave him. She was afraid. They drove along in silence. Bertha waited for her husband to speak, herself daring to say nothing lest he should hear the tears in her voice. At last she made an effort.

'Are you sorry I'm going?'

'I think it's for your good, and I don't want to stand in the way of that.'

Bertha asked herself what love a man had for his wife who could bear her out of his sight, no matter what the necessity. She stifled a sigh.

They reached the station and he took her ticket. They waited in silence for the train, and Edward bought *Punch* and the *Sketch* from the newspaper boy. The horrible train steamed up, Edward helped her into a carriage, and the tears in her eyes now could not be concealed. She put out her lips.

'Perhaps for the last time,' she whispered.

22

72 Eliot Mansions,
Chelsea, S.W.

April 18

Dear Edward,

I think we were wise to part. We were too unsuited to one another, and our difficulties could only have increased. The knot of marriage between two persons of different temperament is so intricate that it can only be cut; you may try to unravel it, and think you are succeeding; but another turn shows you that the tangle is only worse than ever. Even time is powerless. Some things are impossible: you cannot heap water up like stones, you cannot measure one man by another man's rule. I am certain we were wise to separate. I see that if we had continued to live together our quarrels would have perpetually increased. It is horrible to look back upon those vulgar brawls. We wrangled like fish-wives. I cannot understand how my mouth could have uttered such things.

It is very bitter to look back and compare my anticipations with what has really happened. Did I expect too much from life? Ah, me, I only expected that my husband would love me. It is because I asked so little that I have received nothing; in this world you must ask much, you must spread your praises abroad, you must trample underfoot those that stand in your path, you must take up all the room you can, or you will be elbowed away. You must be irredeemably selfish, or you will be a thing of no account, a frippery that man plays with and flings aside.

Of course I expected the impossible. I was not satisfied with the conventional unity of marriage. I wanted to be really one with you. One-self is the whole world and all other people are merely strangers. At first in my vehement desire I used to despair because I knew you so little; I was heart-broken at the impossibility of really understanding you, of getting right down into your heart of hearts. Never, to the best of my knowledge, have I seen your veritable self; you are really as much a stranger to me as if I had known you but an hour. I bared my soul to you, concealing nothing – there is in you a man I do not know and have never seen. We are so absolutely different, I don't know a single thing that we have in common; often when we have been talking and fallen into silence, our thoughts, starting from the same standpoint, have travelled in different directions, and on speaking again we found how widely they had diverged. I hoped to know you to the bottom of your soul; oh, I hoped that we should be united so as to have but one soul between us; and yet on the most commonplace occasion I can never know your thoughts. Perhaps it might have been different if we had had children; they might have formed between us a truer link, and perhaps in the delight of them I should have forgotten my impracticable dreams. But fate was against us, I come from a rotten stock; it is written in the book that the Leys should depart from the sight of man, and return to their mother earth to be incorporated with her; and who knows in the future what may be our lot? I like to think that in the course of ages I may be the wheat on a fertile plain or the smoke from a fire of brambles on the common. I wish I could be buried in the open fields, rather than in the grim coldness of a churchyard, so that I might anticipate the change and return more quickly to the life of Nature.

Believe me, separation was the only possible outcome. I loved you too passionately to be content with the cold regard which you gave me. Oh, of course I was exacting and tyrannical and unkind; I can confess all my faults now; my only excuse is that I was very unhappy. For all the pain I have caused you I beg you to forgive me. We may as well part friends, and I freely forgive you for all you have made me suffer. Now I can afford also to tell you how near I was to not carrying out my intention. Yesterday and this morning I scarcely held back my tears, the parting seemed too hard, I felt I could not leave you. If you had asked me not to go, if you had even showed the smallest sign of regretting my departure, I think I should have broken down. Yes, I can tell you now that I would have given anything to stay. Alas! I am so weak. In the train I cried bitterly. It is the first time we have been apart since our marriage, the first time that we have slept under different roofs. But now the worst is over. I have taken the step and I shall adhere to what I have done. I am sure I have acted for the best. I see no harm in our writing to one another occasionally if it pleases you to receive letters from me. I think I had better not see you – at all events for some time. Perhaps when we are both a good deal older we may without danger see one another now and then; but not yet. I should be afraid to see your face.

Aunt Polly has no suspicion. I can assure you it has been an effort to laugh and talk during the evening, and I was glad to get to my room. Now it is past midnight, and I am still writing to you. I felt I ought to let you know my thoughts, and I can tell them more easily by letter than by word of mouth. Does it not show how separated in heart we have become that I shall hesitate to say to you what I think? And I had hoped to have my heart always open to you; I fancied that I need never conceal a thing, nor hesitate to show you every emotion and every thought. Good-bye.

Bertha.

72 Eliot Mansions,

April 23 Chelsea, S.W.

My poor Edward,

You say you hope I shall soon get better and come back to Court Leys. You misunderstood my meaning so completely that I almost laughed. It is true I was out of spirits and tired when I wrote, but that was not the reason of my letter. Cannot you conceive emotions not entirely due to one's physical condition? You cannot understand me, you never have; and yet I would not take up the vulgar and hackneyed position of a *femme incomprise*. There is nothing to understand about me. I am very simple and unmysterious; I only wanted love, and you could not give it me. No, our parting is final and irrevocable. What can you want me back for? You have Court Leys and your farms, everyone likes you in the neighbourhood, I was the only bar to your complete happiness. Court Leys I freely give you for my life; until you came it brought in nothing, and the income now arising from it is entirely due to your efforts; you earn it and I beg you to keep it. For me the small income I have from my mother is sufficient.

Aunt Polly still thinks I am on a visit, and constantly speaks of you; I throw dust in her eyes, but I cannot hope to keep her in ignorance for long. At present I am engaged in periodically seeing the doctor for an imaginary ill and getting one or two new things.

Shall we write to one another once a week? I know writing is a trouble to you; but I do not wish you to forget me altogether. If you like I will write to you every Sunday, and you may answer or not as you please.

Bertha.

P.S. Please do not think of any *rapprochement*. I am sure you will eventually see that we are both much happier apart.

72 Eliot Mansions,
Chelsea, S.W.

May 15

My dear Eddie,

I was pleased to get your letter. I am a little touched at your wanting to see me. You suggest coming to town; perhaps it is fortunate that I shall be no longer here. If you had expressed such a wish before much might have gone differently. Aunt Polly, having let her flat to friends goes to Paris for the rest of the season; she starts tonight, and to Paris I have offered to accompany her, I am sick of London. I do not know whether she suspects anything, but I notice that she never mentions your name now; she looked a little sceptical the other day when I explained that I had long wished to go to Paris and that you were having the inside of Court Leys painted. Fortunately, however, she makes it a practice not to inquire into other people's business, and I can rest assured that she will never ask me a single question.

Forgive the shortness of this letter, but I am very busy packing.

Your affectionate wife,
Bertha.

41 Rue des Ecoliers,
Paris.

May 16

My dearest Eddie,

I have been unkind to you. It is nice of you to want to see me, and my repugnance to it was, perhaps, unnatural. On consideration, I cannot think it will do any harm if we should see one another. Of course, I can never come back to Court Leys; there are some chains that, having broken, you can never weld together; and no fetters are so intolerable as those of love. But if you want to see me I will put no obstacle in your way, I will not deny that I also should like to see you. I am further away now, but if you care for me at all you will not hesitate to make the short journey.

We have here a very nice apartment, in the Latin Quarter, away from the rich people and the tourists. I do not know which is more vulgar, the average tripper or the part of Paris which he infests; I must say they become one another to a nicety. I loathe the shoddiness of the boulevards, with their gaudy cafés over-gilt and over-sumptuous, and their crowds of ill-dressed foreigners. But if you come I can show you a different Paris, a restful and old-fashioned Paris; theatres to which tourists do not go, gardens full of pretty children and nurse-maids with long ribbons to their caps. I can take you down innumerable grey streets with funny shops, in old churches where you see people praying; and it is all very quiet, calming to the nerves, and I can take you to the Louvre at hours when there are few visitors, and show you beautiful pictures and statues that have come from Italy and Greece, where the gods have their homes to this day. Come, Eddie.

Your ever loving wife,
Bertha.

41 Rue des Ecoliers,
Paris.

My dearest Eddie,

I am disappointed that you will not come. I should have thought, if you wanted to see me you could have found time to leave the farms for a few days. But perhaps it is really better that we should not meet. I cannot conceal from you that sometimes I long for you dreadfully. I forget all that has happened and desire with all my heart to be with you again. What a fool I am. I know that we can never meet again, and you are never absent from my thoughts. I look forward to your letters almost madly, and your handwriting makes my heart beat as if I were a school-girl. Oh, you don't know how your letters disappoint me, they are so cold, you never say what I want you to say. It would be madness if we came together. I can only preserve my love to you by not seeing you. Does that sound horrible? And yet I would give anything to see you once more. I cannot help asking you to come here. It is not so very often I have asked you anything. Do come. I will meet you at the station and you will have no trouble or bother. Everything is perfectly simple, and Cook's interpreters are everywhere. I'm sure you would enjoy yourself so much.

> If you love me, come.
> Bertha.

	Court Leys,
May 30	Blackstable, Kent.

My dearest Bertha,

Sorry I haven't answered yours of 25 inst before but I've been up to my eyes in work. You wouldn't think that there would be so much to do on a farm at this time of year unless you saw it with your own eyes. I can't possibly get away to Paris and besides I can't stomach the French. I don't want to see the capital and when I want a holiday London's good enough for me. You'd better come back here, people are asking after you and the place seems all topsy-turvy without you. Love to Aunt P.

> In haste
> Your affectionate husband
> E. Craddock.

	41 Rue des Ecoliers,
June 1	Paris.

My dearest, dearest Eddie,

You don't know how disappointed I was to get your letter, and how I longed for it. Whatever you do, don't keep me waiting so long for an answer. I imagined all sorts of things – that you were ill or dying. I was on the point of wiring. I want you to promise me that if you are ever ill you will let me know. If you want me urgently I shall be pleased to come. But do not think that I can ever come back to Court Leys for good. Sometimes I feel ill and weak and I long for you, but I know I must not give way. I'm sure, for your good as well as for mine, I must never risk the unhappiness of our old life again. It was too degrading. With firm mind and the utmost resolution I swear that I will never, never return to Court Leys.

> Your affectionate and loving wife,
> Bertha.

Telegram.

> Gare du Nord. 9.50 a.m. June 2.
> Craddock, Court Leys. Blackstable.
> Arriving 7.25 tonight. Bertha.

My dear young Friend,

I am perturbed. Bertha, as you know, has for the last six weeks lived with me, for reasons the naturalness of which aroused my strongest suspicions. No one, I thought, would need so many absolutely conclusive motives to do so very simple a thing. I resisted the temptation to write to Edward (her husband – a nice man, but stupid!) to ask for an explanation, fearing that the reasons given me were the right ones (although I could not believe it), in which case I should have made myself ridiculous. Bertha in London pretended to go to a physician, but never was seen to take medicine, and I am certain no well-established specialist would venture to take two guineas from a *malade imaginaire* and not administer copious drugs. She accompanied me to Paris, ostensibly to get dresses, but has behaved as if their fit were of no more consequence than a change of ministry. She has taken great pains to conceal her emotions, and thereby made them the more conspicuous. I cannot tell you how often she has gone through the various stages from an almost hysterical elation to an equal despondency; she has mused as profoundly as it was fashionable for the young ladies of fifty years ago, (we were all young ladies then – not girls,) she has played *Tristan and Isolde* to the distraction of myself, she has snubbed an amorous French artist to the distraction of his wife; finally she has wept, and after weeping overpowdered her nose and eyes, which in a pretty woman is an infallible sign of extreme mental prostration.

This morning when I got up, I found at my door the following message: '*Don't think me an utter fool, but I couldn't stand another day away from Edward. Leaving by the 10 o'clock train. B.*' Now at 10.30 she had an appointment at Paquin's to try on the most ravishing dinner dress you could imagine.

I will not insult you by drawing inferences from all these facts. I know you would much sooner draw them yourself, and I have a sufficiently good opinion of you to be certain that they will coincide with mine.

Yours very sincerely,
Mary Ley.

23

BERTHA'S relief was unmistakable when she landed on English soil; at last she was near Edward, and she had been extremely seasick. Though it was less than thirty miles from Dover to Blackstable, the communications were so bad that it was necessary to wait for hours at the port, or take the boat train to London and then come sixty miles down again. Bertha was exasperated at the delay, forgetting that she was now (thank Heaven!) in a free country, where the railways were not run for the convenience of the passengers, but the passengers necessary evils to earn dividends for an ill-managed company. Bertha's impatience was so great that she felt it impossible to wait at Dover, and made up her mind to go up to London and down again, thus saving herself ten minutes, rather than spend the afternoon in the dreary waiting-room or wandering about the town. The train seemed to crawl, and her restlessness became quite painful as she recognized the Kentish country, the fat meadows with trim hedges, the portly trees and the general air of prosperity.

Bertha had hoped, against her knowledge of him, that Edward would meet her at Dover, and it had been a disappointment not to see him; then she thought he might come up to London, though not explaining to herself how he could possibly have divined that she would be there; and her heart beat absurdly when she saw a back that might have been his. Still later, she comforted herself with the notion that he would certainly be at Faversley, which was the next station to Blackstable, and when they reached that place she put her head out of the window, looking along the platform – but he was not there.

'He might have come as far as this,' she thought.

Now, the train steaming on, she recognized the country more precisely, the desolate marsh and the sea. The line ran almost at the water's edge. The tide was out, leaving a broad expanse of shining mud, over which the sea-gulls flew, screeching. Then the houses were familiar, cottages beaten by wind and weather, 'The Jolly Sailor,' where in the old days many a smuggled keg of brandy had been hidden on its way to the cathedral city of Tercanbury. The coast-guard station was passed, low buildings painted pink; and finally they rattled across the bridge over the High Street, and the porters, with their Kentish drawl, called out, 'Blackstable, Blackstable.'

Bertha's emotions were always uncontrolled and so powerful as sometimes to unfit her for action. Now she had hardly strength to open the carriage door.

'At last!' she cried, with a gasp of relief.

She had never loved her husband so passionately as then; her love was a physical sensation that almost turned her faint. The arrival of the moment so anxiously awaited left her half afraid; she was of those who eagerly look for an opportunity and then can scarcely seize it. Bertha's heart was so full that she was afraid of bursting into tears when at last she should see Edward walking towards her; she had pictured the meeting so often, her husband advancing with his swinging stride, waving his stick, the dogs in front, rushing towards her, and barking furiously. The two porters waddled, with their seaman's walk, to the van to get out the luggage; people were stepping from the carriages. Next to her a pasty-faced clerk descended, in dingy black, with a baby in his arms; his pale-faced wife followed with another baby and innumerable parcels, then two or three children. A labourer sauntered down the platform, three or four sailors, and a couple of trim infantrymen. They all surged for the wicket at which stood the ticket collector. The porters got out the boxes and the train steamed off; an irascible city man was swearing volubly because his luggage had gone on to Margate. The station-master, in a decorated hat and a self-satisfied air, strolled up to see what was the matter. Bertha looked along the platform wildly. Edward was not there.

The station-master passed her and nodded patronisingly.

'Have you seen Mr Craddock?' she asked.

'No, I can't say I have. But I think there's a carriage below for you.'

Bertha began to tremble. A porter asked whether he should take her boxes; she nodded, unable to speak. She went down and found the brougham at the station door; the coachman touched his hat and gave her a note.

Dear Bertha,

Awfully sorry I can't come to meet you. I never expected you, so accepted an invitation of Lord Philip Dirk to a tennis tournament and a ball afterwards. He's going to sleep me, so I shan't be back till to-morrow. Don't get in a wax. See you in the morning.

E. C.

Bertha got into the carriage and huddled herself into one corner so that no one should see her. At first she hardly understood, she had spent the last hours on such a height of excitement that the disappointment deprived her of the power of thinking. She never took things reasonably and was now stunned. It was impossible. It seemed to be so callous that Edward should go playing tennis when she, looking forward so eagerly to seeing him, was coming home. And it was no ordinary homecoming, it was the first time she had ever left him, and then she had gone, hating him, as she thought for good. But her absence having revived her love, she had returned, yearning for reconciliation. And he was not there, he acted as though she had been to town for a day's shopping.

'Oh, God, what a fool I was to come!'

Suddenly she thought of going away, there and then. Would it not be easier? She felt she could not see him. But there were no trains. The London, Chatham and Dover Railway has perhaps saved many an elopement. But he must have known how bitterly disappointed she would be, and the notion flashed through her that he would leave the tournament and come home. Perhaps he was already at Court Leys, waiting; she took fresh courage and looked at the well-remembered scene. He might be at the gate. Oh, what joy it would be, what a relief! But they came to the gate and he was not there; they drove to the portico and he was not there. Bertha went into the house expecting to find him in the hall or in the drawing-room, not having heard the carriage; but he was nowhere to be found, and the servants corroborated his letter.

The house was empty, dull and inhospitable; the rooms had an uninhabited air, the furniture was primly rearranged, and Edward had caused antimacassars to be placed on the chairs; these Bertha, to the housemaid's surprise, took off one by one, and without a word threw into the empty fireplace. And still she thought it incredible that Edward should stay away. She sat down to dinner, expecting him every moment; she sat up very late, feeling sure that eventually he would come. But he did not.

'I wish to God I'd stayed away.'

Her thoughts went back to the struggle of the last few weeks. Pride, anger, reason, everything had been on one side and only love on the other; and love had conquered. The recollection of Edward had been seldom absent from her, and her dreams had been filled with his image. His letters had caused her an indescribable thrill, the sight of his handwriting had made her tremble; and she wanted to see him; she woke at night with his kisses on her lips.

167

She begged him to come, and he would not, or could not. At last the yearning grew beyond control; and that very morning, not having received the letter she awaited, she had resolved to throw off all pretence of resentment and come. What did she care if Miss Ley laughed at her, or if Edward scored the victory in the struggle? She could not live without him. He still was her life and her love.

'Oh, God, I wish I hadn't come.'

She remembered how she had prayed that Edward might love her as she wished to be loved. The passionate rebellion after her child's death had ceased insensibly, and in her misery, in her loneliness, she had found a new faith. Belief with some comes and goes without reason; with them it is not a matter of conviction, but rather of sensibility; and Bertha found prayer easier in Catholic churches than in the cheerless meeting-houses she had been used to. She could not gabble prayers at stated hours with three hundred other people; the crowd caused her to shut away her emotions, and her heart could expand only in solitude. In Paris she had found quiet chapels, open at all hours, to which she could go for rest when the light without was over-dazzling; and in the evening, when the dimness, the fragrance of old incense and the silence were very restful. Then the only light came from the tapers, burning in gratitude or in hope, throwing a fitful, mysterious glimmer; and Bertha prayed earnestly for Edward and for herself.

But Edward would not let himself be loved. Her efforts all were useless. Her love was a jewel that he valued not at all, that he flung aside and cared not if he lost. But she was too unhappy, too broken in spirit to be angry. What was the use of anger? She knew that Edward would see nothing extraordinary in what he had done; he would return, confident, well-pleased with himself, having slept well, and entirely unaware that she had been grievously disappointed.

'I suppose the injustice is on my side. I am too exacting. I can't help it.' She only knew one way to love, and that, it appeared, was a foolish way. 'Oh, I wish,' she cried, 'I wish I could go away again now – for ever.'

She got up and ate a solitary breakfast, busying herself afterwards in the house. Edward had left word that he would be in to luncheon, and was it not his pride to keep his word? But all her impatience had gone, Bertha felt no particular anxiety now to see him. She was on the point of going out, the air was warm and balmy; but did not, in case Edward should return and be disappointed at her absence.

'What a fool I am to think of his feelings! If I'm not in he'll just go about his work and think nothing more about me till I appear.'

But, notwithstanding, she stayed in. He arrived at last, and she did not hurry to meet him; she was putting things away in her bedroom, and continued, though she heard his voice below. The difference was curious between her intense and almost painful expectation of the previous day and her present indifference. She turned as he came in the room, but did not move towards him.

'So you've come back? Did you enjoy yourself?'

'Yes, rather.'

'But I say, it's ripping to have you home. You weren't in a wax at my not being here?'

'Oh, no,' she said, smiling. 'I didn't mind at all.'

'That's all right. Of course I'd never been to Lord Philip's before, and I couldn't wire the last minute to say that my wife was coming home and I had to meet her.'

'Of course not, it would have made you appear too absurd.'

'But I was jolly sick, I can tell you. If you'd only let me know a week ago that you were coming, I should have refused the invitation.'

'My dear Edward, I'm so unpractical, I never know my own mind. I'm always doing things on the spur of the moment – to my own inconvenience and other people's. And I should never have expected you to deny yourself anything for my sake.'

Bertha had been looking at her husband since he came into the room, unable in astonishment to avert her eyes; she was perplexed, almost dismayed; she scarcely recognized him. In the three years of their common life Bertha had never noticed a change in him, and with her great faculty for idealization had carried in her mind always his image as he appeared when first she saw him, the slender, manly youth of eight-and-twenty. Miss Ley had discovered alterations, and spiteful feminine tongues had said that he was going off dreadfully; but his wife had seen nothing; and the separation had given further opportunity to her fantasy. In absence she had thought of him as the handsomest of men, delighting over his clear features, his fair hair, his inexhaustible youth and strength. The plain facts would have disappointed her even if Edward had retained the looks of his youth, but seeing now as well the other changes the shock was extreme. It was a different man she saw, almost a stranger. He did not wear well; though not thirty-one, he looked older. He had broadened and put on flesh; his features had lost their delicacy and the red of his cheeks was growing blotchy. He wore his clothes in a slovenly way and had fallen into a lumbering walk as if his boots were always heavy with clay; and there was in him besides the heartiness and intolerant joviality of the prosperous farmer. Edward's good looks had given her the keenest pleasure, and now, rushing, as was her habit, to the other extreme, she found him almost ugly. This was an exaggeration, for though he was no longer the slim youth of her first acquaintance, he was still in a heavy, massive way better looking than the majority of men.

Edward kissed her with marital calm, and the propinquity wafted to Bertha's nostrils the strong scents of the farmyard, which, no matter what his clothes, hung perpetually about him. She turned away, hardly concealing a little shiver of disgust; yet they were the same masculine odours as once had made her nearly faint with desire.

24

BERTHA'S imagination seldom permitted her to see things in any but a false light; sometimes they were pranked out in the glamour of the ideal, and at others the process was reversed. It was astonishing that so short a break should have destroyed the habit of years; but the fact was plain that Edward had become a stranger, so that she felt it irksome to share the same room with him. She saw him now with jaundiced eyes, and told herself that at last she had discovered his true colours. Poor Edward was paying heavily because the furtive years had robbed him of his looks and given him in exchange a superabundance of fat, because responsibility, the east wind and good living had taken the edge off his features and turned his cheeks plethoric.

Bertha's love, indeed, had finally disappeared as suddenly as it had arisen, and she began to detest her husband. She had acquired a certain part of Miss Ley's analytic faculty, which now she employed upon Edward's character with destructive effect. Her absence had increased the danger to Edward's connubial happiness in another way, for the air of Paris had exhilarated her and sharpened her wits, she had bought many books, had been to the theatres, had read the French papers, whose sparkle offers at first a pleasing contrast to the sobriety of their British contemporaries; with the general result that her alertness to find fault was doubled and her impatience with the dull and the stupid, extreme.

And Bertha soon found that her husband's mind was not only commonplace, but common. His ignorance no longer seemed touching, but merely shameful; his prejudices no longer amusing, but contemptible. She was indignant at having humbled herself so abjectly before a man of such narrowness of mind and insignificance of character. She could not conceive how she had ever passionately loved him. He was bound by the stupidest routine; it irritated her beyond measure to see the regularity with which he went through the unvarying process of his toilet; nothing interfered with the order in which he washed his teeth and brushed his hair. She was indignant with his presumption and self-satisfaction and conscious rectitude. Edward's taste was contemptible in books, in pictures and in music; and his pretensions to judge upon such matters filled her with scorn. At first his deficiencies had not affected her, and later she had consoled herself with the obvious truism that a man may be ignorant of the arts and yet have every virtue under the sun. But now she was less charitable. Bertha wondered that because her husband could read and write as well as most board-scholars he should feel himself competent to judge books – even without reading them. Of course it was unreasonable to blame the poor man for a foible common to the vast majority of mankind. Everyone who can hold a pen is confident of his ability to criticize, and to criticize superciliously. It never occurs to the average citizen that, to speak modestly, almost as much art is needed to write a book as to adulterate a pound of tea; nor that the author has busied himself with style and contrast, characterization, light and shade, and many other things to which the practice of haberdashery, greengrocery, company promotion or pork-butchery is no sure key.

One day, Edward, coming in, caught sight of the yellow cover of a French book that Bertha was reading.

'What, reading again?' said he. 'You read too much, it's not good for people to be always reading.'

'Is that your opinion?'

'My idea is that a woman oughtn't to stuff her head with books. You'd be much better out in the open air or doing something useful.'

'Is that your opinion?'

'Well, I should like to know why you're always reading.'

'Sometimes to instruct myself; always to amuse myself.'

'Much instruction you'll get out of an indecent French novel.'

Bertha without answering handed him the book and showed the title; they were the letters of Madame de Sevigné.

'Well?' he said.

'You're no wiser, dear Edward?' she asked, with a smile; such a question in such a tone revenged her for much. 'I'm afraid you're very ignorant. You see I'm not reading a novel and it is not indecent. They are the letters of a mother to her daughter, models of epistolary style and feminine wisdom.'

Bertha purposely spoke in a somewhat formal and elaborate manner.

'Oh,' said Edward, looking mystified, feeling that he had been confounded but certain, none the less, that he was in the right. Bertha smiled provokingly. 'Of course, I've no objection to your reading if it amuses you.'

'It's very good of you to say so.'

'I don't pretend to have any book-learning. I'm a practical man and it's not required. In my business you find that the man who reads books comes a mucker.'

'You seem to think that ignorance is creditable.'

'It's better to have a good and pure heart, Bertha, and a clean mind than any amount of learning.'

'It's better to have a grain of wit than a collection of moral saws.'

'I don't know what you mean by that, but I'm quite content to be as I am, and I don't want to know a single foreign language. English is quite good enough for me.'

'So long as you're a good sportsman and wash yourself regularly you think you've performed the whole duty of man.'

'You can say what you like, but if there's one man I can't stick it's a measly book-worm.'

'I prefer him to the hybrid of a professional cricketer and a Turkish-bath man.'

'Does that mean me?'

172

'You can take it to yourself if you like,' said Bertha, smiling, 'or apply it to a whole class. Do you mind if I go on reading?'

Bertha took up her book; but Edward was the more argumentatively inclined since he saw he had not so far got the better of the contest.

'Well, what I must say is,' he rejoined, 'if you want to read, why can't you read English books? Surely there are enough. I think English people ought to stick to their own country. I don't pretend to have read any French books, but I've never heard anybody deny that at all events the great majority of them are indecent, and not the sort of thing a woman should read.'

'It's always incautious to judge from common report.' answered Bertha, without looking up.

'And now that the French are always behaving so badly to us, I should like to see every French book in the kingdom put into a huge bonfire. I'm sure it would be all the better for we English people. What we want now is purity and reconstitution of the national life. I'm in favour of English morals, English homes, English mothers and English habits.'

'What always astounds me, dear, is that though you invariably read the *Standard* you always talk like the *Daily Telegraph*.'

Bertha went on with her book and paid no further attention to Edward, who thereupon began to talk with his dogs. Like most frivolous persons, he found silence very onerous. Bertha thought it disconcerted him by rendering evident even to himself the vacuity of his mind. He talked with every animate thing, with the servants, with his pets, with the cat and the birds; he could not read even a newspaper without making a running commentary upon it. It was only a substantial meal that could induce in him even a passing taciturnity. Sometimes his unceasing chatter irritated Bertha so intensely that she was obliged to beg him, for Heaven's sake, to hold his tongue. Then he would look up with a good-natured laugh.

'Was I making a row? Sorry, I didn't know it.'

He remained quiet for ten minutes, and then began to hum a hackneyed melody, than which there is no more detestable habit.

Indeed the points of divergence between the couple were innumerable. Edward was a man who had the courage of his opinions; he disliked also whatever was not clear to his somewhat

173

narrow intelligence, and was inclined to think it immoral. Bertha played the piano well and sang with a cultivated voice, but her performances were objectionable to her husband because whether she sang or whether she played there was never a rollicking tune that a fellow could get his teeth into. He had upbraided her for this singular taste, and could not help thinking that there was something wrong with a woman who shrugged her shoulders disdainfully at the music-hall ditties that everyone was singing. It must be confessed that Bertha exaggerated, for when a dull musical afternoon was given in the neighbourhood she took a malicious pleasure in playing a long recitative from a Wagner opera that no one could make head or tail of.

On such an occasion at the Glovers', the elder Miss Hancock turned to Edward and remarked upon his wife's admirable playing. Edward was a little annoyed, because everyone had vigorously applauded and to him the sounds had been meaningless.

'Well, I'm a plain man,' he said, 'and I don't mind confessing that I never can understand the stuff Bertha plays.'

'Oh, Mr Craddock, not even Wagner?' said Miss Hancock, who had been as bored as Edward, but, holding the contrary modest opinion that the only really admirable things are those you can't understand, would not for worlds have confessed it.

Bertha looked at him, remembering her dream that they should sit at the piano together in the evening and play for hour after hour; as a matter of fact he had always refused to budge from his chair, and gone to sleep regularly.

'My idea of music is like Dr Johnson's,' said Edward, looking round for approval.

'Is Saul also among the prophets?' murmured Bertha.

'When I hear a difficult piece I wish it was impossible.'

'You forget, dear,' said Bertha, 'that Dr Johnson was a very ill-mannered old man whom dear Fanny would not have allowed in her drawing-room for one minute.'

'You sing now, Edward,' said Miss Glover. 'We've not heard you for ever so long.'

'Oh, bless you,' he retorted, 'my singing's too old-fashioned. My songs have all got a tune in them and some feeling. They're only fit for the kitchen.'

'Oh, please give us "Ben Bolt,"' said Miss Hancock. 'We're all so fond of it.'

174

Edward's repertory was limited, and everyone knew his songs by heart.

'Anything to oblige,' he said; he was, as a matter of fact, very fond of singing, and applause was always grateful to his ears.

'Shall I accompany you, dear?' said Bertha.

> 'Oh! don't you remember sweet Alice, Ben Bolt,
> Sweet Alice with hai-air so brow-own?
> She wept with delight when you gave her a smile,
> And trembled with feaar at your frown.'

Once upon a time Bertha had found a subtle charm in these pleasing sentiments and in the honest melody that adorned them; but it was not strange that constant repetition had left her a little callous. Edward sang the ditty with a simple, homely style – which is the same as saying with no style at all – and he made use of much pathos. But Bertha's spirit was not forgiving; she owed him some return for the gratuitous attack on her playing; and the notion came to her to improve upon the accompaniment with little trills and flourishes that amused her immensely, but quite disconcerted her husband. Finally, just when his voice was growing flat with emotion over the grey-haired schoolmaster who had died, she wove in the strains of 'The Blue Bells of Scotland' and 'God Save the Queen,' so that Edward broke down. For once his even temper was disturbed.

'I say, I can't sing if you go playing the fool.'

'I'm very sorry,' smiled Bertha, 'I forgot what I was doing. Let's begin all over again.'

'No, I'm not going to sing any more. You spoil the whole thing.'

'Mrs Craddock has no heart,' said Miss Hancock.

'I don't think it's fair to laugh at an old song like this,' said Edward. 'After all, anyone can sneer. My idea of music is something that stirs one's heart. I'm not a sentimental chap, but "Ben Bolt" almost brings the tears to my eyes every time I sing it.'

Bertha difficultly abstained from retorting that sometimes she felt inclined to burst into tears over it herself – especially when he sang out of tune. Everyone looked at her as if she had behaved very badly; she smiled at Edward calmly, but she was not amused. On the way home she asked him if he knew why she had spoilt his song.

'I'm sure I don't know, unless you were in one of your beastly tempers. I suppose you're sorry now.'

'Not at all,' she answered. 'I thought you were rude to me just before, and I wanted to punish you a little. Sometimes you're really too supercilious. And besides that, I object to being rowed in public. You will have the goodness in future to keep your strictures till we are alone.'

'I should have thought you could stand a bit of good-natured chaff by now,' he replied.

'Oh, I can, dear Edward. Only, perhaps you may have noticed that I am fairly quick at defending myself.'

'What d'you mean by that?'

'Merely that I can be horrid when I like, and you will be wise not to expose yourself to a public snub.'

Edward had never heard from his wife a threat so calmly administered, and it somewhat impressed him.

But as a general rule Bertha checked the sarcasms that constantly rose to her tongue. She treasured in her heart the wrath and hatred that her husband excited in her, feeling that it was a satisfaction at last to be free from love of him. Looking back, the fetters that had bound her were intolerably heavy. And it was a sweet revenge, although he knew nothing of it, to strip the idol of his ermine cloak and his crown and the gewgaws of his sovereignty. In his nakedness he was a pitiable figure. Edward was totally unconscious of all this. He was like a lunatic reigning in a madhouse over an imaginary kingdom. He did not see the curl of Bertha's lips upon some foolish remark of his, or the contempt with which she treated him. And since she was a great deal less exacting, he found himself far happier than before. The ironic philosopher might find some cause for moralizing in the fact that it was not till Bertha began to dislike Edward that he found marriage quite satisfactory. He told himself that his wife's stay abroad had done her no end of good and made her far more amenable to reason. Mr Craddock's principles, of course, were quite right; he had given her plenty of run and ignored her cackle, and now she had come home to roost. There is nothing like a knowledge of farming and an acquaintance with the habits of domestic animals to teach a man how to manage his wife.

25

I F the gods, who scatter wit in sundry unexpected places, so that it is sometimes found beneath the bishop's mitre, and once in a thousand years beneath a king's crown, had given Edward two-pennyworth of that commodity he would undoubtedly have been a great as well as a good man. Fortune smiled upon him uninter-ruptedly; he enjoyed the envy of his neighbours, he farmed with profit, and having tamed the rebellious spirit of his wife he rejoiced in domestic happiness. And it must be noticed that he was rewarded only according to his deserts. He walked with upright spirit and contented mind along the path that it had pleased a merciful providence to set before him. He was lighted on the way by a strong sense of duty, by the principles that he had acquired at his mother's knee, and by a conviction of his own merit. Finally a deputation waited on him to propose that he should stand for the County Council election that was shortly to be held. He had been unoffi-cially informed of the project, and received Mr Atthill Bacot with seven committee men in his frock-coat and a manner full of responsibility. He told them he could do nothing rashly, must consider the matter and would inform them of his decision. Edward had already made up his mind to accept, and having showed the deputation to the door went to Bertha.

'Things are looking up,' he said, having given her the details. The Blackstable district, for which Edward was invited to stand, being composed chiefly of fishermen, was intensely Radical. 'Old Bacot said I was the only moderate candidate who'd have a chance.'

Bertha was too much astonished to reply. She had so low an opinion of her husband that she could not understand why on earth they should make him such an offer. She turned over in her mind possible reasons.

'It's a ripping thing for me, isn't it?'

'But you're not thinking of accepting?'

'Not? Of course I am. What d'you think!'

This was not an inquiry, but an exclamation.

'You've never gone in for politics, you've never made a speech in your life.' She thought he would make an abject fool of himself, and for her sake, as well as his, decided to prevent him from standing. 'He's too stupid,' she thought.

'What! I've made speeches at cricket dinners; you set me on my legs and I'll say something.'

'But this is different; you know nothing about the County Council.'

'All you have to do is to look after steam-rollers and get glandered horses killed. I know all about it.'

There is nothing so difficult as to persuade men that they are ignorant. Bertha, exaggerating the seriousness of the affair, thought it charlatanry to undertake a post without knowledge and without capacity. Fortunately that is not the opinion of the majority, or the government of this enlightened country could not proceed.

'I should have thought you'd be glad to see me get a lift in the world,' said Edward.

'I don't want you to make a fool of yourself, Edward. You've told me often that you don't go in for book-learning; and it can't hurt your feelings when I say that you're not very well informed. I don't think it's honest to take a position you're not competent to fill.'

'Me – not competent?' cried Edward with surprise. 'That's a good one. Upon my word, I'm not given to boasting, but I must say I think myself competent to do most things. You just ask old Bacot what he thinks of me, and that'll open your eyes. The fact is, everyone appreciates me but you; but they say a man's never a hero to his valet.'

'Your proverb is most apt, dear Edward. But I have no intention of thwarting you in any of your plans. I only thought you didn't know what you were going in for and that I might save you some humiliation.'

'Humiliation, where? Oh, you think I shan't get elected. Well, look here, I bet you any money you like that I shall come out top of the poll.'

Next day Edward wrote to Mr Bacot expressing pleasure that he was able to fall in with the views of the Conservative Association; and Bertha, who knew that no argument could turn him from his purpose, determined to coach him, so that he should not make too arrant a fool of himself. Her fears were proportionate to her estimate of Edward's ability. She sent to London for pamphlets and blue-books on the rights and duties of the County Council, and begged Edward to read them. But in his self-confident manner he pooh-poohed her, and laughed when she read them herself in order to be able to teach him.

'I don't want to know all that rot,' he cried. 'All a man wants is gumption. Why, d'you suppose a man who goes in for Parliament knows anything about politics? Of course he doesn't.'

Bertha was indignant that her husband should be so satisfied in his own ignorance that he stoutly refused to learn. Happily men don't realize how stupid they are, or half the world would commit suicide. Knowledge is a will-of-the-wisp, fluttering ever out of the traveller's reach; and a weary journey must be endured before it is even seen. It is only when a man knows a good deal that he discovers how unfathomable is his ignorance. The man who knows nothing is satisfied that there is nothing to know, consequently that he knows everything; and you may more easily persuade him that the moon is made of green cheese than that he is not omniscient. The County Council elections in London were being held just then, and Bertha, hoping to give Edward useful hints, diligently read the oratory that they occasioned. But he refused to listen to her.

'I don't want to crib other men's stuff. I'm going to talk on my own.'

'Why don't you write out a speech and get it by heart?'

Bertha fancied that so she might influence him a little and spare herself and him the humiliation of utter ridicule.

'Old Bacot says when he makes a speech he always trusts to the spur of the moment. He says that Fox made his best speeches when he was blind drunk.'

'D'you know who Fox was?' asked Bertha.

'Some old buffer or other who made speeches.'

The day arrived when Edward was to make his first address in the Blackstable town hall; and for days placards had been pasted on every wall and displayed in every shop announcing the glad news. Mr Bacot came to Court Leys, rubbing his hands.

'We shall have a full house. It'll be a big success. The hall will hold four hundred people, and I think there won't be standing room. I daresay you'll have to address an overflow meeting at the Forester's Hall afterwards.'

179

'I'll address any number of meetings you like,' replied Edward.

Bertha grew more and more nervous. She anticipated a horrible collapse; they did not know – as she did – how limited was Edward's intelligence. She wanted to stay at home in order to avoid the ordeal, but Mr Bacot had reserved for her a prominent seat on the platform.

'Are you nervous, Eddie?' she said, feeling more kindly disposed to him from his approaching trial.

'Me – nervous? What have I got to be nervous about?'

The hall was indeed crammed with the most eager, smelly, enthusiastic crowd Bertha had ever seen. The gas-jets flared noisily, throwing ugly lights on the people, sailors, shopkeepers and farm hands. On the platform in a semi-circle like the immortal gods sat the notabilities of the neighbourhood; they were Conservative to the backbone. Bertha looked round with apprehension, but tried to calm herself with the thought that they were stupid people and she had no cause to tremble before them.

Presently the vicar took the chair, and in a few well-chosen words introduced Mr Craddock.

'Mr Craddock, like good wine, needs no bush. You all know him, and an introduction is superfluous. Still it is customary on such an occasion to say a few words on behalf of the candidate, and I have great pleasure, etc., etc. . . .'

Now Edward rose to his feet, and Bertha's blood ran cold. She dared not look at the audience. He advanced with his hands in his pockets; he had insisted on dressing himself up in a frock-coat and the most dismal pepper-and-salt trousers.

'Mr Chairman, Ladies and Gentlemen, unaccustomed to public speaking as I am. . . .'

Bertha looked up with a start. Could a man at the end of the nineteenth century seriously begin an oration with those words? But he was not joking; he went on gravely, and looking round, Bertha caught not the shadow of a smile. Edward was not in the least nervous; he quickly got into the swing of his speech: it was awful! He introduced every hackneyed phrase he knew, he mingled slang incongruously with pompous language, and his silly jokes, chestnuts of great antiquity, made Bertha sweat coldly. She wondered that he could go on with such self-possession; did he not see that he was making himself perfectly absurd? She dared not look up for fear of catching the sniggers of Mrs Branderton and the

Hancocks: 'One sees what he was before he married Miss Ley. Of course, he's a quite uneducated man. I wonder his wife didn't prevent him from making such an exhibition of himself. The grammar of it, my dear; and the jokes and the stories!' Bertha clenched her hands, furious because the flush of shame would not leave her cheeks. The speech was even worse than she had expected. He used the longest words and, getting entangled in his own verbosity, was obliged to leave his sentence unfinished. He began a period with an elaborate flourish and waddled in confusion to the tamest commonplace; he was like a man who set out to explore the Andes and then, changing his mind, took a stroll in the Burlington Arcade. How long would it be, asked Bertha, before the audience broke into jeers and hisses? She blessed them for their patience. And what would happen afterwards? Would Mr Bacot ask Edward to withdraw his candidature? And supposing Edward refused, would it be necessary to tell him that he was really too great a fool? Bertha heard already the covert sneers of her neighbours.

'Oh, I wish he'd finish!' she muttered between her teeth. The agony, the humiliation of it, were unendurable.

But Edward was still talking and gave no sign of an approaching termination. Bertha thought miserably that he had always been long-winded; if he would only sit down quickly the failure might not be irreparable. He made a vile pun, and everyone cried, 'Oh! Oh!' Bertha shivered and set her teeth, she must bear it to the end now. Why wouldn't he sit down? Then Edward told an agricultural story, and the audience shouted with laughter. A ray of hope came to Bertha; perhaps his vulgarity might save him with the vulgar people who formed the great body of the audience. But what must the Brandertons and the Molsons and the Hancocks and all the rest of them be saying? They must utterly despise him.

But worse was to follow. Edward came to his peroration, and a few remarks on current politics (of which he knew nothing) brought him to his country, England, Home and Beauty. He turned the tap of patriotism full on; it gurgled out in a stream. He blew the penny trumpets of English purity, and the tin whistles of the British Empire, and he beat the big drum of the great Anglo-Saxon race. He thanked God he was an Englishman, and not as others are. Tommy Atkins and Jack Tar and Mr Rudyard Kipling

181

danced a jig to the strains of the 'British Grenadiers' and Mr Joseph Chamberlain executed a *pas seul* to the tune of 'Yankee Doodle'. Metaphorically he waved the Union Jack.

The sentimentality and the bad taste and the vulgarity of what he said revolted Bertha; it was horrible to think how absolutely common must be the mind of a man who could foul his mouth with the expression of such sentiments.

He sat down. For one moment the audience were silent and then with one throat broke into thunderous applause. It was no perfunctory clapping of hands; they rose as one man and shouted and yelled with enthusiasm.

'Good old Teddy,' cried a voice. And then the air was filled with 'For he's a jolly good fellow.' Mrs Branderton stood on a chair and waved her handkerchief, Miss Glover clapped her hands as if she were no longer an automaton.

'Wasn't it perfectly splendid?' she whispered to Bertha.

Everyone on the platform was in a frenzy of delight. Mr Bacot warmly shook Edward's hand. Mrs Mayston Ryle fanned herself desperately. The scene might well have been described, in the language of journalists, as one of unparalleled enthusiasm. Bertha was dumbfounded.

Mr Bacot jumped to his feet.

'I must congratulate Mr Craddock on his excellent speech. I am sure it comes as a surprise to all of us that he should prove such a fluent speaker, with such a fund of humour and common-sense. And what is more valuable than these, his last words have proved to us that his heart – his heart, gentlemen – is in the right place, and that is saying a great deal. In fact I know nothing better to be said of a man than that his heart is in the right place. You know me, ladies and gentlemen, I have made many speeches to you since I had the honour of standing for the constituency in '85, but I must confess I couldn't make a better speech myself than the one you have just heard.'

'You could – you could!' cried Edward, modestly.

'No, Mr Craddock. No, I assert deliberately and I mean it, that I could not do better myself. From my shoulders I let fall the mantle, and give it –'

Here Mr Bacot was interrupted by the stentorian voice of the landlord of 'The Pig and Whistle' (a rabid conservative).

'Three cheers for good old Teddy!'

'That's right, my boys,' cried Mr Bacot, for once taking an interruption in good part, 'three cheers for good old Teddy!'

The audience opened its mighty mouth and roared, and then burst again into 'For he's a jolly good fellow.' Arthur Branderton, when the tumult was subsiding, rose from his chair and called for more cheers. The object of all this enthusiasm sat calmly, with a well-satisfied look on his face, taking it all with his usual modest complacency. At last the meeting broke up, with cheers and 'God Save the Queen', and 'He's a jolly good fellow.' The committee and the personal friends of the Craddocks retired to the side room for light refreshment.

The ladies clustered round Edward, congratulating him. Arthur Branderton came to Bertha.

'Ripping speech, wasn't it?' he said. 'I had no idea he could jaw like that. By Jove, it simply stirred me right through.'

Before Bertha could answer, Mrs Mayston Ryle sailed in.

'Where's the man?' she cried in her loud voice. 'Where is he? Show him to me. My dear Mr Craddock, your speech was perfect. I say it.'

'And in such good taste,' said Miss Hancock, her eyes glowing. 'How proud you must be of your husband, Mrs Craddock!'

'There's no chance for the Radicals now,' said the vicar, rubbing his hands.

'Oh, Mr Craddock, let me come near you,' cried Mrs Branderton. 'I've been trying to get at you for twenty minutes. You've simply extinguished the horrid Radicals. I couldn't help crying, you were so pathetic.'

'One may say what one likes,' whispered Miss Glover to her brother, 'but there's nothing in the world so beautiful as sentiment. I felt my heart simply bursting.'

'Mr Craddock,' added Mrs Mayston Ryle, 'you've pleased me! Where's your wife, that I may tell her so?'

'It's the best speech we've ever had down here,' cried Mrs Branderton.

'That's the only true thing I've heard you say for twenty years, Mrs Branderton,' replied Mrs Mayston Ryle, looking very hard at Mr Atthill Bacot.

26

WHEN Lord Rosebery makes a speech, even the journals of his own party report him in the first person and at full length; and this is said to be the politician's supreme ambition: when he has reached such distinction there is nothing left him but an honourable death and a public funeral in Westminster Abbey. Now, the *Blackstable Times* accorded this honour to Edward's first speech, it was printed with numberless I's peppered boldly over it, the grammar was corrected, and the stops inserted just as for the most important orators. Edward bought a dozen copies and read the speech right through in each, to see that his sentiments were correctly expressed and that there were no misprints. He gave it to Bertha and stood over her while she read it.

'Looks well, don't it?' he said.

'Splendid!'

'By the way, is Aunt Polly's address 72 Eliot Mansions?'

'Yes. Why?'

Her jaw fell as she saw him roll up half a dozen copies of the *Blackstable Times* and address the wrapper.

'I'm sure she'd like to read my speech. And it might hurt her feelings if she heard about it and I'd not sent her the report.'

'Oh, I'm sure she'd like to see it very much. But if you send six copies you'll have none left – for other people.'

'Oh, I can easily get some more. The Editor chap told me I could have a thousand if I liked. I'm sending her six because I daresay she'd like to forward some to her friends.'

Almost by return of post came Miss Ley's reply.

My dear Edward,

I perused all six copies of your speech with the greatest interest; and I think you will agree with me that it is high proof of its merit that I was able to read it the sixth time with as unflagging attention as the first. The peroration, indeed, I am convinced that no acquaintance could stale. It is so true that 'every Englishman has a mother' (supposing, of course, that an untimely death has not robbed him of her). It is curious how one does not realize the truth of some things till they are set before one; when one's only surprise is at not having seen them before I hope it will not offend you if I suggest that Bertha's handiwork seems to me not invisible in some of the sentiments; (especially in that passage about the Union Jack); did you really write the whole speech yourself? Come, now, confess that Bertha helped you.

Yours very sincerely,
Mary Ley.

Edward read the letter and tossed it, laughing, to Bertha.
'What cheek her suggesting that you helped me! I like that.'
'I'll write at once and tell her that it was all your own.'

Bertha still could hardly believe genuine the admiration that her husband excited. Knowing his extreme incapacity, she was astounded that the rest of the world should think him an uncommonly clever fellow. To her his pretensions were merely ridiculous; she marvelled that he should venture to discuss with dogmatic glibness subjects of which he knew nothing; but she marvelled still more that people should be impressed thereby; he had an astonishing faculty for concealing his ignorance.

At last the polling-day arrived, and Bertha waited anxiously at Court Leys for the result. Edward eventually appeared, radiant.

'What did I tell you?' said he.

'I see you've got in.'

'Got in isn't the word for it! What did I tell you? My dear girl, I've simply knocked 'em all into a cocked hat. I got double the number of votes that the other chap did, and it's the biggest poll they've ever had. Aren't you proud that your hubby is a County Councillor? I tell you I shall be an M.P. before I die.'

'I congratulate you with all my heart,' said Bertha trying to be enthusiastic.

Edward in his excitement did not observe her coolness. He was walking up and down the room concocting schemes, asking himself how long it would be before Miles Campbell, the member, was confronted by the inevitable dilemma of the unopposed M.P., one horn of which is the kingdom of Heaven and the other the House of Lords.

Presently he stopped: 'I'm not a vain man,' he remarked, 'but I must say I don't think I've done badly.'

Edward for a while was somewhat overwhelmed by his own

greatness, but the opinion came to his rescue that the rewards were only according to his deserts; and presently he entered energetically into the not very arduous duties of the County Councillor. Bertha continually expected to hear something to his disadvantage; but on the contrary everything seemed to proceed very satisfactorily, and Edward's aptitude for business, his keenness in making a bargain, his common-sense, were heralded abroad in a manner that should have been most gratifying to his wife. But as a matter of fact these constant praises exceedingly disquieted Bertha. She asked herself uneasily whether she was doing him an injustice. Was he really as clever, had he indeed the virtues that common report ascribed to him? Perhaps she was prejudiced, and perhaps – he was cleverer than she. The possibility of this made her wince; she had never doubted that her intellect was superior to Edward's; their respective knowledge was not comparable; she occupied herself with thoughts that Edward did not conceive. He never interested himself in abstract things, and his conversation was tedious as only the absence of speculation can make it. It was extraordinary that everyone but she should so highly esteem his intelligence. Bertha knew that his mind was paltry and his ignorance egregious. His pretentiousness made him a charlatan. One day he came to her, his head full of a new idea.

'I say, Bertha, I've been thinking it over, and it seems a pity that your name should be dropped entirely. And it sounds funny that people called Craddock should live at Court Leys.'

'D'you think so? I don't know how you can remedy it, unless you think of advertising for tenants with a more suitable name.'

'Well, I was thinking it wouldn't be a bad idea, and it would have a good effect on the county, if we took the name again.'

He looked at Bertha, who glared at him icily, but answered nothing.

'I've talked to old Bacot about it, and he thinks it would be just the thing, so I think we'd better do it.'

'I suppose you're going to consult me on the subject.'

'That's what I'm doing now.'

'Do you think of calling yourself Ley-Craddock or Craddock-Ley, or dropping the Craddock altogether?'

'Well, to tell you the truth, I hadn't gone so far as that yet.'

Bertha gave a little scornful laugh. 'I think the idea is utterly ridiculous.'

'I don't see that; I think it would be rather an improvement.'

'Really, Edward, if I was not ashamed to take your name, I don't think that you need be ashamed to keep it.'

'I say, I think you might be reasonable. You're always standing in my way.'

'I have no wish to do that. If you think my name will add to your importance, use it by all means. You may call yourself Tompkins for all I care.'

'What about you?'

'Oh, I – I shall continue to call myself Craddock.'

'I do think it's rough. You never do anything to help me.'

'I am sorry you're dissatisfied. But you forget that you have impressed one ideal on me for years; you have always given me to understand that your pattern of a female animal was the common or garden cow. I always regret that you didn't marry Fanny Glover. You would have suited one another admirably. And I think she would have worshipped you as you desire to be worshipped. I'm sure she would not have objected to your calling yourself Glover.'

'I shouldn't have wanted to take her name. That's no better than Craddock. The only thing in Ley is that it's an old county name and has belonged to your people.'

'That is why I don't choose that you should take it.'

27

TIME passed slowly, slowly. Bertha wrapped her pride about her like a cloak, but sometimes it seemed too heavy to bear, and she nearly fainted. The restraint that she imposed upon herself was often intolerable; anger and hatred seethed within her, but she forced herself to preserve the smiling face that people had always seen. She suffered intensely from loneliness of spirit, for she had no one to whom she could tell her unhappiness; it is terrible to have no means of expressing oneself, to keep imprisoned always the anguish that gnaws at one's heart-strings; it is well enough for the writer; he can find solace in his words, he can tell his secret and yet not betray it; but the woman has only silence.

Bertha loathed Edward now with such an angry, physical repulsion that she could not bear his touch; and everyone she knew was his admiring friend. How could she tell Fanny Glover that Edward was a fool who bored her to death, when Fanny Glover thought him the best and most virtuous of mankind? She was annoyed that in the universal estimation Edward should have so entirely eclipsed her; once his only importance lay in the fact that he was her husband, but now the position was reversed. She found it very irksome thus to shine with reflected light, and at the same time despised herself for the petty jealousy.

At last she felt it impossible any longer to endure his company; he made her stupid and vulgar, she was ill and weak and she despaired. She made up her mind to go away again, this time for ever.

'If I stay, I shall kill myself.'

For two days Edward had been miserable; a favourite dog of his had died, and he was brought to the verge of tears. Bertha watched him contemptuously.

'You are more affected over the death of a wretched dog than you have ever been over a pain of mine.'

'Oh, don't rag me now, there's a good girl; I can't bear it.'

'Fool!' muttered Bertha under her breath.

He went about with hanging head and melancholy face, telling everyone the particulars of the beast's demise in a voice quivering with emotion.

'Poor fellow,' said Miss Glover, 'he has such a good heart.'

Bertha could hardly repress the bitter invective that rose to her lips. If people knew the coldness with which he had met her love, the indifference he had shown to her tears and to her despair. She despised herself when she remembered the utter self-abasement of the past.

'He made me drink the cup of humiliation to the very dregs.'

From the height of her disdain she summed him up for the thousandth time. It was inexplicable that she had been subject to a man so paltry in mind, so despicable in character. It made her blush with shame to think how servile had been her love.

Dr Ramsay, who was visiting Bertha for some trivial ill, happened to come in when she was engaged with such thoughts.

'Well,' he said, as soon as she had taken breath, 'and how is Edward today?'

'Good Heavens, how should I know?' she cried, beside herself, the words slipping out unawares after the long constraint.

'Hulloa, what's this? Have the turtle-doves had a tiff at last?'

'Oh, I'm sick of continually hearing Edward's praises. I'm sick of being treated as an appendage to him.'

'What's the matter with you, Bertha?' said the doctor, bursting into a shout of laughter. 'I always thought nothing pleased you more than to hear how much we all liked your husband.'

'Oh, my good doctor, you must be blind or an utter fool. I thought everyone knew by now that I loathe my husband.'

'What!' shouted Dr Ramsay; then, thinking Bertha was unwell: 'Come, come, I see you want a little medicine, my dear. You're out of sorts, and like all women you think the world is consequently coming to an end.'

Bertha sprang from the sofa. 'D'you think I should speak like this if I hadn't good cause? Don't you think I'd conceal my humiliation if I could? Oh, I've hidden it long enough; now I must speak. Oh, God, I can hardly help screaming with pain when I think of all I've suffered and hidden. I've never said a word to anyone but you, and now I can't help it. I tell you I loathe and abhor my husband and I utterly despise him. I can't live with him any more and I want to go away.'

Dr Ramsay opened his mouth and fell back in his chair; he looked at Bertha as if he expected her to have a fit.

'Well, I'm blowed. You're not serious?'

Bertha stamped her foot impatiently: 'Of course I'm serious. Do you think I'm a fool too? We've been miserable for years, and it can't go on. If you knew what I've had to suffer when everyone has congratulated me and said how pleased they were to see me so happy! Sometimes I've had to dig my nails in my hands to prevent myself from crying out the truth.'

Bertha walked up and down the room, letting herself go at last. The tears were streaming down her cheeks, but she took no notice of them. She was giving full vent to her passionate hatred.

'Oh, I've tried to love him. You know how I loved him once, how I adored him. I would have laid down my life for him with pleasure. I would have done anything he asked me; I used to search for the smallest indication of his wishes so that I might carry them out. I used to love to think that I was his abject slave. But he's destroyed every vestige of my love, and now I only despise him, I utterly despise him. Oh, I've tried to love him, but he's too great a fool.'

The last words Bertha said with such force that Dr Ramsay was startled.

'My dear Bertha!'

'Oh, I know you all think him wonderful. I've had his praises thrown at me for years. But you don't know what a man really is till you've lived with him, till you've seen him in every mood and in every circumstance. I know him through and through, and he's a fool. You can't conceive how stupid, how utterly brainless he is. He bores me to death.'

'Come now, you don't mean what you say. You're exaggerating as usual. You must expect to have little quarrels now and then; upon my word, I think it took me twenty years to get used to my wife.'

'Oh, for God's sake, don't be sententious,' Bertha interrupted fiercely. 'I've had enough moralizing in these five years. I might have loved Edward better if he hadn't been so moral. He's thrown his virtues in my face till I'm sick of them. He's made every goodness ugly to me till I sigh for vice just for a change. Oh, you can't imagine how frightfully dull is a really good man. Now I want to be free; I tell you I can't stand it any more.'

Bertha again walked up and down the room excitedly.

'Upon my word,' cried Dr Ramsay, 'I can't make head or tail of it.'

'I didn't expect you would. I knew you'd only preach at me.'

'What d'you want me to do? Shall I speak to him?'

'No! No! I've spoken to him endlessly. It's no good. D'you suppose your speaking to him will make him love me? He's incapable of it; all he can give me is esteem and affection. Good God, what do I want with esteem! It requires a certain intelligence to love, and he hasn't got it. I tell you he's a fool. Oh, when I think that I'm shackled to him for the rest of my life I feel I could kill myself.'

'Come now, he's not such a fool as all that. Everyone agrees that he's a very smart man of business. And I can't help saying that I've always thought you did uncommonly well when you insisted on marrying him.'

'It was all your fault,' cried Bertha. 'If you hadn't opposed me I might not have married so quickly. Oh, you don't know how I've regretted it. I wish I could see him dead at my feet.'

Dr Ramsay whistled. His mind worked somewhat slowly and he was becoming confused with the overthrow of his cherished opinions and the vehemence with which the unpleasant operation was conducted.

'I didn't know things were like this.'

'Of course you didn't!' said Bertha scornfully. 'Because I smiled and hid my sorrow you thought I was happy. When I look back on the misery I've gone through I wonder that I can ever have borne it.'

'I can't believe that this is very serious. You'll be of a different mind tomorrow and wonder that such things ever entered your head. You mustn't mind an old fellow like me telling you you're very headstrong and impulsive. After all, Edward is a fine fellow, and I can't believe that he would willingly hurt your feelings.'

'Oh, for God's sake don't give me more of Edward's praises.'

'I wonder if you're a little jealous of the way he's got on?' asked the doctor, looking at her sharply.

Bertha flushed, for she had asked herself the same question; much scorn was needed to refute it.

'I? My dear doctor, you forget! Oh, don't you understand that it isn't a passing whim? It's dreadfully serious to me. I've borne the misery till I can bear it no longer. You must help me to get away. If you have any of your old affection for me, do what you can. I want to go away; but I don't want to have any more rows with Edward; I just want to leave him quietly. It's no good trying to make him understand that we're incompatible. He thinks that it's enough for my happiness just to be his wife. He's of iron and I am pitifully weak. I used to think myself so strong.'

'Am I to take it that you're absolutely serious? Do you want to take the extreme step of separating from your husband?'

'It's an extreme step that I've taken before. Last time I went with a flourish of trumpets, but now I want to go without any fuss at all. I still loved Edward then, but I have even ceased to hate him. Oh, I knew I was a fool to come back, but I couldn't help it. He asked me to return and I did.'

'Well, I don't know what I can do for you. I can't help thinking that if you wait a little things will get better.'

'I can't wait any longer. I've waited too long. I'm losing my whole life.'

'Why don't you go away for a few months, and then you can

191

see? Miss Ley is going to Italy for the winter as usual, isn't she? Upon my word, I think it would do you good to go too.'

'I don't mind what I do as long as I can get away. I'm suffering too much.'

'Have you thought that Edward will miss you?' asked Dr Ramsay, gravely.

'No, he won't. Good Heavens, don't you think I know him by now? I know him through and through. And he's callous and selfish and stupid. And he's making me like himself. Oh, Dr Ramsay, please help me.'

'Does Miss Ley know?' asked the doctor, remembering what she had told him on her visit to Court Leys.

'No, I'm sure she doesn't. She thinks we adore one another. And I don't want her to know. I'm such a coward now. Years ago I never cared a straw for what anyone in the world thought of me; but my spirit is broken. Oh, get me away from here, Dr Ramsay, get me away.'

She burst into tears, weeping as she had been long unaccustomed to do; she was exhausted after the outburst of all that for years she had kept hid.

'I'm still so young, and I almost feel an old woman. Sometimes I should like to lie down and die, and have done with it all.'

A month later Bertha was in Rome. But at first she was hardly able to realize the change in her condition; for her life at Court Leys had impressed itself upon her with ghastly distinctness, so that she could not imagine its cessation. She was like a prisoner so long immured that freedom dazes him, and he looks for his chains and cannot understand that he is free.

They had taken an apartment in the Via Gregoriana, and Bertha, waking in the morning, did not know where she was. The relief was so great that she could not believe it true, and she lived in fear that her vision would be disturbed and she find herself again within the prison walls of Court Leys. It was a dream that she wandered in sunlit places, where the air was scented with violets and roses. The people were unreal, the models lounging on the steps of the Piazza di Spagna, the ragged urchins, quaintly costumed and importunate, the silver speech that caressed the air. How could she believe that life was true when it gave blue sky and sunshine, so that the heart thrilled with joy; when it gave rest and peace and the most delightful idleness. Real life was gloomy and strenuous; and its setting a Georgian mansion, surrounded by desolate, wind-swept fields. In real life everyone was deadly virtuous and deadly dull; the Ten Commandments hedged one round with the menace of hell-fire and eternal damnation. They are a dungeon more terrible because it has not walls, nor bars and bolts. But beyond those gloomy stones with the harsh 'thou shalt not' written upon them, is a land of fragrance and light, where the sunbeams send the blood running gaily through the veins, where the flowers give their perfume freely to the air, in token that riches must be spent and virtue must be squandered; where the amorets flutter here and there on the spring breezes, unknowing whither they go, uncaring. This land beyond the Ten Commandments is a land of olive-trees and pleasant shade, and the sea kisses the shore gently to show the youths how they must kiss the maidens; there lips are not vehicles for grotesque strenuosities, but Cupid's bows; and there dark eyes flash lambently, telling the traveller he need not fear, Love may be had for the asking. Blood is warm, and hands linger with grateful pressure in hands, and red lips ask for the kisses that are so sweet to give. There the flesh and the spirit walk side by side, and each is well satisfied with the other. Ah, give me the sunshine of this blissful country, and a garden of roses, and the murmur of a pleasant brook; give me a shady bank, and wine, and books, and the coral lips of Amaryllis, and I will live in complete felicity for at least ten days.

To Bertha the life in Rome seemed like a play. Miss Ley left her much freedom, and she wandered alone in strange places. She went often to the market and spent the morning wandering in and out of the booths, looking at a thousand things she did not want to buy; she fingered rich silks and antique bits of silver, smiling at the compliments of a friendly dealer. The people bustled round her, volubly talking, intensely alive, and yet, because she could not understand that what she saw was true, strangely unreal. She went to the galleries, to the Sistine Chapel or the Stanze of Raphael; and, lacking the hurry of the tourist and his sense of duty, she would spend a whole morning in front of one picture or in a corner of an old church, weaving with whatever she looked at the fantasies of her imagination.

And when she felt the need of her fellow-men she went to the Pincio and mingled with the throng that listened to the band. But the Franciscan monk in his brown cowl, standing apart, was a figure of a romantic play, and the soldiers in gay uniforms, the Bersaglieri with the bold cock's feathers in their hats, were the chorus of a comic opera. And there were black-robed priests, some old and fat, taking the sun and smoking cigarettes, at peace with themselves and the world; others young and restless, with the flesh unsubdued shining out of their dark eyes. And everyone seemed as happy as the children who romped and scampered with merry cries.

But gradually the shadows of the past fell away and Bertha was able more consciously to appreciate the beauty and the life that surrounded her. And knowing it fleeting, she set herself to enjoy it as best she could. Care and youth are difficultly yoked together, and merciful time wraps in oblivion the most gruesome misery. Bertha stretched out her arms to embrace the wonders of the living world, and she put away the dreadful thought that it must end so quickly. In the spring she spent long hours in the gardens that surround the city; the remains of ancient Rome mingled exotically with the half-tropical luxuriance, and excited in her new and subtle emotions. The flowers grew in the sarcophagi with a wild exuberance, wantoning, it seemed, in mockery of the tomb whence they sprang. Death is hideous, but life is always triumphant; the rose and the hyacinth arise from man's decay; and the dissolution of man is but the signal of other birth; and the world goes on, beautiful and ever new, revelling in its vigour.

Bertha went to the Villa Medici and sat where she could watch the light glowing on the mellow façade of the old palace and Syrinx peeping between the reeds; the students saw her and asked who was the beautiful woman who sat so long and so unconscious of the eyes that looked at her. She went to the Villa Doria-Pamphili, majestic and pompous, the fitting summer-house of princes in gorgeous habit, and bishops and cardinals. And the ruins of the Palatine, with its cypresses and well-kept walks, sent her thoughts back and back, and she pictured to herself the glories of bygone powers.

But the wildest garden of all, that of the Mattei, pleased her best. Here was a greater fertility and a greater abandonment; the distance and the difficulty of access kept strangers away, and Bertha could wander through it as if it were her own. She thought she had never enjoyed such exquisite moments as were given her by its solitude and its silence. Sometimes a troop of scarlet seminarists sauntered along the grass-grown avenues, vivid colour against the desolate verdure.

Then she went home, tired and happy; she sat at her open window and watched the setting sun. The sun set over St Peter's and the mighty cathedral was transfigured into a temple of fire and gold; the dome was radiant, formed no longer of solid stone, but of light and sunshine: it was the crown of a palace of Hyperion. Then with the night, St Peter's stood out in darkness, stood out in majestic profile against the splendour of heaven.

28

BUT after Easter Miss Ley proposed that they should travel slowly back to England. Bertha had dreaded the suggestion, not only because she regretted to leave Rome, but still more because it rendered necessary some explanation. The winter had passed comfortably enough with the excuse of indifferent health, but now another reason must be found to account for the continued absence from her husband's side, and Bertha's racked imagination gave her nothing. She was determined, however, under no circumstances to return to Court Leys; after the happy freedom of six months the confinement of body and soul would be doubly intolerable.

Edward had been satisfied with the pretext, and had let Bertha go without a word. As he said, he was not the man to stand in his wife's way when her health required her to leave him, and he could pig along all right by himself. Their letters had been fairly frequent, but on Bertha's side a constant effort. She was always telling herself that the only rational course was to make Edward a final statement of her intentions, then break off all communication; but the dread of fuss and bother, and of endless explanation, restrained her; and she compromised·by writing as seldom as possible and adhering to the merest trivialities. She was surprised once or twice when she had delayed her answer, to receive from him a second letter, asking with some show of anxiety why she did not write.

Miss Ley had never mentioned Edward's name, and Bertha surmised that she knew much of the truth. But she kept her own counsel; blessed are they who mind their own business and hold their tongues! Miss Ley, indeed, was convinced that some catastrophe had occurred, but true to her habit of allowing people to work out their lives in their own way, without interference, took care to seem unobservant; which was really very noble, for she prided herself on nothing more than on her talent for observation.

'The most difficult thing for a wise woman to do,' she said, 'is to pretend to be a foolish one.'

She guessed Bertha's present difficulty; and it seemed easily surmountable.

'I wish you'd come back to London with me instead of going to Court Leys,' she said. 'You've never had a London season, have you? On the whole I think it's amusing; the opera is very good, and sometimes you see people who are quite well dressed.'

Bertha did not answer, and Miss Ley, seeing her wish to accept and at the same time her hesitation, suggested that she should come for a few weeks, well knowing that a woman's visit is apt to spin itself out for an indeterminate time.

'I'm sorry I shan't have room for Edward too,' said Miss Ley, smiling drily, 'but my flat is very small, you know.'

Irony is a gift of the gods, the most subtle of all the modes of speech. It is an armour and a weapon; it is a philosophy and a perpetual entertainment; it is food for the hungry of wit and drink to those thirsting for laughter. How much more elegant is it to slay your foe with the roses of irony than to massacre him with the axes of sarcasm or to belabour him with the bludgeons of invective. And the adept in irony enjoys its use when he alone is aware of his meaning, and he sniggers up his sleeve to see all and sundry, chained to their obtuseness, take him seriously. In a strenuous world it is the only safeguard of the flippant. To the man of letters it is a missile that he can fling in the reader's face to disprove the pestilent heresy that a man writes books for the subscriber to Mudie's Library, rather than for himself. Be not deceived gentle reader, no self-respecting writer cares a twopenny damn for you.

They had been settled a few days in the flat in Eliot Mansions, when Bertha, coming in to breakfast one morning, found Miss Ley in a great state of suppressed amusement. She was quivering all over like an uncoiled spring, and she pecked at her toast and her egg in a bird-like manner, which Bertha knew could only mean that someone, to the entertainment of her aunt, had made a fool of himself. Bertha began to laugh.

'Good Heavens,' she cried, 'what has happened?'

'My dear, a terrible catastrophe,' Miss Ley repressed a smile, but her eyes gleamed and danced as though she were a young woman. 'You don't know Gerald Vaudrey, do you? But you know who he is.'

'I believe he's a cousin of mine.'

Bertha's father, who made a practice of quarrelling with his relations, had found in General Vaudrey a brother-in-law as irascible as himself; so that the two families had never been on speaking terms.

'I've just had a letter from his mother to say that he's been philandering rather violently with her maid, and they're all in despair. The maid has been sent away in hysterics, his mother and his sisters are in tears, and the General's in a passion and says he won't have the boy in his house another day. And the little wretch is only nineteen. Disgraceful, isn't it?'

'Disgraceful,' said Bertha, smiling. 'I wonder what there is in a French maid that small boys should invariably make love to her.'

'Oh, my dear, if you only saw my sister's maid. She's forty if she's a day, and her complexion is like parchment very much the worse for wear. But the awful part of it is that your Aunt Betty beseeches me to look after the boy. He's going to Florida in a month, and meanwhile he's to stay in London. Now, what I want to know is how am I to keep a dissolute infant out of mischief? Is it the sort of thing that one would expect of me?'

Miss Ley waved her arms with comic desperation.

'Oh, but it'll be great fun. We'll reform him together. We'll lead him on to a path where French maids are not to be met at every turn and corner.'

'My dear, you don't know what he is. He's an utter young scamp. He was expelled from Rugby. He's been to half a dozen crammers, because they wanted him to go to Sandhurst, but he refused to work; and he's been ploughed in every exam. he's gone in for – even for the Militia. So now his father has given him five hundred pounds and told him to go to the devil.'

'How rude! But why should the poor boy go to Florida?'

'I suggested that. I know some people who've got an orange

plantation there. And I daresay that the view of several miles of orange blossoms will suggest to him that promiscuous flirtation may have unpleasant results.'

'I think I shall like him,' said Bertha.

'I have no doubt you will; he's a perfect scamp and rather pretty.'

Next day, when Bertha was in the drawing-room, reading, Gerald Vaudrey was shown in. She got up smiling, to reassure him, and put out her hand in the friendliest manner; she thought he must be a little confused at meeting a stranger instead of Miss Ley, and unhappy in his disgrace.

'You don't know who I am?' she said.

'Oh, yes, I do,' he replied, with a very pleasant smile. 'The slavey told me Aunt Polly was out, but that you were here.'

'I'm glad you didn't go away.'

'I thought I shouldn't frighten you, you know.'

Bertha opened her eyes. He was certainly not at all shy, although he looked even younger than nineteen. He was quite a boy, very slight and not so tall as Bertha, with a small, girlish face. He had a tiny nose, but it was very straight, and his somewhat freckled complexion was admirable. His hair was dark and curly; he wore it long, evidently aware that it was very nice; and his handsome eyes had a charming expression. His sensual mouth was always smiling.

'What a pretty boy!' thought Bertha. 'I'm sure I shall like him.'

He began to talk as if he had known her all his life, and she was struck by the contrast between his innocent appearance and his shocking past. He looked about the room with boyish ease and stretched himself comfortably in a big armchair.

'Hulloa, that's new since I was here last,' he said, pointing to an Italian bronze.

'Have you been here often?'

'Rather! I used to come here whenever it got too hot for me at home. It's no good scrapping with your governor, because he's got the ooftish. It's a jolly unfair advantage that fathers have, but they always take it. So when the old chap flew into a passion, I used to say: "I won't argue with you. If you can't treat me like a gentleman, I shall go away for a week." And I used to come here. Aunt Polly always gave me five quid and said: "Don't tell me how you spend it, because I shouldn't approve, but come again when you want more." She is a ripper, ain't she?'

'I'm sorry she's not in.'

'I'm rather glad, because I can have a long talk with you till she comes. I've never seen you before, so I have such a lot to say.'

'Have you?' said Bertha laughing. 'That's rather unusual in young men.'

He looked so absurdly young that Bertha could not help treating him as a schoolboy; she was amused at his communicativeness. She wanted him to tell her all his escapades, but was afraid to ask.

'Are you very hungry?' She thought that boys always had appetites. 'Would you like some tea?'

'I'm starving.'

She poured him out a cup, and taking it and three jam sandwiches at once, he sat on a footstool at her feet. He made himself quite at home.

'You've never seen my Vaudrey cousins, have you?' he asked, with his mouth full. 'I can't stick 'em at any price, they're such frumps. I'll tell 'em all about you; it'll make them beastly sick.'

Bertha raised her eyebrows: 'And do you object to frumps?'

'I simply loathe them. At the last tutor's I was at the old chap's wife was the most awful old geyser you ever saw. So I wrote and told my mater that I was afraid my morals were being corrupted.'

'And did she take you away?'

'Well, by a curious coincidence, the old chap wrote the very same day and told the pater if he didn't remove me he'd give me the shoot. So I sent in my resignation and told him his cigars were poisonous and cleared out.'

'Don't you think you'd better sit on a chair?' said Bertha. 'You must be very uncomfortable on that footstool.'

'Oh, no, not at all. After a Turkey carpet and dining-room table, there's nothing so comfy as a footstool. A chair always makes me feel respectable, and dull.'

Bertha thought Gerald a nice name.

'How long are you staying in London?'

'Oh, only a month, worse luck. Then I've got to go to the States to make my fortune and reform.'

'I hope you will.'

'Which? One can't do both at once, you know. You make your money first and you reform afterwards if you've got time. But whatever happens, it'll be a damned sight better than sweating away at an everlasting crammer's. If there is one man I can't stick at any price it's the army crammer.'

'You have a large experience of them, I understand.'

'I wish you didn't know all my past history. Now I shan't have the sport of telling you.'

'I don't think it would be edifying.'

'Oh, yes, it would. It would show you how virtue is down-trodden (that's me) and how vice is triumphant. I'm awfully unlucky; people sort of conspire together to look at my actions from the wrong point of view. I've had jolly rough luck all through. First I was bunked from Rugby. Well, that wasn't my fault. I was quite willing to stay, and I'm blowed if I was worse than anybody else. The pater blackguarded me for six weeks and said I was bringing his grey hairs with sorrow to the grave. Well, you know, he's simply awfully bald, so at last I couldn't help saying that I didn't know where his grey hairs were going to; but it didn't much look as if he meant to accompany them. So after that he sent me to a crammer who played poker; well, he skinned me of every shilling I'd got, and then wrote and told the pater I was an immoral young dog and corrupting his house.'

'Isn't there something else we could talk about?'

'Oh, but you must have the sequel. The next place I went to, I found none of the other fellows knew poker; so of course I thought it a sort of merciful interposition of providence to help me to recoup myself. I told 'em not to lay up treasure in this world, and walloped 'em thirty quid in four days; then the old thingamyjig (I forget his name, but he was a parson) told me I was making his place into a gambling hell and he wouldn't have me another day in his house. So off I toddled, and I stayed at home for six months. That gave me the fair hump, I can tell you.'

The conversation was disturbed by the entrance of Miss Ley.

'You see we've made friends,' said Bertha.

'Gerald always does that with everybody. He's the most gregarious person. How are you, Lothario?'

'Flourishing, Belinda,' he replied, flinging his arms round Miss Ley's neck to her great delight and pretended indignation.

'You're irrepressible,' she said. 'I expected to find you in sack-cloth and ashes, penitent and silent.'

'My dear Aunt Polly, ask me to do anything you like except to repent and to hold my tongue.'

'You know your mother has asked me to look after you.'

'I like being looked after. And is Bertha going to help?'

'I've been thinking it over,' added Miss Ley, 'and the only way I can see to keep you out of mischief is to make you spend your evenings with me. So you'd better go home now and dress. I know there's nothing you like better than changing your clothes.'

Meanwhile Bertha observed with astonishment that Gerald was devouring her with his eyes. It was impossible not to see his evident admiration.

'The boy must be mad,' she thought, but could not help feeling flattered.

'He's been telling me some dreadful stories,' she said to Miss Ley when he had gone. 'I hope they're not true.'

'Oh, I think you must take all Gerald says with a grain of salt. He exaggerates dreadfully, and all boys like to seem Byronic; so do most men, for the matter of that.'

'He looks so young, I can't believe that he's really very naughty.'

'Well, my dear, there's no doubt about his mother's maid. The evidence is of the most conclusive order. I know I should be dreadfully angry with him, but everyone is so virtuous nowadays that a change is quite refreshing. And he's so young, he may reform. Englishmen start galloping to the devil, but, as they grow older, they nearly always change horses and amble along gently to respectability, a wife and seventeen children.'

'I like the contrast of his green eyes and his dark hair.'

'My dear, it can't be denied that he's made to capture the feminine heart. I never try to resist him myself. He's never so convincing as when he tells you an outrageous fib.'

Bertha went to her room and looked at herself in the glass, then put on her most becoming dinner-dress.

'Good gracious,' said Miss Ley, 'you've not put that on for Gerald? You'll turn the boy's head; he's dreadfully susceptible.'

'It's the first one I came across,' replied Bertha innocently.

29

'You've quite captured Gerald's heart,' said Miss Ley to Bertha a day or two later. 'He's confided in me that he thinks you perfectly stunning.'

'He's a very nice boy,' said Bertha, laughing.

The youth's outspoken admiration could not fail to increase her liking; and she was amused by the stare of his green eyes, which, with a woman's peculiar sense, she felt even when her back was turned. They followed her, they rested on her hair and on her beautiful hands; when she wore a low dress they burnt themselves on her neck and breast; she felt them travel along her arms and embrace her figure. They were the most caressing, smiling eyes, but with a certain mystery in their emerald depths. Bertha did not neglect to put herself in positions in which Gerald could see her to advantage; and when he looked at her hands she could not be expected to withdraw them as though she were ashamed. Few Englishmen see anything in a woman but her face, and it seldom occurs to them that her hand has the most delicate outlines, all grace and gentleness, with tapering fingers and rosy nails; they never look for the thousand things it has to say.

'Don't you know it's very rude to stare like that?' said Bertha, with a smile, turning round suddenly.

'I beg your pardon, I didn't know you were looking.'

'I wasn't, but I saw you all the same.'

She smiled at him most engagingly and she saw a sudden flame leap into his eyes. He was a pretty boy; of course a mere child.

A married woman is always gratified by the capture of a boy's fickle heart; it is an unsolicited testimonial to her charms, and has the advantage of being completely free from danger. She tells herself that there is no better training for a young man than to fall in love with a really nice woman a good deal older than himself. It teaches him how to behave and keeps him from getting into scrapes. How often have callow youths been known to ruin their lives by falling into the clutches of an adventuress with yellow hair and painted cheeks! Since she's old enough to be his mother, the really nice woman thinks there can be no harm in flirting with the poor boy, and it seems to please him; so she makes him fetch and carry, and dazzles him, and generally drives him quite distracted, till his youthful fickleness comes to the rescue and he falls passionately in love with a barmaid; when, of course, she calls him an ungrateful and low-minded wretch, regrets she was so mistaken in his character, and tells him never to come near her again. This, of course, only refers to the women whom men fall in love with; it is well known that the others have the strictest views on the subject and would sooner die than flirt.

Gerald had the charming gift of becoming intimate with people at the shortest notice, and a cousin is an agreeable relation (especially when she's pretty) with whom it is easy to get on. The relationship is not so close as to warrant chronic disagreeableness, and close enough to permit personalities, which are the most amusing part of conversation.

Within a week Gerald took to spending his whole day with Bertha, and she found the London season much more amusing than she had expected. She looked back with distaste to her only two visits to town; one had been her honeymoon, and the other the first separation from her husband; it was odd that in retrospect they both seemed equally dreary. Edward had almost disappeared from her thoughts, and she exulted like a captive free from chains. Her only worry was his often-expressed desire to see her. Why could he not leave her alone, as she left him? He was perpetually asking when she would return to Court Leys, and she had to invent excuses to prevent his coming to London. She loathed the idea of seeing him again.

But she put aside these thoughts when Gerald came. It is no wonder that the English are a populous race, when one observes how many are the resorts supplied by the munificence of governing bodies for the express purpose of philandering. On a hot day what spot can be more enchanting than the British Museum, cool, and silent, and roomy, with harmless statues that tell no tales and afford matter for conversation to break an awkward pause? The parks also are eminently suited for those whose fancy turns to thoughts of platonic love. Hyde Park is the fitting scene for an idyll in which Corydon wears patent-leather boots and a shiny top-hat, and Phyllis an exquisite frock. The well-kept lawns, the artificial water and the trim paths give a mock rurality that is infinitely amusing to persons who do not wish to take things too seriously. Here, in the summer mornings, Gerald and Bertha spent much time. It pleased her to listen to his chatter and to look into his green eyes; he was such a very nice boy, and seemed attached to her. Besides, he was only in London for a month, and she could afford to let him fall in love with her a little.

'Are you sorry you're going away so soon?' she asked.

'I shall be miserable at leaving you.'

'It's nice of you to say so,' she answered, smiling.

Bit by bit she extracted from him his discreditable history.

Bertha was possessed by a curiosity to know details, which she elicited artfully, making him confess his iniquities so that she might pretend to be angry. It gave her a curious thrill, partly of admiration, to think that he was such a depraved young person, and she looked at him with a sort of amused wonder. He was very different from the virtuous Edward. A childlike innocence shone out of his handsome eyes, and yet he had already tasted the wine of many emotions. Bertha felt somewhat envious of the sex that gave opportunity, and the spirit that gave power, to seize life boldly and wring from it all it had to offer.

'I ought to refuse to speak to you any more,' she said; 'I ought to be ashamed of you.'

'But you're not. That's why you're such a ripper.'

How could she be angry with a boy who adored her? He might be utterly vicious, in fact he was; but his perversity fascinated her. Here was a man who would never hesitate to go to the devil for a woman, and Bertha was pleased at the compliment to her sex.

One evening Miss Ley was dining out, and Gerald asked Bertha to come to dinner with him, and then to the opera. She refused, thinking of the expense; but he was so eager, and she really so anxious to go, that at last she consented.

'Poor boy, he's going away so soon, I may as well be nice to him.'

Gerald arrived in high spirits. Evening clothes suited him admirably, but he looked even more boyish than usual.

'I'm really afraid to go out with you,' said Bertha. 'People will think you're my son. "Dear me, who'd have thought she was forty"!'

'What rot!' He looked at her beautiful gown. Like all nice women, Bertha was extremely careful to be always well dressed. 'By Jove, you are a stunner!'

'My dear child, I'm old enough to be your mother.'

They drove off, to a restaurant which Gerald, boy-like, had chosen because common report pronounced it the dearest in London. Bertha was amused by the bustle, the glitter of women in diamonds, the busy waiters gliding to and fro, the glare of the electric light; and her eyes rested with approval on the handsome lad in front of her. She could not keep in check the recklessness with which he insisted on ordering the most expensive things; and when they arrived at the opera she found he had a box.

'Oh, you wretch,' she cried. 'You must be utterly ruined.'

'Oh, I've got five hundred quid,' he replied, laughing. 'I must blue some of it.'

'But why on earth did you get a box?'

'I remembered that you hated any other part of the theatre.'

'But you promised to get cheap seats.'

'And I wanted to be alone with you.'

He was by nature a flatterer; and few women could withstand the cajolery of his eyes and his charming smile.

'He must be very fond of me,' thought Bertha, as they drove home, and she put her arm in his to express her thanks and her appreciation.

'It's very nice of you to have been so good to me. I always thought you were a nice creature.'

'I'd do more than that for you.'

He would have given the rest of his five hundred pounds for one kiss. She knew it and was pleased; but gave him no encouragement, and for once he was bashful. They separated at her doorstep with a discreet handshake.

'It's awfully kind of you to have come.'

He appeared immensely grateful to her. Her conscience pricked her now that he had spent so much money; but she liked him all the more. A woman would rather have a bunch of weeds that cost a fortune than a basket of roses that cost a shilling.

Gerald's month was nearly over, and Bertha was astonished that he occupied her thoughts so much. She did not know that she was so fond of him; it had never occurred to her that she would miss him.

'I wish he weren't going,' she said, and then quickly: 'But of course it's much better that he should.'

At that moment the boy appeared.

'This day week you'll be on the sea, Gerald,' she said. 'Then you'll be sorry for all your iniquities.'

'No,' he answered, sitting in the position he most affected, at Bertha's feet.

'No – which?'

'I shan't be sorry,' he replied, with a smile, 'and I'm not going away.'

'What d'you mean?'

'I've changed my plans. The man I'm going to said I could start

205

at the end of this month or at the end of next. And I shall start at the end of next.'

'But why?' It was a foolish question, because she knew.

'I had nothing to stay for. Now I have, that's all.'

Bertha looked at him and caught his shining eyes, fixed intently upon her. She became grave.

'You're not angry?' he asked, changing his tone. 'I thought you wouldn't mind. I don't want to leave you.'

He looked at her earnestly, and tears were in his eyes. Bertha could not help being touched.

'I'm very glad that you should stay, dear. I didn't want you to go so soon. We've been such good friends.'

She passed her fingers through his curly hair and over his ears; but he started, and shivered.

'Don't do that,' he said, pushing her hand away.

'Why not?' she cried, laughing. 'Are you frightened of me?'

And caressingly she passed her hand over his ears again.

'Oh, you don't know what pain that gives me.'

He sprang up, and to her astonishment Bertha saw that he was pale and trembling.

'I feel I shall go mad when you touch me.'

Suddenly she saw the burning passion in his eyes: it was love that made him tremble. Bertha gave a little cry, and a curious sensation pressed her heart. Then without warning, the boy seized her hands and falling on his knees before her kissed them repeatedly. His hot breath made Bertha tremble too, and the kisses burnt themselves into her flesh. She snatched her hands away.

'I've wanted to do that so long,' he whispered.

She was too much moved to answer, but stood looking at him.

'You must be mad, Gerald.'

'Bertha!'

They stood very close together. He was about to put his arms around her, and for an instant she had an insane desire to let him do what he would, to let him kiss her lips as he had kissed her hands; she wanted to kiss his mouth and his curly hair and his cheek as soft as a girl's. But she recovered herself.

'Oh, it's absurd! Don't be silly, Gerald.'

He could not speak, he looked at her with his green eyes sparkling with desire.

'I love you,' he whispered.

'My dear boy, do you want me to succeed your mother's maid?'

'Oh!' He gave a groan and turned red.

'I'm glad you're staying on. You'll be able to see Edward, who's coming to town next week. You've never met my husband, have you?'

His lips twitched and he seemed to struggle to compose himself. Then he threw himself on a chair and buried his face in his hands. He seemed so little, so young – and he loved her. Bertha looked at him for a moment, and the tears came to her eyes. She put her hand on his shoulder.

'Gerald!' He did not look up. 'Gerald, I didn't mean to hurt your feelings. I'm sorry for what I said.'

She bent down and drew his hands away from his face.

'Are you cross with me?' he asked, almost tearfully.

'No,' she answered, caressingly. 'But you musn't be silly, dearest. You know I'm old enough to be your mother.'

He did not seem consoled, and she felt still that she had been horrid. She took his face between her hands and kissed his lips. And as if he were a little child she kissed away the teardrops that shone in his eyes.

30

BERTHA still felt on her hands Gerald's passionate kisses; they were like little patches of fire; and on her lips was still the touch of his boyish mouth. What magic current had passed from him to her that she should feel this sudden happiness? It was enchanting to think that Gerald loved her; she remembered how his eyes had sparkled, how his voice had grown hoarse so that he could hardly speak: ah, those were the signs of real love, of the love that is mighty and triumphant. Bertha put her hands to her heart with a rippling laugh of pure joy – for she was loved. The kisses tingled on her fingers so that she looked at them with surprise; she seemed almost to see a mark of burning. She was very grateful to him, she wanted to take his head in her hands and kiss his hair and his boyish eyes and again the soft lips. She told herself that she would be a mother to him.

The following day he had come to her almost shyly, afraid that she would be angry, and the bashfulness contrasting with his usual happy audacity had charmed her. It flattered her extremely to think that he was her humble slave, to see the pleasure he took in doing as she bade; but she could hardly believe it true that he loved her, and she wished to reassure herself. It gave her a queer thrill to see him turn white when she held his hand, to see him tremble when she leant on his arm. She stroked his hair, and was delighted with the anguish she saw in his eyes.

'Don't do that,' he cried. 'Please. You don't know how it hurts.'

'I was hardly touching you,' she replied, laughing.

She saw in his eyes glistening tears: they were tears of passion, and she could scarcely restrain a cry of triumph. At last she was loved as she wished; she gloried in her power: here at last was one who would not hesitate to lose his soul for her sake. She was grateful. But her heart grew cold when she thought that it was too late, that it was no good; he was only a boy, and she was married and nearly thirty.

But even then, why should she attempt to stop him? If it was the love she dreamt of, nothing could destroy it. And there was no harm; Gerald said nothing to which she might not listen, and he was so much younger than she; he was going away in less than a month and it would all be over. Why should she not enjoy the modest crumbs that the gods let fall from their table? It was little enough in all conscience! How foolish is he who will not bask in the sun of St Martin's summer because it heralds the winter as surely as the east wind!

They spent the whole day together, to Miss Ley's amusement, who for once did not use her sharp eyes to much effect.

'I'm so thankful to you, Bertha, for looking after the boy. His mother ought to be eternally grateful to you for keeping him out of mischief.'

'I'm very glad if I have,' said Bertha. 'He's such a nice boy and I'm so fond of him. I should be very sorry if he got into trouble. I'm rather anxious about him afterwards.'

'My dear, don't be; because he's certain to get into scrapes – it's his nature; but it's likewise his nature to get out of them. He'll swear eternal devotion to half a dozen fair damsels, and ride away rejoicing, while they are left to weep upon one another's bosoms. It's some men's nature to break women's hearts.'

'I think he's only a little wild; he means no harm.'

'Those sort of people never do; that's what makes their wrong-doing so much more fatal.'

'And he's so affectionate.'

'My dear, I shall really believe that you're in love with him.'

'I am,' said Bertha, 'madly!'

The plain truth is often the surest way to hoodwink people, more especially when it is told unconsciously. Women of fifty have an irritating habit of treating as contemporaries all persons of their own sex who are over twenty-five, and it never struck Miss Ley that Bertha might look upon Gerald as anything but a little boy.

But Edward could no longer be kept in the country. Bertha was astonished that he should wish to see her, and a little annoyed, for now of all times his presence would be importunate. She did not wish to have her dream disturbed, she knew it was nothing else; it was a mere spring day of happiness in the long winter of life.

She looked at Gerald now with a heavy heart, and she could not bear to think of the future. How empty would existence be without that joyous smile; above all, without that ardent passion! His love was wonderful; it surrounded her like a mystic fire and lifted her up so that she seemed to walk on air. But things always come too late or come by halves. Why should all her passion have been squandered and flung to the winds, so that now when a beautiful youth offered her his virgin heart she had nothing to give in exchange?

She was a little nervous at the meeting between him and Edward; she wondered what they would think of one another, and she watched – Gerald. Edward came in like a country wind, obstreperously healthy, jovial, large and rather bald. Miss Ley trembled lest he should knock her china over as he went round the room. He kissed her on one cheek and Bertha on the other.

'Well, how are you all? And this is my young cousin, eh? How are you? Pleased to meet you.'

He wrung Gerald's hand, towering over him, beaming good-naturedly; then sat on a chair much too small for him, which creaked and grumbled at his weight. There are few sensations more amusing to a woman than to look at the husband she has once adored and to think how very unnecessary he is; but it is apt to make conversation a little difficult.

Miss Ley soon carried Gerald off, thinking that husband and wife should enjoy a little of that isolation to which marriage had indissolubly doomed them. Bertha had been awaiting, with great discomfort, the necessary ordeal. She had nothing to tell Edward, and she was much afraid that he would be sentimental.

'Where are you staying?' she asked.

'Oh, I'm putting up at the "Inns of Court", I always go there.'

'I thought you might care to go to the theatre tonight. I've got a box so that Aunt Polly and Gerald can come too.'

'I'm game for anything you like.'

'You always were the best-tempered man,' said Bertha, smiling gently.

'You don't seem to care very much for my society all the same.'

Bertha looked up quickly. 'What makes you think that?'

'Well, you're a precious long time coming back to Court Leys,' he replied, laughing.

Bertha was relieved, for he was evidently not taking the matter seriously. She had not the courage to say that she meant never to return; the endless explanation, his wonder, the impossibility of making him understand, were more than she could bear.

'When are you coming back? We all miss you like anything.'

'Do you?' she said. 'I really don't know. We'll see after the season.'

'What? Aren't you coming for another couple of months?'

'I don't think Blackstable suits me very well. I'm always ill there.'

'Oh, nonsense. It's the finest air in England. Death-rate practically *nil*.'

'D'you think our life was very happy, Edward?'

She looked at him anxiously to see how he would take the tentative remark: but he was only astonished.

'Happy? Yes, rather. Of course we had our little tiffs. All people do. But they were chiefly at first; the road was a bit rough, and we hadn't got our tyres properly blown out. I'm sure I've got nothing to complain about.'

'That, of course, is the chief thing,' said Bertha.

'You look as well as anything now; I don't see why you shouldn't come back.'

'Well, we'll see later. We shall have plenty of time to talk it over.'

She was afraid to speak the words on the tip of her tongue; it would be easier by correspondence.

'I wish you'd give some fixed date, so that I could have things ready and tell people.'

'It depends upon Aunt Polly; I really can't say for certain; I'll write to you.'

They kept silence for a moment, and then an idea seized Bertha.

'What d'you say to going to the Natural History Museum? Don't you remember, we went there on our honeymoon?'

'Would *you* like to go?' asked Edward.

'I'm sure it would amuse you,' she replied.

Next day while Bertha was shopping with her husband, Gerald and Miss Ley sat alone.

'Are you very disconsolate without Bertha?' she asked.

'Utterly miserable!'

'That's very rude to me, dear boy.'

'I'm awfully sorry, but I can never be polite to more than one person at a time: and I've been using up all my good manners upon Mr Craddock.'

'I'm glad you like him,' replied Miss Ley, smiling.

'I don't!'

'He's a very worthy man.'

'If I hadn't seen Bertha for six months, I shouldn't take her off at once to see bugs.'

'Perhaps it was Bertha's suggestion.'

'She must find Mr Craddock precious dull if she prefers black-beetles and stuffed kangaroos.'

'You shouldn't draw such rapid conclusions, my friend.'

'D'you think she's fond of him?'

'My dear Gerald, what a question! Is it not her duty to love, honour and obey him?'

'If I were a woman I could never honour a man who was bald.'

'His locks are growing scanty; but he has a strong sense of duty.'

'It oozes out of him whenever he gets hot, like gum.'

'He is a County Councillor, and he makes speeches about the Union Jack, and he's virtuous.'

'I know that too. He simply reeks of the Ten Commandments; they stick out all over him, like almonds in a tipsy cake.'

'My dear Gerald, Edward is a model; he is the typical Englishman, as he flourishes in the country, upright and honest, healthy, dogmatic, moral and rather stupid. I esteem him enormously, and

211

I ought to like him much better than you, who are a disgraceful scamp.'

'I wonder why you don't.'

'Because I'm a wicked old woman; and I've learnt by long experience that people generally keep their vices to themselves, but insist on throwing their virtues in your face. And if you don't happen to have any of your own, you get the worst of the encounter.'

'I think that's what's so comfortable in you, Aunt Polly, that you're not obstreperously good. You're charity itself.'

'My dear Gerald,' said Miss Ley, putting up an admonishing forefinger, 'women are by nature spiteful and intolerant; when you find one who exercises charity, it proves that she wants it very badly herself.'

Miss Ley was glad that Edward could not stay more than two days for she was always afraid of surprising him. Nothing is more tedious than to talk with persons who treat your most ordinary remarks as startling paradoxes; and Edward suffered likewise from that passion for argument which is the bad talker's substitute for conversation. People who cannot talk are always proud of their dialectic; they want to modify your most obvious statements, and if you do no more than observe that the day is fine insist on arguing it out. Miss Ley's opinion on the subject was that no woman under forty was worth talking to at all, and a man only if he was an attentive listener. Bertha, in her husband's presence, had suffered singular discomfort; it had been such a constraint that she found it an effort to talk with him, and had to rack her brain for subjects of conversation. Her heart was lightened when she returned from Victoria after seeing him off, and it gave her a thrill of pleasure to hear Gerald jump up when she came in. He ran towards her with glowing eyes.

'Oh, I'm so glad. I've hardly had a chance of speaking to you these last two days.'

'We have the whole afternoon before us.'

'Let's go for a walk, shall we?'

Bertha agreed, and like two school-fellows they sallied out, wandering by the river in the sunlight and the warmth: the banks of the Thames about Chelsea have a pleasing trimness, a levity that is infinitely grateful after the staidness of the rest of London. The embankments in spite of their novelty recall the days when the huge city was a great, straggling village, when the sedan-chair was a means of locomotion, and ladies wore patches and hoops; when epigram was the fashion and propriety was not.

Presently, as they watched the gleaming water, a penny-steam-boat approaching the adjoining stage gave Bertha a sudden idea.

'Would you like to take me to Greenwich?' she cried. 'Aunt Polly's dining out; we can have dinner at the "Ship" and come back by train.'

'By Jove, it will be ripping.'

They bolted down the gangway and took their tickets; the boat started, and Bertha, panting, sank on a seat. She felt a little reckless, rather pleased with herself, and amused to see Gerald's unmeasured delight.

'I feel as if we were eloping,' she said with a laugh. 'I'm sure Aunt Polly will be dreadfully shocked.'

The boat went on, stopping every now and then to take people in. They came to the tottering wharves of Millbank, and then to the footstool turrets of St John's, the eight red blocks of St Thomas's Hospital and the Houses of Parliament. They passed Westminster Bridge and the massive strength of New Scotland Yard, the hotels and flats and public buildings that line the Albert Embankment, the Temple Gardens: and opposite this grandeur, on the Surrey side, were the dingy warehouses and factories of Lambeth. At London Bridge, Bertha found new interest in the varying scene; she stood in the bows with Gerald by her side, not speaking; they were happy in being near one another. The traffic became denser and their boat more crowded, with artisans, clerks, noisy girls, going eastwards to Rotherhithe and Deptford. Great merchantmen lay by the riverside or slowly made their way downstream under the Tower Bridge; and here the broad waters were crowded, with every imaginable craft, with lazy barges as picturesque, with their red sails, as the fishing-boats of Venice, with little tugs, puffing and blowing, with ocean tramps and with great liners. And as they passed in the penny-steamer, they had swift pictures of groups of naked boys, wallowing in the Thames mud, diving from the side of an anchored coal-barge.

A new atmosphere enveloped them now; grey warehouses that lined the river and the factories announced the commerce of a mighty nation, and the spirit of Charles Dickens gave to the passing scenes a fresh delight. How could they be prosaic when the great master had described them? An amiable stranger put names to the various places.

'Look, there's Wapping Old Stairs.'

And the words thrilled Bertha like poetry.

They passed innumerable wharves and docks, London Dock, John Cooper's Wharves and William Gibbs's Wharves (who are John Cooper and William Gibbs?), Limehouse Basin and West India Dock. Then with a great turn of the river they entered Limehouse Reach, and soon the noble lines of the Hospital, the immortal monument of Inigo Jones came in view, and they landed at Greenwich Pier.

31

THEY stood for a while on a terrace by the side of the hospital. Immediately below them a crowd of boys were bathing, animated and noisy, chasing and ducking one another, running to and fro with many cries and splashing in the mud, a fine picture of youthful movement.

The river was stretched more widely before them. The sun played on the yellow wavelets so that they shone like gold. A tug grunted past with a long tail of barges, and a huge East Indiaman glided noiselessly. In the late afternoon there was over the scene an old-time air of ease and spaciousness. The stately flood carried the mind away, so that the onlooker followed it with his thoughts, and went down, as it broadened, crowded with traffic; and presently a sea-smell reached the nostrils, and the river, ever majestic, flowed into the sea; and the ships went East and West and South, bearing their merchandise to the uttermost parts of the earth, to Southern sunnier lands of palm trees and dark-skinned peoples, bearing the name and wealth of England. The Thames became an emblem of the power of the mighty Empire, and those who watched felt strong in its strength and proud of their name and the undiminished glory of their race.

But Gerald looked sadly.

'In a very little while it must take me away from you, Bertha.'

'But think of the freedom and the vastness. Sometimes in England one seems oppressed by the lack of room; one can hardly breathe.'

'It's the thought of leaving you.'

She put her hand on his arm, caressingly; and then, to take him away from his sadness, suggested that they should stroll about.

Greenwich is half London, half country town, and the unexpected union gives it a peculiar fascination. If the wharves and docks of London still preserve the spirit of Charles Dickens, here it is the happy breeziness of Captain Marryat that fills the imagination. Those tales of a freer life and of the sea-breezes come back amid the grey streets still peopled with the vivid characters of *Poor Jack*. In the park, by the side of the labourers asleep on the grass, navvies from the neighbouring docks, and the boys who play a primitive cricket, may be seen fantastic old persons who would have delighted the grotesque pen of the seaman-novelist.

Bertha and Gerald sat beneath the trees, looking at the people till it grew late; and then wandered back to the 'Ship' for dinner. It amused them immensely to sit in the old coffee-room and be waited on by a black waiter, who extolled absurdly the various dishes.

'We won't be economical today,' cried Bertha: 'I feel utterly reckless. It takes all the fun away if one counts the cost.'

'Well, for once let us be foolish and forget the morrow.'

And they drank champagne, which to women and boys is the acme of dissipation and magnificence. Presently Gerald's green eyes flashed more brightly, and Bertha turned red before their ardent gaze.

'I shall never forget today, Bertha,' said Gerald. 'As long as I live I shall look back upon it with regret.'

'Oh, don't think that it must come to an end; or we shall both be miserable.'

'You are the most beautiful woman I've ever seen.'

Bertha laughed, showing her exquisite teeth, and was glad that her own knowledge told her she looked her best.

'But come on the terrace again and smoke there. We'll watch the sunset.'

They sat alone, and the sun was already sinking. The heavy western clouds were rich and vivid red, and over the river the bricks and mortar stood out in ink-black masses. It was a sunset that singularly fitted the scene, combining in audacious colour with the river's strength. The murky wavelets danced like little flames of fire.

Bertha and the youth sat silently, very happy, but with the regret gnawing at their hearts that their hour of joy would have no morrow.

The night fell, and one by one the stars shone out. The river flowed noiselessly, restfully, and around them twinkled the lights of the riverside towns. They did not speak, but Bertha knew the boy thought of her, and she wanted to hear him say so.

'What are you thinking of, Gerald?'

'What should I be thinking of but you, and that I must leave you?'

Bertha could not help the pleasure that his words gave her: it was so delicious to be really loved; and she knew his love was real. She half turned her face, so that he saw her dark eyes, darker in the night.

'I wish I hadn't made a fool of myself before,' he whispered. 'I feel it was all horrible; you've made me so ashamed.'

'Oh, Gerald, you're not remembering what I said the other day. I didn't mean to hurt you. I've been so sorry ever since.'

'I wish you loved me. Oh, Bertha, don't stop me now. I've kept it in so long, and I can't any more. I don't want to go away without telling you.'

'Oh, my dear Gerald, don't,' said Bertha, her voice almost breaking. 'It's no good, and we shall both be dreadfully unhappy. My dear, you don't know how much older I am than you. Even if I weren't married, it would be impossible for us to love one another.'

'But I love you with all my heart. I wish I could tell you what I feel.'

He seized her hands and pressed them; she made no effort to resist.

'Don't you love me at all?' he asked.

Bertha did not answer, and he bent nearer to look into her eyes. Then, letting her hands go, he flung his arms about her and pressed her to his heart.

'Bertha, Bertha!'

He kissed her passionately.

'Oh, Bertha, say you love me. It would make me so happy.'

'My dearest,' she whispered, and taking his head in her hands, kissed him.

But the kiss that she had received had fired her blood, and she could not resist now from doing as she had wished. She kissed him on the lips and on the eyes, and she kissed his curly hair. But she tore herself away from him, and sprang to her feet.

'What fools we are! Let's go to the station, Gerald; it's growing late.'

'Oh, Bertha, don't go yet,' he pleaded.

'We must. I daren't stay.'

He tried to take her in his arms again, begging her passionately to remain.

'Please don't, Gerald,' she said. 'Don't ask me; you make me too unhappy. Don't you see how hopeless it is? What is the use of our loving one another? You're going away in a week and we shall never meet again. And even if you were staying, I'm married, and I'm twenty-six and you're only nineteen. My dearest, we should only make ourselves ridiculous.'

'But I can't go away. What do I care if you're older than I? And it's nothing if you're married; you don't care for your husband and he doesn't care two straws for you.'

'How do you know?'

'Oh, I saw it. I felt so sorry for you.'

'You dear boy!' murmured Bertha, almost crying. 'I've been dreadfully unhappy. It's true Edward never loved me, and he didn't treat me very well. Oh, I can't understand how I ever cared for him.'

'I'm glad.'

'I would never allow myself to fall in love again. I suffered too much. I wonder I didn't kill myself.'

'But I love you with all my heart, Bertha; don't you see I love you? Oh, this isn't like what I've felt before; it's something quite new and different. I can't live without you, Bertha. Oh, let me stay.'

'It's impossible. Come away, dearest; we've been here too long.'

'Kiss me again.'

Bertha, half smiling, half in tears, put her arm round his neck and kissed the soft, boyish lips.

'You are good to me,' he whispered.

Then they walked to the station, silently; and eventually reached Chelsea. At the flat door Bertha held out her hand, and Gerald looked at her with a sadness that almost broke her heart; then he just touched her fingers and turned away.

But when Bertha was alone in her room she threw herself down on her bed and burst into tears. For she knew at last that she loved him. Gerald's kisses still burned on her lips and the touch of his hands was tremulous on her arms. Suddenly she knew that she had deceived herself; it was more than friendship that held her heart as in a vice, it was more than affection: it was eager, passionate love.

For a moment she was overjoyed, but quickly she remembered that she was married, that she was years older than he: to a boy of nineteen a woman of twenty-six must appear almost middle-aged. She seized a hand-mirror and looked at herself, she took it under the light so that the test might be more searching, and scrutinized her face for wrinkles and crow's-feet, the signs of departing youth.

'It's absurd,' she said. 'I'm making an utter fool of myself.'

Gerald was fickle; in a week he would be in love with some girl he met on the steamer. Well, what of it? He loved her now, with all his heart and with all his soul; he trembled with desire at her touch, and his passion was an agony that blanched his cheek. She could not mistake the eager longing of his eyes. Ah, that was the love she wanted, the love that kills and the love that engenders. She stood up, stretching out her arms in triumph, and in the empty room her lips formed the words:

'Come, my beloved, come, for I love you.'

But the morning brought an intolerable depression. Bertha saw then the futility of her love; her marriage, his departure, made it impossible; the disparity of age made it even grotesque. But she could not dull the aching of her heart, she could not stop her tears.

Gerald arrived about midday and found her alone. He approached almost timidly.

'You've been crying, Bertha.'

'I've been very unhappy,' she said. 'Oh, please, Gerald, forget our idiocy of yesterday. Don't say anything to me that I mustn't hear.'

'I can't help loving you.'

'Don't you see that it's all utter madness?'

'I can't leave you, Bertha. Let me stay.'

'It's impossible; you must go, now more than ever.'

They were interrupted by the appearance of Miss Ley. She began to talk; but to her surprise neither Bertha nor Gerald showed any vivacity.

'What is the matter with you both today?' she asked. 'You're usually attentive to my observations.'

'I'm tired,' said Bertha, 'and I have a headache.'

Miss Ley looked at Bertha more closely and fancied she had

been crying; Gerald also seemed profoundly miserable. Surely –
Then the truth dawned on her, and she could hardly conceal her
astonishment.

'Good Heavens!' she thought, 'I must have been blind. How
lucky he's going away in a week!'

Miss Ley now remembered a dozen occurrences that had escaped
her notice. She was confounded.

'Upon my word,' she thought, 'I don't believe you can put a
woman of seventy for five minutes in company of a boy of fourteen
without their getting into mischief.'

The week to Gerald and to Bertha passed with terrible quickness.
They scarcely had a moment alone, for Miss Ley, under the pretence of making much of her nephew, arranged little pleasure
parties, so that all three might be continually together.

'We must spoil you a little before you go; and the harm it does
you will be put right by the rocking of the boat.'

Bertha was in a torment. She knew that her love was impossible,
but she knew also that it was beyond control. She tried to argue
herself out of the infatuation, but without avail; Gerald was never
absent from her thoughts, and she loved him with her whole soul.
The temptation came to bid him stay. If he remained in England
they might give rein to their passion and let it die of itself. But she
dared not ask him. And his sorrow was more than she could bear;
she looked into his eyes, and seemed there to see the grief of a
breaking heart. It was horrible to think that he loved her and that
she must continually distress him. And then a more terrible temptation beset her. There is one way in which a woman can bind a man
to her for ever, there is one tie that is indissoluble; her very flesh
cried out, and she trembled at the thought that she could give
Gerald the inestimable gift of her body. Then he might go, but that
would have passed between them which could not be undone; they
might be separated by ten thousand miles, but there would always
be the bond between them. Her flesh cried out to his flesh, and the
desire was irresistible. How else could she prove to him her wonderful love? How else could she show her immeasurable gratitude?
The temptation was very strong, incessantly recurring, and she
was weak. It assailed her with all the violence of her fervid imagination. She drove it away with anger, she loathed it with all her heart;
but she could not stifle the appalling hope that it would be too
strong.

32

AT last Gerald had but one day more. A long-standing engagement of Bertha and Miss Ley forced him to take leave of them in the afternoon, for he was to start from London at seven in the morning.

'I'm dreadfully sorry that you can't spend your last evening with us,' said Miss Ley. 'But the Trevor-Jones will never forgive us if we don't go to their dinner-party.'

'Of course it was my fault for not finding out before when I sailed.'

'What are you going to do with yourself this evening, you wretch?'

'I'm going to have one last unholy bust.'

'I'm afraid you're very glad that for one night we can't look after you.'

In a little while Miss Ley, looking at her watch, told Bertha that it was time to dress. Gerald got up, and kissing Miss Ley thanked her for her kindness.

'My dear boy, please don't sentimentalize. And you're not going for ever. You're sure to make a mess of things and come back; the Leys always do.'

Then Gerald turned to Bertha and held out his hand.

'You've been awfully good to me,' he said, smiling; but there was in his eyes a steadfast look that seemed intent on making her understand something. 'We've had a ripping time together.'

'I hope you won't forget me entirely. We've certainly kept you out of mischief.'

Miss Ley watched them, admiring their composure. She thought they took the parting very well.

'I daresay it was nothing but a little flirtation and not very serious. Bertha's so much older than he and so sensible that she's most unlikely to have made a fool of herself.'

But she had to fetch the gifts that she had prepared for Gerald.

'Wait just a moment, Gerald,' she said. 'I want to fetch something.

She left the room, and immediately the boy bent forward.

'Don't go out tonight, Bertha. I must see you again.'

Before Bertha could reply, Miss Ley called from the hall.

'Good-bye,' said Gerald aloud.

'Good-bye. I hope you'll have a nice journey.'

'Here's a little present for you, Gerald,' said Miss Ley, when he was outside. 'You're dreadfully extravagant; and as that's the only virtue you have I feel I ought to encourage it. And if you want money at any time, I can always scrape together a tenner, you know.'

She put into his hand two fifty-pound notes, and then, as if she were ashamed of herself, bundled him out of doors. She went to her room; and as she had somewhat seriously inconvenienced herself for the next six months, for an entirely unworthy object, she began to feel remarkably pleased.

In an hour Miss Ley returned to the drawing-room to wait for Bertha, who presently came in, dressed, but ghastly pale.

'Oh, Aunt Polly, I simply can't come tonight. I've got a racking headache, I can scarcely see. You must tell them that I am sorry, but I'm too ill.'

She sank on a chair and put her hands to her forehead. Miss Ley lifted her eyebrows; the affair was evidently more serious than she thought. However, the danger was over; it would ease Bertha to stay at home and cry it out. She thought it brave of her niece even to have dressed.

'You'll get no dinner,' she said. 'There's nothing in the place.'

'Oh, I want nothing to eat.'

Miss Ley expressed her concern, and promising to make excuses, went away. Bertha started up when she heard the door close, and went to the window. She looked round for Gerald, fearing he might be already there: he was incautious and eager; but if Miss Ley saw him, it would be fatal. The hansom drove away and Bertha breathed more freely. She could not help it, she too felt that she must see him; if they had to part it could not be under Miss Ley's cold eyes.

She waited at the window, but he did not come. Why did he delay? He was wasting the precious minutes; it was past eight. She walked up and down the room and looked again, but still he was not in sight. She fancied that while she watched he would not come, and forced herself to read, but how could she? Again she looked out of the window; and this time Gerald was there. He stood in the porch of the opposite house, looking up; and immediately he saw her crossed the street. She went to the door and opened it gently.

He slipped in, and on tip-toe they entered the drawing-room.

'Oh, it's so good of you,' he said. 'I couldn't leave you like that. I knew you'd stay.'

'Why have you been so long? I thought you were never coming.'

'I dared not risk it before. I was afraid something might happen to stop Aunt Polly.'

'I said I had a headache. I dressed so that she might suspect nothing.'

The night was falling, and they sat together in the dimness. Gerald took her hands and kissed them.

'This week has been awful. I've never had the chance of saying a word to you. My heart has been breaking.'

'My dearest.'

'I wondered if you were sorry I was going.'

She looked at him and tried to smile; she could not trust herself to speak.

'Every day I thought you would tell me to stop, and you never did, and now it's too late. Oh, Bertha, if you loved me you wouldn't send me away.'

'I think I love you too much. Don't you see it's better that we should part?'

'I daren't think of tomorrow.'

'You are so young; in a little while you will fall in love with someone else.'

'I love you. Oh, I wish I could make you believe me. Bertha, Bertha, I can't leave you. I love you too much.'

'For God's sake don't talk like that. It's hard enough to bear already; don't make it harder.'

The night had fallen, and through the open window the summer breeze came in, and the softness of the air was like a kiss. They sat side by side in silence, the boy holding Bertha's hand; they could not speak, for words were powerless to express what was in their hearts. But presently a strange intoxication seized them and the mystery of passion wrapped them about invisibly. Bertha felt the trembling of Gerald's hand, and it passed to hers. She shuddered and tried to withdraw, but he would not let go. The silence became suddenly intolerable. Bertha tried to speak, but her throat was dry, and she could utter no word.

A weakness came to her limbs and her heart beat painfully. Her eyes met Gerald's, and they both looked aside, as if caught in some crime. Bertha began to breathe more quickly. Gerald's intense desire burned itself into her soul; she dared not move. She tried to implore God's help, but could not. The temptation, which all the week had terrified her, returned with double force, the temptation that she abhorred, but that she had a horrible longing not to resist.

And now she asked what it mattered. Her strength was dwindling; Gerald had but to say a word. And now she wished him to say the word; he loved her and she loved him. She gave way, she no longer wished to resist, flesh called to flesh, and there was no force on earth more powerful. Her whole frame was quivering with passion. She turned her face to Gerald, she leant towards him with parted lips.

'Bertha!' he whispered, and they were nearly in one another's arms.

But a fine sound pierced the silence; they started back and listened. They heard a key being put into the front door, and the door being opened.

'Take care,' whispered Bertha.

'It's Aunt Polly.'

Bertha pointed to the electric switch and, understanding, Gerald turned on the light. He looked round instinctively for some way to escape, but Bertha, with a woman's quick invention, sprang to the door and flung it open.

'Is that you, Aunt Polly?' she cried. 'How fortunate you came back! Gerald is here to bid us definitely good-bye.'

'He makes as many farewells as a *prima-donna*,' said Miss Ley. She came in, breathless, with two spots of red on her cheeks.

'I thought you wouldn't mind if I came back here to wait till you returned,' said Gerald. 'And I found Bertha.'

'How funny that our thoughts should have been identical,' said Miss Ley. 'It occurred to me that you might come, and so I hurried home as quickly as I could.'

'You're quite out of breath,' said Bertha.

Miss Ley sank on a chair exhausted. As she was eating her fish and talking to a neighbour, it suddenly dawned upon her that Bertha's indisposition was assumed.

'Oh, what a fool I am! They've hoodwinked me as if I were a child. Good Heavens, what are they doing now?'

The dinner seemed interminable, but immediately afterwards she took leave of her astonished hostess and gave the cabman orders to drive furiously. She arrived, inveighing against the deceitfulness of the human race. She had never run up the stairs so quickly.

'How is your headache, Bertha?'

'Thanks, it's much better. Gerald has driven it away.'

This time Miss Ley's good-bye to the precocious youth was chilly; she was devoutly thankful that his boat sailed next morning.

'I'll show you out, Gerald,' said Bertha. 'Don't trouble, Aunt Polly, you must be dreadfully tired.'

They went into the hall, and Gerald put on his coat. He stretched out his hands to Bertha, without speaking; but she, with a glance at the drawing-room door, beckoned Gerald to follow her and slid out of the front door. There was no one on the stairs. She flung her arms around his neck and pressed her lips to his. She did not try to hide her passion now, she clasped him to her heart, their very souls flew to their lips and mingled. Their kiss was rapture, madness; it was an ecstasy beyond description, complete surrender; their senses were powerless to contain their pleasure. Bertha felt herself about to die. In the bliss, in the agony her spirit failed and she tottered; Gerald pressed her more closely to him.

But there was a sound of someone coming upstairs. She tore herself away.

'Good-bye for ever,' she whispered, and slipping in, closed the door between them.

She sank down half-fainting, but in fear struggled to her feet and dragged herself to her room. Her cheeks were glowing and her limbs trembled. Oh, now it was too late for prudence. What did she care for her marriage? What did she care that he was younger than she? She loved him, she loved him insanely; the present was there with its infinite joy, and if the future brought misery it was worth suffering. She could not let him go, he was hers; she stretched out her arms to take him in her embrace. She would surrender everything; she would bid him stay; she would follow him to the end of the earth. It was too late now for reason.

She walked up and down her room excitedly. She looked at the door; she had a mad desire to go to him now, to abandon everything for his sake. Her honour, her happiness, her station, were only precious because she could sacrifice them for him. He was her life and her love, he was her body and her soul. She listened at the door. Miss Ley would be watching, and she dared not go. Miss Ley knew or suspected.

'I'll wait,' said Bertha.

She tried to sleep, but could not. The thought of Gerald distracted her. She dozed, and his presence became more distinct. He seemed to be in the room, and she cried: 'At last, my dearest, at last!'

She woke and stretched out her hands to him; she could not realize that she had dreamt.

The day came, dim and grey at first, but lightening with the brilliant summer morning; the sun shone in the windows and the sunbeams danced in the room. Now the moments were very few, she must make up her mind quickly; and the sunbeams promised life and happiness and the glory of the unknown. Oh, what a fool she was to waste her life, to throw away her chance of happiness! How weak she was not to grasp the love thrown in her way! She thought of Gerald packing his things, getting off, the train speeding through the summer country. Her love was irresistible. She sprang up, and bathed, and dressed. She put her jewels and one or two things in a tiny handbag. It was past six; she slipped out of the room and made her way downstairs. The street was empty as in the night, but the sky was blue and the air fresh and sweet. She took a long breath and felt marvellously gay. She walked till she found a cab, and told the driver to go quickly to Euston. The cab crawled along, and she was in an agony of impatience. Supposing she arrived too late? She told the man to hurry.

The Liverpool train was full. Bertha walked up the crowded platform and quickly saw Gerald. He sprang towards her.

'Bertha, you've come. I felt certain you wouldn't let me go without seeing you.'

He took her hands and looked at her with eyes full of love.

'I'm so glad you've come so that I can say what I wanted. I meant to write to you. I shall always be grateful. I wanted to tell you how sorry I am that I've caused you unhappiness. I almost ruined your life. I was selfish and brutal; I forgot how much you had to lose. Of course I see now that it is all for the best that I'm going away. Will you forgive me?'

Bertha looked at him. She wanted to say that she adored him

and would accompany him to the world's end, but the words stuck in her mouth. An inspector came along to look at the tickets.

'Is the lady going?' he asked.

'No,' said Gerald; and then when the man had passed on: 'You won't forget me, Bertha, will you? You won't think badly of me?'

Bertha's heart was breaking. He had only to ask her once more to go with him, and she would go. But he thought her refusal of the night before was final, and in his misery saw the obstacles that passion now hid from her.

'Gerald,' she murmured.

He had but to ask. She dared not speak. Did he want her? Was he repenting already? Was his love already on the wane? Oh, why did he not repeat that he adored her and say once more that he could not live without her? Bertha tried to make herself speak. She could not.

'Take your seats, please. Take your seats, please.'

A guard ran along the platform: 'Jump in, sir.'

'Right behind!'

'Good-bye,' said Gerald.

He kissed her quickly and jumped into the carriage.

'Right away!'

The guard blew his whistle and waved a flag, and the train puffed slowly out of the station.

33

MISS LEY was alarmed when she got up and found that Bertha had flown.

'Upon my word, I think that Providence is behaving scandalously. Am I not a harmless middle-aged woman who minds her own business? What have I done to deserve these shocks?'

She suspected that her niece had gone to the station; but the train started at seven, and it was ten. She started as it occurred to her that Bertha might have – eloped; and like a swarm of abominable little demons came thoughts of the scenes she must undergo if such were the case – the writing of the news to Edward, his consternation, the comfort that she must administer, and the fury of Gerald's father, the hysterics of his mother.

'She can't have done anything so stupid,' she cried in distraction. 'But if women can make fools of themselves, they always do.'

Miss Ley was extraordinarily relieved when at last she heard Bertha come in and go to her room.

Bertha for a long time had stood motionless on the platform, staring haggardly before her. She was stupefied. The excitement of the previous hours was followed by an utter blankness. Gerald was speeding to Liverpool, and she was still in London. She walked out of the station and turned towards Chelsea. The streets were endless and she was already tired, but she dragged herself along. She did not know the way, and wandered hopelessly, scarcely conscious. In Hyde Park she sat down to rest, feeling utterly exhausted; but the weariness of her body relieved the aching of her heart. She walked on after a while – it never occurred to her to take a cab – and eventually came to Eliot Mansions. The sun had grown hot and burned the crown of her head. Bertha crawled upstairs to her room, and throwing herself on the bed burst into tears of bitter anguish. She wept desperately.

'Oh, I daresay he was as worthless as the other,' she cried at last.

Miss Ley sent to inquire if she would eat, but Bertha had now really a bad headache, and could touch nothing. All day she spent in agony; she could not think; she was in despair. Sometimes she reproached herself for denying Gerald when he had asked her to let him stay; she had wilfully let go the happiness that was within her reach; and then, with a revulsion of feeling, she repeated that Gerald was worthless and thanked Heaven that she had escaped the danger. The dreary hours passed, and when the night came Bertha scarcely had strength to undress, and not till the morning did she get rest. But the early post brought a letter from Edward, repeating his wish that she should return to Court Leys. She read it listlessly.

'Perhaps it's the best thing to do,' she groaned.

She hated London now, and the flat; the rooms must be horribly bare without the joyous presence of Gerald. To return to Court Leys seemed the only course left to her, and there at least she would have quiet and solitude. She thought almost with longing of the desolate shore, the marshes and the dreary sea; she wanted rest and silence. But if she went she had better go at once; to stay in London was only to prolong her woe.

Bertha got up and dressed, and went into Miss Ley. Her face

was deathly pale, and her eyes were heavy and red with weeping. She made no attempt to hide her distress.

'I'm going down to Court Leys today, Aunt Polly. I think it's the best thing I can do.'

'Edward will be pleased to see you.'

'I think he will.'

Miss Ley hesitated, looking at Bertha.

'You know, Bertha,' she said after a pause, 'in this world it is very difficult to know what to do. One struggles to know good from evil, but really they're often so very much alike. I always think those people fortunate who are content to stand, without question, by the Ten Commandments, knowing exactly how to conduct themselves and propped up by the hope of Paradise on the one hand and by the fear of a cloven-footed devil with pincers on the other. But we who answer *Why* to the crude *Thou shalt not* are like sailors on a wintry sea without a compass: reason and instinct say one thing, and convention says another; but the worst of it is that one's conscience has been reared on the Decalogue and fostered on hell-fire, and one's conscience has the last word. I daresay it's cowardly, but it's certainly discreet, to take it into consideration; it's like lobster salad: it's not immoral to eat it, but you will very likely have indigestion. One has to be very sure of oneself to go against the ordinary view of things; and if one isn't, perhaps it's better not to run any risks, but just to walk along the same secure old road as the common herd. It's not exhilarating, it's not brave, and it's rather dull; but it's eminently safe.'

Bertha sighed, but did not answer.

'You'd better tell Jane to pack your boxes,' said Miss Ley. 'Shall I wire to Edward?'

When Bertha had at last started, Miss Ley began to think.

'I wonder if I've done right,' she murmured, uncertain as ever. She was sitting on the piano-stool, and as she meditated, her finger passed idly over the keys. Presently her ears detected the beginning of a well-known melody, and almost unconsciously she began to play the air of Rigoletto. *La Donna è mobile*, the words ran, *Qual piuma al vento*. Miss Ley smiled: 'The fact is that few women can be happy with only one husband. I believe that the only solution of the marriage question is legalized polyandry.'

In the train at Victoria Bertha remembered with relief that the cattle-market was held at Tercanbury that day, and Edward would not come home till the evening; she would have the opportunity to settle herself at Court Leys without fuss or bother. Full of her painful thoughts, the journey passed quickly, and Bertha was surprised to find herself at Blackstable. She got out, wondering whether Edward would have sent the trap to meet her, but to her extreme surprise Edward himself was on the platform, and running up, helped her out of the carriage.

'Here you are at last!' he cried.

'I didn't expect you,' said Bertha. 'I thought you'd be at Tercanbury.'

'I got your wire just as I was starting, so of course I didn't go.'

'I'm sorry I prevented you.'

'Why? I'm jolly glad. You didn't think l was going to the cattle-market when my missus was coming home?'

She looked at him with astonishment; his honest, red face glowed with the satisfaction he felt at seeing her.

'By Jove, this is ripping!' he said. 'I'm tired of being a grass widower, I can tell you.'

They came to Corstal Hill, and he walked the horse.

'Just look behind you,' he said in an undertone. 'Notice anything?'

'What?'

'Look at Parker's hat.'

Parker was the footman. Bertha looked again and observed a cockade.

'What d'you think of that, eh?' Edward was almost exploding with laughter. 'I was elected Chairman of the Urban District Council yesterday; that means I'm *ex officio* J.P. So as soon as I heard you were coming I bolted off and got a cockade.'

When they reached Court Leys he helped Bertha out of the trap quite tenderly. She was taken aback to find the tea ready, flowers in the drawing-room, and everything possible done to make her comfortable.

'Are you tired?' asked Edward. 'Lie down on the sofa, and I'll give you your tea.'

He waited on her and pressed her to eat, and was, in fact, unceasing in his attentions.

'By Jove, I am glad to see you here again!'

His pleasure was obvious, and Bertha was touched.

229

'Are you too tired to come for a little walk in the garden? I want to show you what I've done for you, and just now the place is looking its best.'

He put a shawl round her shoulders, so that the evening air might not hurt her, and insisted on giving her his arm.

'Now, look here; I've planted rose trees outside the drawing-room window; I thought you'd like to see them when you sat in your favourite place, reading.'

He took her further to a place that offered a fine view of the sea.

'I've put a bench here between those two trees, so that you can sit down sometimes and look at the view.'

'It's very kind of you to be so thoughtful. Shall we sit there now?'

'Oh, I think you'd better not. There's a good deal of dew, and I don't want you to catch cold.'

For dinner Edward had ordered the dishes that he knew Bertha preferred, and he laughed joyously as she expressed her pleasure.

Afterwards when she lay down on the sofa he arranged the cushions for her. No one could have been kinder or more thoughtful.

'Ah, my dear,' she thought, 'if you'd been half as kind three years ago you might have kept my love.'

She wondered whether absence had increased his affection, or whether it was she who had changed. Was he not as unchanging as a rock? She knew that she was as unstable as water and variable as the summer winds. Had he always been kind and considerate; and had she, demanding a passion that it was not in him to feel, been blind to his deep tenderness? Expecting nothing from him now, she was astonished to find he had so much to offer. But she felt sorry if he loved her, for she could give him nothing in return but complete indifference; she was even surprised to find herself so utterly callous.

At bedtime she bade him good night, and kissed his cheek.

'I've had the spare bedroom arranged for me,' she said.

'Oh, I didn't know,' he replied; then, after glancing at her: 'I don't want to do anything that is disagreeable to you.'

There was no change in Blackstable; Bertha's friends still lived, for the death-rate of that fortunate place was their pride, and they could do nothing to increase it. Arthur Branderton had married a

230

pretty, fluffy-haired girl, nicely bred and properly insignificant; but the only result of that was to give his mother a new topic of conversation. Bertha, resuming her old habits, had difficulty in realizing that she had ever been away. She set herself to forget Gerald, and was pleased to find the recollection of him not too importunate. A sentimentalist turned cynic has observed that a woman is only passionately devoted to her first lover, afterwards it is love itself of which she is enamoured; and certainly the wounds of second and subsequent attachments heal easily. Bertha was devoutly grateful to Miss Ley for her opportune return on Gerald's last night; she shuddered to think of what might have happened, and was thoroughly ashamed of the madness that had driven her to Euston intent upon the most dreadful courses. She could hardly forgive Gerald that, on his account, she had almost made herself ridiculous; she saw that he was a fickle boy, prepared to philander with every woman he met, and told herself scornfully that she had never really cared for him.

But in two weeks Bertha received a letter from America, forwarded by Miss Ley. She turned white as she recognized the handwriting; the old emotions came tumbling back, she thought of Gerald's green eyes, and of his boyish lips, and she felt sick with love. She looked at the address and at the post-mark, and then put the letter down.

'I told him not to write,' she murmured.

A feeling of anger seized her that the sight of a letter from Gerald should bring her such pain. She almost hated him now; and yet with all her heart she wished to kiss the paper and every word that was written upon it. But the violence of her emotion made her set her teeth, as it were, against giving way.

'I won't read it,' she said.

She wanted to prove to herself that she had strength, and this temptation at least she was determined to resist. Bertha lit a candle and took the letter in her hand to burn it, but then put it down again. That would settle the matter too quickly, and she wanted rather to prolong the trial so as to receive full assurance of her fortitude. With a strange pleasure at the pain she was preparing for herself, Bertha placed the letter on the chimney-piece of her room, prominently, so that whenever she went in or out she could not fail to see it. Wishing to punish herself her desire was to make the temptation as distressing as possible.

She watched the unopened envelope for a month, and sometimes the craving to open it was almost irresistible; sometimes she awoke in the middle of the night, thinking of Gerald, and told herself that she must know what he said. Ah, how well she could imagine it! He vowed he loved her, and he spoke of the kiss she had given him on that last day, and he said it was dreadfully hard to be without her. Bertha looked at the letter, clenching her hands so as not to seize it and tear it open; she had to hold herself forcibly back from covering it with kisses. But at last she conquered all desire; she was able to look at the handwriting indifferently; she scrutinized her heart and found no trace of emotion. The trial was complete.

'Now it can go,' she said.

Again she lit a candle, and held the letter to the flame till it was all consumed; and she gathered up the ashes, putting them in her hand, and blew them out of the window. She felt that by that act she had finished with the whole thing, and Gerald was definitely gone out of her life.

But rest did not come to Bertha's troubled soul. At first she found her life fairly tolerable; but she had now no emotions to distract her, and the routine of the day was unvarying. The weeks passed and the months; the winter came upon her, more dreary than she had ever known it. The country became insufferably dull. The days were grey and cold, and the clouds so low that she could almost touch them. The broad fields, which had once offered such wonderful emotions, were now only tedious, and all the rural sights sank into her mind with a pitiless monotony; day after day, month after month, she saw the same things. She was bored to death.

Sometimes Bertha wandered to the sea-shore and looked across the desolate waste of water. She longed to travel as her eyes and her mind travelled, South, South to the azure skies, to the lands of beauty and sunshine beyond the greyness. Fortunately she did not know that she was looking almost directly North, and that if she really went on and on as she desired, she would reach no Southern lands of pleasure, but the North Pole.

She walked along the beach, among the countless shells; and not content with present disquietude, tortured herself with anticipation of the future. She could only imagine that it would bring an increase of this frightful ennui, and her head ached as she looked forward to the dull monotony of her life. She went home, entering the house with aversion as she thought of the tiresome evening.

Bertha was seized with restlessness. She would walk up and down her room in a fever of almost physical agony. She would sit at the piano, and cease playing after half a dozen bars; music seemed as futile as everything else. She seemed to have done everything so often. She tried to read, but could hardly bring herself to begin a new volume; the very sight of the printed pages was distasteful; the books of information told her things she did not want to know, the novels related deeds of persons about whom she could not raise the least interest. She read a few pages and threw the book down in disgust. Then she went out again – anything seemed preferable to what she was actually doing. She walked rapidly, but the motion, the country, the very atmosphere about her, were wearisome, and almost immediately she returned home.

Bertha was forced to take the same walks day after day, and the deserted roads, the trees, the hedges, the fields, impressed themselves on her mind with a dismal insistence. When she was driven to go out merely for exercise, she walked a certain number of miles, trying to get it over quickly. The winds of the early year blew that season more persistently than ever, and they impeded her steps, and chilled her to the bone.

Sometimes Bertha paid visits, and the restraint she had to put upon herself relieved her for the moment, but as soon as the door was closed behind her she felt more desperately bored than ever.

Yearning suddenly for society, she would send out invitations for some function, then, as it approached, felt it inexpressibly irksome to make preparations, and she loathed and abhorred her guests. For a long time she refused to see anyone, protesting her feeble health; and sometimes in the solitude she thought she would go mad. She turned to prayer as the only refuge of those who cannot act, but she only half believed, and therefore found no comfort. She accompanied Miss Glover on her district visiting, but she disliked the poor and hated their inane chatter.

Her head ached, and she put her hands to her temples, pressing them painfully; she felt she could take great wisps of her hair and tear it out. She threw herself on her bed and wept in the agony of boredom. Edward once found her thus and asked what was the matter.

'Oh, my head aches so that I feel I could kill myself.'

He sent for Ramsay, but Bertha knew that the doctor's remedies were useless. She imagined that there was no remedy for her ill – not even time – no remedy but death. She knew the terrible distress of waking in the morning with the thought that still another day must be gone through, she knew the relief of bedtime, with the thought that she would enjoy a few hours of unconsciousness. She was racked with the imagination of the future's frightful monotony: night would follow day, and day would follow night, the months passing one by one and the years slowly, slowly. They say that life is short: to those who look back perhaps it is; but to those who look forward it is long, horribly long, endless. Sometimes Bertha felt it impossible to endure. She prayed that she might fall asleep at night and never awake. How happy must be the lives of those people who can look forward to eternity! To Bertha the idea of living for ever and ever was merely ghastly; she desired nothing but the long rest, the rest of an endless sleep, the dissolution into nothing.

Once in her depression she wished to kill herself, but she was afraid. People say it requires no courage to commit suicide. Fools! They cannot realize the horror of the needful preparations, the anticipation of the pain, the terrible fear that one may regret when it is too late, when life is ebbing away. And there is the dread of the Unknown; above all, the awful fear of hell-fire. It is absurd and revolting, but so ingrained that no effort is sufficient entirely to destroy it; there is still, notwithstanding reason and argument, the fear that it may be true, the fear of a jealous God who will doom one to eternal punishment.

34

BUT if the human soul, or the heart, or the mind – call it what you will – is an instrument upon which countless melodies may be played, it is capable of responding to none for very long. Time dulls the most exquisite emotions and softens the most heart-rending grief; the story is told of a philosopher who sought to console a woman in distress by the account of tribulations akin to hers, and upon losing his only son was sent by her a list of kings similarly bereaved. He read it, acknowledged its correctness, but wept none the less. Three months later the philosopher and the lady were surprised to find one another quite gay, and they erected a fine statue to Time, with the inscription: *A celui qui console*.

When Bertha vowed that life had lost all savour, that her ennui was unending, she exaggerated as usual; and almost grew angry on discovering that existence could be more supportable than she thought.

One gets used to all things. It is only very misanthropic persons who pretend that they cannot accustom themselves to the stupidity of their fellows; after a while one gets hardened to the most desperate bores, and monotony even ceases to be quite monotonous. Accommodating herself to circumstances, Bertha found life less tedious; it was a calm river, and presently she came to the conclusion that it ran more easily without the cascades and waterfalls, the eddies, whirlpools and rocks, that had disturbed its course. The man who can still humbug himself has before him a future not lacking in brightness.

The summer brought a certain variety, and Bertha found amusement in things that before had never interested her. She went to sheltered parts to see if favourite wild flowers had begun to blow: her love of liberty made her prefer the hedge-roses to the pompous blooms of the garden, the buttercups and daisies of the field to the prim geraniums, the calceolarias. Time fled, and she was surprised to find the year pass imperceptibly.

She began to read with greater zest, and in her favourite seat, on the sofa by the window, spent long hours of pleasure. She read as fancy prompted her, without a plan, because she wanted to, and not because she ought. She obtained pleasure by contrasting different writers, getting emotions out of the gravity of one and the frivolity of the next. She went from the latest novel to Orlando Furioso, from the Euphues of John Lyly (most entertaining and whimsical of books) to the tender melancholy of Verlaine. With a lifetime before her, the length of books was no hindrance, and she started boldly upon the eight volumes of the *Decline and Fall*, upon the many tomes of St Simon; and she never hesitated to put them aside after a hundred pages.

Bertha found reality tolerable when it was merely a background, a foil to the fantastic happenings of old books: she looked at the green trees, and the song of birds mingled agreeably with her thoughts, still occupied with the Dolorous Knight of La Mancha, with Manon Lescaut or the joyous band that wanders through the *Decameron*. With greater knowledge came greater curiosity, and she forsook the broad high-roads of literature for the mountain pathways of some obscure poet, for the bridle-track of the Spanish picaroon. She found unexpected satisfaction in the half-forgotten masterpieces of the past, in poets not quite divine whom fashion had left on one side, in the playwrights, novelists and essayists whose remembrance lives only with the bookworm. It is a relief sometimes to look away from the bright sun of perfect achievement; and the writers who appealed to their age and not to posterity have by contrast a subtle charm. Undazzled by their splendour, one may discern more easily their individualities and the spirit of their time; they have pleasant qualities not always found among their betters, and there is even a certain pathos in their incomplete success.

In music also Bertha developed a taste for the half-known, the half-archaic. It suited the Georgian drawing-room, with its old pictures, with its Chippendale and chintz, to play the simple melodies of Couperin and Rameau; the rondos, the gavottes, the sonatinas in powder and patch that delighted the rococo lords and ladies of a past century.

Living away from the present, in an artificial paradise, Bertha was happy. She found indifference to the whole world a trusty armour: life was easy without love or hate, hope or despair, without ambition, desire of change or tumultuous passion. So bloom the flowers; unconscious, uncaring, the bud bursts from the enclosing leaf, and opens to the sunshine, squanders its perfume to the breeze, and there is none to see its beauty; and then it dies.

Bertha found it possible to look back upon the past with something like amusement: it seemed now melodramatic to have loved the simple Edward with such violence; she was even able to smile at the contrast between her vivid expectations and the flat reality. Gerald was a pleasantly sentimental memory, she did not want to see him again, but she thought of him often, idealizing him until he became a mere figure in one of her favourite books. Her winter in Italy also formed the motive of some of her most delightful thoughts, and she determined never to spoil the impression by another visit. She had advanced a good deal in the science of life when she realized that pleasure came by surprise, that happiness was a spirit that descended unawares, and seldom when it was sought.

Edward had fallen into a life of such activity that his time was entirely taken up. He had added largely to the Ley estate, and, with the second-rate man's belief that you must do everything yourself to have it well done, he kept the farms under his immediate supervision. He was an important member of all the rural bodies: he was on the School Board, on the Board of Guardians, on the County Council; he was Chairman of the Urban District Council, president of the local Cricket Club, and of the Football Club; patron of the Blackstable Regatta, on the committee of the Tercanbury Dog Show, and an enthusiastic supporter of the Mid-Kent Agricultural Exhibition. He was a pillar of the Blackstable Conservative Association, a magistrate, and a churchwarden. Finally, he was an ardent Freemason, and flew over Kent to attend the meetings of the half-dozen lodges of which he was a member. But the work did not disturb him.

'Lord bless you,' he said, 'I love work. You can't give me too much. If there's anything to be done, come to me and I'll do it, and say thank you for giving me the chance.'

Edward had always been even-tempered, but now his good nature was angelic. It became a by-word. His success was according to his deserts, and to have him concerned in any matter was an excellent insurance. He was always jovial and gay, contented with himself and with the world at large; he was a model squire, landlord, farmer, Conservative, man, Englishman. He did everything thoroughly, and his energy was such that he made a point of putting into every concern twice as much work as it really needed. He was busy from morning to night (as a rule quite unnecessarily), and he gloried in it.

'It shows I'm an excellent woman,' said Bertha to Miss Glover. 'to support his virtues with equanimity.'

'My dear, I think you ought to be very proud and happy. He's an example to the whole country. If he were my husband, I should be grateful to God.'

'I have much to be thankful for,' murmured Bertha.

Since he let her go her own way and she was only too pleased that

237

he should go his, there was really no possibility of difference, and Edward, wise man, came to the conclusion that he had effectively tamed his wife. He thought, with good-humoured scorn, that he had been quite right when he likened women to chickens, animals which, to be happy, required no more than a good run, well fenced in, where they could scratch about to their heart's content.

'Feed 'em regularly, and let 'em cackle; and there you are!'

It is always satisfactory when experience proves the hypothesis that you formed in your youth.

One year, remembering by accident their wedding day, Edward gave his wife a bracelet; and feeling benevolent in consequence, and having dined well, he patted her hand and said:

'Time does fly, doesn't it?'

'I have heard people say so,' she replied, smiling.

'Well, who'd have thought we'd been married so many years; it doesn't seem above eighteen months to me. And we've got on very well, haven't we?'

'My dear Edward, you are such a model husband. It quite embarrasses me sometimes.'

'Ha, that's a good one! But I can say this for myself, I do try to do my duty. Of course at first we had our little tiffs, people have to get used to one another, and one can't expect to have all plain sailing just at once. But for years now – well, ever since you went to Italy, I think – we've been as happy as the day is long, haven't we?'

'Yes, dear.'

'When I look back at the little rumpuses we used to have, upon my word, I wonder what they were all about.'

'So do I.' And this Bertha said quite truthfully.

'I suppose it was just the weather.'

'I daresay.'

'Ah, well, all's well that ends well.'

'My dear Edward, you're a philosopher.'

'I don't know about that, but I think I'm a politician which reminds me that I've not read about the new men-of-war in today's paper. What I've been agitating about for years is more ships and more guns. I'm glad to see the Government have taken my advice at last.'

'It's very satisfactory, isn't it? It will encourage you to persevere. And of course it's well to know that the Cabinet read your speeches in the *Blackstable Times*.'

'I think it would be a good sight better for the country if those in power paid more attention to provincial opinions. It's men like me who really know the feeling of the nation. You might get me the paper, will you? It's in the dining-room.'

It seemed quite natural to Edward that Bertha should wait upon him: it was the duty of a wife. She handed him the *Standard*, and he began to read; he yawned once or twice.

'Lord, I am sleepy.'

Presently he could not keep his eyes open, the paper dropped from his hand and he sank back in his chair with his legs out-stretched and his hands resting comfortably on his stomach; his head lolled to one side and his jaw dropped; he began to snore. Bertha read. After a while he woke with a start.

'Bless me, I do believe I've been asleep,' he cried. 'Well, I'm dead beat; I think I shall go to bed. I suppose you won't come up yet?'

'Not just yet.'

'Well, don't stay up too late, there's a good girl; it's not good for you; and put the lights out properly when you come.'

She turned her cheek to him, which he kissed, stifling a yawn; then rolled upstairs.

'There's one advantage in Edward,' murmured Bertha. 'No one could accuse him of being uxorious.'

Mariage à la Mode.

Bertha's solitary walk was to the sea. The shore between Black-stable and the mouth of the Thames was very wild. At distant intervals were the long, low buildings of the coastguard stations, and the prim gravel walk, the neat railings came as a surprise, but they made the surrounding desolation more forlorn. One could walk for miles without meeting a soul, and the country spread out from the sea low and flat and marshy. The beach was strewn with countless shells, and they crumbled underfoot, and here and there were great banks of seaweed and bits of wood and rope, the jetsam of a thousand tides. In one spot, a few yards out at sea, high and dry at low water, were the remains of an old hulk, whose wooden ribs stood out weirdly like the skeleton of some huge sea-beast. And then all round was the grey sea, with never a ship nor even a fishing-smack in sight. In winter it was as if a spirit of loneliness, like a mystic shroud, had descended on the shore and the desert waters.

There in the melancholy, in the dreariness, Bertha found a bitter fascination. The sky was a lowering cloud, the wind tore along shouting and screaming and whistling; there was panic in the turbulent sea, murky and yellow; the waves leaped up, one at the other's heels, and beat down on the beach with an angry roar. It was desolate, desolate; the sea was so merciless that the very sight appalled one: it was a wrathful power, beating forwards, ever wrathfully beating forwards, roaring with pain when the chains that bound it wrenched it back; and after each desperate effort it shrank with a yell of pain. And the seagulls swayed above the waves in their disconsolate flight, rising and falling with the wind.

Bertha loved the calm of winter, when the sea-mist and the mist of heaven are one, when the sea is silent and heavy, and the solitary gull flies screeching over the grey waters, screeching mournfully. She loved the calm of summer, when the sky is cloudless and infinite. Then she spent long hours, lying at the water's edge, delighted with the solitude and the peace of her heart. The sea, placid as a lake, unmoved by the slightest ripple, was a looking-glass reflecting the glory of heaven, and it turned to fire when the sun sank in the west; it was a sea of molten copper, shining, so that the eyes were dazzled. A troop of seagulls slept on the water; there were hundreds of them, motionless, silent; one arose now and then, and flew for a moment with heavy wing, and sank down, and all was still.

Once the coolness was so tempting that Bertha could not resist it. Timidly, rapidly she slipped off her clothes, and looking round to see that there was really no one in sight, stepped in; the wavelets about her feet made her shiver a little, and then with a splash, stretching out her arms, she ran forward, and half fell, half dived into the water. Now it was delightful; she rejoiced in the freedom of her limbs; it was an unknown pleasure to swim unhampered by a bathing-dress. It gave her a wonderful sense of freedom, and the salt water lapping round her was so exhilarating that she felt a new strength. She wanted to sing aloud in the joy of her heart. Diving below the surface, she came up with a shake of the head and a little cry of delight; her hair was loosened, and with a motion it all came tumbling about her shoulders and trailed out in its ringlets over the water.

She swam out, a fearless swimmer; and it gave her a sense of power to have the deep waters all about her, the deep calm sea of summer. She turned on her back and floated, trying to look the sun in the face: the sea glimmered with the sunbeams and the sky was dazzling. Then, returning, Bertha floated again, quite near the shore; it amused her to lie on her back, rocked by the tiny waves, and to sink her ears so that she could hear the shingle rub together curiously with the ebb and flow of the tide. She shook her long hair, and it stretched about her like an aureole.

She exulted in her youth – in her youth? Bertha felt no older than when she was eighteen, and yet she was thirty. The thought made her wince; she had never realized the passage of the years, she had never imagined that her youth was waning. Did people think her already old? The sickening fear came to her that she resembled Miss Hancock attempting by archness and by an assumption of frivolity to persuade her neighbours that she was juvenile. Bertha asked herself whether she was ridiculous when she rolled to the water like a young girl: you cannot play the mermaid with crow's-feet about your eyes and with wrinkles round your mouth. In a panic she dressed herself, and going home flew to a looking-glass. She scrutinized her features as she had never done before, searching anxiously for the signs she feared to see; she looked at her neck and at her eyes: her skin was as smooth as ever, her teeth as perfect. She gave a sigh of relief.

'I see no difference.'

Then, doubly to reassure herself, a fantastic idea seized Bertha to dress as though she were going to a great ball; she wished to see herself to all advantage. She chose the most splendid gown she had, and took out her jewels. The Leys had sold every vestige of their old magnificence, but their diamonds, with characteristic obstinacy, they had invariably refused to part with; and they lay aside, year after year unused, the stones in their old settings dulled with dust and neglect. The moisture still in Bertha's hair was an excuse to do it capriciously, and she placed in it the tiara that her grandmother had worn in the Regency. On her shoulders she wore two ornaments exquisitely set in gold-work, purloined by a great uncle from the saint of a Spanish church in the Peninsular War. She slipped a string of pearls round her neck, bracelets on her arms, and fastened a gleaming row of stars to her bosom. Knowing she had beautiful hands, Bertha disdained to wear rings, but now she covered her fingers with diamonds.

Finally she stood before the looking-glass, and gave a laugh of pleasure. She was not old yet.

But when she sailed into the drawing-room, Edward jumped up in surprise.

'Good Lord!' he cried. 'What on earth's up? Have we got people coming to dinner?'

'My dear, if we had I should not have dressed like this.'

'You're got up as if the Prince of Wales were coming. And I'm only in knickerbockers. It's not our wedding-day?'

'No.'

'Then I should like to know why you've got yourself up like that.'

'I thought it would please you,' she said, smiling.

'I wish you'd told me, I'd have dressed too. Are you sure no one's coming?'

'Quite sure.'

'Well, I think I ought to dress. It would look so queer if someone turned up.'

'If anyone does, I promise you I'll fly.'

They went in to dinner, Edward feeling very uncomfortable, and keeping his ear on the front-door bell. They ate their soup, and then was set on the table the remainder of a cold leg of mutton and some mashed poatoes. Bertha looked blank, and then, leaning back, burst into peal upon peal of laughter.

'Good Lord, what is the matter now?' asked Edward.

Nothing is more annoying than to have people violently hilarious over a joke that you cannot see. Bertha held her sides and tried to speak.

'I've just remembered that I told the servants they might go out tonight, there's a circus at Blackstable; and I said we'd just eat up the odds and ends.'

'I don't see any joke in that.'

And really there was none, but Bertha laughed again immoderately.

'I suppose there are some pickles,' said Edward.

Bertha repressed her gaiety and began to eat.

'That is my whole life,' she murmured under her breath, 'to eat cold mutton and mashed potatoes in a ball dress and all my diamonds.'

35

BUT in the winter of that very year Edward, while hunting, had an accident. For years he had made a practice of riding unmanageable horses, and he never heard of a vicious brute without wishing to try it. He knew that he was a fine rider, and since he was never shy of parading his powers nor loth to taunt others with their inferior skill or courage, he preferred difficult animals. It gratified him to see people point to him and say: 'There's a good rider'; and his best joke with some person on a horse that pulled or refused was to cry: 'You don't seem friends with your gee; would you like to try mine?' And then, touching its sides with his spurs, he set it prancing. He was merciless with cautious hunters who looked for low parts of a hedge or tried to get through a gate instead of over it; and when anyone said a jump was dangerous, Edward with a laugh promptly went over it, shouting as he did so:

'I wouldn't try it if I were you. You might fall off.'

He had just bought a roan for a song, because it jumped un-uncertainly and had a trick of swinging a foreleg as it rose. He took it out on the earliest opportunity, and the first two hedges and a ditch the horse cleared easily; Edward thought that once again he had got for almost nothing a hunter that merely wanted riding properly to behave like a lamb. They rode on and came to a post and rail fence.

'Now, my beauty, this'll show what you're made of.'

He took his horse up in a canter and pressed his legs; the horse did not rise, but swerved round suddenly.

'No, you don't,' said Edward, taking him back.

He dug his spurs in, and the horse cantered up, but refused again. This time Edward got angry. Arthur Branderton came flying by, and having many old scores to pay, laughed loudly.

'Why don't you get down and walk over?' he shouted, as he passed Edward and took the jump.

'I'll either get over or break my neck,' said Edward, setting his teeth.

But he did neither. He set the roan at the jump for the third time, hitting him over the head with his crop. The beast rose and then, displaying his habit of letting the fore-leg swing, came down with a crash. Edward fell heavily, and for a minute was stunned; when he recovered consciousness he found someone pouring brandy down his neck.

'Is the horse hurt?' he asked, not thinking of himself.

'No; he's all right. How d'you feel?'

A young surgeon was in the field, and rode up.

'What's the matter? Anyone injured?'

'No,' said Edward, struggling to his feet, angry at the exhibition he thought he was making of himself. 'One would think none of you fellows had ever seen a man come down before. I've seen most of you come off often enough.'

He walked up to the horse and put his foot in the stirrup.

'You'd better go home, Craddock,' said the surgeon. 'I expect you're a bit shaken up.'

'Go home be damned. Blast!' As he tried to mount Edward felt a pain at the top of his chest. 'I believe I've broken something.'

The surgeon went up to him and helped him off with his coat. He twisted Edward's arm.

'Does that hurt?'

'A bit.'

'You've broken your collar-bone,' said the surgeon, after a moment's examination. 'You'll want a Sayer's strapping, my friend.'

'I thought I'd smashed something. How long will it take to mend?'

'Only three weeks. You needn't be alarmed.'

'I'm not alarmed, but I suppose I shall have to give up hunting for at least a month.'

Edward was driven to Dr Ramsay's, who bandaged him, and then went back to Court Leys. Bertha was surprised to see him in a dog-cart. He had by now recovered his good temper, and explained the occurrence laughing.

'It's nothing to make a fuss about. Only I'm bandaged up so that I feel like a mummy, and I don't know how I'm going to get a bath. That's what worries me.'

Next day Arthur Branderton came to see him.

'You've found your master at last, Craddock.'

'Me? Not much! I shall be all right in a month, and then out I go again.'

'I wouldn't ride him again if I were you. It's not worth it. With that trick of his of swinging his leg, you'll break your neck.'

'Bah,' said Edward scornfully. 'The horse hasn't been built that I can't ride.'

'You're a good weight now, and your bones aren't as supple as when you were twenty. The next fall you have will be a bad one.'

'Rot, man! One would think I was eighty. I've never funked a horse yet, and I'm not going to begin now.'

Branderton shrugged his shoulders and said nothing more at the time; but afterwards spoke to Bertha privately.

'You know, I think if I were you I'd persuade Edward to get rid of that horse. I don't think he ought to ride it again. It's not safe. However well he rides, it won't save him if the beast has got a bad trick.'

Bertha had in this particular great faith in her husband's skill. Whatever he could not do, he was certainly one of the finest riders in the country; but she spoke to him notwithstanding.

'Pooh, that's all rot!' he said. 'I tell you what, on the eleventh of next month we go over pretty well the same ground, and I'm going out, and I swear he's going over that post and rail in Coulter's Field.'

'You're very incautious.'

'No, I'm not. I know exactly what a horse can do. And I know that horse can jump it if he wants to, and by George, I'll make him. Why, if I funked it now I could never ride again. When a chap gets to be near forty and has a bad fall, the only thing is to go for it again at once, or he'll lose his nerve and never get it back. I've seen that over and over again.'

Miss Glover later on, when Edward's bandages were removed and he was fairly well, begged Bertha to use her influence with him.

'I've heard he's a most dangerous horse, Bertha. I think it would be madness for Edward to ride him.'

'I've begged him to sell it, but he merely laughs at me,' said Bertha. 'He's dreadfully obstinate, and I have very little power over him.'

'Aren't you frightened?'

Bertha laughed. 'No, I'm really not. You know, he always has ridden dangerous horses, and he's never come to any harm. When we were first married I used to go through agonies; every time he hunted I used to think he'd be brought home dead on a stretcher. But he never was, and I calmed down by degrees.'

'I wonder you could.'

'My dear, no one can keep on being frightfully agitated for ten years. People who live on volcanoes forget all about it; and you'd soon get used to sitting on barrels of gunpowder if you had no armchair.'

'Never!' said Miss Glover with conviction, seeing a vivid picture of herself in such a position.

Miss Glover was unaltered. Time passed over her head powerlessly; she still looked anything between five-and-twenty and forty, her hair was no more washed-out, her figure in its armour of black cloth was as young as ever, and not a new idea nor a thought had entered her mind. She was like Alice's queen who ran at the top of her speed and remained in the same place; but with Miss Glover the process was reversed: the world moved on, apparently faster and faster as the century drew near its end, but she remained fixed – an incarnation of the eighteen-eighties.

The day before the eleventh arrived. The hounds were to meet at 'The Share and Coulter', as when Edward had been thrown. He sent for Dr Ramsay to assure Bertha that he was quite fit; and after the examination brought him into the drawing-room.

'Dr Ramsay says my collar-bone is stronger than ever.'

'But I don't think he ought to ride the roan notwithstanding. Can't you persuade Edward not to, Bertha?'

Bertha looked from the doctor to Edward, smiling.

'I've done my best,' she said.

'Bertha knows better than to bother,' said Edward. 'She doesn't think much of me as a churchwarden, but where a horse is concerned she does trust me; don't you, dear?'

'I really do.'

'There,' said Edward, much pleased. 'That's what I call a good wife.'

Next day the horse was brought round and Bertha filled Edward's flask.

'You'll bury me nicely if I break my neck, won't you?' he said, laughing. 'You'll order a handsome tombstone.'

'My dear, you'll never do that. I feel certain you will die in your bed when you're a hundred and two, with a crowd of descendants weeping round you. You're just that sort of man.'

'I don't know where the descendants are coming in,' he laughed.

'I have a presentiment that I am doomed to make way for Fanny Glover. I'm sure there's a fatality about it. I've felt for years that you will eventually marry her; it's horrid of me to have kept you waiting so long, especially as she pines for you, poor thing.'

Edward laughed again. 'Well, good-bye!'

'Good-bye. Remember me to Mr Arthur.'

She stood at the window to see him mount, and as he flourished his crop at her waved her hand.

The winter day closed in, and Bertha, interested in the novel she was reading, was surprised to hear the clock strike. She wondered that Edward had not yet come in, and ringing for tea and the lamps, had the curtains drawn. He could not now be long.

'I wonder if he's had another fall,' she said with a smile. 'He really ought to give up hunting, he's getting too fat.'

She decided to wait no longer, but poured out her tea and arranged herself so that she could get at the scones and see comfortably to read. Then she heard a carriage drive up. Who could it be?

'What bores these people are to call at this time!'

Bertha put down her book to receive the visitor, as the bell was rung. But no one was shown in; there was a confused sound of voices without. Could something have happened to Edward, after all? She sprang to her feet and walked half across the room. She heard an unknown voice in the hall.

'Where shall we take it?'

It. What was *it* – a corpse? Bertha felt a coldness travel through all her body; she put her hand on a chair, so that she might steady herself if she felt faint. The door was opened slowly by Arthur Branderton, and he closed it quietly behind him.

'I'm awfully sorry, but there's been an accident. Edward is rather hurt.'

She looked at him, growing pale; but found nothing to answer.

'You must nerve yourself, Bertha. I'm afraid he's very bad. You'd better sit down.'

He hesitated, and she turned to him with sudden anger.

'If he's dead, why don't you tell me?'

'I'm awfully sorry. We did all we could. He fell at the same post and rail fence as the other day. I think he must have lost his nerve.

247

I was close by him. I saw him rush at it blindly, and then pull just as the horse was rising. They came down with a crash.'

'Is he dead?'

'Death must have been instantaneous.'

Bertha did not faint. She was a little horrified at the clearness with which she was able to understand Arthur Branderton. She seemed to feel nothing at all. The young man looked at her as if he expected that she would weep or swoon.

'Would you like me to send my wife to you?'

'No, thanks.'

Bertha understood quite well that her husband was dead, but the news seemed to make no impression upon her. She heard it as unmovedly as though it referred to a stranger. She found herself wondering what young Branderton thought of her unconcern.

'Won't you sit down?' he said, taking her arm and leading her to a chair. 'Shall I get you some brandy?'

'I'm all right, thanks. You need not trouble about me. Where is he?'

'I told them to take him upstairs. Shall I send Ramsay's assistant to you? He's here.'

'No,' she said in a low voice. 'I want nothing. Have they taken him up already?'

'Yes, but I don't think you ought to go to him. It'll upset you dreadfully.'

'I'll go to my room. Do you mind if I leave you? I should prefer to be alone.'

Branderton held the door open and Bertha walked out, her face very pale, but showing not the least trace of emotion. Branderton walked to Leanham Vicarage to send Miss Glover to Court Leys, and then home, where he told his wife that the wretched widow was absolutely stunned by the shock.

Bertha locked herself in her room. She heard the hum of voices in the house; Dr Ramsay came to the door, but she refused to open; then all was quite still.

She was aghast at the blankness of her heart; the calmness was inhuman and she wondered if she was going mad; she felt no emotion whatever. But she repeated to herself that Edward was killed; he was lying quite near at hand, dead, and she felt no grief. She remembered her anguish years before when she thought of his

248

death, and now that it had taken place she did not faint, she did not weep, she was untroubled. Bertha had hidden herself to conceal her tears from strange eyes, and the tears did not come! After the sudden suspicion was confirmed she had experienced no emotion whatever; she was horrified that the tragic death affected her so little. She walked to the window and looked out, trying to gather her thoughts, trying to make herself care; but she was almost indifferent.

'I must be frightfully cruel,' she muttered.

Then the idea came of what her friends would say when they saw her calm and self-possessed. She tried to weep, but her eyes remained dry.

There was a knock at the door, and Miss Glover's voice.

'Bertha, Bertha, won't you let me in? It's me, Fanny.'

Bertha sprang to her feet, but did not answer. Miss Glover called again: her voice was broken with sobs. Why could Fanny Glover weep for Edward's death, who was a stranger, when she, Bertha, remained insensible?

'Bertha!'

'Yes.'

'Open the door for me. Oh, I'm so sorry for you. Please let me in.'

Bertha looked wildly at the door; she dared not let Miss Glover in.

'I can see no one now,' she cried hoarsely. 'Don't ask me.'

'I think I could comfort you.'

'I want to be alone.'

Miss Glover was silent for a minute, crying audibly.

'Shall I wait downstairs? You can ring if you want me. Perhaps you'll see me later.'

Bertha wanted to tell her to go away, but had not the courage.

'Do as you like,' she said.

A second voice was added to Miss Glover's, and Bertha heard a whispered conversation. There was another knock.

'Bertha, what do you wish done?'

'What can be done?'

'Oh, why don't you open the door? Don't you understand?' Miss Glover's voice shook. 'Shall we send for a woman to wash the body?'

Bertha paused, and the blood fled from her lips.

'Do whatever you like.'

There was silence again, an unearthly silence, more trying than hideous din. It was a silence that tightened the nerves and made them horribly sensitive: one dared not breathe for fear of breaking it.

And one thought came to Bertha, assailing her like a devil tormenting. She cried out in horror. This was more odious than anything. Intolerable. She threw herself on the bed and buried her face in the pillow to drive it away. For shame she put her hands to her ears in order not to hear the invisible fiends that whispered silently.

She was free.

'Has it come to this?' she murmured.

And then came back the recollection of the beginnings of her love. She recalled the passion that had thrown her blindly into Edward's arms, her bitter humiliation when she realized that he could not respond to her ardour; her love was a fire playing ineffectually over a rock of basalt. She recalled the hatred that followed the disillusion, and finally the indifference. It was the same indifference that chilled her heart now. Her life seemed all wasted when she compared her mad desire for happiness with the misery she had in fact endured. Bertha's many hopes stood out like phantoms, and she looked at them despairingly. She had expected so much and got so little. She felt a terrible pain at her heart as she considered all she had gone through, her strength fell away, and, overcome by pity for herself, she sank to her knees and burst into tears.

'Oh, God,' she cried, 'what have I done that I should have been so unhappy?'

She sobbed aloud, not caring to restrain her grief.

Miss Glover, good soul, was waiting outside the room in case Bertha wanted her, crying silently. She knocked again when she heard the impetuous sobs within.

'Oh, Bertha, do let me in. You're tormenting yourself so much more because you won't see anybody.'

Bertha dragged herself to her feet and undid the door. Miss Glover entered, and throwing off all her reserve in her overwhelming sympathy clasped Bertha to her heart.

'Oh, my dear, my dear, it's utterly dreadful. I'm so sorry for you. I don't know what to say. I can only pray.'

Bertha sobbed unrestrainedly – not because Edward was dead.

'All you have now is God,' said Miss Glover.

At last Bertha tore herself away and dried her eyes.

'Don't try and be too brave, Bertha. It'll do you good to cry. He was such a good, kind man, and he loved you so.'

Bertha looked at her in silence.

'I must be horribly cruel,' she thought.

'Do you mind if I stay here tonight, dear?' said Miss Glover. 'I've sent word to Charles.'

'Oh, no, please don't. If you care for me, Fanny, let me be alone. I don't want to be unkind, but I can't bear to see anyone.'

Miss Glover was deeply pained. 'I don't want to be in the way. If you really wish me to go, I'll go.'

'I feel if I can't be alone I shall go mad.'

'Would you like to see Charles?'

'No, dear. Don't be angry. Don't think me unkind or ungrateful, but I want nothing but to be left entirely by myself.'

36

ALONE in her room once more, memories of the past crowded upon her. The last years passed from her mind, and Bertha saw vividly again the first days of her love, the visit to Edward at his farm, and the night at the gate of Court Leys when he asked her to marry him. She recalled the rapture with which she had flung herself into his arms. Forgetting the real Edward who had just died, she remembered the tall strong youth who had made her faint with love, and her passion returned, overwhelming. On the chimney-piece stood a photograph of Edward as he was then; it had been before her for years, but she had never noticed it. She took it and pressed it to her heart, and kissed it. A thousand things came back, and she saw him again standing before her as he was then, manly and strong so that she felt his love a protection against all the world.

But what was the use now?

'I should be mad if I began to love him again when it's too late.'

Bertha was appalled by the regret that she felt rising within her, a devil that wrung her heart in an iron grip. Oh, she could not risk the possibility of grief, she had suffered too much, and she must kill in herself the springs of pain. She dared not leave things that in future years might be the foundation of a new idolatry. Her only chance was to destroy everything that might recall him.

She took the photograph and, without daring to look again, withdrew it from its frame and quickly tore it in bits. She looked round the room.

'I mustn't leave anything,' she muttered.

She saw on a table an album containing pictures of Edward at all ages, the child with long curls, the urchin in knickerbockers, the schoolboy, the lover of her heart. She had persuaded him to be photographed in London during their honeymoon, and he was there in half a dozen positions. Bertha thought her heart would break as she destroyed them one by one, and it needed all the strength she had to prevent her from covering them with passionate kisses. Her fingers ached with the tearing, but in a little while they were all in fragments in the fireplace. Then she added the letters Edward had written to her, and applied a match. She watched them curl and frizzle and burn; and presently they were ashes.

She sank on a chair, exhausted by the effort, but quickly roused herself. She drank some water nerving herself for a more terrible ordeal; she knew that on the next few hours depended her future peace.

By now the night was late, a stormy night with the wind howling through the leafless trees. Bertha started when it beat against the windows with a scream that was nearly human. A fear seized her of what she was about to do, but she was driven on by a greater fear. She took a candle, and opening the door listened. There was no one; the wind roared with its long, monotonous voice, and the branches of a tree beating against a window in the passage gave a ghastly tap-tap, as if unseen spirits were near.

The living in the presence of death feel that the air about them is full of something new and terrible. A greater sensitiveness perceives an inexplicable feeling of something present, or some horrible thing happening invisibly. Bertha walked to her husband's room, and for a while dared not enter. At last she opened the door; she lit the candles on the chimney-piece and on the dressing-table, then went to the bed. Edward was lying on his back, with a handkerchief bound round his jaw to hold it up, his hands crossed.

Bertha stood in front of the corpse and looked. The impression of the young man passed away, and she saw him as in truth he was, stout and red-faced; the vesicles of his cheeks stood out distinctly in a purple network; the sides of his face were bulgy as of late years they had become; and he had little side-whiskers. His skin was lined already and rough, the hair on the front of his head was scanty, and the scalp showed through, shining and white. The hands that had once delighted her by their strength, so that she compared them with the porphyry hands of an unfinished statue, now were repellent in their coarseness. For a long time their touch had a little disgusted her. This was the image Bertha wished to impress upon her mind. At last, turning away, she went out and returned to her own room.

Three days later was the funeral. All the morning wreaths and crosses of beautiful flowers had poured in, and now there was quite a large gathering in the drive in front of Ley House. The Blackstable Freemasons (Lodge No. 31,899), of which Edward at his death was Worshipful Master, had signified their intention of attending, and now lined the road, two and two, in white gloves and aprons. There were likewise representatives of the Tercanbury Lodge (4169), of the Provincial Grand Lodge, the Mark Masons and the Knights Templars. The Blackstable Unionist Association sent one hundred Conservatives who walked two and two after the Freemasons. There was some dispute as to precedence between Bro. G. W. Havelock, C.P.W.U., who led the Blackstable Lodge (31,899), and Mr Atthill Bacot, who marched at the head of the politicians; but it was settled in favour of the Lodge, as the older established body. Then came the members of the Local District Council, of which Edward had been chairman, and after them the carriages of the gentry. Mrs Mayston Ryle sent a landau and pair, but Mrs Branderton, the Molsons and the rest only broughams. It needed a prodigious amount of generalship to marshal these forces, and Arthur Branderton lost his temper because the Conservatives would start before they were wanted to.

'Ah,' said Bro. A. W. Rogers (the landlord of 'The Pig and Whistle'), 'they want Craddock here now. He was the best organizer I've ever seen; he'd have got the procession into working order and the funeral over half an hour ago.'

The last carriage disappeared, and Bertha, alone at length, lay

253

down by the window on the sofa. She was devoutly grateful to the old convention that prevented the widow's attendance at the funeral.

She looked with tired and listless eyes at the long avenue of elm trees, bare of leaf. The sky was grey and the clouds were heavy and low. Bertha was now a pale woman of more than thirty, still beautiful, with curly and abundant hair, but her dark eyes had under them still darker lines, and their fire was dimmed; between her brows was a little vertical line, and her lips had lost the joyousness of youth; the corners of her mouth turned down sadly. Her face was very thin. She seemed weary. Her apathetic eyes said that she had loved and found love wanting, that she had been a mother and that her child had died, and that now she desired nothing very much but to be left in peace.

Bertha was indeed tired out, in body and mind, tired of love and hate, tired of friendship and knowledge, tired of the passing years. Her thoughts wandered to the future, and she decided to leave Blackstable; she would let Court Leys, so that in no moment of weakness might she be tempted to return. And first she intended to travel; she wished more easily to forget the past, to live in places where she was unknown. Bertha's memory brought back Italy, the land of those who suffer in unfulfilled desire, the lotus-land; she would go there and she would go further, ever towards the sun. Now she had no ties on earth, and at last, at last she was free.

The melancholy day closed in, and the great clouds hanging overhead darkened with the approach of night. Bertha remembered how ready in her girlhood she had been to give herself to the world. Feeling intense fellowship with all human beings, she wished to throw herself into their arms, thinking that they would stretch them out to receive her. Her life seemed to overflow into the lives of others, becoming one with theirs as the waters of rivers become one with the sea. But very soon the power she had felt of doing all this departed; she recognized a barrier between herself and human kind, and felt that they were strangers. Hardly understanding the impossibility of what she desired, she placed all her love, all her faculty of expansion, on one person, on Edward, making a final effort as it were to break the barrier of consciousness and unite her soul with his. She drew him towards her with all her might, Edward the man, seeking to know him in the depths of his heart, yearning to lose herself in him. But at last she saw that what she had striven for was unattainable. I myself stand on one side, and the rest of the world on the other. There is an abyss between that no power can cross, a strange barrier more insuperable than a mountain of fire. Husband and wife know nothing of one another. However ardently they love, however intimate their union, they are never one; they are scarcely more to one another than strangers.

And when she had discovered this, with many tears and after bitter heartache, Bertha retired into herself. But soon she found solace. In her silence she built a world of her own, and kept it from the eyes of every living soul, knowing that none could understand. And then all ties were irksome, all earthly attachments unnecessary.

Confusedly thinking these things, Bertha's thoughts reverted to Edward.

'If I had been keeping a diary of my emotions, I should close it today with the words, "My husband has broken his neck".'

But she was pained at her own bitterness.

'Poor fellow,' she murmured. 'He was honest and kind and forbearing. He did all he could, and tried always to act like a gentleman. He was very useful in the world, and in his own way he was fond of me. His only fault was that I loved him – and ceased to do so.'

By her side lay the book she had been reading while waiting for Edward. Bertha had put it down open, face downwards, when she rose from the sofa to have tea; it had remained as she left it. She was tired of thinking and, taking it now, began reading quietly.

Fiction

☐	**Castle Raven**	Laura Black	£1.75p
☐	**Options**	Freda Bright	£1.50p
☐	**Bad Company**	Liza Cody	£1.50p
☐	**Chances**	Jackie Collins	£2.50p
☐	**Brain**	Robin Cook	£1.75p
☐	**The Entity**	Frank De Felitta	£1.95p
☐	**The Dead of Jericho**	Colin Dexter	£1.50p
☐	**Whip Hand**	Dick Francis	£1.75p
☐	**Saigon**	Anthony Grey	£2.50p
☐	**The White Paper Fan**	Unity Hall	£1.75p
☐	**Solo**	Jack Higgins	£1.75p
☐	**The Rich are Different**	Susan Howatch	£2.95p
☐	**Smash**	Garson Kanin	£1.75p
☐	**Smiley's People**	John le Carré	£1.95p
☐	**The Conduct of Major Maxim**	Gavin Lyall	£1.75p
☐	**The Master Mariner Book 1: Running Proud**	Nicholas Monsarrat	£1.50p
☐	**Fools Die**	Mario Puzo	£1.95p
☐	**The Throwback**	Tom Sharpe	£1.75p
☐	**Wild Justice**	Wilbur Smith	£2.50p
☐	**Cannery Row**	John Steinbeck	£1.50p
☐	**That Old Gang of Mine**	Leslie Thomas	£1.75p
☐	**Caldo Largo**	Earl Thompson	£1.75p
☐	**Ben Retallick**	E. V. Thompson	£1.95p

All these books are available at your local bookshop or newsagent, or
can be ordered direct from the publisher. Indicate the number of copies
required and fill in the form below   11

....

Name_____
(Block letters please)

Address_____

_____

Send to CS Department, Pan Books Ltd, PO Box 40, Basingstoke, Hants
Please enclose remittance to the value of the cover price plus:
35p for the first book plus 15p per copy for each additional book ordered
to a maximum charge of £1.25 to cover postage and packing
Applicable only in the UK

While every effort is made to keep prices low, it is sometimes
necessary to increase prices at short notice. Pan Books reserve
the right to show on covers and charge new retail prices which
may differ from those advertised in the text or elsewhere